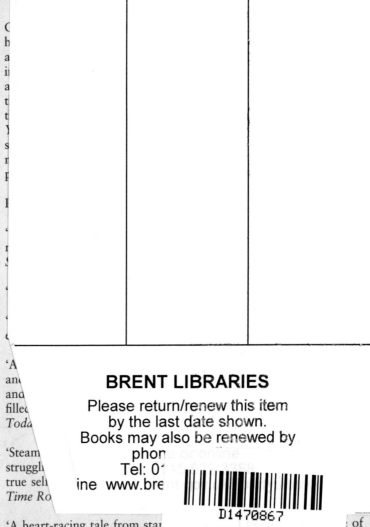

'A
an
and
filled
Toda

'Steam
struggl
true sel
Time Ro

'A heart-racing tale from star   of
it!' *The Romance Reader's Co*

'[A] brilliantly plotted book. The love story, as always, is hot and
emotive and balanced well with the exciting and well-crafted
mystery. Her main characters are vulnerable yet strong, and even
the villain   strokes
haunting y   *on*

By Christy Reece

Last Chance Rescue Series
Rescue Me
Return to Me
Run to Me
No Chance
Second Chance
Last Chance
Sweet Justice
Sweet Revenge
Sweet Reward

Second Chance
CHRISTY REECE

ETERNAL
ROMANCE

First published in the United States of America in 2010
by Ballantine Books, an imprint of
The Random House Publishing Group,
a division of Random House, Inc.

First published in Great Britain in 2011

an imprint of HEADLINE PUBLISHING GROUP

ISBN 978 0 7553 9797 6

Offset in Sabon by Avon DataSet Ltd, Bidford-on-Avon, Warwickshire

Printed and bound by CPI Group (UK) Ltd, Croydon, CR0 4YY

Headline's policy is to use papers that are natural, renewable and
recyclable products and made from wood grown in sustainable forests.
The logging and manufacturing processes are expected to conform to the
environmental regulations of the country of origin.

HEADLINE PUBLISHING GROUP
An Hachette UK Company
338 Euston Road
London NW1 3BH

www.eternalromancebooks.co.uk
www.headline.co.uk
www.hachette.co.uk

In memory of my sweet mother-in-law,
who was the complete opposite
of Elizabeth Fairchild in every way

prologue

Fairview, South Carolina

He sat on a hillside and surveyed the estate below. Icy gusts of wind blasted around him, swirling up frozen dust particles from the dry earth. Undeterred by the elements, Cole Mathison maintained his focus on his target below—a modern-day fortress. The massive brick wall surrounding the Southern-style mansion would stop all but the most determined. Hidden sensors covered the vast estate, designed to alert the owner to the presence of any intruder within seconds.

Keeley Fairchild and her daughters were well protected.

She had been given detailed instructions on how to protect her family and had taken that advice to heart. Other than its lack of armed guards, the estate's security could rival some embassies'. This was a woman intent on ensuring her children's safety.

Cole lowered his high-powered binoculars and released a harsh breath. Why the hell was he even here? There was no indication that she was in trouble or under any kind of threat. It had been more than a year since her husband's abduction and death. From all accounts, there'd never been a threat to anyone else in the family. So why couldn't he just forget about her and let this obsession go?

He stood and stretched his long legs, wincing at the

stiffness. Three days of doing nothing but watching the nonexistent comings and goings at the estate was wearing. For a man used to a daily routine of physical activity, sitting on his ass for any amount of time exhausted him faster than a ten-mile uphill run.

None of the family had left the grounds since he'd been here. Two visitors, both young women, had come by for brief visits. That had been the only outside activity. Other than the occasional shadow that flitted by a window, he never saw Keeley Fairchild or her children.

She was fine; the kids were fine. So why didn't he leave?

There was no reason to believe that she or her daughters were in the slightest bit of danger. Despite that knowledge, he came here every few weeks just to reassure himself. Damn stupid obsession had to end sometime. The need to protect this family was a bizarre and useless pastime. They didn't need his help. Hell, they didn't even know he existed. And with any luck, he could keep it that way.

His phone vibrated in his pocket. Grabbing it, he held the phone to his ear as he perused the perimeter once more. "Yeah?"

"We found him." Noah McCall's hard voice held a tinge of triumph.

Cole's entire body stiffened at the news. "Where?"

"Still in his home base."

The bastard had never left Mexico. Good, that'd make it easier for everyone.

"Figured he'd get out of the country," Cole said.

"He may have tried . . . just couldn't."

"He suspect anything?"

"No. Staying below radar, but he's set up shop. Got himself a little lab in the basement of an abandoned building."

Sounded like the freak. A fanatical need to experiment had ruined lives, caused untold death and destruction. But now the man's sick fascination to screw with people's minds was playing right into their hands.

"You coming?" McCall asked.

Cole took another sweeping glance at the scenic and peaceful valley below. His instincts were off, had been since his capture. There was no hint of threat, no evidence of danger. Keeley Fairchild had gotten on with her life; he needed to get on with his.

Jerking his backpack up, he swung it over his shoulder and started down the hill. "Be there tomorrow."

one

A female shriek, loaded with drunken laughter, ripped through the air. *Oh yeah*. The Saturday night crowd at Bug-n-Booze was alive and kicking. The aroma of roasted peanut shells covering the floor blended with the lusty smells of women who only wanted two things—to get drunk and to get laid.

Wesley Tuttle's mouth slid up in an easy smile . . . his favorite kind of woman.

"Are you listening to me?"

With deliberate slowness, Wes turned back to his companion. She'd asked to meet him hundreds of miles from Fairview; least she could do was let him enjoy himself for a little while. This was his first time here and Wes already knew it wouldn't be his last.

He eyed the woman sitting at the table with him. With her upper-crust, snooty attitude and expensive clothes, she looked as out of place here as a possum would at a pie-throwing contest. It was all for show; everything about her was fake. He knew more than most anybody about this particular rich bitch. Those clothes might make her look high class, but when she had a little liquor inside her or needed a favor, she could make a Saturday night slut look like a nun.

He gave her the smile he reserved especially for her, knowing it'd piss her off. "I want the woman, too."

Shock reflected on her face for barely a second, then a skinny, manicured hand waved dismissively. "Don't be ridiculous. If you make this more complicated, it will never work. You'll get more than enough for the kids."

He stared hard. This point was non-negotiable. If she wanted him to do the job, she'd come around.

Her eyes skittered away from his face. Good. She might be his employer for this particular gig, but she was scared of him. Just the way he liked it.

She chewed at her lower lip, smearing red lipstick over her teeth. "What do you want her for? Ransom?"

A grin tugged on his mouth. "You know money ain't the reason I want her."

Jealousy dripping from every word, she said, "What is it with you men? Her ass is the size of a double-wide and those boobs are freakishly large."

It was all he could do not to laugh in her face. "If double-wide trailers were shaped like her ass, I wouldn't mind living in one the rest of my life."

The woman continued her rant. Wes ignored her, as he did most of the time. When she said something he wanted to hear, he'd tune in again.

She was pissed he wasn't still trying to get into her panties. He'd been there and done that more times than he liked to count. Every time he made the return trip, he always swore he'd never go back again, but when he was horny, sometimes he needed the itch scratched without preliminaries. Given the proper incentive, this bitch was always willing.

"Are you listening to me?"

"I will when you say something worth hearing."

Eyes flashed with a haughty fury; she reared back as only her kind could.

Wes snorted, not one bit impressed with her highbrow attitude. "Listen, we may be in business together, but I ain't taking no shit off you. You tell me where I can nab the brats and the woman. I'll take care of the rest. That sure as hell don't mean we gotta be bosom buddies."

Wes swallowed another snort. Like she had any kind of bosom he could buddy up to. Hell, she barely had anything up top at all. Another reason she was so jealous of the woman. The difference between them was like an ocean to a mud puddle.

The anger in her eyes seemed to dim for the moment. Talking business was one way to keep that jealousy under control. "They'll be hard to get to; she barely lets them out of her sight. And it'll have to be done somewhere out of the house. It'd take a tank to get inside that estate."

Wes shrugged. "So? Find a way to get them out in the open. I can get rid of anybody who sees me."

"No, I don't want anyone killed. That would attract too much attention."

He cackled. Hell, she was dumber than he thought. "You don't think kidnapping two little girls with that last name in this state ain't going to cause an uproar? Especially after what happened to their daddy? FBI's gonna be on it like flies on chicken shit."

A small bit of fear flashed in her face and then she shrugged. "You do what I tell you to do and no one will ever find them . . . it doesn't matter who's looking for them."

Man, she sure hated the woman. Wes wasn't one to question other people's motives. Most times he didn't care. If he got money for it, there wasn't a lot he wouldn't do. He'd always prided himself on having no limits. Took balls of steel and major smarts to do what he'd done most of his life and not get caught. He eyed the woman again. Hell, might as well make the offer. It'd be some extra dough and no skin off his nose. "If you hate her that much, I can off her once I'm finished with her."

Her eyes widened with what looked like genuine

shock. "I don't want her dead, you idiot. I don't want anyone killed." She leaned forward. "Understood?"

Fine with him. He sure as hell wasn't going to do extra stuff he wouldn't get paid for. "Fine. I'll wear a mask or something. Don't know why you're so against killing all of a sudden. You sure didn't seem to have a problem with it when you got rid of her husband."

Her face went still for an instant and then her mouth tilted in a smirk. "Now, what makes you think I had anything to do with that?"

" 'Cause I saw you right after they got married. Never seen you so pissed before. Besides, it sounds like something you'd do."

She pressed a hand against her heart in fake outrage. "I can't believe you think I'd be so vindictive." The slight humor he'd seen in her eyes disappeared and the ice-bitch look returned. "Despite all the evidence that pointed to her, she was barely even considered a suspect."

"Well, least you got the money for it."

She waved a negligent hand. "Money is inconsequential."

Spoken like a woman who had it to spare. To Wes, money would never be inconsequential. "What'd you have him kidnapped for then?"

A skinny, haughty brow lifted. "I never said I did."

Wes swallowed a guffaw. Wasn't no use denying it. He knew what the bitch was capable of. "Bet the outcome really honked you off, too. She got the money, the mansion, and got rid of a cheating husband to boot. I'd say you got screwed."

"The only reason they believed her is because of her looks. Idiot men take one look at her and start thinking with their dicks. It's disgusting."

Unable to resist needling her, Wesley quipped, "Thought you said she wasn't good-looking."

Her mouth tightened at the reminder, but she stayed focused on business. "One hundred thousand to snatch both of them, plus the money you get from each buyer." She slid a piece of paper toward him. "Here are the names, phone numbers, and addresses." A blood-red nail tapped on the paper. "The dark-haired one goes to these people in Florida; the blonde to this couple in Pennsylvania. As soon as you make the delivery, they'll give you the money. It's all yours."

Like he needed her telling him how to conduct business. Whatever she said didn't mean squat. He'd do it his way. He already had a buyer set up for the blond one and would be getting a whole hell of a lot more than the fifteen thousand the people in Pennsylvania were willing to cough up. The dark-haired one might have to go to the Florida people, though. The blond one would be easier to pass off as his till he could drop her off; the dark-haired one looked too different to belong to him.

She continued with her instructions. "You'll need to get out of town immediately after you take them."

He knew how to take care of his business. Just 'cause she'd started the process didn't mean she was going to run the show.

Once he got rid of the kids, he'd keep the woman for as long as he wanted, then drop her somewhere when he was through. Using her brats as leverage would ensure she'd do everything he told her to do. Wes squirmed in his chair as he thought about all the things that plump pink mouth would do to him.

Putting those needs on the back burner, he leaned forward, eager to get things into motion. The sooner he got the plans in place, the sooner he'd be getting what he'd been wanting for years. "Here's what you're going to do."

Her face lit up and became more animated than he'd ever seen it.

Man, if she really hated Keeley Fairchild that much, why the hell didn't she want her dead?

Two weeks later
Fairview, South Carolina

A gurgling giggle caused Keeley to smile. Even without looking, she knew the giggle belonged to Hailey. It had a tinkling, musical quality to it. Her sister Hannah's giggle was softer and sounded more like a wind chime.

"Mommy, look at me!"

She turned and grabbed Hailey's waist just in time to pull her down from the monkey bars she was trying to climb. The little knot on her head from last week's adventure was barely gone. "Hailey, I told you not to go up there."

She sat her daughter down on the ground and tried for a hard look. When her angel just gave her an innocent, adorable grin, Keeley figured she'd failed the stern-mother-glare test. With her light blue eyes and fair complexion, Hailey looked so much like her father that Keeley felt that familiar painful twist to her heart.

Going to her knees, Keeley brushed a blond curl from her daughter's forehead and gave her button nose a gentle tap. "No climbing . . . promise Mommy."

Another gap-toothed grin was her response. Keeley held back a sigh. How on earth had she managed to create a daredevil daughter? Hailey wasn't happy unless she was doing something she knew her mother would definitely not want.

"Mommy, can I have some juice?"

She pressed a kiss to Hailey's forehead and twisted around to Hannah, Hailey's sister. Though the girls were twins, they were as unalike as if they came from different parents. Hannah was a miniature version of Keeley—light olive skin, ebony hair, and black eyes. Her personality was easygoing and pleasant. She could be entertained with a book for hours; her sister might hold out for five minutes.

Sometimes it amazed her how these two precious little girls had come from something so disastrous as her marriage to Stephen. Not that she'd known how bad it was until just before he died. But the gifts of her daughters more than made up for the other things. No doubt about it, they were heaven-sent.

Keeley pulled a small juice box from the thermal picnic bag and inserted the straw into the box. Turning back to her daughter, she pressed a small kiss to Hannah's silky head and then handed her the juice. "Here you go, sweet pea."

Smiling her thanks, Hannah headed toward her sister, her tiny hands wrapped tight around the juice box as she sipped. Little Miss Careful never wanted to spill a drop.

Keeley turned to grab another juice from her bag, knowing once Hailey saw her sister with juice, she'd want some, too. She was putting the straw in when she heard the first scream.

"Mommy!"

Keeley whirled around. In an instant, she dropped the juice and ran. A large man in a black ski mask had both her babies in his arms and was running down the sidewalk toward the parking lot.

Her heart pounded as her feet flew toward the monster. "What are you doing? Stop!"

Focused only on her children, Keeley barely noticed when another masked man ran up beside her. He threw his arm around her waist, picked her up, and started carrying her. Her only instinct to get to her girls, Keeley kicked and beat at him until he dropped her to the ground.

Terror exploding inside her, Keeley was back on her feet in an instant and running. Her babies were screaming for her; the man carrying them never looked back.

A hard arm grabbed her from behind. "Come on, bitch." The voice sounded breathless and angry.

Barely pausing, Keeley slugged the man in the face and kept on running. She screamed, "Don't you take my babies!"

"Bitch!" The second masked man was beside her again. He made another grab for her. Wasting precious seconds, Keeley turned around and put everything she had into the punch; her fist slammed into his head. She turned and started running again.

Their faces red and puckered with fear, her babies screamed, shouting for her. With a gasping sob, Keeley stretched her hand out and managed to claw at the man's sleeve.

He shot a quick glance back and wrenched his arm away.

Oh God, don't let him get away. "No!" Keeley screamed.

He reached the parking lot and ran toward the open side door of a white van. Keeley took a leap and sprang toward him, her arms outstretched. Once again she felt the brush of his jacket on her fingertips. He pulled away sharply and Keeley felt herself falling. Pain slammed into her as she smacked face-first onto the concrete pavement. On the edge of consciousness, the last sound Keeley heard was the cry of her daughters screaming "Mama!"

Wes glanced in his rearview mirror at the two sleeping kids. Seeing them with their arms wrapped around each other for comfort and warmth kind of tugged at his heart. They'd been so upset he'd given them orange juice laced with Valium to calm them down. They'd fallen asleep almost immediately. Had he given them too much? Maybe he should check and make sure they were still breathing.

Damned if he needed anything else to go wrong with this job. He had two kids, hopefully alive, but no woman. The bitch had double-crossed him; the grab hadn't gone down like he'd instructed. The email he got on his BlackBerry just seconds ago indicated that as far as she was concerned, the job was finished: "Your money's at the P.O. box. Get out of town and don't come back."

Like hell.

Wes turned down the gravel path to his cabin. The first thing he needed to do was get off the road. He'd paid Fletch the money he owed him for his help, though not as much as Wes had promised. Hell, even if the setup wasn't right, the bastard should've been able to grab Keeley.

Since Wesley was the larger of the two men, he'd decided to be the one to nab the kids. Squirmy kids, even young ones like these, could be a pain in the ass to carry. He'd thought Fletch could handle the woman, though. That'd been his only job. In Wes's estimation, if a man couldn't take down a woman, he wasn't much of a man. *Stupid prick.*

Wes parked in front of his cabin and turned the ignition off. Twisting around, he eyed the unconscious kids, and then reached out a hand and touched the pulses at their necks. Yeah, both still beating. At least that was one thing that hadn't got messed up.

Weird that they were twins when they didn't even look related. One had blond hair; the other one had black hair . . . the color of her mother's. The dark-haired one would be going to some people in Georgia. He'd found somebody who was willing to pay five thousand more than what the Florida people had promised. Fifteen thousand had a nicer ring to it than ten.

The blond one was going to bring him almost double what the dark-haired one had. With the hundred thousand he'd gotten for the grab, he was going to be sitting pretty for a long time.

First, he had a call to make.

Wes pressed a key on his cellphone. She answered on the first ring in that haughty voice he hated. "I told you not to call me."

"You're going to pay. Nobody double-crosses me and gets away with it."

She laughed. The bitch had the nerve to laugh at him!

"I did pay you. With that kind of money, you can find plenty of women to do anything you want. And I got what I wanted. We're even."

His teeth ground so hard his jaw ached. "We ain't even and you know it. I'll be back. You're going to get me what you promised or else."

He ended the call before she could say anything else. Wouldn't matter what she said. He wanted what he wanted. And he had wanted Keeley Fairchild for years.

In high school, she'd been focused on other things, never dated. Not that he'd ever asked. She wouldn't have anything to do with him or any of the other boys who'd panted after her. She was always too serious, had her head in a book, or was busy practicing for track. But her body . . . Wes hardened at the mental image. Keeley's hot-damn body was the kind boys dreamed of and men salivated for.

After high school, he'd tried a few times to get her to go out with him, but she'd always turned him down. She'd always been nice about it, though, and he figured she was just shy. Then what'd she do but up and marry that rich bastard Stephen Fairchild. Whatever good feelings he'd had about Keeley had been lost. Most everybody knew Fairchild couldn't keep his pants zipped. Wes figured Keeley had gotten what she deserved.

Things were different now. Fairchild's ass was ashes, and Wes had been dreaming and salivating way too long. When he got back to town, the waiting would be over.

First things first . . . get rid of her brats. Other than getting a nice chunk of money, the only satisfaction this job gave him was the knowledge that the bitch would be pissed he hadn't dropped the kids where she'd told him to go.

Wes snorted. Like he was going to take orders from a woman.

Once he took care of his transactions, he'd lay low and enjoy his rewards for a while. Let the bitch get comfortable, think he'd forgotten about her. He'd be back and show her that nobody double-crosses Wesley Tuttle and gets away with it. She'd either pony up the other part of the bargain and get him the woman or he'd be announcing to the world just who was responsible for Keeley Fairchild's misery. Wouldn't the good citizens of Fairview be surprised?

two

Six weeks later
Last Chance Rescue headquarters
Paris, France

Fury vibrated in every step as Cole shoved open the door to his boss's office. Noah McCall was sprawled in his chair, that cool, implacable expression firmly in place.

"Damn you, McCall. Why wasn't I told?"

Other than the tic in McCall's right jaw, the man didn't move. Cole forced several deep breaths to quiet the roar of fury inside him. Teeth clenched, he spoke softly. "I want this case."

Reining in the rage wasn't easy; anger felt more natural than breathing. Being pumped full of supercharged steroids, along with a bunch of other shit, for almost a year will do that to a man. It'd taken months of detox and meditation before he felt his control returning. Now it took only a few seconds to calm the roaring beast inside him. Besides, if there was one man who didn't give a damn about having someone pissed at him, it was McCall.

His boss didn't bother to pretend he didn't know which case. He raised his head slowly and waited a palpable second before saying, "Eden and Jordan are on it. I don't need you."

"I don't care who you've got on it. I want in."

McCall shook his head. "You haven't finished up the job in Mexico."

"We got the doctor . . . he's the one we wanted the most. I left Dylan in charge. The few that are left have been targeted . . . he's got plenty of backup to take them down. If they still need help after I rescue the kids, I'll go back."

Unmoved, McCall shook his head. "I'll keep you informed. Give you access to all the information we have, but I'm not going to—"

"This is a courtesy call, Noah. Whether you put me on the case or not, I'm working it."

McCall leaned back into his chair, his black eyes assessing. "FBI's been all over it. It's over a month old and the trail's gone ice-cold. Keeley Fairchild called me right after it happened. We've been on the case from the beginning."

Cole ground his teeth to keep from snarling. Getting more pissed with McCall for not telling him wouldn't accomplish a damn thing. His boss would have assigned the people he believed were the best operatives to get the kids back.

Personal issues could screw up an op. Cole was more than aware that he wasn't the best person for the job. Staying objective would be critical. Didn't matter. Objectivity for this family had gone out the window a long time ago. If it was the last thing he did, he was going to get those kids back to their mother.

If fury should be directed at anyone, Cole was more than aware that it should be directed at himself. It was his failing that something had happened to the Fairchild children. He'd chosen revenge over protection. While he'd been rounding up the assholes who'd tortured him, he'd failed at his one major responsibility—keeping Keeley Fairchild and her children safe. The knowledge of that failure burned through him like acid. He wouldn't screw up again.

"I have to be on this case, McCall."

"Eden's developed a special bond with Keeley Fairchild. Jordan's got a good relationship going with the investigators. You go in and that might disrupt the balance. Let them handle this. Either one could single-handedly bring in those kids. If the children are still alive, there's no doubt they'll get them back. I'll keep you updated on all the progress."

He couldn't argue the point. Eden and Jordan Montgomery were the best of LCR. No question. But that wouldn't stop him. "Doesn't matter. I want this case."

McCall stared long and hard, then asked quietly, "Have you thought about the cost to yourself?"

Cole snorted. That was the least of his worries. "I don't have anything left to lose."

McCall's eyes flashed. "Don't say that. You have a lot of people who care—"

Cole waved an impatient hand. "You know what I mean. Eden and Jordan are more than capable, but they have a lot to lose if something goes wrong. I don't."

Noah McCall's hard-eyed stare had intimidated many—Cole wasn't one of them. He knew the man too well. Noah's first responsibility would always be to the victims, but that would never negate his concern for his operatives.

"You think sacrificing yourself is going to get these kids back?"

"I've been on plenty of rescue missions and didn't get killed. I don't plan on dying on this one."

"You didn't plan on getting captured and tortured either."

"I screwed up. It won't happen again."

"We all screwed up, Cole. Not just you."

Cole held back his automatic denial. Everyone felt so damned guilty for what he'd gone through, but it'd been his stupid-assed decision to go into that warehouse without backup. There was no one else to blame, but if it got him on the case, he'd use what he had to.

"There's no one more motivated than I am to get those children back to their mother."

The flicker in his boss's eyes told Cole he'd scored a point. Seeing that, Cole stiffened his spine, shut down his conscience, and went for the kill. "You owe me, Noah."

In spite of his determination to feel nothing, a slash of pain ripped through his head at the guilt in his boss's eyes. He'd lied. McCall didn't owe him a damn thing. He'd saved Cole's life years ago by giving him an opportunity and purpose few could. Noah McCall was the most decent man Cole knew, but if pushing this particular button got him on the case, he'd push the hell out of it. He had no choice.

McCall gave a curt nod. "Fine. I'll give you all the intel. You can work it from here or Florida. Another set of eyes can only help. I can—"

"No. I'm going to South Carolina."

"Dammit, there's no reason to meet the woman."

"I'm not in the habit of running from my demons."

"Are you going to tell her who you are?"

"There's no reason to bring her more pain. I'll be another LCR operative working to find her children. What's done is done."

"Here's all the intel we have." McCall slid a thick folder across his desk. A telling gesture. He'd known Cole was coming and had been prepared. "Police report, interviews, investigators' notes. FBI has been extraordinarily cooperative. They've allowed Jordan to sit in on all of the interviews. And Eden's been Keeley's shadow. I think having Eden there has helped the woman about as much as anything. From the sound of it, she has few friends in Fairview."

Cole took the folder and dropped into a chair in front of the desk. He'd take the file apart tonight when he was alone. Right now, he wanted more than what the papers in his hand would reveal . . . he wanted a gut feeling. Noah's take on the situation would give him important insight. The man had overseen more rescues than all his operatives combined.

"I know her parents are gone. Doesn't she have any other family?"

"No family other than the children . . . and her in-laws." Noah's tone indicated antipathy.

"In-laws not like her?"

"From what we can tell, the sister-in-law's a good friend. Mother-in-law sounds like one of those witches Samara reads to Micah about."

"Wicked stepmother type?"

McCall's mouth lifted. "Yeah. Without the poisoned apple."

"What's her problem?"

"Not sure other than Keeley wasn't good enough for her son. Elizabeth Fairchild has made no secret of how she feels. Did her best to have Keeley blamed when Stephen Fairchild was abducted. Local law's a bunch of idiots, and since she apparently has them in her pocket, they tried to charge Keeley without any real evidence. FBI stepped in and stopped them before it went that far."

Guilt skewered through Cole. Bad enough that her husband had been killed, but to be accused of that crime only added to her pain. Through no fault of her own, the woman had suffered tremendously already. Even more incentive for him to find her children.

"What about the kids . . . there's been no ransom demand?"

"No."

His gut twisted. "Hell, it's been too long."

McCall's grim expression was an acknowledgment of what they both knew. The lack of communication for that length of time meant dire consequences. If the kids were even alive, they'd probably been sold. And there were all too many places for that kind of transaction to take place. Those children could be anywhere.

Cole forced his mind away from the harsh reality to get more facts. "How'd it go down?"

"Keeley Fairchild watched a man take the children. Fought like hell to prevent it."

"Watched?"

"Yeah, she was within a few feet of catching up with him and fell flat on her face. Another man tried to grab her . . . she got away from him, but suffered a broken wrist and a concussion."

Cole stiffened. "They tried to grab her along with the kids?"

"Yeah. That's why Eden's sticking so close to her. She may be in danger as well. And it's one of the reasons no one's surprised there's not been a ransom."

"One of the reasons?"

Propping his arms on his desk, McCall leaned forward as he explained. "The kidnappings seemed odd enough . . . what with two kids taken and what happened to her husband. About a week after they were nabbed, the emails started."

"What kind of emails?"

"Not your normal wacko stuff . . . though those kinds of creeps do seem to come out of the woodwork when things like this happen. These comments are targeted and constant, with only one apparent purpose—to hurt Keeley."

Cole held up the folder. "Copies in here?"

Noah nodded. "FBI is keeping the emails under their hat for now, along with the information that she was almost taken, too. As far as the media knows, it's a kidnapping, not a personal vendetta. Press doesn't need more fodder."

"Media circus?"

"It was for a while. They've backed off since there's been no developments."

"So what's your take?"

"The woman's definitely got an enemy. Whether the emails are being sent by the kidnappers is less clear. They make no mention of the kids . . . where they could be, why they were taken, no admission of guilt. Just very pointed and cruel remarks toward her."

"So it could still just be some sick creep who gets off on hurting those who are already hurting."

"Possibly. Thanks to her mother-in-law, Keeley isn't the most popular person in town. Could be one of them."

"The whole town dislikes her?"

Even though it was intentional, Cole cursed his lack of knowledge of Keeley Fairchild. His goal had been to make sure she stayed safe. Finding out personal information about her was a line he hadn't wanted to cross.

"Elizabeth Fairchild owns many of the businesses in Fairview and most of the land in the county. She's got the money and the influence to control the vast majority of the town's employment. Apparently they stay in her good graces by ostracizing Keeley."

Cole clenched his jaw. Getting involved in small-town dramatics would be pointless. Still, hearing how Keeley Fairchild had been treated in her own town didn't sit well with him.

"Any reference to the husband's abduction in the emails?"

"No, nothing about him. Just remarks about what a terrible mother she must be to lose her kids. The writer knows exactly where to stick the knife to do the most damage."

"How many FBI are on the case?"

"Seven when they started. It's dropped to one. Honor Stone . . . you've worked with her before. You remember?"

A vague mental picture of a pretty, freckle-faced woman with a no-nonsense attitude and compassionate green eyes flashed in his mind.

When Cole nodded, Noah continued, "She's worked well with Eden and Jordan but I wouldn't be surprised if she's reassigned soon." He lifted a shoulder. "They'll still work it, of course."

Noah didn't need to add the obvious. The FBI would continue to work it, but there were hundreds of other missing-persons cases they were working, too. Fortunately, Cole had two things the FBI didn't have. Time and total focus. He would never give up until those kids were found.

"Where'd it happen? Her place is like a fortress. Hell, the wall that surrounds her property would stop ninety-nine percent of the population."

"The park. She took the kids for a picnic. An older couple close by called the cops, but their description was as vague as Keeley's. Masked men, white van, no tags or identifying features."

"FBI have any suspects?"

"No strong ones. That's what makes it so damned frustrating."

"Two abductions in two years in the same family," Cole muttered. "No way the two aren't related. Somebody hates Keeley Fairchild enough to take her husband and then her children."

McCall blew out a sigh. "Question is, who?"

"What's your gut say?"

"No one was ever fingered for hiring the husband's abduction." McCall's gaze narrowed on Cole. "You still think it was someone Fairchild knew?"

"Yeah. Rosemount's records never said for sure, but there was something in his insane ramblings that made me believe someone who knew the family hired him."

"Then it stands to reason it's the same person. Someone who either sees Keeley as a cash cow or . . ."

"Or has an intense hatred for her."

"Or both," Noah said.

"If money was the primary motivator, they could've got a hell of a lot by demanding a ransom."

Noah's eyes went bleak. "Yeah. But if there's an additional reason, like hurting Keeley, selling the kids off would make some money and accomplish the other, too."

"And the local law . . . they any help on this case?"

McCall snorted his disgust. "Despite eyewitness accounts, they waited till Keeley regained consciousness before they put out any kind of alert on the kids. Keeley ended up calling the FBI herself. They got there within hours of her call and took over. Did a round of interviews. Got squat. Either no one knows anything . . ."

"Or they're not talking." Cole finished his boss's sentence, then asked, "Jordan and Eden come up with anything yet?"

"Pretty much what we think. Someone has it out for her. Taking her kids is the best way to hurt her."

Yeah, he knew all about that. To truly tear someone to pieces, you go for the heart. "If taking her kids doesn't satisfy them, Keeley could be next," Cole said.

McCall nodded. "If it's a personal vendetta, whoever it is won't be satisfied until she's destroyed."

Having heard enough to give him a good start, Cole stood. "I'll head out tonight."

"I'll let them know you're coming."

Unable to leave alone the words he'd used earlier, Cole turned at the door. "For what it's worth, you don't owe me anything, Noah. What happened wasn't your fault."

McCall's mouth tightened into a grim line as if he were fighting back words. Finally he nodded and said, "Be safe."

When the door closed behind Cole, Noah released a ragged breath. No way in hell could he not feel responsible for what Cole had experienced. There wasn't a person at LCR who didn't feel some sort of guilt. Noah felt the grief and guilt deeper than anyone. He was responsible for every individual at LCR. He'd recruited, trained, encouraged, and, when necessary, disciplined every operative. Noah took his responsibilities seriously. He'd let Cole down.

Instead of investigating the possibility that Cole had been kidnapped and not killed in the warehouse explosion, Noah had concentrated on getting the man responsible for Cole's death. While they'd been searching for a murderer, Cole had been drugged and tortured for months. Used as a killing machine without any concept of what he was doing, he had endured mindless, anguished agony. The scars on his body were only a glimpse of the damage done inside him.

When he'd hired Cole, he'd been impressed with the man's strength of character. Having survived this past year with his sanity intact told Noah he had underestimated that strength.

Having Cole work this particular op wasn't something he could feel comfortable about. He owed it to Cole to let him have the job, but he'd seen that look in other operatives' eyes before. Cole had lost everything and felt he had nothing left to lose. Getting those kids back would be his only aim and focus.

While all LCR operatives understood that the victim always came first and self-sacrifice might well be necessary to get the job done, most of his people had more than an ounce of self-preservation. Cole didn't have that.

Noah picked up a frame from his desk and felt a strong tug to a heart he hadn't even known existed until he'd met Samara. The photo was of his beautiful wife holding their infant son, Micah. He never knew he could feel such love. And if he lost them . . . his life would be destroyed.

A few years back, Cole had lost his wife and daughter in an act of senseless violence. Noah had heard about the case and did his own investigating. He had learned what he needed to know, and had given Cole a few months to grieve. Then Noah had called him. After only one meeting with Cole, he'd offered him a job.

It had been one of the best decisions Noah had ever made. LCR had given the man the purpose he needed. Cole's terrible ordeal and his own innate strength had made him an excellent operative. Compassion tempered with steely determination. And then Cole had been captured; the torture he'd suffered had almost destroyed him. Now all he felt he had left was the payment of this one debt.

If Keeley Fairchild's children could be found, Noah had no doubt that his operative would rescue them. Problem was, would Cole survive it?

three

Dampness cloaked her, saturating Keeley's skin with a welcome layer of moisture. Legs pumping with furious energy and urgency, she raced through the woods. On a deep breath, she inhaled the fragrant scents of pine and cedar. Already budding, dogwood and redbud trees would soon unfurl their blooms, scattering pink and white petals along the trail. Another month or so after that, magnolia trees would fill the air with a subtle lemony fragrance and blend with the sweet scent of honeysuckle. She drew in another breath; she could almost smell them.

To her left, the bright glow of the sun peeking just over the horizon told her it was time to go in. Despite the fact that she'd been running for over an hour, she felt a pang of regret. Sometimes she wanted to run forever.

This was her favorite time of day. The gentle music of nature, along with an invigorating run, always filled her with tranquillity. As a single mom of two rambunctious little girls, her day was filled to the brim. She loved every second of being a mother, but this hour alone, before they woke, was just for her.

Today was Sunday and she'd planned for it by running an extra mile.

Sunday was Hannah's day to choose breakfast, which meant pancakes, with strawberries and whipped cream. If asked what she wanted, at breakfast or anytime, "Pancakes" was always Hannah's answer.

Saturday was Hailey's breakfast choice. Yesterday's had been cereal and toast with grape jelly. Her answer for most meals was an eclectic variety.

Her girls might be twins, but they were polar opposites in almost everything.

A sudden need to see their angelic faces had her increasing her pace. Her lungs working at full capacity, Keeley raced toward the white Southern-style mansion in the distance. It was almost time for them to wake up. She loved being in the room when they opened their eyes.

An unexplained urgency suddenly gripping her, Keeley unlocked the door, keyed in the security code, and raced up the winding staircase. Her breath soughing from overtaxed lungs, she ran down the wide landing toward the children's wing. Within feet of their door, she stopped. The sight of her gasping and wide-eyed with anxiety wasn't something she wanted in their minds.

She bent over and pulled in deep breaths till her rapid breathing slowed to almost normal. Then, putting on her happy face, Keeley walked into the bedroom. She stopped. Their unmade beds were empty. Shaking her head in confusion, Keeley backed out of the room. Were they already up?

Wait. Her friend Jenna . . . did she stay over last night? Of course, how could she have forgotten? They were probably all in the playroom. Keeley ran to the playroom and pushed open the door. Filled with every imaginable toy a child could want, the room was empty of what Keeley wanted most . . . her children.

She hurried back downstairs. Maybe they'd been impatient and had already demanded breakfast. Jenna was a softie when it came to giving in to them . . . that must be what had happened. Her heart pounding with an unknown dread, she pushed opened the kitchen door. Empty.

Telling herself there was nothing to worry about, Keeley called out, "Okay, little chicks. Time for breakfast. Come on out."

Silence.

Her heart picking up a deep, ominous rhythm, Keeley ran through the house. Every door she opened, every closet she peered into, every piece of furniture she looked under, she just knew she'd see two pairs of glinting eyes, proud of themselves for fooling their mama.

On the third floor, where no one ever went, panic set in. Where were her babies? Was that a giggle? She smiled. They were playing a trick on her. Silly gooses.

Keeley raced downstairs, back to their bedroom, and found nothing. Her mind screamed: Where are my babies!

A cry of agony woke Keeley. She shot out of bed; sobs tore and rippled through her body as she ran through her door and into the children's bedroom.

A nightmare . . . only a nightmare. Please, God, oh please God, oh please . . . they had to be there.

Keeley pushed the door open and faced a living nightmare. One she'd been living for over a month. Her children were gone.

Dropping to her knees in the middle of the room, she bent over and wrapped her arms around her body. Tears flooded her eyes, blurring the empty beds in front of her. Keening cries of pain filled the empty room as she rocked her body, reaching for a comfort she'd never find. *My babies . . . Oh God, my babies.*

It took several seconds to realize a slender arm had wrapped around her shoulders and soft, soothing sounds were being whispered in her ear. Breath shuddered through her as she struggled for control. This had turned into almost a daily ritual to wake, believing it had all been a nightmare. Then when she realized the reality, she dissolved into a basket case. The woman beside her had become a rock for her to cling to.

She looked up into the soft gray eyes of LCR operative Eden Montgomery. "I'm sorry." Keeley winced at the hoarseness of her voice. "I keep doing this, don't I?"

"There's no reason to apologize. Nightmares have a tendency to strike when we're the most vulnerable."

Keeley closed her eyes to block out the sight of the empty beds. "If only this was a sleeping nightmare."

"Sometimes the worst nightmares are the ones that exist without the benefit of sleep."

The words were softly spoken but Keeley got the impression that this beautiful woman knew more than her share about waking nightmares. But when she looked at Eden, behind the concern she always showed, there was peace. As if whatever nightmare Eden had endured, she had overcome and found what she was looking for. It was a peace Keeley once thought she had but didn't know if she'd ever feel again.

Eden helped her to her feet. "Why don't you go shower and then come down for breakfast."

Keeley's stomach took a somersault. Considering she'd always had to be careful of every morsel that touched her mouth, not having an appetite was unprecedented. Gut-wrenching grief tended to be the only way she'd ever lost weight. She didn't recommend it as a permanent diet plan. "You and Jordan go ahead and eat. I'm not—"

"I know you're not hungry, but you've got to keep up your strength. What are Hailey and Hannah going to think when they come back and find their mom too weak to hug them?"

Unless she was dead, that would never happen, but she nodded and headed back to her bedroom. Eden was right. It would serve no purpose to starve herself. She had to be strong to get her babies back.

Eden blew out a long sigh as she watched Keeley leave the room. This was the fourth time this week she'd found the young mother in her children's bedroom. What sleep Keeley had been able to catch always ended with the nightmare that had her up and then screaming the moment she realized her children had been taken.

Shaking her head at the sheer heartlessness of the situation, Eden left the room and headed downstairs. The fragrance of freshly brewed coffee drew her to the kitchen. She stopped at the door and took in the sight of Jordan preparing breakfast. They'd been married over two years now, but her heart still pounded like a teenager's when she caught sight of her gorgeous husband. And that would never change.

"Good morning, my love." Jordan's masculinity and sexy smile were not one bit diminished by the small, frilly apron he'd wrapped around his waist.

Rarely able to be in the same room without touching him, Eden crossed the room and reached for her husband, suddenly needing the comfort of his strong embrace. As his arms wrapped around her, she breathed in the deliciously familiar scent of warm, sexy male.

Jordan pulled away slightly to look down at her. "You okay?"

"Yes, just needed an extra hug this morning."

Jordan pressed a kiss to her forehead and held her close again. "Keeley wake up the same way this morning?"

Eden nodded against his chest. "And I know for a fact she didn't go to bed until after three. I got up several times and found her in the girls' room."

"Cases like this are never easy, but you're taking this harder than most. Why?"

She pulled away to pick up the coffee Jordan had poured for her and took an appreciative sip. "I guess because what she's already gone through . . . losing her husband. And now her kids are gone."

"And because we're about to become parents?"

Eden smiled softly. He knew her so well. "Even though I've only seen pictures of him, I already love him."

"So do I," Jordan said.

She and Jordan couldn't have children of their own. A few months ago, they'd made the decision to begin adoption proceedings. Fate had intervened. McKenna, another LCR operative, was in Bangkok on an op and found a little boy, no older than three, who'd been abandoned on the streets. She had called Eden immediately and sent a photo over her cellphone. It had been love at first sight for both Eden and Jordan.

Though Eden wasn't long on patience and didn't have any real issues with bending the law to get things done, she and Jordan were jumping through hoops and doing all the proper things to get this child. No way in hell would anyone ever question whether he belonged to them. Paulo had become their son the second they saw him. Unfortunately, going the legal route also took an enormous amount of time. But they would succeed; she had no doubt about that.

The wait, though, had been agonizing. Eden had welcomed this assignment, knowing that staying busy would make the time go faster. It had, but it had also produced a surprising vulnerability she hadn't expected. She already loved her son without ever having met him and would be devastated if something happened to him. How much more anguish was Keeley Fairchild feeling?

Not only had she lost her husband last year, both of her babies had been stolen from her.

"Noah called," Jordan said.

"Anything new?"

"Yes."

By the look in his eyes, Eden knew he had conflicting feelings about the call. "What's up?"

"Cole's coming."

Eden shrugged. "We knew he would once he learned about it. Noah say how he's doing?"

Jordan's mouth lifted in a slight smile. "Pissed."

"Yeah. I figured. Other than that, how's he doing?"

"For a man who a year ago didn't know who the hell he was, Noah said he was doing remarkably well . . . physically. The rest . . ." He shrugged. "You know better than anyone how that is."

"Day-to-day kind of thing." She pulled a stool away from the bar and sat down, enjoying watching her husband make his famous pancakes. "Are we off the case?"

Jordan flipped a pancake with the expertise of a short-order cook. "Not yet. I told Noah I'd get back to him after we talked. What do you think?"

"I think we should wait. Despite Cole's understandable desire to handle this case, Keeley not only requires our protection, she needs a support system. Cole won't be able to give her that."

"You're right," Jordan said. "He'll want to stay as removed as possible."

Eden bit her lip, feeling an unusual reluctance to bring the subject up, even though it had to be addressed. "I'm assuming we're supposed to tell Keeley that Cole is just another operative on the case and nothing more?"

"Right. Anything else Keeley learns will be up to him."

"When's he getting here?"

"Tomorrow." Jordan shot her a glance. "How do you

feel about backing off and letting Cole take over the op?"

"If anyone has a right to run it, he does. Don't you agree?"

Jordan nodded. "Absolutely. There's no one who could be more motivated to get those kids back to their mother."

She stood and headed to the door. "I'll call Honor and give her a heads-up. She'll want to be prepared."

Jordan turned, a slight furrow of his brow indicating his confusion. "Why? She's been more than cooperative with us. Having another LCR operative shouldn't make that much difference for her."

Eden grimaced. "This one will. Only a few people know about it, but she and Cole had a small fling not long after he started with LCR. It never developed into anything. I think Honor might have wanted something more, but Cole never pursued it. She was as upset as any of us when we thought Cole died. She'll want to be prepared."

Jordan flipped another pancake. "Better warn her then. Last thing we need is that kind of complication."

Eden stepped out onto the back porch and pulled out her cellphone. She only hoped this wasn't going to cause problems for Honor. The woman was a professional, but working with a man you had feelings for who didn't feel the same way could destroy your concentration. She knew that all too well.

Hopefully, Honor was strong enough to handle this.

Keeley frowned at the washed-out, fragile-looking woman staring back at her in the mirror. The ghostlike reflection made her want to turn around and go back to bed. Unfortunately, that would only result in more nightmares. Awake or asleep, they were there, haunting her with thousands of questions for which she had no answers.

With a ragged breath, she opened the shower door and turned on the spray, allowing the tears to mingle with the water. If only her mother were here. She'd been gone almost eight years and Keeley missed her every day. Since Hailey and Hannah had been taken, the void created by her death seemed darker and deeper than ever.

Keeley's childhood hadn't been the easiest, but thanks to her mother, she'd learned early that the true measure of a person was found in the heart, not their bank account. Kathleen Daniels had a way of making everything make sense. Even during the hardest and darkest times, when they'd lived at the poverty level, her mother's natural optimism could soothe Keeley's deepest hurts. Whenever some kid at school had been particularly cruel, her mother's wise words would alleviate the pain and somehow Keeley would end up feeling sorry for the kid.

After rinsing the soap from her hair and body, Keeley turned the shower off and grabbed a towel. Just thinking about her mother gave her a sense of peace.

Resolved to follow her mother's example and be strong for her children, she quickly dried off and slipped into a pair of jeans and a button-up cotton blouse. Though the clothes hung on her body, Keeley didn't care. Apparently whoever had taken her children wanted to see her suffer. Maybe if they saw they had achieved their goal, they'd bring her babies back. Flawed, irrational reasoning, but it gave her some kind of hope and God knew she needed it.

Keeley braided her wet hair, then, barely glancing at the results, steeled her backbone and headed downstairs. Today was Monday, which meant she had a full day ahead of her in the office. Sending a blast of emails all over the world twice a week was her Monday and Thursday ritual. Each day of the week was devoted to a special task or event . . . all having one thing in common—getting her children back.

Tomorrow would be devoted to sending flyers with the girls' photographs to hospitals, daycare centers, and grocery stores throughout the country.

Wednesday morning Honor Stone, the special FBI agent in charge of the case, would come for their weekly meeting. In the afternoon, Keeley devoted her time to updating all the social networking sites she'd joined right after the girls had been taken.

Friday was devoted to answering correspondence and updating the website she'd set up a few days after their abduction. Saturday and Sunday were filled with strategizing what she would do the next week.

Next Monday it would begin all over again. And would continue until her girls were back home. This she vowed.

No one had said they were giving up, but she couldn't help but wonder if that day would come soon.

The FBI had been helpful and professional. It'd been hard to accept, but Keeley understood their need to reduce the number of agents assigned to the case. Thankfully, the agent they'd left in charge was the most compassionate of the lot. Unlike some of the others, who'd only looked upon her children's disappearance as a job, Honor's empathy and humanity came through.

The press had been another matter. She resented and hated their voracious, never-ending questions. At first they'd been like vultures, with only one thing on their minds—a dramatic or lurid story to tell. She allowed them entrance because she needed their assistance. Getting as much publicity into the world about her babies could only help.

As much as she had resented their personal, often painful questioning, what hurt even more was when they began to dwindle away, leaving only a handful of local reporters. She told herself it was because more sensational stories were happening and not because they believed the case was over.

She would not give up and refused to allow anyone else to give up either. Her daughters were coming back to her. Period.

Her mind out of victim mode and into mission mode, Keeley pushed open the door to the kitchen. She stopped at the entrance, not wanting to disrupt the tender moment Eden and her husband, Jordan, were sharing. Whispering words she couldn't make out, Jordan pressed a soft kiss to Eden's lips and held her close in his arms.

She observed these tender moments almost on a daily basis, and every time she did, a lump developed in her throat. What a beautiful and loving relationship they seemed to have. That kind of close bond in a marriage was foreign to her. Her mother had never married. And Keeley's marriage to Stephen had never developed into the kind of loving intimacy Jordan and Eden seemed to share.

Spotting Keeley at the door, Eden pulled away from her husband's arms and smiled. "Come eat some of Jordan's pancakes. You'll love them."

Tears sprang to her eyes before she could stop them.

Eden was at her side immediately. "What's wrong?"

Keeley shook her head. What a wimp she was. "I'm sorry. It's just that pancakes are Hannah's favorite meal." She smiled through her tears. "She calls them 'mama cakes.'"

Eden gave her a bracing hug. "You have to have faith, Keeley. Soon you'll be eating them again with both your daughters. Okay?"

Keeley nodded. Eden was right. She had to stay positive that her girls would be returned to her soon.

Taking a breath to calm herself, Keeley poured a cup of coffee from the glass carafe on the counter and sat down at the kitchen table.

Jordan handed her a plate stacked with fluffy pancakes and then dropped into a chair across from her. "We have another operative coming tomorrow."

In the middle of pouring maple syrup on her stack of pancakes, she stopped to look at him. "Oh really . . . who?"

"Cole Mathison. He's worked a lot of these cases." He glanced at his wife and then back to Keeley. "And he's worked with Agent Stone before."

A burst of optimism hit Keeley. The more people on the case, the quicker her babies would be found. "What will Mr. Mathison do?"

"Cole's one of our best interrogators, excellent at ferreting out secrets. We'll sit down and come up with a plan where his talents can be best used."

The hopeful news giving her a bit of appetite, Keeley attacked the pancakes with determination, managing six bites, along with a half a glass of orange juice and her requisite three cups of coffee. Then, pulling in another deep breath, she smiled at the two people across the table from her eyeing her with such concern. "I'll be in my office if anything comes up."

"Jordan's headed out to follow up on the tips that came in last night."

Every few days, Jordan mysteriously disappeared for several hours. Though she knew he was working closely with the FBI, Keeley knew he had contacts that weren't necessarily considered aboveboard.

Eden had assured her that Jordan's methods of getting information from all kinds of sources were legal. Keeley didn't care if they were legal. She just wanted results. So far nothing substantial had come from his contacts, but that didn't keep Jordan from trying.

Eden continued, "I'll help him clean up in here and join you. Are Jenna or Miranda coming today?"

Jenna Banks, Keeley's best friend since they were children, and Miranda, Stephen's sister, took turns helping her in the office. Since Jenna ran a successful business and Miranda had a six-year-old daughter, they both led very busy lives. Keeley was enormously grateful for their help. Not that it surprised her. Jenna and Miranda loved Hailey and Hannah almost as much as she did.

"Unless I hear differently, I don't think Miranda will be here until Friday." Keeley laughed softly. "I expect we'll see Jenna again tonight . . . she's been dropping by around dinnertime a lot since Mrs. Thompkins has been cooking for us."

"I can't blame her," Eden said. "Her pot roast is out of this world."

Jordan gently nudged Eden toward the door. "I'll clean up . . . there's not that much to do. Go on with Keeley."

"You'll be careful?"

"Always," Jordan said.

At the tender look Jordan gave his wife, Keeley turned away and headed to her office. She wasn't jealous of their relationship, but after her own failed marriage, seeing what was possible was sometimes painful.

Flipping the light switches, she went about getting what she thought of as her control room up and running. She called it that because at least here she felt as though she had a modicum of control over the hell her life had become.

The day she'd returned from the hospital, Keeley had converted what had once been Stephen's home office into command central. Updating the website she'd set up after her girls were taken and generally making

herself a pain in the ass had become a full-time job. She
didn't care. Until her children were back in her arms,
this would be her life, and if she had to bug the hell out
of every person in the universe, then she would.

The FBI and LCR had the most-advanced technology
and could accomplish much more than she ever could.
It didn't matter. She had to do something, and if she got
even one clue, it would have all been worth it.

She clicked on her email and was soon immersed, barely
hearing Eden quietly enter and begin work at the other
desk. She tackled every email as she came to it, refusing to
flinch at the sheer cruelty of some people. Within this correspondence could well be the key they'd been searching
for for so long.

Many of the emails were from well-meaning, sympathetic people only wanting an update or to express sympathy. A few didn't bother with sympathy; they were the
nosy ones, wanting to know information without any
offer to help. And then there were the sadists who apparently got their rocks off by telling her she was a rotten
mother. She printed each one, even the nice ones. Honor,
Jordan, and Eden could read them and determine much
more than she. Just because the emails seemed nice
didn't mean there wasn't some underlying message she
was missing. She could leave no stone unturned.

The emailer who insisted on torturing her with the
most horrific observations and cruel remarks hadn't sent
anything in the last few days, and unless he finally
decided to admit he was the one who took her girls, she
hoped she didn't hear from him today. Some days she
handled them better than others. Today, for some reason,
she felt even more fragile. As if something was about to
happen and she wasn't as prepared as she needed to be.

Unfortunately, she wasn't going to get her wish. An
email with the same subject line as usual showed up in
her in-box. Closing her eyes, Keeley took a long, brac-

ing breath. Then, determined to weather whatever the creep had to say to her, she clicked on the email.

SUBJECT: Stupid Bitch loses babies

Hi Bad Mama Bitch, over a month and still no sightings. Are the brats gone for good? Hopefully they found a better mother than you. Ha! A rabid half-dead hyena would be a better mother than you. Later, Bitch.

After another shaky breath, Keeley hit the print button. Actually this message had an almost friendly tone. Others had been horrendously cruel, giving graphic details of what might have happened to her girls. Maybe he was getting tired of sending them. She sincerely hoped that was the case.

Keeley didn't question why she assumed this person was a man. There were plenty of mean-spirited women in the world, but for some reason she could not accept that there was a woman out there who would do something like this. A woman should be able to identify with how gut-wrenchingly painful it was to have your children snatched from you. She realized she was being unfair to the many good men in the world, but she refused to believe another woman could be so cruel.

"Another one?" Eden's sympathetic face peered over the top of her computer.

Keeley released a shaky sigh. "Not as mean as he usually is."

Tilting her head a little, Eden posed the question Keeley had just been thinking. "Why do you always refer to this person as 'he'?"

"It was a man—or men—who took them." She shrugged. "And it's just hard for me to believe that a woman could be that cruel."

"First of all, we don't know that the person sending

these emails took your girls. And secondly, don't kid yourself, women can often be much crueler than men."

"So you still don't think this person took them?"

"No."

"Why?"

"Gut mostly . . . but also, why don't the emails ever mention where the children are, why they were taken, or how they were taken? There's no mention that you were almost abducted, too, no details given at all. I think this person is taking advantage of a horrific situation to hurt you even more."

"But why?"

"Why does anyone hurt another person?"

"Do you think it's someone I know?"

"It's possible. Or it could just be someone half a world away who read about this and enjoys inflicting this kind of pain. I gave up asking why people are the way they are a long time ago. Just don't assume that a woman isn't capable of this type of cruelty. I was raised by a mother who would take great delight in something like this."

Unable to comprehend anyone being so vicious, Keeley asked, "How did you escape from being like her?"

A small sad smile curved her mouth. "I had a stepfather who was the total opposite . . . and I had Jordan."

"You knew Jordan as a child?"

Eden stood and stretched. "Let's take a walk outside; I'll tell you our story."

Biting her lip, Keeley glanced down at her monitor. As much as she wanted to get some fresh air and learn more about Eden and Jordan, she was torn. "You go on, I'll—"

"No arguments. It might help you sleep."

Appreciating Eden's gentle bullying, Keeley stood and followed Eden out the door. Fresh air could only help.

Still, she couldn't get Eden's comments out of her mind. The emails could be coming from a woman . . . even possibly one she knew? Keeley couldn't accept that. No one she knew could be so incredibly evil.

four

Cole took a long swallow of coffee, hoping to sideline the oncoming headache. They were less frequent now. Doctors said that at some point, they'd go away completely. Couldn't be soon enough for him.

A glance at his watch assured him he had four more hours before the plane touched down at the Fairview airport. The remaining hours of the flight he would devote to reviewing the files one more time, including the things he'd avoided last night.

The vibration of his cellphone in his pocket delayed the inevitable a little longer. He checked the readout and instantly felt a lift to his spirits. *Shea.* Though he figured he'd be getting a lecture, that didn't keep him from enjoying talking to her.

"Hello, Shea."

"I can't believe you're going to do this."

"What happened to 'Hello, how are you'?"

"Why would you put yourself through this?"

"You, of all people, shouldn't have to ask me that. In fact, I'm damn pissed that you and Ethan kept it from me."

"Because we knew exactly how you would react. Besides, Eden and Jordan can—"

"I'm not disputing Eden and Jordan's qualifications. But you had to know I'd be on it as soon as I found out."

"We thought you had enough on your plate. How'd

you find out? You were supposed to be incommunicado for months."

"McKenna."

Her sigh held exasperation. "Remind me to have a talk with her next time I see her."

Picturing the determined and feisty McKenna battling the spirited Shea was almost amusing.

"She did the right thing. I need to be on this case."

"You've been hurt enough." The thickness in her voice told him she was close to tears. He didn't like to think of her crying, but he would not back down.

"You risked your life to avenge me when you thought I was dead. Do you think I can do anything less for this woman?"

"Dammit, what happened wasn't your fault."

"Doesn't matter. It still happened." He softened his voice. "I'll be fine. I promise."

He heard an audible swallow. "How are you feeling?"

Thankful she'd dropped the subject, he said, "Better each day. You?"

"Almost completely recovered. No nightmares in weeks. Headaches are almost completely gone, too."

"I'm glad."

The knowledge that Rosemount had found Shea because of Cole's drug-induced ramblings was bad enough. But after she'd been captured, Cole had stood and watched while she was being tortured and had done nothing to stop it. Those memories tore at his insides like shards of glass. Didn't matter that he'd been drugged and hadn't even known what the hell was going on. The recollections of her torture had come back quickly . . . were still featured in his nightmares.

"Are you really feeling better?" Shea asked.

"I'm getting there. Finding those kids will help a lot."

"You want us to help?"

A smile lifted his lips. Cole touched his fingers to his

mouth, unable to resist feeling it. Smiling was more spontaneous now, but still felt odd on his face.

"I thought you and Ethan were concentrating on something else."

Shea laughed. "Well, we have to come up for air sometime."

Cole heard a growl in the background. Just as he figured, Ethan had been listening the entire time, and this was probably the only part of the discussion he'd disagreed with.

"Thanks for the offer, but I'll be fine. You guys stay busy making me a godfather."

Another laugh. Thank God Shea had almost completely recovered. Hearing her laugh eased the pain inside him. She deserved every happiness. Finally marrying the man she'd been in love with forever had helped her heal more than anything.

"You'll be the first to know when that happens."

"How're Gabe and Skylar doing?"

Another soft laugh. "Behaving like two fools in love. I've never seen a man smile as much as Gabe has since they got back together. And Skylar is glowing like the sun. They came over last night and we celebrated the house they closed on yesterday. It's just a few miles down the road from us."

"Give them my congratulations, will you?"

"Will do. And please, Cole, let us know if we can help."

"I will, Shea. Thanks."

Somewhat heartened by talking to his former wife, Cole pocketed his phone. She sounded so much like the old Shea, and hopefully, soon, she would learn she was expecting.

Though she and Ethan had married several months ago, the doctors had advised Shea to wait awhile before trying to conceive, giving her body time to completely heal. She'd recently been given the go-ahead, and knowing his friends, he fully expected to hear good news very soon.

If there was anything worthwhile that came out of the hellacious experience he and Shea had suffered, it was that Ethan and Shea finally got their happy ending.

Taking a deep breath, Cole forced his mind back to his new mission. Opening the file, he quickly reviewed the pages he'd read last night. Keeley Fairchild was a young woman who'd lost too much already. She'd been raised by a single mother who had died during Keeley's second year of college. Dying from breast cancer at the age of forty was a sad ending for woman who'd apparently struggled all her life.

A year after her mother's death, Keeley had married the son of one of the wealthiest families in South Carolina. They'd had a seemingly happy marriage until Stephen was kidnapped last year by Donald Rosemount's organization.

Just before the abduction, rumors of Stephen Fairchild's infidelities had become rampant, leading to accusations from Stephen's mother that Keeley set up the abduction. The infidelity proved to be true; the accusations against Keeley were denounced.

Ransom had been demanded, and Keeley Fairchild had paid. However, two days after the ransom drop, Stephen's body was found in the woods close to the abduction site, his neck broken. Donald Rosemount had been in charge of the abduction, but who'd hired him was still a mystery. Though Stephen Fairchild wasn't supposed to die, finding out who had hired Rosemount could lead to who had taken the children. Solving one mystery might well solve another.

Turning the page, Cole caught his breath and then expelled a long, shaky sigh. He'd never seen pictures of Keeley Fairchild. Had avoided them along with any personal information. In his mind, knowing more would

have put him in the category of a stalker. Now he regretted not seeing photos of her before. If he'd known what
to expect, then maybe he wouldn't feel as though he'd
been gut-punched and thrown off a cliff.

To say Keeley was beautiful would be wrong. What
Keeley had was something women all over the world
spent thousands on each year. Her light olive skin was
so clear and creamy that wearing makeup would be like
adding paint to a rose. Thick, lustrous shoulder-length
black hair famed a heart-shaped face. Eyes the color of
dark chocolate were surrounded by long, thick black
lashes. Full, luscious lips were the color of pink rose
petals and little creases on either side of her mouth indicated that those lips probably lifted a lot in laughter. A
softly pointed chin and high cheekbones completed
what was one of the most exotic and loveliest women he
had ever seen.

Cole swallowed hard. That wasn't where her outward
beauty ended. The photograph was a full-body shot.
Faded jeans emphasized impossibly long legs and
rounded womanly hips. The white T-shirt she wore, lov-
ingly molded over . . .

He slammed the file shut, feeling like a voyeur and a
sleaze. Here he was trying to make amends and all he
could think about was what those beautiful lips would
taste like against his. How her gorgeous ass would feel
cupped in his hands. Or how it would feel to bury his
head between what anyone in their right mind could
only term world-class breasts.

He shifted in his seat. Of all the freaking times for his
libido to come back full force. And of all people, for this
woman. Cole had often felt that his life was one giant
irony; his attraction to Keeley proved the point even
more.

It'd been years . . . he pressed a finger to his temple.
Hell, had he slept with anyone since Jill? Though he and

Shea had been briefly married, they'd never felt that way about each other and had never slept together.

No. As far as he could remember, there had been no one since his first wife. As usual, when he thought of Jill, a dull ache thudded in his chest. She'd been gone over five years now, and thanks to Rosemount's drugs, many of his memories of her were gone, too. She had been his childhood sweetheart and he'd planned to spend his life with her. Fate had stepped in and taken her from him.

But Cassidy . . . in some ways, losing Jill had been easier than losing his precious daughter. Adults die . . . children shouldn't, especially not in the way his little girl had.

Cole rubbed at his eyes, not surprised to feel the sting of tears. Cassidy had been seven years old, just a few days shy of her eighth birthday. Seven too-short years on this earth. Then some freaking kid with no sense of right or wrong because of a head full of drugs and a gun had taken her away.

Of all the things he would like to never remember, the most painful was the moment he walked into the kitchen and found Jill and Cassidy lying on the floor in a pool of blood, wrapped in each other's arms. There were still large patches of his memory missing. Why the hell couldn't that be one of them?

The doctors told him he could probably force out any missing memories with drugs, but damned if he wanted to put any more garbage into his body. Whatever he never remembered, he would never remember. That was just the way it would be.

Another irony. He remembered the horror of his family's murder, remembered Shea's torture, his own agonizing pain, but many of the good memories were gone. He knew there were some . . . he'd felt small blips and shadows . . . knew they were of happiness. Sometimes he saw Jill's face, heard Cassidy's laughter . . . but those memories were much too few. Just another way that Rosemount's drugs continued to torture.

His only hope was that Donald Rosemount was enjoying his own torture in hell.

Cole forced himself to open the file again. Any other photographs of Keeley he came to, he ignored. Having any kind of interest in the woman beyond rescuing her children would be a million miles past off-limits.

He turned a page and his chest tightened with an almost excruciating squeeze. Hannah and Hailey Fairchild—Keeley's four-year-old twin girls—looked up at him with the precious eyes of innocence and candor.

Hannah had her mother's coloring—olive skin, deep, dark brown eyes, thick black hair. Her sister, Hailey, supposedly resembled her father, who'd been blond with light blue eyes. Cole remembered those eyes all too well. He still saw them in his nightmares.

Another memory he'd love to forget.

His head pressed back against the seat cushion, he closed his eyes. There were certain degrees of hell; he figured he'd experienced almost all of them. Meeting Keeley Fairchild for the first time would just be one more.

five

Something about Cole Mathison bothered Keeley on sight. At first glance, she got the impression of a tall, muscular man with thick black hair, oddly colored eyes, and a grim expression.

Eden, who stood beside the large, fierce-looking man, looked like a beautiful delicate flower standing beside a giant, weathered oak.

When Eden saw Keeley hesitate at the door, she gave her an encouraging smile. "Keeley, this is Cole Mathison, the other operative we told you about."

As Eden made the introductions, Keeley tried to pinpoint why the man bothered her so much. His outward attractiveness was undeniable. With his striking looks, Cole Mathison might well be considered movie-star handsome. But something was missing . . . keeping his good looks in check. An underlying danger, a hollow sadness.

He was very tall . . . maybe around six-five. Tall men certainly didn't bother her. She stood close to five feet eleven in her stocking feet. Perhaps it was his eyes that disturbed her. They were an unusual color—dark charcoal, with striations of silver and electric blue. Or maybe it was just the sheer bleakness of his face. Did he ever smile? Lines around his eyes and mouth indicated that he might have at one time, but she couldn't imagine that happening. His face was cold and austere, almost emotionless. He didn't look as though he had an ounce of humanity or sympathy inside him.

Not that it mattered what he looked like. Her only priority was finding her children. Still, he worried her on a level she couldn't fully comprehend.

Despite her uneasiness, Keeley forced stiff legs to move forward as she held out her hand. "Thank you for your help, Mr. Mathison."

A brisk, hard press of her hand and a quick nod was his response.

An awkward silence surrounded them, finally broken by Eden saying, "Cole has read your file and all the interviews conducted by the FBI and by us. He'd like to talk with you now, if you feel up to it."

Keeley nodded. While she hated having to repeat for the thousandth time what she'd told a seemingly endless amount of people, she would do it a million times more if it brought her girls home.

Eden gave her arm a reassuring squeeze. "I'm going to go make us some tea."

Before Keeley could respond, Eden left the room, leaving her alone with Cole Mathison. Forcing herself to look up at him, she was surprised by the quick expression of what looked like pain flashing across his face.

"Are you all right?" she asked.

In an instant, the cold remoteness returned. "I'm fine." He indicated a chair across from him. "Have a seat."

Fighting her odd nervousness, Keeley perched on the edge of the seat and wrapped her arms around herself.

"Let's start on the day your girls were taken. See where that leads."

"Okay. We were at the park and I—"

Cole held up his hand. "Start earlier. When you got up that day. Take me through as much as you can remember."

"We started out early . . . only an hour or so after

breakfast. I packed a picnic lunch for all of us. My friend, Jenna Banks, was supposed to meet us there, but had to work instead. Miranda, my sister-in-law, and her daughter, Maggie, were supposed to come, too, but Miranda called the night before and said Maggie was coming down with a cold and was running a temperature. She didn't want my girls to get sick.

"It's a public park . . . I thought we would be safe." She cleared her throat and continued. "It was a warm and sunny day, the first one we'd had in months . . . a perfect day for a picnic."

Cole forced a cold stoicism as he listened to the pain in Keeley's voice. After his year of hell, much of the emotion and compassion he'd once felt was gone. He didn't know if it would ever return. There was an odd sort of comfort in that kind of emptiness. Today was the first day he'd felt anything close to breaking through that impenetrable void.

This woman bore little resemblance to the photographs he'd seen of her. Then she'd been healthy and tanned, vibrantly alive. The camera had captured a serenity and peacefulness in her expressive face. A love of life. Today, she looked washed out, tortured, and almost thin—a shadowed image of what she used to be. Losing her husband had taken a toll; having her children taken was destroying her.

"Why'd you decide to go to the park? I checked out back. You have a big yard and almost everything a park would have."

A slight lift of her lips was barely a smile. "It's something different for them. They play in the backyard every day. Saturdays are park days."

"How long have you been going on Saturdays and do you go the same time each Saturday?"

"We started a few weeks after Stephen's death. We don't usually stay more than an hour or two . . . the picnic was unusual. But yes, it's usually around the same time."

"And do your friends Jenna and Miranda usually join you?"

"Almost always. It's not only a chance for the girls to play, it's an opportunity for Jenna, Miranda, and I to catch up."

"You said you started going to the park after your husband's death. Why then?"

"Playing in the backyard was something Stephen did with the girls when he got home from work. It was their time together. They missed him so much, I just wanted them to be able to play without wondering why their daddy wasn't with them."

"Did it help?"

Her dark brows shifted slightly as though she was surprised by the question.

"It helped a little. Stephen's been gone well over a year now . . . they were barely three years old when he died, still babies really, so their memories of him aren't as vivid as they once were. They've adjusted better than I thought they would."

"And you?"

"Me?"

"Have you adjusted?"

Her expressive face was telling him she thought his questions were not the least bit related to her children's disappearance. Cole knew he needed to back off and focus on the abduction. This one last question and he would.

"Yes, I think so."

Had she? From all accounts, she had little social life. Her children and running on her trail were her only outlets. Keeley Fairchild was only twenty-nine years old. Much too young to bury herself in a tiny town, especially since most of the residents seemed to dislike her.

As Cole continued, taking her through the series of events of what happened the day her children were stolen, he began to see why Keeley seemed to have no life outside of her small world. She lived for her children. It was obvious in the way she spoke of them as individuals, relating little tidbits of information on each child. Her mobile mouth moved up in a small smile as if talking about them brought her comfort.

"So Hailey was on the monkey bars and Hannah was heading toward her?"

"Yes, I was getting a juice box for Hailey when I heard them scream. I turned. Saw that a man had both of them in his arms. I started running . . . then another man tried to grab me."

"The man who tried to grab you. Did he say anything to you?"

Her smooth brow wrinkled in concentration. "He said, 'Come on, bitch,' once, and then another time, he shouted, 'Bitch.'" She lifted a slender shoulder. "He might have cursed a couple more times, but nothing more."

"And the voice didn't sound familiar at all?"

"No."

"Anyone else around to see what was going on?"

"Just an older couple—the Wilsons. They're the ones who called the sheriff's office. By the time they realized what was happening, the van had disappeared. I was unconscious."

"How were you injured?"

"I was chasing the man who had my girls . . . they were screaming for me." Her throat moved convulsively. "My hand was on the man's sleeve. I wasn't fast enough . . . he pulled away." She closed her eyes briefly; when she opened them, Cole saw unending horror. "I tripped and fell. The next thing I knew, I was in the hospital. Jenna was there." Her eyes sparkled with contempt as she added, "And the sheriff."

"I understand he didn't want to send out an alert about the children until he talked with you. Why is that?"

She gave a soft snort. "Hiram Mobley is an imbecile. Despite what the Wilsons told him, he insisted he had to hear my report first. When I woke up, he became more cooperative. When the FBI arrived, he backed off completely."

Though he figured Keeley's mother-in-law had control of the local sheriff, Cole made a mental note to talk to Sheriff Mobley very soon.

He glanced down at a previous interview Jordan had done with her. "You gave a description of the two men. One was stocky, between five-eight and five-ten; the other was more muscular and about six feet tall. They were masked and wore jackets, but you were able to see that both men were Caucasian?"

"Yes. The man who grabbed me . . . I clawed at his arm, his sleeve jacket slipped, and I glimpsed pale skin."

"And the other?"

Her eyes anguished, she bit her lip and said, "Hannah was crying, tugging on the man's ski mask. She pulled enough of it away for me to see his neck. . . . He was white, very fair."

Telling himself this was just like any other case he'd been on, Cole worked hard to avoid revealing how Keeley's obvious grief affected him. In his years with LCR, he'd interviewed many grieving mothers. This should be no different.

"Tell me about your family. I see your mother passed away several years ago. What about your father and his family?"

"My father died before I was born. He was from Venezuela, here on a work visa. He met my mother and they fell in love. They'd planned to marry but he was killed in a car accident. She found out she was pregnant with me a few weeks after his death."

"And you're sure there's no one from his side of the family who could be involved in this?"

"Quite sure. My mother didn't know his family and they never knew about us."

"Your husband's family . . . tell me about them."

The deep breath she exhaled revealed much about her feelings. "There's only Stephen's sister and mother left. His father died long before Stephen and I became involved."

"No aunts, uncles, cousins?"

"No close relatives . . . just some distant cousins in Kansas. Stephen didn't know them and never talked about them. Nolan Fairchild, Stephen's great-grandfather, founded the town of Fairview over a hundred years ago. The Fairchilds were once a large, thriving family, but Baker Fairchild, Stephen's father, was an only child. So is Elizabeth, Stephen's mother."

"I understand that Miranda, Stephen's sister, is a good friend."

A small smile. "Yes, she was a few years behind me in school, so we didn't really get to know each other until after Stephen and I got married."

"And Miranda's mother? Tell me about Elizabeth Fairchild."

As if unable to sit still while she talked about her former mother-in-law, Keeley stood and went to the large window that overlooked the backyard. Her face averted, she spoke softly, reflectively. "She's very protective of the Fairchild name. Anything that could bring shame or tarnish the family's reputation is something she'd do anything to stop."

"And she thinks you tarnished it? How?"

"By marrying her son."

"Do you trust her?"

She looked at him then. "Absolutely not. But if you're asking if I believe she was involved with my children's disappearance, then the answer is no. Elizabeth might not love them, but she would've done anything to prevent the media circus their disappearance caused."

"What makes you say your mother-in-law doesn't love her grandchildren?"

"Elizabeth despises me and, in turn, hates my children."

Though Cole knew enough about her background to know the answer to many of these questions, getting her perspective was vital. "Why does your mother-in-law hate you?"

A wry smile twisted her full mouth. "I'm a walking cliché. Poor girl from the wrong side of the tracks marries the richest boy in the county. My mother was an unwed mother. In small towns, especially this small town, that means something. Elizabeth was horrified to have me as a member of her family."

Cole looked down at his notes. "But Miranda, her daughter, is also a single mother, isn't she?"

"Even though Miranda and Maggie live with Elizabeth, she barely acknowledges their existence." She shrugged. "I'm not necessarily the only one Elizabeth ostracizes, I just happen to be her favorite target."

"Hailey and Hannah are her son's children, too. Surely she feels some affection for them."

"Affection is an emotion for normal people. Elizabeth isn't normal. To her, my girls are tainted with my blood."

Could Elizabeth Fairchild really be so cold and hate her daughter-in-law so much that she didn't care that her own grandchildren had been abducted? She might hate the mother, but the children were her son's—her own—flesh and blood.

When he'd lost his daughter, Cassidy, his in-laws had grieved almost as much as he did. A grandparent with this kind of cold, uncaring attitude was foreign to him. If Elizabeth could hate that deeply and severely, what better way to destroy the woman she despised than to take her children from her?

"The person who arranged your husband's abduction was never found. And from all accounts, there are still no suspects. Correct?"

Returning to her chair, Keeley nodded. "Yes. The final theory was that someone saw an opportunity to make some money and they knew we could pay the ransom. Though it's my understanding from LCR that Stephen wasn't supposed to die. Another kidnap victim inadvertently killed him."

Refusing to give himself an out by avoiding her gaze, Cole faced her and answered, "That's true."

Keeley hadn't thought Cole Mathison's expression could get any grimmer, but for some reason, it had. Perhaps she was wrong about him. His questions were thorough and his demeanor gave every indication that he took this assignment very seriously. Something inside her began to ease.

"I know you're new to the case, but Eden, Jordan, and the FBI believe that the same person who had Stephen kidnapped could also be responsible for Hailey and Hannah's disappearance. Do you agree?"

"The person who paid for the abduction could well be the same person." Cole Mathison's eyes went icy cold as he continued, "Donald Rosemount, the man responsible for the actual abduction, is dead."

"Yes, I was told he was killed by one of his victims."

"That's true, also."

"You seem to know a lot about Stephen's case. You worked on it, too?"

"Yes."

"So you think it's possible it's the same person?"

"Abductions are rare enough in this country. To have two in the same family is too much of a coincidence."

"But if that's the case . . . who? And why would they try to take me, too?"

"I know you've been asked this before, but are you sure there's no one in your past who could hold a grudge against you?"

"I'm certainly not the most popular person in town, but other than Elizabeth hating me for marrying her son, I can't think of anyone in my past who hates me."

"No old boyfriends?"

"No. I didn't date a lot. Stephen was my first serious relationship."

The man across from her leaned forward. They locked gazes, and she saw a flash of something intense as he said, "We will find your children, Keeley. I promise you that."

Behind that hard exterior, Keeley glimpsed not only determination but also compassion. That strange tension she'd felt on meeting him disappeared. Cole Mathison did indeed care. For some reason, he wanted to hide it, but she sensed his kindness and his resolve. He shared the same conviction that everyone else did.

Without any concrete reason, Keeley felt more optimistic than she had in weeks. Somehow, just seeing the steady, resolute look in this man's eyes, hearing his deep, masculine voice filled with purpose, reassured her. There were too many people working for the same goal for it not to come true.

She was going to get her babies back. She was sure of it.

A door slammed somewhere in the house. Elizabeth jerked, losing her concentration on the book in front of her. This time of night, no one should be up. It was probably Miranda coming in late as usual. She'd left her daughter, Maggie, in the care of one of the servants while she, no doubt, went slumming around again.

Elizabeth couldn't care less where she had been or what she did as long as she brought no more shame to the Fairchild name. She'd done enough for a lifetime.

When Stephen lived at home, he had often come in this late, sometimes later, and had made no effort to be quiet. She had never been able to break him of that irritating habit, but he'd been so charming, she'd often overlooked his less desirable qualities.

Melancholy hit her, as it often did, when she thought about her son. Why, oh why, couldn't he have taken after her instead of his philandering father?

Her husband, Baker, had been undisciplined, emotional and fiery, uncaring of his status in the community. She had saved his ass on numerous occasions, and saved him from destroying what his ancestors had worked so hard for. Without her, the Fairchild name would have been forever soiled.

She'd never expected great things from Miranda. She'd been a whiny, irritating child; Elizabeth hadn't seen much improvement in her as an adult. Though Miranda hadn't seemed to be anything like her father, getting pregnant in the midst of her sophomore year of college by a man she refused to even name changed Elizabeth's mind. And Maggie, no doubt, would grow up to be just like her. Another Fairchild failure.

At one time she'd thought Stephen had inherited at least some of his mother's qualities. She took pride in the family name and their stature in this world. She had thought Stephen did, too, but when he'd married that tramp, he had deeply disappointed her.

She'd had such plans for Stephen. With the Fairchild money and influence behind him, the sky had been the limit. And as his devoted mother, she would have been at his back, pushing him gently toward a grand future. With his good looks and charm, he could have been anything she wanted . . . even possibly president someday.

Instead his hormones and the weakness he inherited from his father had overruled any good qualities he'd inherited from her. His stunt of marrying the one woman he knew his mother would definitely not approve of had sealed her opinion of him. Though she could never admit it to anyone publicly, she had often thought that Stephen got what he deserved.

Now the children he'd spawned with that slut were gone. Of course, being the lady that she was and with her status in the community, she had to show at least a modicum of concern.

The damnable FBI and those humorless people from that do-good organization had questioned her repeatedly. Though she refused to hide her disgust for their mother—she wasn't that good of an actress—showing outright antipathy toward the brats would have garnered suspicion. Something she couldn't afford.

A soft sound penetrated her thoughts. Elizabeth put her book aside and marched to the door. It was after eleven. No one should be about this time of night. Any servants would be immediately fired if she saw them.

Opening the door, she peeked out. Saw no one. Perhaps it had been the wind. Elizabeth closed the door and, instead of going back to her reading chair, headed to the bathroom. It was time for her facial. Though weariness pulled at her, she was too disciplined not to complete her nightly ritual. Her appearance was an integral part of her persona. How many people had she heard comment that Elizabeth Fairchild looked at least twenty years younger than her real age? Society valued youth and beauty. With her looks and wealth, she would continue to control her part of the world and the people in it. After all, she was a Fairchild. It was not only her duty; it was her right.

six

As he sat reading at the small desk in his bedroom, Cole massaged his temples, where a headache had set up residence. He reviewed the pages of notes he'd taken in his interview with Keeley. From what he could tell, she was hiding nothing. Whatever he asked, she'd given him a straightforward and sometimes heartbreaking answer. Clearly her only desire was to find her children.

He remembered being the same way when his wife and daughter were murdered. Stripping himself bare, he'd share even the most minute detail in an effort to find the bastards who'd destroyed his family and taken the two people who meant everything to him. Though they'd been identified and punished, he hadn't felt any satisfaction. His family was gone and nothing could be done to bring them back. Another incentive to help Keeley. He could and would return her children to her . . . she would have the peace he'd been denied. He owed her that.

A knock at the door jerked him from his grim thoughts. Jordan stuck his head in. "Ready?"

Cole nodded.

Jordan and Eden came into the room and settled onto the sofa across from him.

"Who do you like?" Cole asked.

Eden answered first. "I'm still going with the grandmother. There's an aura of evilness around her." She shrugged. "Can't explain it other than I feel there's something more there than just her hatred of Keeley."

She gave a sidelong glance at her husband. "Jordan's got another theory."

Jordan shook his head. "I don't deny the grandmother's evil, but she just seems too obvious. Her hatred of Keeley is blatant. There's not a soul in this county who doesn't know about it. If she was behind it, I think she'd back off a little. She hasn't."

"Who's your pick then?" Cole asked.

Jordan huffed a disgusted sigh. "Hell if I know. FBI profiler believes there's someone out there who hates Keeley and seeing her suffer is their primary motive."

Cole gave a slow nod. "Based on what I've read and heard so far, I agree that Elizabeth Fairchild is evil. However, I also agree that she's too obvious. Sounds like she's perfectly capable of doing something like this, though."

"That's what Keeley keeps saying," Eden said. "She believes Elizabeth is vicious enough, but that she wouldn't because of the publicity."

"What are your thoughts about the two abductions being tied together?" Cole asked.

"Got to be related in some way," Jordan said. "And it reinforces the idea that someone wants to see Keeley suffer."

"It was Elizabeth who wanted Keeley charged with Stephen's abduction," Eden reminded them.

"True. But that could just be the woman being who she is. She'd want Keeley to pay whether she really believed she had anything to do with it or not," Cole said.

Flipping to a clean piece of paper, he jotted Elizabeth's name down. "So who are the closest people to Keeley? We'll put them on the short list for the time being." He shot Eden a glance. "Elizabeth's at the top. But who else?"

"Mrs. Pickens . . . the housekeeper. She comes in once a week. Mary Thompkins, a woman who comes in three or four times a week to cook. Miranda Fairchild, Keeley's sister-in-law. And Keeley's friend Jenna Banks."

"What about the sister-in-law? Seems odd that Elizabeth hates Keeley but her daughter is one of Keeley's closest friends."

"Won't seem strange when you meet mother and daughter," Eden said. "They're polar opposites."

Cole grunted. From the sound of it, being the polar opposite of Elizabeth Fairchild would put a person in line for sainthood.

"What do you think about her friend Jenna?"

"Keeley and Jenna have been friends since grammar school," Eden said. "It's pretty obvious she adores Keeley and her daughters."

Cole glanced down at the meager list of suspects. "Anyone else?"

"There's the weekly yardman and the gardener. They've been questioned repeatedly, too."

Cole's gaze darted between the two LCR operatives across from him. "So has Keeley angered one of them so much they arranged for her husband's abduction? And then, when that didn't destroy her, they took her children, too?"

"FBI has questioned every one of them extensively, as have Eden and I. Elizabeth is openly hostile, but the others appear to be almost as devastated as Keeley."

"What about someone in town? Someone from her past?"

Eden shook her head. "She keeps a very low profile, hardly ever goes into town. And if that woman has a past, it's invisible. Other than going to Tahiti on her honeymoon, she's rarely even been out of Fairview. Grew up here, went to the community college the next town over. Married the local golden boy. From what we can tell, this is all she's ever known."

Cole stretched his long legs out in front of him. "Any other terrible events in her life besides the kidnapping of her husband and now her children?"

"Nothing that would indicate someone has it in for her," Eden said.

"So the real problems started after she'd been married to Stephen for several years. I understand he had several affairs. What about those women? Anyone talked with them?"

Jordan grimaced. "Yeah, I had the dubious pleasure of talking to the ones we know about. None of them live in Fairview, and from what I can tell, none of them had any real regret that Stephen Fairchild was dead. Sex was pretty much their only relationship."

Cole had to agree with that assessment. Rarely did sex, even good sex, create the kind of hatred and need for revenge this person seemed to have toward Keeley.

He tapped his pen on the notepad as his mind searched for an answer. "It's been over a year since Stephen was killed. Why would the children be taken now?"

"I think the saddest part is that Keeley was finally getting her life back together," Eden said. "She was even in the process of putting this house on the market."

Cole straightened in his chair. "She didn't mention that."

"She'd talked to a realtor a few weeks before. She said she wanted to get out of Fairview before the children got much older."

His heart kicking up a beat, Cole stood and began to pace as he pieced his thoughts together. "So what if the knowledge that Keeley was thinking about leaving triggered this?"

Eden leaned forward. "You mean having Keeley leave Fairview was something this person didn't want to see happen?"

"That," Cole said. "Or seeing Keeley get her life back

together wasn't something this person could tolerate. Leaving Fairview meant she was getting on with her life. Maybe he or she is only happy when Keeley is unhappy."

"Now, that's sick."

Jordan nodded. "It's a definite possibility. If that's the case, then it's someone close to her. Only someone she would've shared her deepest thoughts with." He eyed Cole. "What's our strategy?"

Not for the first time, Cole felt pride in working for an organization where being the lead dog didn't mean shit. Egos were checked at the door when one became an LCR operative. The only thing that mattered was the mission. Getting credit never came into play.

Jordan and Eden had been first on the case. If this were any other organization, heads would be butting to determine who should be in charge. Jordan was indicating that if Cole wanted the lead dog position, he and Eden would back off and let him take over. Having control of this case wasn't an issue with Cole either. Like everyone else, finding these children was his only motivation.

"Let's proceed the way you and Eden have been going." He looked at the slender blonde. "Eden, you stick with Keeley. Noah told me you've developed a good relationship with her. With her attempted abduction, we have to assume she's still in danger."

Eden raised a brow. "There's a twist we haven't discussed. If we go with the theory that someone just wanted to see her suffer, having her abducted, too, wouldn't have accomplished this."

"You're right . . . that's not consistent. Which means someone could want more than just seeing Keeley suffer emotionally. Let's make sure she goes nowhere alone." He eyed Jordan. "Sounds like you've made some good connections with our underground leads. Why don't you continue with that?"

Jordan nodded. "What are you going to do?"

"I'm going to talk to the townspeople. This is a small town . . . everyone knows everyone's business. Secrets are hard to keep. I'm betting someone out there is willing to tell us exactly who hates Keeley Fairchild so much and why."

Wes eased his way up the stairs to the second floor. Security system wasn't worth a damn in this house. Imagine having all that money and not putting in a decent system. Damn rich were too damn arrogant. If he wanted to, he could kill the bitch and there'd be no one the wiser. How he wanted to do just that. She had betrayed him, and no one did that to Wes and got away with it.

The vacation he had indulged in hadn't been as much fun as he hoped. Not getting what he wanted usually did that to him. He'd driven into Mexico after making the drop-off in California. Found himself a nice little tourist town. The tequila had been free-flowing and the women wild and horny . . . more than willing to do whatever he wanted. Still, he couldn't forget about the one who got away . . . and the one responsible for letting her get away.

After several weeks, his dissatisfaction had grown and he'd left with only one thing on his mind—returning to Fairview and getting what had been denied him. It was time for the bitch to pay up.

He pushed the bedroom door open and stood there, watching the skinny bitch get ready for bed. The thin nightgown she wore made her look a little meatier than she actually was. An idea popped into his head, causing a certain body part that he rarely denied to stand up. Maybe he'd just have a little more fun than he had originally planned.

Why he was suddenly jonesing for the bitch he didn't

bother to question. When he wanted it, he wanted it . . . the reason didn't matter. Maybe it was because he knew she wouldn't give it up without a fight. Her kind only gave it up when they wanted something in return. But she made no secret that she enjoyed a little rough play. In a few minutes, she'd be begging for it. Hell, who didn't like a little violence with their sex?

"Bet you thought you'd never see me again."

She jerked her head around and stifled the scream in her throat. Yeah, she wouldn't want anyone to know she had a night visitor. There'd be questions she'd never be able to answer.

"How did you get in?"

Wes snorted. "Your security system sucks."

She straightened and gave him that haughty stare he hated. "What are you doing here?"

"Like you don't know. You double-crossed me. You think I was just going to go my merry way and forget about what you owe me?"

Her nose tilted up as if the stench of him was more than she could bear. Like she was a queen looking down on some lowly peasant.

"You're the one that double-crossed me. You didn't take them where you were supposed to."

Wes shrugged. "You paid me to get rid of them. I fulfilled my end of the bargain . . . done my job."

She glared for several seconds as if there was something else she wanted to say, but then, with an aristocratic sniff, turned away. "Then consider it over with. Get out."

"Like hell."

"You got what you wanted. I got what I want. We're even."

In a flash, Wes crossed the room and grabbed her arm, whipping her around. He heard the startled gasp and got harder. "We ain't ever going to be even till I get everything I want. I want the woman . . . that's what we agreed to."

Her eyes flashing contempt, she laughed in his face.

A fiery mist covered his vision. His hand tightening into a fist, he popped her one in the stomach. As she bent over, gagging, Wes ripped the flimsy nightgown from her body and pushed her face-first onto the bed. He was mad now, and whether she liked it or not, his pound of flesh was about to get a little rougher than what even she liked.

Unzipping his pants, he lifted her up and shoved inside before she caught her breath. He knew he was hurting her, but she muffled her cries of pain against the bedspread.

Though she was as dry as an August creekbed, he worked back and forth till he could ram all the way inside her. His hands wrapped around her neck, he bent over as he plunged and retreated. "You screwed me over, seems only fair that I screw you. Don't it?"

When she didn't immediately answer, he tightened his hands on her neck until she whispered hoarsely, "I won't do it again."

"You got that right. You're going to bring the woman to me or I'll come back and show you just how rough it can really get."

Again, when she didn't answer, his hand tightened just enough to cut off all air. When she started squirming and bucking under him, trying to knock him off, he finally got the ride he was looking for. Wes pumped deep and hard for a few seconds. He'd done it this way a few times before . . . though not with her. He knew how to time it just right . . . almost to the edge of unconsciousness. He didn't want to kill the bitch . . . leastways not yet. He grunted and flooded inside her, finally letting go of her neck.

She lay gasping beneath him, her lungs rasping for breath like a chain-smoker with emphysema.

Wes pulled out and eased off the bed. "Find a way to get her to me, or I'll be back." He zipped up and swaggered out the door, more than a little pleased at how the night had gone down.

Minutes passed before she could move. Finally and with great effort, she rolled over and blew out a long shaky breath. She supposed she was lucky he hadn't killed her. It infuriated her that she hadn't anticipated the attack. He'd told her he'd be back and she had ignored his warning.

She should've been prepared and been able to do something to stop him. Not that she would've killed him in her own bedroom. She had her reputation to maintain. Having a sleaze like Wes anywhere near her, even if he'd broken in, wasn't something she wanted known.

Wincing, she pulled herself from the bed. Every muscle in her body ached as she padded painfully to the door and peeked out into the hallway. Holding her breath, she listened intently . . . no sound.

The bastard's threat was real. He would be back if she didn't find a way to get Keeley alone so Wes could have her and get it out of his system. She wouldn't let it get too rough . . . just painful enough for a much-needed lesson.

Wes had a way with lessons; she'd learned her own tonight. He had become a liability she couldn't afford. They'd known each other a long time and their relationship had been useful and mutually beneficial. Sex and money were Wes's motivators; power and revenge were hers. Whenever someone angered her, Wes had always been a reliable weapon. He was very good at getting his point across and not getting caught.

However, his usefulness had ended. The idiot apparently believed they had a partnership. Little did he know he was being manipulated right along with everyone else in town.

A slow smile lifted her mouth as she considered exactly how she would manipulate Wesley one final time.

seven

From his vague memory of Honor Stone, she looked just the way Cole thought she would. With shoulder-length strawberry blond hair, a hundred freckles on her face, golden-green eyes, and a warm friendly smile that invited secrets. He barely remembered the case they'd worked on together, but remembered enough to know that she was both professional and compassionate. They were damn lucky to have her working this case.

Cole held out his hand to her. "It's good to see you again, Honor."

She shook his hand, a small frown furrowing her brow. Somehow he got the feeling she was uncomfortable with him. Her warm words seemed to deny that. "It's wonderful to see you as well, Cole. When I heard you'd been killed, I couldn't believe it. Thank God it wasn't true."

Aware that Keeley was watching and listening to the exchange with great interest, he nodded his thanks and dropped into one of the chairs that had been set out for their meeting.

This office was what Keeley had termed her "control station." She had two monitors on a large desk, several maps on the walls, and numerous photographs of Hailey and Hannah throughout the room.

The office looked like a mini-version of an LCR office. Eden had described how Keeley worked here for hours every day, doing everything she could to assist in finding her children. If determination and sheer will could accomplish her goal, Cole knew they'd be found.

"Keeley," Honor said, "I reviewed the emails you sent over yesterday."

He didn't ask, but Keeley glanced over at him, apparently feeling the need to explain. "I get between fifty and a hundred emails a day," she said. "Most of them are asking questions on how the case is going, offering condolences, things like that. I show all of them to Eden and Jordan and forward a copy over to Honor."

"I think you're right . . . the email from our friendly sadist was different," Honor said.

Cole sat up. He'd read the other emails in the file Noah had given him. They'd been cruel and sick, some of them describing in detail what might have happened to her children. Others were just pointed and spiteful comments about how it was her fault that they'd been taken.

"How was it different?" Cole asked.

Honor pulled out a piece of paper from a file folder she held. "Take a look."

Cole scanned the email and had to agree. This one did seem less mean-spirited. He handed the page back to Honor. "Maybe the bastard's getting bored with the harassment."

"We can only hope," Eden said.

"Still no news or tips on your end?" Keeley asked.

"No, we still have no real suspects. All of our interviews have been conducted . . . without any real leads." Honor leaned forward, her expression one of compassionate concern. "I'm being relocated, Keeley. I'll still be working on your case, but I'll be working it from Greenville."

Keeley's dark eyes filled with tears and Cole could tell she was doing everything in her power not to lose control. He watched her throat move convulsively before she asked, "Does that mean that—"

Honor dropped to her knees in front of Keeley. "It only means I'll be farther away but I will still be working on this case. I'm not giving up." She looked over her shoulder and took in everyone's gazes before turning back around to add, "None of us are giving up."

Cole's opinion of Honor shot up a thousand percent.

Keeley's audible swallow echoed in the silent room. "Thank you."

Giving Keeley's hand a small pat for comfort, Honor stood and turned to Eden, speaking to her in a low voice.

The sorrow on Keeley's face was almost more than Cole could take. Despite having known this woman only a couple of days, he had to grip the arms of his chair to keep from going to her and holding her.

She was biting her lip, obviously doing her best not to break down. Even with Honor's assurance that she would continue on the case, she had to know that having the FBI backing away even further meant that the odds of finding her children were becoming remote.

Unable to watch her without offering some kind of support, Cole reached over and touched her hand that was digging into the arm of her chair. "Honor's right. We're never going to stop. Not until we find them. Okay?"

Her eyes swimming with unshed tears, she stood and a gave him a brief "Thank you." Barely glancing at the others, she whispered, "I've got some calls to make," then turned and almost ran from the room.

Honor sighed as she glanced at the door Keeley had just gone through. "I hated telling her, but I didn't have a choice."

"I'll go talk to her," Eden said.

Jordan stood, his eyes on Honor. "I'm assuming we'll continue to meet once a week, just not in person?"

"Yes. I'll leave all the numbers for you before I leave."

Giving Cole an odd, searching look, Jordan said, "I'll go check and see how Keeley's doing."

Cole was getting the feeling that everyone other than he and Keeley knew a secret. Something that he should know.

Glancing over at Honor, he was surprised to see her studying him so intently.

"Is there something going on I need to know about?" he asked.

Her head tilted slightly. "You don't remember me, do you?"

"I remember we worked on a case together."

"Have all of your memories come back?"

"The significant things, I guess. Why?"

When she flinched, he instantly wished he could withdraw the word *significant*. Dammit, had he had a relationship with this woman? Why the hell hadn't anyone told him?

He ignored the sudden throbbing in his temple. "Were we more than just friends, Honor?"

Though she smiled, he saw the hurt in her eyes. "We had a small fling. Nothing major, really. Just two people comforting each other."

Cole muttered, "I'm sorry."

"It's not important, really it's not." She touched his arm lightly. "I'm just glad you're okay. When they told me you'd been found alive, after almost a year of thinking you were dead . . ."

He felt a gut punch when tears brightened her eyes and she smiled again. "That was a very good day."

Feeling like a slug for having to ask, he did anyway. "Did we date?"

"Not exactly. We spent a weekend together after a job we worked was finished. It's okay that you don't remember."

"Was this something a lot of people knew?"

"Not a lot. But LCR's a small organization. It happened just a few months after you joined them. We rescued a missing kid."

"And celebrated together."

She giggled. "Like two drunken bunnies." She touched his arm again. "We were on adrenaline overload. Working out a bit of steam, nothing more. Okay?"

Hell no, it wasn't okay. He wasn't the type to sleep around. Going to bed with this woman should have meant more to him. And he sure as shit should be able to remember it.

"Cole, really . . . I can tell you're bothered by it and I don't want you to be. I'd just come off of a bad breakup. One thing led to another."

Cole nodded, but the guilt was still there. She may have said it meant nothing; her eyes said something else.

Not for the first time, Cole wished Donald Rosemount was alive so he could kill him again.

"Keeley, we got another donation. That makes a thousand dollars just this week."

Her focus on what was happening outside her window, she twisted her head slightly to answer Jenna. "Any name on this one?"

"No. Just like most of the others, they're anonymous."

Keeley rubbed the back of her neck. While it was kind of people to want to help, it added a burden that she really didn't have time for. She didn't need the money. There were so many other people who could use it.

"Just deposit it in the fund we set up. When this is over and the girls are home, we'll find an organization to donate it to. I just can't think of that right now."

She heard her friend come up behind her.

"What are you looking at?"

Keeley lifted her shoulder in an overexaggerated non-chalant shrug. She was about to be caught staring.

"Oh my," Jenna's tone revealed wonder and awe.

Keeley silently agreed. Cole Mathison stood in the middle of the front courtyard replacing a security light that had gone out last night. Dressed in running shorts and a navy blue T-shirt, he'd just finished his morning run. The shirt, damp with sweat, clung to every sinew and muscle as if it were a second skin.

As someone who once had a daily regimen that might put some Olympic athletes to shame, Keeley recognized Cole Mathison's physical fitness was at that level. She could quite honestly say that she had never seen a man in such top physical shape, nor one that was so incredibly appealing.

"Who on earth is that?" Jenna asked.

"Cole Mathison. He's the LCR operative I told you about."

"Honey, you told me another man had come to help. I can barely look at Jordan Montgomery without getting all tingly inside, and now this. You could've at least warned me that a Greek god had arrived."

Her eyes never straying from Cole, she said, "He is nice-looking, isn't he?"

Jenna snorted. "Stephen was nice-looking. This man is a thousand times past nice-looking. Think he's a bodybuilder?"

"I don't think so. His muscles don't overbulge like most bodybuilders'. He's just . . ."

"Absolutely gorgeous," Jenna finished for her.

That Keeley couldn't deny. Though Cole had been here over a week, other than the initial interview he had with her, she'd not talked to him other than to nod in passing or say good morning as he headed out the door. He went for a run each day, and somehow Keeley always found herself at the window at the exact time he left and came back. Funny how that worked.

"Is he married?"

Jenna's question brought her back to reality. The last thing she had time for was lusting after a man she barely knew. Turning away from the window, she seated herself at her desk again. "I don't know."

With another long sigh, Jenna stepped away from the window.

Immersed in adding information to the website, she felt eyes on her and glanced up to see Jenna staring at her. "What's wrong?"

"I just realized that Cole Mathison is the first man you've shown any interest in since Stephen."

"I'm not interested . . . I'm just . . ." She paused to swallow. She didn't have time to be interested, but something about Cole Mathison fascinated her. And it wasn't just his incredible looks . . . though she couldn't deny that every time she saw him, her heartbeat spiked toward a gallop.

"You're just . . . ?"

Unable to explain her feelings, she said, "So? What about you? After Frank died, you told me you were off men for good."

Another snort. "Frank Banks and Cole Mathison aren't even in the same species. And just 'cause I'm off men doesn't mean I'm blind. That man could make any woman break her vow of celibacy."

Yet another comment Keeley couldn't argue with. And she also agreed with her friend's comment on Frank Banks. Even though Jenna's husband had been dead for five years, it still astounded Keeley that her young, very attractive friend had married the owner of the town's only funeral home. The man had not only been twice Jenna's age, he'd been three times her size and wasn't the least bit attractive. Frank Banks gave

Keeley the creeps just thinking about him, and it had nothing to do with his occupation.

She'd asked Jenna when they first announced their engagement what she saw in him, but her friend had been evasive. Keeley finally came up with the theory that Jenna had grown up without a father and was trying to find someone to replace him. It was the only one that made any sense to her.

"Eden would know, wouldn't she?" Jenna asked.

"Know what?"

"Whether Cole Mathison is married or not."

"I'm sure she would, but I'm not going to ask her."

"Mind if I do?"

The stabbing pain in her chest was jealousy. Though she tried her best to ignore it, the emotion was there. She didn't want her best friend interested in Cole Mathison. And just what kind of friend did that make her?

Jenna's soft little laugh brought Keeley's head up. "What?"

"Those dark brown eyes are turning green."

A smile tugged at Keeley's mouth. "Okay, I'll scratch your eyes out if you make a play for him. Better?"

"Honest." Jenna's head tilted slightly. "Why don't you have a little fling with him?"

Keeley shrugged. "For one thing, I doubt that he'd be interested. Besides, I'm not a fling kind of girl. And—" Her gaze went back to the screen in front of her. The home page of the website had several pictures of Hailey and Hannah, together and separate. The girls were opposites in so many ways, but one thing they shared was their love for each other. As much as she missed them, besides praying with all her might that they were safe and healthy and that they would soon be home, she prayed that they were still together. They could comfort each other and maybe they wouldn't be so scared.

Tears blurred her vision and she suddenly felt a wave of loneliness so great and vast she almost cried out. A hand on her shoulder had her looking up.

"Sweetie, you need to take a break."

Keeley could only smile at her friend. "You've been here the same amount of time I have."

"I've been in and out of this office half a dozen times, and you haven't even noticed."

Taking a trembling breath, Keeley stood and stretched. The pop in her neck told her she did indeed need a break.

"Why don't you get something to eat?"

"I'm not—"

"Keeley, your clothes are practically hanging off you . . . your body's not designed to be thin."

Even though her friend's comments were said out of love, Keeley couldn't help the inward wince at her words. Stephen had often made pointed comments about Keeley's flaws, particularly when it came to her body. Her ongoing weight issue was one of the reasons he'd built a running trail for her. Having her stay in shape had been important. Why, she had no idea, since his interest in her had waned only a few months after their marriage.

Jenna continued, "If you don't start taking care of yourself, you're going to get sick."

"You're right . . . I know. It's just hard to—"

"I know it is, but you have to take care of yourself first. Okay?"

"I'll go make myself a sandwich or something. How's that?"

"Use extra mayo."

A surge of affection went through her. This nightmare would have been so much worse if she hadn't had Jenna standing beside her. Leaning down, she enveloped the smaller woman in a big hug. Jenna stiffened as she always did, but that didn't stop Keeley. She was a hugger; Jenna wasn't. Everyone needed hugs, whether they returned them or not.

Leaving her friend ripping into a stack of mail, Keeley headed to the kitchen. A motion outside caught her attention. She walked toward the double doors that led to the front porch and looked out the window.

Cole Mathison was getting into his car in the driveway. Now dressed in tan khakis and a royal blue shirt, he once again did that something to her heart he'd been doing since she met him. What was it about him? Admittedly, he was a handsome man, but there was something else there . . . something she couldn't place. Something that told her this man had more to him than just good looks. There was depth there. Dependability. Trustworthiness. Characteristics her handsome husband had sadly lacked.

How she knew there was more to Cole Mathison, she couldn't really say. Other than the interview and the illicit peeps she took when he was outside for his run, the most she'd seen of him was the back of his head. After saying a brief good morning, he left each day. Where he went and what he did during those hours was a mystery. She'd mentioned his absence to Eden, who'd said that Cole was talking to the townspeople. She'd assured Keeley he was working very hard on her case.

The citizens of Fairview had been questioned extensively already. Just how much more could Cole learn by talking to them? Though she'd told him of Elizabeth Fairchild's antipathy and influence, he was no doubt getting the full flavor of it. The townspeople wouldn't talk. Most of them worked in businesses owned by the Fairchild family and would be too fearful to speak out.

If they spoke out against anyone, it would be Keeley. Would Cole understand this? She told herself what he thought of her personally shouldn't matter. Getting her children back wasn't predicated on anyone having a good opinion of her.

Usually she could shrug off the negative stuff people thought about her, but she couldn't this time. Whether she wanted to admit it or not, Cole Mathison's opinion did matter. She told herself it was because he was searching for her babies.

Her babies. Nothing had happened. It had been almost two months and there had been no reliable sightings, no clues. She'd stopped watching the news. Couldn't bear to see their faces flashed on the screen while strangers speculated on where they were, who had taken them, and whether they were alive. She knew they were alive! A mother would know these things about her own children. It was all she had to go on . . . the only hope she had. They had to be alive.

No one needed to tell her that the longer they were missing, the lower the chances of her ever seeing them again. But she would never give up hope.

Someone, somewhere, had her children. It was still so hard to believe that not only were they gone, but that someone could be doing this to hurt her. Why? Who could she have angered so much?

If only this person would identify themselves, tell her what she'd done wrong, she would apologize profusely, literally beg if only they would return her children. Whatever it was they wanted, she would gladly give it.

eight

"So you've known Keeley most of her life?"

"Yep."

The clink of silverware and the hum of low-key conversation from the patrons of Lilly's Diner shouldn't have been able to drown out Dwayne Henderson. However, the man's apparent discomfort in talking to Cole made him mumble his monosyllabic answers.

Cole leaned forward, hoping if the guy thought no one other than Cole could hear him, he'd be willing to say more. "You went to school with her?"

"Uh-huh."

"How well did you know her?"

A halfhearted shrug.

"Do you know her children?"

"No."

"Do you know anyone who dislikes Keeley?"

A headshake.

"How about her husband? Did you know him?"

The first enthusiastic nod. "Oh yeah, he was a fine man. Such a shame what happened."

Maybe if he could get him talking about Stephen Fairchild, the man might open up more. "What did happen?"

Dwayne mumbled as he looked down at his plate. "You know . . . he died and all."

Since it was a bit more involved than just a mere death, Cole had to add, "He was abducted . . . no one was ever charged with that."

"Yeah, that was a real shame."

"Do you know anyone who disliked Stephen?"

His head shot up with a rapid headshake. "Oh no, everyone liked Stephen. He was a good man."

Wondering if the shock factor would work, Cole leaned back into his chair and said, "Couldn't have been too good and fine . . . he cheated on his wife."

His lips pursed like he'd eaten something sour. "Yeah . . . well. That's what *she* said."

According to the reports Cole read, just days before Stephen was abducted, rumors of the man's numerous infidelities had run rampant. His wife had not been responsible for those rumors. They'd spread like wild-fire and not a soul had been able to tell him where the information had come from. Cole was getting a grim picture of what Keeley had faced most of her life. Arrogant self-righteous idiots.

"Several women admitted they'd had affairs with him."

Another halfhearted shrug.

Cole ground his teeth in frustration. Getting information from the citizens of Fairview, South Carolina, was like chiseling granite with a plastic spoon. Southerners were known for their hospitality and openness. Fairview had apparently never gotten that memo.

Either the South had changed since he'd lived in it, or this town was an exception to that rule. Someone was keeping them from talking. His number one and only suspect was Elizabeth Fairchild.

"Were you in the same class as Keeley?"

"Yeah." Dwayne looked at his watch. "Look, I got to get back to work. Nice talking to you." He stood, put a small tip down for the waitress, and walked away.

Cole clenched his jaw to keep from snarling out a sarcastic reply. Making the townspeople angry would get him nowhere. Hell, what was he thinking . . . he *was* getting nowhere.

"I went to school with Keeley, too."

Cole looked up into the worst bloodshot eyes he'd ever seen. His clothes ragged and torn, the poor guy looked as though he'd had a hell of a life. He also looked years older than Keeley.

"Oh, I know I don't look like I went to school at all, but I did. Keeley was a couple of years behind me. But it was a small school. Everybody knew everybody."

What the hell, no one else would talk to him. Cole pulled out a chair for the stranger and watched as he plopped down with a tired sigh.

"So tell me about Keeley."

He smiled, showing that it had been years, if ever, since he'd visited a dentist. "She was the nicest and best-looking girl in the county. Of course, she was the poorest, too. Even poorer than me. Kids used to make fun of her . . . wearing hand-me-downs and the like. She was always neat and clean as a pin, but she was dirt poor. There was no hiding that. People used to say all sorts of bad stuff about her mama, too. You know, her not being married when she had Keeley. But neither one of them ever let on that any of that bothered them."

As Cole listened to Myron Gurganus, he became convinced not only that Myron had indeed gone to school with Keeley, but that the man might well be the fount of information he'd been digging for.

"Keeley didn't have many friends in school. Jenna was about the only one who'd have anything to do with her. They went everywhere together, like two peas in a pod. Keeley was always so sweet and pleasant. Never had a bad thing to say about anybody. Of course, when she got to be a teenager and started looking like she does now, the boys took a shine to her."

Despite his determination to avoid the thought, a vision of the dark-haired and curvaceous beauty appeared in his mind. Keeley Fairchild had the kind of exotic looks and figure that made grown men drool. If she looked like that in school, he knew exactly how the teenaged boys of Fairview County High School had reacted. Like ravenous wolves.

"She didn't pay them no mind, though. Even when she started winning all them awards, she never got the big head."

"Awards?"

Myron nodded. "For running track. Won several state finals . . . mostly long-distance running. Paper only printed one little article about her, though."

"Why's that?"

"Don't really know. Made the excuse they had too much news that week or some such thing."

That seemed odd. Why would the town's newspaper not write an article about a local student winning a statewide award? Keeley didn't have a lot of friends because of her poverty, but would that have made a difference to a newspaper? Had someone perhaps pulled strings and prevented them from publishing the article? Someone like Elizabeth Fairchild? But why would Elizabeth hate a teenaged Keeley? From what he'd been able to glean from the few people who would talk to him, Stephen only started seeing Keeley well after she'd graduated from high school.

"Can you think of anyone who would hate Keeley enough to want to take her children?"

Myron's face drooped with sorrow. "I wish I could tell you something about that. I'd do just about anything for Keeley, but I don't know anybody who'd hate her that much. Townsfolk might not like her, but I don't know of anybody that hates her . . . other than old lady Fairchild, that is."

"Do you think she's capable of doing something like this?"

"Oh, she's capable all right. She's 'bout as mean as they come."

Cole had yet to meet the woman, but he already shared Myron's opinion of her.

"You're the first person to open up about Keeley. Most of the people act like they know nothing about her."

Myron snorted. "That's 'cause old lady Fairchild thinks she owns everybody in town. She don't own me, though." His eyes gleamed. "You got a pen and some paper?"

Cole pulled a notepad and pen from his pocket and handed them to Myron.

"I'll give you some names of people who'll talk to you. A lot of them have been down on their luck at one time or another. . . . Keeley's one of the few people who'll give them some work or a helping hand. Not a lot of people know about her doing stuff like that, 'cause . . . well, that's just the way she is. But these people here . . . you tell 'em Myron sent you. They'll tell you what kind of lady she is. They ain't beholden to Elizabeth Fairchild, so they'll talk and tell you the truth, too."

Myron scribbled several names on the pad and handed it back to Cole. Then, with a dignified nod, he stood and shuffled away. Several people in the small diner glared at him, which, by the small chuckle Cole heard as Myron went out the door, seemed to amuse him.

Cole got to his feet. As he made his way through the diner to pay for his meal, he could feel the stares boring a hole into his back. Elizabeth Fairchild had to be very pleased with how the townspeople kowtowed to her. Fear of losing your job was a powerful motivator.

He pushed open the diner door and took a moment to survey the small town of Fairview. No doubt about it, the town was thriving. Businesses were open, people were bustling here and there, and the many cars parked up and down the street indicated a steady and healthy clientele. With the economy, most people were struggling these days. The people in Fairview probably felt they had it good. They might have to pay homage to the town's matriarch, but they had jobs, food to eat, and a roof over their heads.

List in hand, Cole went searching for the few people who obviously didn't have to feel beholden to the Fairchilds.

By the time he drove through the gates of Keeley's home, he'd talked to three people from Myron's list. The picture they'd given him was of a young woman who'd suffered prejudice and poverty as a child. And, as an adult, had used what she'd learned to help others.

Lila Atkinson, a young pregnant teen, he'd found working at a daycare center. She explained that Keeley had helped her find a job where she could bring her child with her after it was born and was also paying for her prenatal care.

At the local body shop, he found Buck Stafford, a mechanic who'd lost his other part-time job at a yard service. Keeley had hired him to take care of her grounds. Buck also explained that because Keeley owned several acres, he'd been able to hire two of his friends.

And he'd talked to Myra Redmond, who'd lost her job at the Fairchilds' mansion after she'd missed a day of work. Keeley had called her the very next day and asked her to help her around the house.

His last meeting had been with Miranda Fairchild. This morning, before he'd left Keeley's house, he'd called her and she had agreed to meet him at a coffee shop on the outskirts of town. He hadn't suggested meeting her at her house, since her mother would no doubt be in attendance.

With the exception of her blond hair, Miranda Fairchild looked nothing like her brother, Stephen. She was petite and delicate-looking, with fair skin, light brown eyes, and a serious, somewhat anxious demeanor. At twenty-six years of age, she seemed too young to be so solemn. Perhaps it was her concern for her nieces that made her appear so sad.

She'd offered little information that he didn't already know, but the statement she'd given him right before he left her was the most telling. He'd thanked her for meeting him and then, hoping to catch her off guard, asked, "Do you believe your mother had anything to do with the children's disappearance?"

Her soft eyes had hardened. "If I were running the investigation, she would be my only suspect."

When he'd asked why she thought that, she'd shrugged and said, "Talk to her . . . then you'll see."

Cole had walked away oddly unsettled. Though Miranda seemed sincerely concerned about her nieces, she was also evasive about the day they had disappeared. When he'd mentioned that her daughter, Maggie, had been sick and was unable to go on the picnic as they'd planned, something had flickered in her face that told him that wasn't the reason they hadn't gone that day.

The woman was hiding something, but other than accusing her of an outright lie, he could only bide his time and keep a watch on her.

Elizabeth Fairchild was an entirely different kettle of fish. After careful consideration of how he would approach Keeley's nemesis, he had an idea he planned to implement soon. Even if the woman wasn't responsible for her grandchildren's disappearance, she damned well needed to learn some lessons. Cole was of a mind to be her teacher.

Tonight he would be meeting Jenna Banks for the first

time. She was having dinner with Keeley and promised to stay until he got there. Just in the five-minute conversation he'd had with her yesterday, he got the impression that Jenna was one of Keeley's staunchest supporters.

He was beginning to get the idea that Keeley was actually very well liked in Fairview, with the exception of those Elizabeth could influence and buy. The question was, had she paid someone to abduct her grandchildren?

Getting out of his vehicle, he scanned the large, well-manicured lawn. Despite his knowledge that the security system was state-of-the-art and working fine, Cole felt a sudden uneasiness. One he hadn't felt before.

Standing in the middle of the drive, he made a slow 360-degree turn, inspecting the perimeter. Nothing. Birds continued to twitter as a light spring breeze fluttered the budding flowers of a nearby dogwood tree. Still the feeling lingered.

An urgent need to see Keeley had Cole running toward the house. Jordan was probably still out, but he knew Eden was inside with her. Despite this assurance, he had to see for himself that she was all right.

He unlocked the door, swung it open, and promptly lost his breath. Keeley stood in the middle of the giant foyer. She was dressed casually in jeans and a pink, sleeveless cotton shirt. There was nothing remotely sexy about her clothing. But somehow Keeley made them sexy.

The jeans emphasized her long, shapely legs, and the fitted shirt was just snug enough to hug those luscious curves. Thick, lustrous, shoulder-length hair gleamed blue-black under the large chandelier. A sudden image of that hair spread out on a white pillowcase had him swallowing a groan. Why the hell this woman?

He'd spent as little time in Keeley's presence as he could. Any information he didn't get in their initial interview, he could pick up from Eden or Jordan. Spending time with her wouldn't help him find her children. She was the only person he knew for sure was innocent. But that was only half the reason why he stayed away from her.

She stirred something in him. Something he hadn't felt in years. . . . Actually, he wasn't sure he'd ever felt anything like it. Sure, she was beautiful. Her exotic beauty and lush curves made him long for things he dared not put a name to. She reminded him of the movie stars from years ago, a Sophia Loren exoticness with the classic loveliness of Grace Kelly. After his interviews today, Cole was beginning to see that her inward beauty might well rival her outward beauty.

Whatever the reason for this odd attraction, he needed to stay focused. Being around her for any length of time blurred that focus. Guilt? Definitely. But something more than that. Something he needed to stay the hell away from. Having any kind of feelings for her other than obligation would be damned stupid.

A slight movement beside her jerked him out of his lustful thoughts. She wasn't alone. He turned to see another woman, about Keeley's age. She was shorter, much smaller than Keeley. Very pretty, with light brownish-blond hair and a thin, somewhat angular face.

"Cole, this is my friend Jenna Banks."

Cole drew closer and held out his hand. "Nice to meet you, Jenna."

"Jenna came over for dinner."

Jenna Banks snorted softly as she shook his hand. "More like I invited myself to dinner." She winked at Keeley. "Have to make sure the girl's eating."

Keeley laughed softly. "That and the fact that Mrs. Thompkins made her famous chicken and dumplings."

Her eyes twinkling, Jenna nodded. "Not going to lie, that's the primary reason. It was exceptional tonight."

"And I appreciate you staying so I could talk with you," Cole said.

She shot a mysterious smile at Keeley. "Anything for Keeley."

A wide-eyed, almost panicked look flickered on Keeley's face. What was that about? He shifted his attention back to Jenna. "Would you be available to talk now?"

"Absolutely." She gave Keeley another long look. "I'll see if I can find out that information we were discussing earlier."

A pink blush added a lovely color to Keeley's face. After whispering "Behave" to Jenna, she shot Cole an awkward look. "I'll go make sure Mrs. Thompkins keeps dinner warm for you."

Before Cole could ask her if something was wrong, she turned and almost ran toward the back of the house, toward the kitchen.

His eyes followed Keeley until she disappeared from view. When he turned back to Jenna, he was surprised to see a small smile on her face.

"Something amusing?"

She shrugged and the smile disappeared, making her look years older. "How can I help you get her children back for her?"

"Let's go into the sitting room."

He followed behind her, noting that she had a slight limp and favored her right knee. She settled onto the couch and Cole chose a chair across from her.

"How long have you and Keeley known each other?"

"Since we were six years old. Her mother was like a mother to me."

"What about your own parents?"

Her expression became shuttered for just an instant. Then, as if realizing it, she immediately altered that look with a wry smile. "My dad took off when I was kid. We never saw him again. My mother was too busy drowning her sorrows to notice me. Keeley's mama pretty much raised me."

"So Keeley is more like your sister than friend."

"Absolutely."

"Any idea why anyone would want to hurt her by taking her children?"

"If you've been around town asking questions, then you probably already know the answer to that. Keeley doesn't have a lot of friends in Fairview . . . thanks to Elizabeth Fairchild."

After a day of talking with people who did indeed like Keeley, he didn't agree with Jenna's assessment. However, he nodded, keeping his opinion to himself.

"So you believe it could be one of the townspeople?"

Jenna shrugged. "It could be just about anyone that Elizabeth has influence over . . . which is basically everyone within a hundred-mile radius of Fairview, along with plenty of politicians and the like all over the state."

"But she has no influence over you?"

She gave a self-satisfied smile. "The town of Fairview needs my services. Elizabeth has no control over that."

"But before you had the business, how'd you escape her attention?"

"Before I married Frank, I had no money, which meant I had no significance to Elizabeth. After I married, I had almost as much money as the Fairchilds. She couldn't touch me."

"You're a widow now, though?"

"Thankfully, yes."

Noting his obvious look of surprise at her blunt statement, Jenna grimaced and said, "Sorry, but I can't play the grieving widow. Frank was years older than me and a son of a bitch."

"Why did you marry him?"

"Why does anyone marry? We both had something the other wanted. He liked my looks, I liked his money."

Though he didn't share her opinion on marriage, Cole couldn't help but be impressed with Jenna's honesty. Not many people would be willing to admit they'd married for money.

"Tell me about Keeley's husband."

"You mean the other SOB in town. Well, at least until someone had the good sense to kill him."

"You didn't care for Stephen?"

"He cheated on her, Mr. Mathison. If you hadn't noticed, Keeley is one of the sweetest people in the world. I'm not in the habit of forgiving or forgetting. He broke her heart."

"You're very protective of her, aren't you?"

"Keeley's the only family I have. Aren't you protective of yours?"

Cole ground his teeth together. He thought he had been, until it was too late.

"Did other people dislike Stephen?"

She snorted. "The fair-haired Fairchild? If they did, they wouldn't dare show it. Openly disliking a Fairchild can get you into the unemployment line very quickly."

"If you dislike the town so much, why stay?"

She shrugged. "The business I inherited from my husband is very lucrative, and even with its faults, Fairview is my home. Besides, Keeley's here."

"So if Keeley moved, would you move?"

"I might consider it. After Stephen died, we talked about moving in together. Hailey and Hannah mean the world to me, too. They're my family."

"What would happen to your business if you moved?"

"I would sell it." A wry smile lifted her mouth. "Despite my antipathy for some of the townspeople, I don't really enjoy seeing them in my business."

Since he knew she ran the town's only funeral home, Cole could understand her reasoning.

"You were supposed to be at the park with Keeley that day . . . but you had to work?"

Her expression one of sorrow, she said, "Yes, something I'll never forgive myself for. You'll never know how many times I wished I'd postponed my meeting so I could have been there."

He refrained from telling her that since she looked as though a stiff wind could knock her down, he doubted that she could have been any help. Instead he moved on to his primary suspect. "What about Keeley's mother-in-law? Could she be responsible?"

Her nose scrunched in distaste. "Absolutely. She's not only mean enough but she's got the money to get away with it. Seems her only joy in life is making Keeley's life miserable."

"How does she do that?"

Jenna held up her hand and began ticking off items. "Tickets ranging from speeding to driving too slow, running red lights, parking. If there's a ticket to be issued, Keeley will get it. Haven't you noticed that she rarely leaves the house?"

A sudden anger that had nothing to do with her children's disappearance flooded him.

"What else does Mrs. Fairchild do?"

"You name it, she's tried it. She continues to try to contest Stephen's will. She accused Keeley of having something to do with Stephen's disappearance and death. Made insinuations that it was Keeley who cheated on Stephen. And those are just the ones I know about."

Cole was determined to return the Fairchild children back home safely, but before he left Fairview, he had every intention of changing the town's attitude toward

Keeley. And that would begin with convincing Elizabeth Fairchild to stop her harassment.

"Are you married, Mr. Mathison?"

Somewhat surprised by the question, Cole said, "No. Why?"

With a mysterious smile, she said, "No reason. Just wondered." Her expression turned grim as she leaned forward. "There's nothing I wouldn't do for Keeley. Seeing her hurting like this is killing me. I'll do anything to help you bring her girls home."

nine

The house was quiet as Cole went through his nightly ritual of ensuring that everything was locked up tight. Though the security system was of the highest quality, he'd taken to double-checking all locks before he went up to his room. Despite the fact that what was most precious to her had already been stolen, Cole had to make sure that she was safe each night. As if this too-late, lame-assed routine would make up for the hell Keeley was going through.

Eden and Jordan had headed to bed about an hour ago. Keeley had gone up to her room minutes after Jenna had left.

As he wandered through the house, he couldn't help but appreciate the way Keeley had made the enormous mansion so comfortable and livable. On the outside, it had an elegant and pretentious glamour, as if whoever designed the house wanted to impress onlookers.

On the inside, Keeley had somehow turned the giant structure into a home. He could imagine two little girls running through this house and their mother not agonizing over the mess they might create.

Rubbing away the tension at the back of his neck, he tugged on one last window in the sitting room and then headed toward the stairway. Staying up as late as possible was the norm for him. If he went to bed too soon, before extreme exhaustion hit, nightmares would attack. He had them every night, but if he was tired enough, he could sometimes avoid remembering them. Waking up with the vagueness of horror was a hell of a lot better than remembering the agony in vivid, Technicolor detail.

At the top of the landing, he jerked to a stop. The unmistakable sound of weeping hit his ears. Unable to prevent himself, Cole went toward the sound. At Keeley's bedroom door, he stopped. His chest tightened to an unbearable pain as he listened to the soft, heart-wrenching sobs coming from within.

His hand on the doorknob, he twisted it, all the while telling himself he was crazy. She wouldn't appreciate his sympathy, would resent his intrusion. That didn't stop him from opening the door.

The room was dark with the exception of a light from the bathroom. It cast enough brightness for him to see the huddled figure in the middle of the bed, holding a pillow in her arms as she shuddered with grief.

Cole's heart cracked wide open.

Refusing to back away, refusing to think about all the reasons he shouldn't be in this room with her, Cole went to the bed. "Keeley?"

When she didn't appear to hear him, he sat on the edge of the bed and said softly, "Keeley?"

The sobs stopped abruptly as she sat up and looked at him. Her beautiful face was wet with tears, and he watched a teardrop glide to her full, trembling lips. Everything within him tightened.

Instead of patting her hand, assuring her that things would get better, doing the normal, impersonal stuff to ease the agony of grief, Cole went with his instincts. He opened his arms.

And Keeley, instead of demanding that he leave, screaming that he came uninvited to her bedroom, threw herself into them. Though he knew he was just a warm body to her, Cole held her close, and as she sobbed her heartbreak against his chest, he smoothed her hair and whispered soothing, inarticulate words of comfort.

When was the last time anyone just held her? Petted her? This woman was going through hell, yet when he'd walked into her room, she'd been holding a pillow for comfort. If things had been different, she'd at least have the solace of her husband's arms.

He told himself he owed her—that this was the only reason he was here, holding her. Deep down, Cole knew that to be a lie. This woman stirred something in him that had nothing to do with guilt, obligation, or sorrow. He just damn well needed to keep that part of himself as separate as possible.

After several minutes, she pulled in several ragged breaths and then stiffened in his arms, as if she'd just realized where she was. He held her tight for just another second and then let her go.

Her voice husky and thick with tears, she asked, "Did I wake you?"

"No, I was about to go to bed . . . heard you."

"I'm sorry, I—"

"No. Don't apologize. I wish I could do something to help you."

Instead of backing away, she leaned into him again, rubbed her face against his chest, and said, "This helps. Thank you."

Aw hell. Arousal surged hard, thick . . . unrelenting. Cole ground his teeth as she nuzzled against him, her soft, womanly body pressing into his. This wasn't about him and his inappropriate lust . . . it was about comforting her. Unfortunately, the erection throbbing insistently wasn't receiving the message.

She shifted slightly, and before Cole could pull away from her, she felt him. Her body stiffened for just an instant. He fully expected her to jerk out of his arms and tell him to leave. But then she released a trembling sigh that seemed to go through her entire body as she relaxed against him again.

Cole closed his eyes. Hell no, this was not an invitation. She probably thought his arousal was a normal male reaction to a beautiful female body pressed against his. There was no reason to tell her that he hadn't felt this kind of physical reaction in a very long time. She didn't need to know that it wasn't just her beautiful body he found alluring but everything about her. He ground his teeth, determined to endure.

A soft mouth pressed against his neck. Cole stopped breathing. Just an accidental caress . . . nothing more. At the feel of her hot, moist tongue in the hollow of his throat, denial was no longer possible.

"Keeley?"

She backed away a little so she could look up at him. He didn't know what to expect. Didn't know what she would say. Her eyes searched his face for several seconds, and Cole allowed her to see everything. Want. Need. Compassion. It was all there for her. Whatever she wanted . . . whatever she needed. He waited for her response.

All she said was "Please."

With a growl that began deep within his soul, Cole lowered his head and covered her mouth with his. She was soft, warm . . . delicious. When he pressed deeper, she opened her mouth and let him in.

And Cole lost his mind.

Pushing her back against the bed, he came over her and devoured her sweet mouth, eating at her lips, surging, retreating, thrusting inside the hot, sweet cavern. She moaned, opened wider and offered her tongue. Propping his arms on either side of her, Cole held her head in his hands and concentrated his total focus on her mouth. Licking at and dueling with her tongue, he then angled his mouth fully over hers for maximum penetration, maximum pleasure.

Oh, sweet mercy. Keeley felt as if her entire body was ablaze. Never in her life had she felt anything close to this feeling, this unbelievable, overwhelming need to connect with someone. She undulated beneath Cole's big body, wanting, needing with an intensity she'd never even imagined. Nothing about this encounter made sense but she refused to question its rightness. This man had brought life back to a body that had felt dead and undesirable for so long.

Cole raised his head slightly; beautiful masculine perfection stared down at her. Those amazing eyes glittered with a desire she'd never seen in anyone's eyes . . . and it was all for her. Body throbbing in response to that heated look; her entire being felt drenched in sensual need.

Warm breath bathed her face as he asked softly, "What do you want, sweetheart?"

"I want . . . I need . . ." She stopped on a sobbing breath, unable to articulate the words. How do you ask a man you barely know to devour you until you forget to breathe, to think, to be? How do you ask him to consume you until your very being is changed, cleansed, renewed? How do you ask someone to make you forget for just a few moments that your life is a living hell?

Keeley said the only thing that made sense. "Make me forget, for just a little while, make me forget."

Groaning, Cole lowered his head and reignited the fire; in seconds he returned her body to a full blaze of searing heat. Large, calloused hands glided under her nightgown, moving over her legs slowly, caressing, stroking, and then they were between her thighs, headed for a destination that desperately needed to be filled.

With a sob, Keeley spread her legs open in welcome. Long fingers, at first tentative and then more sure, explored her tenderly, separating the folds. Using the moisture he found there, he gently, slowly penetrated her.

Another soft sob escaped her . . . she had to have more, not just tenderness . . . she wanted it all, everything. Following those needs, her hands went to the hard erection pressing against her leg. Cole shifted slightly. A desperate urgency taking over, Keeley quickly unzipped his pants and delved between the layer of clothing to find him . . . hard, hot, and ready. Coherent thought vanished, consumed by desire. Using both her hands, she brought his hard length to her, opened herself wider and surged upward.

With one powerful thrust, Cole buried himself to the hilt inside her. With a welcoming, gasping "Yes," Keeley wrapped her legs around him, grabbed his hips in her hands, and pressed him harder, deeper into her.

Holding her close, Cole rolled onto his back without breaking their connection. His eyes shimmering with a hot light, he whispered, "Take what you need, sweetheart."

Bracing her knees on either side of his hips, she sat up . . . directly on him, impaled by his shaft. A powerful flush of erotic heat flooded through her. With a cry of need, intermingled with a desperate gratitude, Keeley balanced her hands on the hard planes of his stomach and began to ride, setting a wild but steady rhythm.

Cole's hands were at her hips, but he allowed her full control—how much she wanted and how fast she wanted it. She was well aware that he could take over anytime he wanted; the fact that he was allowing her to take what she needed only added to the intense sensuality of the moment. Those amazing eyes gleamed up at her as he watched her take her pleasure . . . she drew on him and he gave her everything.

Soon it was too much. The rhythm became erratic,

the incredible aching pleasure became wilder, more intense. Cole made one slight adjustment by pressing his pelvis against the very top of her sex, allowing her to grind against him in the exact spot she needed him most. Keeley's eyes widened as the entire universe became one long, glorious, throbbing, explosive moment of ecstasy. Her mouth opened to scream and Cole pulled her down to him, covering her mouth with his to muffle the sound.

An eternity later, Keeley came back to earth and realized the man inside her was still rock hard, his big body shaking with the volcanic need to let go. His face was buried against her neck as harsh breaths rasped from his lungs.

"Cole?"

"Keeley." Her name was a mutilated, tortured sound.

She sat up so she could see him, and he let out a long, low groan at her movement. Self-denial was etched on his handsome face. Why? Why would he give her the most unbelievable physical pleasure she'd ever known and deny himself?

"Cole, let go," she whispered.

"I can't . . . I . . ."

Unwilling to take and not give, Keeley's hands moved down to where they were still joined. Her fingers wrapping around the hot, hard length, she said softly, quietly, "Please . . . I need this, too."

Whether it was her hands or the words, she didn't know. She heard a low, feral growl as he rolled her over onto her back, buried himself deep, and began a hard, relentless rhythm of thrusts. Unbelievably, Keeley felt the resurgence of desire deep within her. Gasping with new need, she locked her legs around his hips and closed her eyes; glorious explosions went off inside her and she reveled in the beauty of sheer physical satiation.

Harsh breaths grating against his lungs, Cole pulled

from the luscious body beneath him and rolled over on his back. When Keeley snuggled against him, he held her tighter. His mind was blurred with pleasure and the deeply intense feeling that something monumental had just occurred. For just a few moments, he closed his eyes and savored a rare sense of peacefulness.

Regret would come . . . but not yet. Though his memory was sketchy in many things, he knew he'd never experienced this kind of sexual, intimate connection in his life. It was more than just physical . . . they had shared something he didn't even know existed.

Even before Rosemount got his drugs in him and tortured the humanity from him, Cole had never been one to delve deeply into his emotions. He loved and was loved, but accepted that emotion without exploring the feeling. Here, with Keeley in his arms, he recognized a joining, a connection, that could never be broken. No matter what happened in the future, this was a bond they would always share.

She moved her head against his chest to peek up at him through her lashes. "I've never experienced anything like that in my life."

He wanted to say the words . . . wanted to agree with her, but he couldn't. What they had shared was incredible, but could never happen again. He'd tried to comfort her and it had become an extraordinary event beyond his comprehension. Most important, for one brief moment in time, she'd forgotten that her life was a hell. He had to remember that was all it had been . . . all it could be.

"Keeley, I—"

Soft fingertips pressed against his mouth. "No, don't say anything." As if she'd read his mind, she raised up on her elbow and whispered, "I know what just happened was crazy and irresponsible. It wasn't like me at all . . . and I don't think it was like you either." She took a breath and added, "For the record, I'm not on birth control, but I'm as regular as clockwork and the timing isn't right. And I haven't, um . . ." She stumbled and then started again. "I haven't been sexually active in a long while, so you don't have to worry about that either."

When she paused, obviously waiting for his health report, Cole provided it. "Neither have I." He didn't bother with details.

She put her head on his chest and he heard her swallow hard before she added, "I don't want to regret it."

Tightening his arms around her again, he said quietly, "Then let's not."

"Thank you."

Seconds later her soft, even breaths told him she was in a deep, restful sleep. At last.

Cole stared at the ceiling, refusing to allow himself the same relief. For this one night, he could ensure that her sleep would be unencumbered by nightmares. In the morning, before she woke, he would leave her. Then he would think and he would regret. But for right now, Cole held this beautiful woman in his arms and let himself wish for the impossible.

The devil's face hovered over him, leering. Shrill laughter, hideous and wicked, echoed around him. He was tied spread-eagle to the ground with ropes so tight they sawed into his skin every time he moved. The sun blazed above him, while insects stung and gnawed at his sizzling skin, feasting on the thousands of oozing cuts all over his body.

Cole struggled against the bonds. If he could free just one hand, the devil would die. Pain speared through him and he fought against its overpowering deadly embrace. If he let go . . . if he gave up . . . all was lost.

Agony seared deeper and the devil whispered his

enticement. High and whiny, his voice pierced Cole's skull like a branding rod. "You can't fight. You'll never escape. I'm your master. You're weak, everything you loved is gone. . . . Let go and all the pain will go away."

Temptation lured. How easy it would be . . . how wonderful to put all the pain behind him. How easy to just . . . let . . . go . . .

A scream penetrated his nightmare. Cole was on his feet and out the door before the agonizing sound stopped. As if a guide other than his senses led him, he found himself at the door of the children's bedroom.

Keeley was on her knees in the middle of the room. Sobs tore through her and the anguish radiating from her crumpled figure cut him to the core. There was his answer. The reason he couldn't let go. Why he'd never let the devil win. He was here for a purpose: to return Hannah and Hailey to their mother.

A slight breeze stirred behind him. Eden passed by, kneeled beside Keeley, and wrapped her arms around the weeping woman.

Cursing himself, Cole stepped back into the hallway. He'd left Keeley's bed just before dawn and returned to his own, telling himself he would lie down for a little while and doze. Instead not only had he endured another nightmare, Keeley had woken up to one also. If she'd still been in his arms, he could have prevented that.

Hell, what was he thinking? That wasn't the reason he was here. Comforting Keeley was best left to someone more qualified. Humanity, even in its most basic form, had been stripped from him. There were only a few things he felt qualified to do any longer. None of them involved the compassion this woman needed. Just because he'd been able to give her sexual pleasure sure as hell didn't qualify him for anything else.

Cole stalked back to his room. A quick glance at the

bedside clock told him he might as well shower and start his day. It was just before six, and if he did manage to go back to sleep, the nightmares would return. No point in inviting them.

Under the hot, hard spray, Cole fought for focus, but his mind battled images: Keeley's beautiful face as she rode him, the way she bit her lip as she sought her pleasure, then her expression of ecstasy when she climaxed; clinching and clasping, her inner muscles had pulsed around him. Leaning his head against the cool, wet wall, he ground his teeth together as he struggled to control the arousal from the imagery.

In an instant, those images were obliterated as he remembered the ravaged expression he'd just witnessed. Hell, that and nothing more had to be his total focus. He had to put an end to the pain she continued to suffer. Nothing else mattered.

After all that had happened to her, she probably felt as though God had turned His back on her, and was trying to figure out what the hell she'd done to incur His wrath.

Cole had endured his own battle with questioning God's vengeance and had never come up with an answer other than to question His existence. Horrendous things happened in random chaos, and to look for reasons or try to make sense of it could only invite insanity.

Slamming the shower door, Cole dried off, wrapped the towel around his waist, and headed into the bedroom. One of the many nice things about staying in a mansion was that each bedroom had its own bath. He rifled through the closet as he thought about the meeting he planned to have today. What did one wear to interview a she-devil?

At the knock on the door, he called out "Come in" without much thought.

The soft gasp behind him had him turning around.

Keeley stood in the doorway. She was still too pale, but the shadows under her eyes seemed less pronounced than they had been yesterday. Perhaps those few hours of sleep had helped after all. Finally her expression snagged his attention—horrified and compassionate. What was that about?

"Keeley. Are you okay?"

"What? Oh yes . . . sorry." Her throat worked convulsively. "I . . . um . . . I wanted to thank you again . . . for last night."

Damned if he wanted her gratitude. "There's nothing to thank me for, Keeley. What happened was . . ." Hell, what happened was indescribable.

A small tilt of her mouth told him she might feel the same way, but all she said was "Since everyone is up early, Eden and Jordan are making breakfast and wanted to know if you'd like to join us."

"I'll be down in about five minutes."

Her face once more showed that flash of compassion before she closed the door. Why had she looked so . . . ? Cole looked down, just now realizing all he had on was a towel. Wouldn't be a big deal except for one thing. He'd had his back to her when she came in, and she'd seen the scars. Last night it had been dark, and though they'd shared an incredible intimacy, they'd actually touched each other very little. She hadn't felt his back . . . hadn't touched the scars.

After seeing them, it was a wonder she hadn't run away screaming. It'd taken him months to be able to look at his back without all the memories slamming into him. Now the scars were just part of him. They were what they were—evidence that even if he found himself questioning God's existence, he would never question the existence of hell. That he'd seen firsthand.

ten

Keeley leaned against the wall outside Cole's bedroom
and took a shuddering breath. Dear God, what had
happened to him? Who could have done that? And how
painful it must have been. You didn't get scars like that
without enduring severe agony. Had he been in some
kind of accident? Could a car wreck create the mass of
thick welts and what looked like hundreds of long, thin
scars?

What kind of horrific event had Cole been through?
And how strong of a man was he to have survived?

How could she have not noticed them last night? Of
course, the fact that she'd been concentrating on other
areas of her body experiencing mind-numbing pleasure
might have something to do with it. Now she regretted
not knowing, not feeling. The man who'd made love to
her so passionately last night was extraordinary in
many ways. Keeley wanted to know them all.

"You okay, Keeley?"

She turned to see Eden standing at the top of the
stairs, a frown of concern furrowing her brow.

Keeley pushed away from the wall and nodded. "I
told Cole breakfast is ready. He said he'd be down in a
moment."

"Good. Let's go on down before Jordan's omelets get
cold."

She followed behind Eden, her mind still focused on
the incredibly giving, sexy, and mysterious man upstairs.

Apparently she hadn't convinced Eden that she was okay, since as soon as they entered the kitchen, she turned to Keeley and said, "Are you sure you're okay? You're awfully quiet."

"How long have you known Cole?" She inwardly winced. So much for subtle questioning.

Jordan answered, "I've only known him since I've worked for LCR, which is around two years."

Eden nodded. "I've known him about four years or so."

"He seems very . . . controlled." Except for that one glorious, incredible moment when he'd exploded and they experienced ecstasy together. Keeley crossed her arms over her chest, hoping no one could see how her nipples peaked in arousal as her body responded to that memory.

When both Eden and Jordan shot her an odd glance, Keeley worried she'd given her thoughts away.

"Cole's had some experiences that might have hardened him a bit . . . but he's an excellent operative," Eden said.

Relieved that they'd apparently not read her mind, she quickly said, "Oh, I'm sure he is." The last thing she wanted was for them to think she didn't like Cole or didn't want him here. He'd made it more than clear that getting her girls back was his number one priority.

"He's also one of the best interrogators LCR has," Jordan added.

Keeley hid a grimace. Cole might be an expert at interrogation, but it was clear she wasn't. "I just wondered—"

"If you have questions about me, ask me."

Heat bloomed in her cheeks. Keeley whirled around and faced the tall, dark man standing at the door. Black brows arched over those amazing eyes; his head was slightly cocked as if in a challenge.

"I was just trying to—" Hell, what could she say? *I want to know more about you because you're the most interesting, gorgeous, sexiest man I've ever met in my entire life.* Uh, no.

Cole let her off the hook with "Totally understandable" as he came toward her. "Ask away."

Her heartbeat tripled as she watched him. For such a tall, muscular man, his movements were silent, graceful. Keeley swallowed hard and lifted her chin. He'd invited the questions; she wasn't going to pass up the opportunity just because her face was blood-red from embarrassment. "Where are you from? Neither Eden or Jordan have an accent, but you have a drawl."

His lips quirked slightly and Keeley focused on that beautiful masculine mouth. Last night he'd kissed her with that mouth. Kissed her? No, more like devoured her . . . and she'd loved every moment of it.

"I grew up in Oklahoma. Lived most of my adult life in Texas."

"What part of Texas?"

"Here and there."

He was being deliberately vague. She should have expected that. By necessity, LCR was a secretive organization. Asking personal questions of their operatives would probably always garner ambiguous answers.

Eden broke into the tense silence. "Why don't we all sit down and have breakfast."

Keeley headed to the kitchen table. About to pull out a chair to sit down, she was a little disconcerted to have it pulled out for her. Muttering "Thank you," she sat down abruptly.

Cole dropped into a chair across from Keeley, her wary expression bothering him. True, he needed to keep a certain distance between them, but her obvious uncertainty around him caused a slight sting he couldn't deny. Was it the scars? Admittedly, they were hideous and would probably disgust most people. He was past the point of being embarrassed by them, but there was no doubt they had disturbed her.

He told himself it didn't matter. He wished he believed it. The thought of her being frightened or disgusted by him bothered him more than he would have liked to admit.

Refocusing once more, Cole took a swallow of coffee and shot a glance at her. "I'm headed over to see Elizabeth Fairchild today."

"Elizabeth agreed to see you?"

He shrugged. "Didn't ask. Figured I'd drop in."

Her lips twitched as if she were struggling not to smile.

"Something wrong with that?"

She shook her head. "It's just that Elizabeth is very big on protocol and proper etiquette. Not calling prior to visiting is an insult to her."

Insulting the woman sounded damn good to him. "It's not a social visit." He watched her closely as he said, "I want you to go with me."

"Why?"

"I want to see her hostility up close."

"Because you think she's behind all this?"

"Maybe." Cole didn't see the need to explain that he intended on learning as much as he could about the woman so he could stop the harassment. He had a feeling Keeley wouldn't appreciate his interference.

"Dropping in on Elizabeth, without having an appointment, to ask her questions?" She smiled. "Yes, I'd be happy to join you."

Cole was glad to see that Keeley didn't mind stirring up her former mother-in-law's ire. So why the hell did she let her get away with so much?

Elizabeth might well refuse to see him. Not that he had any problem busting the door open and making her talk to him. If he could do it peaceably, he would. The last thing he needed was to get arrested. The woman apparently controlled the local law just like she controlled everything else in this town. At her word, they'd lock Cole up and he'd waste valuable time he didn't have. The one meeting he'd had with the sheriff had convinced him the man would do whatever the hell Elizabeth Fairchild wanted.

Taking Keeley along might help . . . or hurt. Either way, he wanted to see that animosity firsthand. Eden had told him Keeley hadn't been out of the house in days. Maybe some sunshine would help.

Cole checked his watch. "Can you be ready to go in about half an hour?"

"Yes, but it might be a little early for Elizabeth. It's only just now six-thirty."

"You got a problem with that?"

Another smile, bigger this time, curved her full lips. "Not at all."

Elizabeth stood on the landing as she listened to Patrick, her butler, argue with some stranger about seeing her. The man had no appointment. Hadn't had the decency to call and arrange a meeting. And he was here at the ungodly hour of seven o'clock in the morning. Some people could be so uncouth. She'd watched from an upstairs window as he drove up, and she'd seen Keeley get out of the car with him. That slut's presence only reinforced her reluctance to meet with him. How like Keeley to be so common.

"I'm sure if you'll explain to Mrs. Fairchild that this concerns her grandchildren, she'll be more than happy to make an exception."

At those words, she stiffened. Grandchildren? More like the slut's children.

"As I have tried to explain to you, sir, Mrs. Fairchild isn't even here."

"Then we'll come in and wait or you can tell me where she is and we'll go see her there."

Really. This man had the gall. How dare he!

"I'm afraid I can't do that, sir."

"Why not?"

"Because . . . well, because it wouldn't be proper."

Her hand tightened on the banister. Patrick wasn't used to anyone being so forceful. Having someone ignore propriety and insist on seeing Elizabeth was unprecedented. The Fairchild name held far more power than that of any other South Carolinian family. And Elizabeth wielded that power with a strong and punishing hand.

The deep voice growled, "Since I'm not really too much into proper, I guess we'll just come on in until she gets back."

Of all the nerve. Huffing with displeasure, Elizabeth descended. She would get rid of this obnoxious man and his whorish companion on her own.

Keeley had stood beside Cole in wide-eyed awe as he argued with Patrick, a man who'd been the Fairchild butler for years. Not that Cole had needed to argue that much. With his height and intimidating scowl, a lesser man might have cried just looking at him. Patrick had done his best to scowl back, but it had done little good. Cole Mathison would not be deterred.

She told herself she was too old for hero worship, but she couldn't deny that her feelings for Cole were nearing that state. Having him on her side was becoming increasingly important to her.

"Let them in, Patrick."

The familiar autocratic voice of Elizabeth Fairchild caused Keeley to stiffen. No one could make her skin crawl quite like this woman.

His eyes showing more than a hint of desperation and fear, Patrick swallowed hard and backed away.

Cole gave a polite nod and went through the door; Keeley followed behind him. It had been years since she had been inside the mansion, and she braced herself for the unpleasantness that was sure to follow. She'd only been inside a handful of times when she and Stephen were married. Not once had she felt welcome.

"Mrs. Fairchild, thank you for seeing us. I apologize for the intrusion."

Keeley jerked to attention at the charm exuding from the man beside her. Gone was the austere, grim-faced stranger demanding to see the lady of the house. In his place was a handsome Southern charmer. Had his Texas drawl gotten just a bit thicker?

She watched Elizabeth's expression change. Even to Keeley's jaded eyes, her former mother-in-law was a beautiful woman. She had to give her that. Thick blond hair just brushed her shoulders and glowed golden in the early-morning sunlight. Elizabeth's delicate, feminine features were in direct contrast to the mean-spirited person Keeley knew her to be. And though she knew the woman had to be fifty or older, she could easily pass for thirty-five, even younger. Of course, with the Fairchild money at her disposal, the best spas and plastic surgeons were only an airplane flight away.

What caught Keeley's attention today were Elizabeth's eyes. They literally lit up when she looked at Cole. Good heavens, the woman was eyeing him as if she'd just found a three-carat diamond at the bottom of her cereal box.

Elizabeth gave a tinkling little laugh. "No apology is necessary, Mr. . . . ?"

"Mathison. Cole Mathison. But please, call me Cole."

"How do you do, Cole?" She held out her hand and Keeley watched as he took her hand and held it. Maybe a little longer than was necessary?

"Feel free to call me Elizabeth." Turning to Patrick, she said, "Bring us some coffee and perhaps a plate of Marvella's delicious scones."

"Yes, ma'am."

Patrick looked relieved to be escaping without a lecture. As Elizabeth linked her arm in Cole's and led him to the sitting room, Keeley remained by the front door and grimly wondered if she was just supposed to stand in the foyer and wait. The woman had yet to even acknowledge her presence. She refused to follow like a puppy and would just damn well stand here.

Elizabeth stopped at the entrance to the parlor. Turning ever so slightly, her tone imperious and condescending as always, she said, "You might as well come, too."

Resisting the temptation to tell her to go to hell, Keeley bit the inside of her check and walked into the room behind Elizabeth and Cole. She stalked over to a chair and sat down. Damned if she'd wait to be told to sit, too.

Elizabeth seated herself in the middle of an overstuffed antique sofa and patted it as if wanting to share it with Cole. Instead of obliging her, he sat in another sofa across from her. Her thin brows arched a bit; no doubt she was surprised someone had actually refused her. Apparently willing to overlook his refusal, she gave him a bright, inviting smile. "Tell me about yourself, Cole."

"Be glad to, Elizabeth. But first, I'd like to ask you a few questions. If that's okay."

"But of course."

Keeley swallowed a snort. Cole glanced at her as if he knew what she was thinking, and she saw his eyes for the first time since they'd arrived. There was amusement in them. He was enjoying playing Elizabeth and knew exactly why he was being treated so nicely.

Keeley bit her lip to control the smile twitching at her mouth.

"I'm with Last Chance Rescue."

Elizabeth's expression flickered for just an instant with distaste, but she quickly controlled it and said, "How rewarding that must be."

Cole flashed another charming smile. "Few could understand that, but since you've known the despair of having your grandchildren abducted, as well as your son, you can identify so much better."

"Well, yes . . . of course."

"You know, it's a strange twist of fate that both your son and his children were abducted. I was wondering, could there be someone perhaps who has a grudge against the Fairchilds?"

Managing to look tragic and offended at the same time was a feat, but Elizabeth handled it quite well. She raised a slender shoulder. "There's no reason for anyone to hold anything against us. We've put hundreds of people to work in our factories and businesses. Without us, many families would starve." Thin brows arched again as she cast a scathing glance at Keeley. "That doesn't mean that other people don't have enemies, though."

"You mean Keeley?"

Another shift of her bony shoulder was Elizabeth's answer.

It was all Keeley could do not to fly across the room and floor her. Her mother-in-law had worked like hell to make everyone believe she'd been responsible for Stephen's abduction. But to have her insinuate she was responsible for her daughters being taken, too, was almost more than Keeley could stomach.

Since this was the woman who'd barely managed a tear at her own son's funeral, Keeley knew she shouldn't be surprised. No wonder Stephen had been cold in so many ways. Keeley slammed the door on that thought. Dwelling on how stupid she'd been in her marriage would not bring her children back to her. She had to concentrate on the here and now.

"We know so little about Keeley's family."

Every muscle in her body clenching with resentment, Keeley said, "*I* know about my family."

As expected, Elizabeth ignored her comment and said, "My family goes back hundreds of years."

"Everyone's family goes back that far . . . thousands in fact. Ever heard of Adam and Eve? And just because someone has more money doesn't make them any better."

Both Cole and Elizabeth shot her a look. Elizabeth's was her usual mixture of haughtiness and disgust. Cole's was a warning of *Let me handle this*.

Keeley straightened and looked away. Fine, there was no point in pretending. Her mother-in-law's opinion didn't matter and hadn't for years. What mattered was finding her girls.

While Cole continued to charm Elizabeth, Keeley watched him . . . and felt her fascination grow. When she'd first met him, his grim, cold demeanor had bothered her. Last night had obliterated that misconception. Controlled? Yes. Focused? Absolutely. Cold? The exact opposite.

Cole Mathison had something that drew her to him, and it wasn't just his extraordinary good looks. He had an air of stability and self-assuredness. This was a man who did what he had to do, no matter what others thought of him—an "I don't give a damn" quality.

A distant buzzing sound caught her attention. Cole pulled his cellphone from his pocket. Holding it to his ear, he stood and said, "Excuse me, please."

Her heartbeat skyrocketing, Keeley watched him anxiously. Had something happened?

She glanced over at Elizabeth, who was sipping her coffee and eyeing Cole, too . . . in an odd, predatory way. Her gaze roaming up and down his body said she liked what she saw.

Cole pocketed his phone and turned back to Elizabeth. "I'm afraid we're going to have to cut our visit short. Would it be all right if I come back again sometime soon?"

Elizabeth beamed. "But of course. Perhaps for dinner one night?"

"That would be delightful. Thank you." Turning to Keeley, he said, "Let's go."

Her heart thumping, she jumped up and almost ran from the room. Something had happened. Had her girls been found?

eleven

Cole could feel the anxiety bouncing from Keeley as they walked out together. The front door had barely shut behind them before she asked, "What is it?"

He gave a subtle shake of his head as he took her arm and guided her toward his Jeep. There was no telling who Elizabeth had listening all around her estate. Though based on what he'd learned in their brief visit, he doubted this new development would be of the slightest interest to her. A good thing, since it was none of her damn business.

He opened the vehicle's passenger door for her, then came around and slid in beside her. Twisting round to face her, he considered how he was going to tell Keeley the news without getting her hopes up. In the next second, he knew there was no way. She was going to get her hopes up no matter what he said.

"Jordan got a tip this morning . . . a couple in Grantham, Georgia, have recently adopted a child. The couple isn't known for their upright citizenship . . . been in and out of jail for various things. Somebody got to wondering who would be stupid enough to give them a child."

His heart literally ached as he saw the joy and sadness on her face. Joy because this child could be hers. Sadness because it was only one child, not two.

His estimation of Keeley's strength shot up as he watched her stiffen her spine, take a deep breath, and say, "Okay, let's go."

Cole stifled a laugh. If only it were that easy. He cranked up the engine and glanced over at her. "Jordan and Eden are already working a rescue scenario. We'll head back to your house, pick them up, and head out."

Her jaw clenched. She was clearly not crazy about the delay. Yeah, he could understand that. Most likely she wanted to go roaring over there, knock on the door, and demand her daughter back. Unfortunately, it wasn't going to be that simple.

"So what's the plan? Is Honor taking over?"

"No."

"Why not?"

He shrugged. "No real need if this doesn't pan out. Our tipster isn't the most reliable source. If it is Hailey or Hannah, we'll work something out with her." He shot her another look. "Okay?"

It was a credit to the character of Keeley Fairchild that she asked, "Will this get you into trouble?"

"None we can't handle. Don't worry about it."

A shudder ran through her and she wrapped her arms around herself. "There's only one girl?"

"Yes. I'm sorry."

"I'll never give up hope. No matter how long it takes, what I have to do . . . I'll never give up looking for them."

His eyes locked with hers as he gave her a promise. "Neither will I."

Jordan and Eden were waiting in the living room when Keeley and Cole walked in. Eden looked determined and excited. For some reason, Jordan looked grim.

Unable to wait any longer, Keeley said, "What's our plan?"

Eden put her arm around her and led her to the couch. Sitting beside Keeley, she took her hand. "Here's what we know. A childless couple, known for their sordid and questionable lifestyle, was seen in their car with a little girl, about four or five years old. Our tipster said they were evasive when asked where she came from. Their explanation is that a distant relative passed away and left the child to them."

Despite the desperate need for this child to be hers, she had to ask, "But that sounds plausible, doesn't it?"

Jordan growled from across the room, "Plausible but oddly coincidental. Especially considering the timing, and the age and description of the little girl."

Keeley closed her eyes and swallowed hard. Then she opened her eyes and asked, "What does she look like?"

"She has dark hair, light olive skin, and black eyes."

Her heart almost pounded through her chest. *Hannah! Oh God, please let it be Hannah. But where is my Hailey?*

Eden squeezed her hand. "You okay?"

She took a long shuddering breath and nodded, determined to be strong and calm. "It sounds like Hannah." Knowing it was useless because they would have told her if they had other news, she had to ask, "Your source had no knowledge of another child? Blond hair, fair complexion?"

Sympathy darkening her gray eyes, Eden shook her head. "Only one child was seen."

Keeley took another breath. "Okay, so what's the plan?"

Jordan's voice grumbled across the room again. "We were just discussing that."

Eden turned to her husband, her exasperation obvious. "Jordan, it's the best way for us to get in. And you know I can take care of myself."

Jordan's grim expression didn't change. "That doesn't keep me from worrying."

For the first time, Cole spoke up. "What are you thinking?"

Eden took in both Cole's and Keeley's gazes. "They live in a rural area. Not a lot of houses close by. I'm going to knock on their door, pretend I have a flat and that my cellphone can't get a signal. I'll ask to use their phone, go in and snoop."

"And if you get caught, there's no telling what they'll do," Jordan said.

"I'm not going to get caught." Eden looked at Cole. "What do you think?"

Cole nodded. "Sounds like a good plan to me. We'll wire you so we can monitor what's happening. The instant you find the child, let us know if it's Hannah. If it is, Jordan and I will come through the doors. If it isn't, you can make a pretend call and then leave without them ever knowing what we suspected."

Keeley couldn't just sit there and do nothing. "Doesn't it make more sense if I go in?" She looked at Eden. "You've only seen photos of Hannah. I could tell immediately and—"

"No," Cole said. "What are you going to do if it is Hannah and she recognizes you? She could blow your cover and get both of you hurt. You willing to risk that?"

"I can't just sit by and—"

"Yes, you can. Hannah needs her mother to be safe and Hailey needs you to keep looking for her."

Cole was right ... she knew he was, but now that there was some hope, she desperately needed to do something. And amazingly, he seemed to understand that.

"You'll be in a car a few yards away. If it's Hannah, the instant we grab her, we'll pass her to you. She'll be scared and will need her mother immediately."

Keeley cast him a grateful look and nodded. "Okay, so when are we going?"

All three LCR operatives glanced at their watches and then in one simultaneous statement said, "One hour."

Dark ominous clouds were rolling in as they started for Grantham, creating an even more somber, anxious feeling inside Keeley. Jordan and Eden were in the car ahead of them. Cole and Keeley followed behind in his SUV. It was a seven-hour drive to Grantham. They had discussed flying, but wanted to go under the radar as much as possible. Once there, Cole said he would give Honor a call.

Honor would likely be upset that she wasn't notified sooner. Keeley couldn't let that concern her. If this was Hannah, nothing else mattered. She didn't care if they broke every law man had ever made. Saving her children was the only thing that mattered.

A shiver of excitement swept through her, followed quickly by a strong surge of hope. Could it be possible that in just a few hours, she could be holding one of her daughters? Her arms ached with the need to hold their soft warm bodies.

"You cold?" Cole's voice sounded rough, gravelly with his concern.

"No, just excited and worried. I feel so torn. On one hand, I can't wait to hold Hannah in my arms, but I can't stop thinking about Hailey. Where could she be?"

"It makes sense they're not together. For one thing, this case was too well publicized to keep them together. And secondly . . ." He glanced over at her as if concerned whether or not she could take what he was about to say.

"And secondly?"

"Since they were likely sold, most people would only be able to purchase one, not both."

Keeley closed her eyes. Yes, that had been a theory all along. Selling her children for profit. What kind of monster would do that to a child? She fell silent, her mind bouncing with worry and the inability to fathom what had caused her entire family to be ripped away from her.

"Tell me about your husband."

Surprised by the question, Keeley was grateful for anything to get her mind off her tortured thoughts. "He was a complex man."

"In what way?"

Her mind envisioned Stephen when they'd first married. Golden hair, golden skin, and perfect smile. Charming. Witty. He'd seemed so uncomplicated and easygoing, so full of life.

At the beginning of their relationship, he'd been good to her . . . respectful and seemingly loving. It was only after they'd been married a few months that she saw that beneath the façade was a flawed, shallow man. She had accepted her marriage wasn't perfect . . . little had she known how incredibly imperfect it had been. Days before Stephen died, she found out just how much he'd duped her.

"I'm sorry, I didn't mean to upset you."

It wasn't until he spoke than she realized she was crying. She wiped at her face and swallowed back the rest of her tears. "I can't believe I'm crying about him. Guess I'm just a little more emotional than usual."

As she'd been doing since Stephen died, she described him as she thought of him before that awful day when the affection she'd felt for him shriveled and died. "He was funny, often kind and generous. When we first started seeing each other, I was still grieving for my mother . . . she'd died just a few months before. Stephen made me laugh . . . feel better."

"You were very close to your mother?"

"Yes. Very. She was my best friend . . . even more so than Jenna. Her illness was long and drawn out. Losing her was devastating . . . I was in a fog of grief for months." Keeley closed her eyes as she remembered that grief—how she'd lost her mother. She had been expecting it, but the day it happened had been a devastating, horrendous blow.

"You okay?"

Drawing in a shaky breath, she pulled herself away from that torturous memory. "Yes . . . sorry. Anyway, I had gone to school with Stephen . . . he was a few years older than me. I hadn't seen him in years, not that he even noticed me in school. One day he came into the diner where I worked, sat down, ordered pie and a side order of a date."

"Smooth."

She laughed at his sarcasm. "You had to be there. He said it so charmingly, I said yes before I knew what I was doing."

"How long did you date?"

"Only about four months. Though no one knew we were dating."

"Why is that?"

She snorted. "Poor girl from the wrong side of the tracks dating the son of the richest family in the county? Even I knew it wasn't a smart idea. But we were young."

"And in love," Cole added.

She shrugged. "I thought so."

"What happened when everyone learned you were dating?"

"No one knew until after we married. We eloped."

"Bet that went over well with his mother."

"Can't say it was the most pleasant experience of my life when we announced it to her. Elizabeth made sure I knew she'd had plans for Stephen. Those plans didn't include him marrying 'trash.'"

Cole blew out an explosive curse.

Keeley smiled. "It doesn't hurt anymore. To be hated by Elizabeth Fairchild is not the worst thing that can happen to a person. She hates many more people than she likes. Actually I'm not sure she likes anyone. However, there are few people she hates more than me."

"I understand that she tried to blame you for Stephen's abduction."

"She did her best. When no one believed that, she found other ways to try to destroy me."

Those grim days were engraved in her memory forever. Learning of Stephen's numerous affairs had torn her apart. Realizing how stupid she'd been was made all the worse by the knowledge that apparently she was once again the cliché: the wife is always the last to know. She'd barely comprehended that pain when she'd learned that Stephen had been abducted, and then his body had been found days later.

And then a new agony had begun when Elizabeth accused her of setting it all up.

"On the surface, it probably looked as though you were guilty."

She huffed out a breath. "Yeah, even Jenna asked me if I did it. Miranda never asked, but I think she wondered, too."

He took his eyes off the road to give her a sympathetic glance. "Bet that hurt."

"It did. What hurt worse was that both of them had known for a long time that Stephen was being unfaithful to me. They never told me."

"They say why?"

She lifted her shoulder in a halfhearted shrug. "Stephen was Miranda's brother; she loved him and didn't want to hurt him or me. I guess I understood that. It hurt, but I understood. Jenna not telling me was worse. She said that by the time she heard about it, I was pregnant with the girls. Then, after they were born, she just couldn't figure out a way to tell me."

"How did you convince the FBI that you had nothing to do with his abduction?"

"I just told the truth. Nothing more. I offered to take a polygraph test and I passed. They questioned me but I don't think they ever looked at me as a real suspect."

He shot her a grave, sorrowful look. "I'm sorry you went through that."

"Thank you. Having Hailey and Hannah helped a lot. They were a blessing."

"Was he good to you? I mean, other than the affairs?"

"Do you mean was he physically abusive? Not at all. Most of the time he was charming and witty."

"Most of the time?"

Long past the stage of being hurt by Stephen's sometimes very barbed and pointed stings, she shrugged. "He had flaws like most of us do."

"Was he a good father?"

"Oddly enough, he was. I'm not sure if that would have continued once the girls got older. Stephen was such a child himself in many ways, being an actual father might have been tougher for him."

"I'm sorry he was taken from them."

"Thank you." She twisted around in her seat to face him. "What about you?"

His entire body jerked as if he were shocked at the question. "Me?"

"Yes, we've been talking so much about me. . . . I know as an LCR operative you can't tell me some things, but other than you grew up in Oklahoma and used to live in Texas, I know almost nothing about you. Can you tell me more than that?"

"Like what?"

"I know you're not married." She offered a tentative

smile, a little embarrassed to have that information. "Jenna told me she asked you."

He didn't return the smile, just said, "No, I'm not married."

Well, that was short and sweet. She could feel the tenseness of his body and knew he was uncomfortable. With that question or any question? It seemed almost ridiculous to not know more about the man she'd shared such intimacy with last night.

"What did you do before you started working for Last Chance Rescue?"

"High school history teacher."

Wow. If he'd told her he was an android from Mars, she couldn't have been more surprised. None of her history teachers had ever looked like him. Probably a good thing, since she would have had some major concentration problems.

"In Texas?"

"Yes."

"I'm not going to tell anyone, if that's why you don't want to talk about yourself."

"I never thought you would. I just don't have that interesting of a past."

"Why did you start working for LCR?"

"My family was murdered. I needed focus. LCR gave me that."

The old adage "Be careful what you wish for" suddenly hit her square in the face. A simple "I'm sorry" seemed woefully inadequate, yet what else could she say? "I'm sorry for your loss."

"It was a long time ago."

"When did it happen?"

He was silent for so long, she was beginning to think he wasn't going to answer. Then he said, "Almost six years ago." After a palpable pause, he whispered, "Six years . . ."

"Does it still seem recent?"

A dry huff of a laugh held no amusement. "Sometimes it seems like only yesterday . . . other times, like it happened to someone else and I read about it." He glanced over at her. "That make any sense?"

"Actually, yes. Maybe that's all part of the healing process."

"Maybe."

"Can you tell me what happened?"

"Kids busted into my house, looking for me. I wasn't there, my wife and daughter were."

Horrified, Keeley whispered, "Why?"

"They failed my class . . . got kicked off the football team. Thought it'd be cool to beat the hell out of me. Unfortunately, one of them was high on drugs. He brought a gun to the party. When they couldn't find me, he shot them instead."

Tears blurred her vision of the grim-faced man beside her. The emotionless way he'd recited the events told her more than if he'd been sobbing. There was such pain and grief and a whole lot of anger there. Maybe she detected it because she'd lived it herself.

"So they caught them?"

"Yeah. Put 'em away for a few years. They'll probably get out before they're thirty." She heard him swallow. "My daughter never saw her eighth birthday. My wife never saw her thirtieth."

"You must have hated those boys."

He nodded. "That hate consumed me for a long time. Then I found LCR, or I should say LCR found me."

"So you never want to go back to teaching again?"

"I'm not the same man I was back then . . . in too many ways to count."

"Where do you live when you're not on a case?"

"Tampa, Florida."

"I've always wanted to go to Florida."

"You've never been out of Fairview, have you?"

She laughed. Did she seem that backward? "I've been to Greenville and Columbia a few times. And Stephen and I honeymooned in Tahiti."

He flashed her a small apologetic smile and Keeley found herself focusing on his well-shaped mouth again. It could look so stern sometimes, but even then, it was beautifully shaped. When he smiled the least little bit, Cole's face transformed from handsome to gorgeous.

"Isn't that right?"

Keeley jerked her attention back to the conversation. "Sorry, what?"

"But you've never lived anywhere else other than Fairview?"

"No."

"Why not?"

She shrugged. "We didn't have enough money for me to go away to college. So I stayed here and went to the community college in Myerstown, the next town over. I was in my second year of college when mama died, and still grieving when I started dating Stephen. Then we got married."

"Why have you put up with Elizabeth's antics all these years?"

Another person might have been offended by his bluntness. Keeley wasn't. It was a fair question. "I didn't know about them for a long time. Oh, I knew she didn't like me, but I was busy with my own life. I was still in school and newly married. I got pregnant before I finished my degree. Stephen didn't want me driving back and forth to school during that time, since I was sick almost the entire nine months. So I stayed home and took online classes to finish up my degree. Then my babies were born." She shrugged. "I had my girls . . . I stayed busy."

Keeley inwardly winced as she heard herself describe

her life. She probably sounded like the most boring person in the universe. "It wasn't until after Stephen died that I realized what a hatchet job she'd done on me. Stephen never told me. Miranda and Jenna never told me." She grimaced a smile. "You must think I'm the dumbest, most idiotic and boring person in the world."

"You sound like someone who believes the best of people."

She cracked a dry laugh. "That's a nice way of saying I was clueless."

"But you don't back down when confronted with Elizabeth's hatred."

"Her opinion isn't important to me. As I said, having Elizabeth or even an entire town hate me isn't the worst thing that can happen. I don't measure my worth by other people's opinion."

His approving glance had Keeley's heart picking up an erratic rhythm.

"Eden said you were in the process of putting your home up for sale and moving somewhere else?"

She nodded. "There's no real reason for us to stay. Other than my mom, Fairview holds few fond memories for me. Moving to another state and starting all over again would be good for all of us. Smearing my name and harassing me is one of Elizabeth's hobbies; I don't see her stopping anytime soon. I refuse to allow my daughters to be exposed to her hatred."

"Did you tell anyone that you were leaving?"

"A few people."

"Like who?"

"Why?"

"I'm just wondering if someone didn't want you to leave and this was a way to keep you here."

"Why would anyone care?"

"I don't know . . . but who did you tell?"

"Let's see . . . Jenna and Miranda, of course. And the

realtor, Mr. Dotson. And I might have mentioned it to Mrs. Thompkins." A gasp caught in her throat as she remembered an event that took place only days before Hailey and Hannah were taken.

"What?"

"I told Elizabeth. I was at the bank. Hailey and Hannah were with me. Elizabeth came in, glanced at the girls as if she were looking down at garbage, and then turned her back to them. I marched up to her, told her that we were leaving town and that I was glad we would never have to see her sour old face ever again."

Cole's shout of laughter surprised her. And from the expression on his face, it surprised him, too. When was the last time he'd laughed?

"I'm sure that went over well."

Remembering the shocked surprise on Elizabeth's cold face, Keeley grinned. "Since we were standing in the middle of a busy bank and everyone heard me, not really. She glared at me as if I was some sort of vagrant and stalked out the door."

"So several people heard you say you were leaving."

"Yeah, so I guess more than a few knew about it."

"Do you remember who was there?"

"No. I was so angry at the way she'd snubbed her own grandchildren, I grabbed the girls and left. I know several people were watching, but I learned a long time ago to ignore them." She sighed. "But in a small town, as soon as a few people know about it, everyone seems to know. And since I'm often their favorite topic of conversation, I'm sure everyone knows about it now."

"You had a tough time growing up, didn't you?"

"No, actually I didn't."

He shot her a surprised look. "I thought—"

"Oh, we were poor, and yes, people whispered about my mother and I heard 'bastard child' more than once, but I would never say I had it tough. My mama made sure of that."

"She sounds like she was an exceptional woman."

"She was the best mother a child could have."

"Jenna told me that your mother basically raised her, too."

"Now, Jenna's the one who had it tough."

"She was poor, too?"

"Poor and abused. When she was thirteen, her mother broke Jenna's kneecap with a hammer."

His expression one of horror, he shook his head and asked, "Hell . . . Why?"

"She was drunk. Jenna gave her lip. Her mother grabbed the first thing she saw to hit her." Keeley swallowed a lump in her throat. "Jenna had to wear a brace for years. By the time she could afford surgery, the damage was already done. She'll always have the limp, but it's a lot less noticeable now."

"I'm sure she was grateful to have you and your mother."

"She's been my best friend since we were in the first grade together. Her mother died when she was seventeen. She came to live with us and was a huge help when mama got sick. We took turns staying with her."

"True friends like that are hard to find."

Cole's compassion continued to surprise her. Not only had he survived a tragedy no one should have to live through, he chose to help others instead of focusing on the hatred he must still feel. When she'd first met him, she'd wondered if he had enough humanity in him to care. She now knew that he probably had more than most. He cared enough to risk his life to save others. Her mother would have liked and approved of Cole Mathison.

She wanted to ask him about his scars but wouldn't. Not only was it none of her business, she wasn't sure that knowing more about Cole was a good thing. The more she knew, the more she wanted to know.

Last night was an anomaly. He'd come to her room to comfort her and had gotten a whole lot more than he had planned. She was the least sexually aggressive person she knew; the fact that she'd practically asked him to make love to her amazed her.

With Stephen, when they'd first married, she had initiated their lovemaking from time to time, but the longer they'd been married, the less secure she became in her sexuality. Stephen had never turned her down, but neither had he acted like it meant that much to him. Of course, after finding out that he had numerous women on the side, she understood why their lovemaking was no big deal. To Stephen, sex had been sex, outside or inside the confines of marriage vows. They made no difference to him.

She knew to her soul that Cole was different . . . in that way . . . in every way from Stephen. But he was here to do a job. Once her children were back with her, he would leave. Having any kind of feelings for him would be futile and could only invite heartache. Something she was all too well acquainted with already.

She'd made a mistake with Stephen. She couldn't make another one, especially where Hailey and Hannah were concerned. If and when she ever had another relationship or marriage, she would make sure that not only would he be the right man for her, but he'd also be the right father for her daughters.

Just because Cole was the opposite of Stephen didn't make him a better choice. Besides, just because she was incredibly attracted to him didn't mean he felt the same way. Yes, he'd been aroused last night, very much so. But that didn't necessarily mean he was interested in anything more. Other than last night, he'd never given any indication that he found her remotely appealing.

That thought depressed her.

Cole took his eyes off the road to shoot a quick glance at Keeley. She had gone silent on him. Had he told her too much about his life? Why he'd felt the need to be so open about his past he didn't question. He was keeping so much from this woman, the least he could do was be truthful about everything else. Problem was, having her know of his loss only drew them closer together, and damned if he needed that to happen.

He was only now getting used to that feeling whenever he looked at her . . . a gut punch. How the hell could he be attracted to this woman? Yes, she was beautiful. But how many other beautiful women had he seen since he'd lost Jill and never felt anything but an appreciation of that beauty?

Even Shea, his ex-wife, as much as he loved her as a friend and as lovely as she was, had never caused this gut-wrenching feeling. And as pretty as Honor was, the fact that he still didn't remember their weekend together and wasn't the slightest bit attracted to her now was an indication that it wasn't just Keeley's outward attractiveness he found so appealing. There was a hell of a lot more to Keeley than just her looks, but he could do nothing about his feelings.

Last night, in her arms, he'd experienced something extraordinary, but damned if it could mean anything more than just a good memory of sexual fulfillment and comfort. He was here for only one purpose. Having any kind of relationship with Keeley would be beyond stupid. If he told her the truth about her husband's death, she'd hate him.

Stephen Fairchild might have been a lousy husband. That didn't mean Keeley wanted him dead or that she would want to be around the man responsible for his death. If she knew the truth, she might demand that he be taken off this case. He couldn't risk that.

This could be his only chance to help this woman. More than anything, he wanted to bring her children back home safely to her. He'd failed his own family . . . hadn't kept them safe. And he'd failed this family, too. He'd never let that happen again, no matter what he had to hide.

Until her children were home and their kidnapper caught, he needed to stay as aloof as possible. Yeah, hard as hell when they'd shared the most intimate of experiences, but that could never happen again. He was here to do a job. When that job was finished, he'd be gone from her life for good.

twelve

They stopped at an off-road clearing about five miles from their intended destination. Her knees weak and shaky, Keeley leaned against Cole's SUV and listened as the three LCR operatives reviewed and confirmed their plans.

Adrenaline, fear, and excitement bounced wildly inside her. This was really going to happen. She was going to get one of her girls back. She refused to believe this child wasn't Hannah. It had to be her. It had to be!

And despite what she'd been told, she couldn't help but hope that Hailey was there, too. Admittedly it was a long shot, but that didn't stop her from hoping.

"Key word is 'macaroni,'" Eden said. "Once I see the child, I'll verify it's Hannah with that word. Jordan, you'll come through the front. Cole will come through the back."

Cole double-checked his gun and then slipped it into the holster under his jacket. "We'll assume they'll be armed, but no drawing unless absolutely necessary."

Jordan and Eden nodded. "Agreed."

"I'll call Honor." Cole pulled out his cellphone and walked several feet from where Keeley stood.

Jordan took Eden's hand and led her away, his face as grim as Keeley had ever seen it. They stopped a few yards away, and from the looks of it, Jordan was giving extra instructions. Eden was gazing up at him with a small, understanding smile and the absolute adoration of a woman in love.

Keeley looked away. Just watching the love they had for each other created an ache she couldn't comprehend. Almost from the beginning, she had known there was something missing in her marriage to Stephen, though she hadn't known what it was at the time. She'd mistaken the gifts he'd given her and the girls for love.

After his death, she had acknowledged that their love had never gone as deeply as it should have. Despite the hurt of learning he'd been unfaithful within months of their marriage, deep down she hadn't really been surprised.

Never having seen her father and mother together, she'd never been exposed to the deep and abiding love a man and woman could have for each other. The kind of love Eden and Jordan had went beyond her realm of understanding and experience, but the knowledge that it existed created a gnawing emptiness inside her.

"You okay?"

She twisted around to look up at Cole. "Just anxious."

"It'll be over soon."

"What did Honor say?"

His mouth lifted in that attractive way of his. "The woman's got a colorful vocabulary."

"She's angry?"

"Yeah, but she'll get over it. Turns out she's in Atlanta on another case. She'll be here soon."

"Before you go in?"

He gave a full-fledged grin. "Hell no."

Despite the worry bubbling inside her, she had to smile at him. "If it is Hannah . . . what's next?"

"FBI will take it from there. Since this is a hunch, they're not approving us to go in, but they're not stopping it either. If it is Hannah, they'll take over as soon as we give them the info. We get Hannah. They do the arrests."

"Will they question the people about Hailey?"

"Absolutely. And so will we. Between the two of us, if they know anything, they'll give it up."

"Do you think they know anything?"

"Hard to say. Depends on whether they actually knew the man who sold them Hannah."

Sold. What a cold, revolting word, especially when applied to her babies. Revulsion shuddered through her. In the next second, a warm jacket, heated with Cole's body heat and smelling deliciously like male musk, appeared on her shoulders. Words of thanks got caught in her throat as she looked at him. She saw gentleness and concern, but also desire and attraction. She shivered again, this time for a completely different reason.

"We ready to roll?" Jordan's deep voice interrupted the moment. His arm around his wife, he looked more at peace, and Eden had a soft glow in her eyes.

Keeley sent up a quick prayer that Eden would be safe. Yes, she desperately wanted her girls back, but the thought of Eden getting hurt in the process was unbearable.

Cole shot a hard look at Keeley. "Stay in my vehicle. Once we know it's Hannah and we get her out, one of us will bring her to you. Until then, you don't move. Right?"

Keeley nodded. The last thing she wanted to do was get in anyone's way.

She got into the driver's seat of Cole's Jeep and watched as he, Jordan, and Eden got into the other one. Once they started moving, Keeley pulled out and followed behind them. She'd driven almost five miles when the lights of the vehicle in front of her blinked—her signal to pull over. Her heart in her throat, Keeley pulled to the side of the road and watched as they continued on. Though the radio transmitter Cole had given her would give her access to everything that was going on, she couldn't stop the anxious fear that she should be there with them, just in case.

Wrapping Cole's jacket around her tighter, Keeley gritted her teeth and waited.

After what seemed an interminable amount of time, she heard a small amount of static and then Eden's voice, soft, low, but very clear. "Okay, guys, stepping up on the porch. Looks pretty damn seedy. There's a light on at the back of the house . . . maybe the kitchen. Here goes."

The distant clang of a doorbell ring and then the squeak of a door opening.

"Yeah?"

"Omigosh," Eden gushed breathlessly. "I'm so glad somebody's home. My car broke down about a mile down the road. And my cellphone . . ." A soft swallowed sob. "My cellphone . . . I can't get a signal. Do you have a phone I can use?"

If Keeley didn't know it was Eden, she would never have recognized her. She sounded young, frightened, and authentically Southern.

A distant female voice said, "Who is it, Bobby?"

The harsh male voice answered, "Nobody, Ava. Get on back upstairs."

"I need to call my husband," Eden said. "We're staying at the Sleepy Time . . . you know that motel on Jackson Street?"

There was such a long silence, Keeley began to think the transmitter had stopped working. Then the man said, "Yeah, come on in. We got a phone in the kitchen you can use."

Eden stepped through the door, resisting the temptation to scrunch her nose at the offensive odor inside the house. A mixture of tobacco, body odor, old grease, and something truly abhorrent assailed her nostrils.

As the door closed behind her, she stood in a small foyer and assessed the area. Living room on the right— sofa and curtains had seen better days. The large area rug, stained and threadbare, had, too. The wide-screen plasma television hanging on the wall and black leather lounge chair in the corner was incongruent with the rest of the sad décor, sticking out like shiny jewels among garbage.

"Phone's this way," the man grumbled beside her.

Her gaze taking everything in while she tried to appear anxious to use the phone, Eden stepped over a small pile of toys in the middle of the hallway floor. Dolls, plastic teacups, coloring books and crayons. Definitely a child here . . . but was it Hannah? She saw no one other than the large, rather obese man leading the way to the kitchen.

"On the wall." He jerked his head at a phone hanging from a paint-cracked wall.

Pretending she didn't notice how he was eyeing her up and down like she was a juicy steak, she asked, "Do you have a phone book I could use?"

He turned around and headed out the door. "I think there's one in the other room. Be right back."

In his absence, Eden took a quick glance around the kitchen. The sink was filled with dishes, and every available counter was cluttered with something . . . much of which had no business being in a kitchen, such as the car battery sitting beside the sink.

The door to the left of the oven would be a good entrance for Cole. She murmured into her mic, "Back door leads to kitchen."

"Here you go."

Eden twisted around and gave him her most charming smile.

The leering interest gleaming in his eyes told her she should have lowered the wattage on the smile.

"Phone book's a couple of years old but the number should still be the same." The words were pleasant enough but would have been less bothersome if his eyes had risen above her chest when he said them.

"Oh, thanks so much." Eden flipped to the hotel's number, picked up the phone and began to dial. There would be someone to pick it up and transfer her to a man who would pretend to be her husband. If the man behind her chose to check the number or wanted to speak with her husband, then he would have someone to talk to.

As she sweetly explained to her fake husband what had happened to her car, the man leaned against the counter, eyed her ass, and listened to every word.

In an effort to keep him as unsuspicious as possible, she hung up the phone and offered him another smile, less wattage this time. "Thank goodness he was there. It's going to take him a few minutes to get here. Mind if I use your bathroom?"

His gaze finally moving to her face, he crossed his arms over his barrel chest and grimaced. "It's not working."

That explained the vile odor. "Then I guess I'll just wait."

His gaze began a slow up-and-down again. "Where you from? You got the look of one of them Stewart girls from up around Minton."

"I'm from Raleigh, North Carolina, but my daddy's family came from around Minton. Maybe they're some distant kin."

"How long you been married?"

"It'll be a year July seventh." No doubt about it, if she acted the least bit interested, she'd have herself a date or even more. Time for a few questions of her own. "Was that your wife I saw?"

His expression one of deep regret, he nodded. "Yeah."

"Do you have children?"

A wary flicker of his eyes told her she was onto something. Before she could say anything, he glanced at a wall clock. "It's getting late and I gotta get up early in the morning. You can wait on the porch till your man gets here."

Since it was just past seven o'clock, she doubted that going to bed early was really on his agenda. Her question had made him nervous.

Her sweetly naïve expression gave no indication of her thoughts. "Mind if I have a glass of water before I leave? I had to walk almost a mile and I'm—"

"Plumbing's out, water's off."

While that could be true, the question about children had definitely made him uneasy. As much as he'd apparently enjoyed staring at her body, he wanted her out of here as soon as possible.

Determined not to leave the house before she found something, she turned to go down the hall and deliberately stepped on one of the small toys. The squeak was amazingly loud in the deadly quiet house.

Eden looked over her shoulder and flashed a bright smile at the man behind her. "Do you have a dog?"

"No."

"Oh, then you do have a child? How old?"

"You don't need to know our business. Get—"

"Bobby? Who is it?"

Eden whirled at the soft voice behind her. A haggard-looking woman in her mid-forties stood at the bottom of the stairway. What caught Eden's attention was the small child she held in her arms. Black hair, light olive skin . . . about five years old.

Eden gave her a warm, friendly "Oh, hello there."

The man barked, "Ava, get back upstairs." He turned to Eden. "Get out."

Widening her eyes in surprised innocence, Eden said, "But I—"

The man grabbed her arm. "Get out of here. Now."

"But why?"

Before Eden realized his intent, his fist slammed toward her face. Her arm blocked the brunt of his punch, but he still got in a glancing blow to her jaw. On the way to the floor, darkness closing in, she managed to whisper, "Macaroni."

Keeley sat up. Her heartbeat tripled in speed. *Hannah!* Opening the Jeep door, she jumped out and began running.

Cole kicked the back door open and ran through the kitchen. Jordan's roar of outrage as he slammed through the front door blended with a woman's shrill scream and the wailing of a child.

Jerking to a halt in the foyer, Cole took in the scene. Eden was pulling herself up from the floor, and Jordan had a heavyset man pinned to the wall. A lank-haired, malnourished-looking woman stood at the bottom of the stairs. In her arms was a crying child—Hannah Fairchild.

The woman's eyes saucer-wide, she held tight to Hannah as she turned and put her foot on the bottom stair.

Cole grabbed her arm. "Hold it right there. That's not your child."

She jerked away and snarled, "You get away from us."

Hannah's little face scrunched up with fear and she let out another wail.

Cole snapped, "This child doesn't belong to you."

The woman twisted her head and shouted at the man Jordan still held. "Bobby, don't just stand there. Do something!"

Cole plucked Hannah from the woman's arms.

Covering her face with her hands, the woman dropped down to the bottom step and sobbed pitifully. Unable to feel any compassion toward anyone who knowingly kept a stolen child, he whispered soothing words to Hannah as he headed to the front door.

"Everything okay here?" Honor Stone appeared at the entrance, her eyes gleaming with excitement.

"Just a couple of folks here with an abducted child," Cole said.

Her smile one of delight, she said, "You don't say."

The woman's sobs grew louder and her husband shouted at her to shut up. Blended with Hannah's cries, the cacophony of noise was ear-shattering. Patting Hannah on her back, Cole strode out of the room, onto the porch. There was only one person who could calm her now.

He halted when he saw Keeley sprinting toward the house. The joy on her face was unlike anything he'd ever seen before. She literally glowed as she screamed, "Hannah!"

The little arms that had wrapped around his neck loosened and Hannah twisted around. "Mommy!"

Cole met Keeley at the bottom step. A lump developed in his throat as her arms reached for Hannah. Tears streaming down her face, she gave a soft sob as she wrapped her arms around her daughter and enveloped her in a tight embrace.

And for the first time in a very long time, Cole realized it was good to be alive.

thirteen

Keeley couldn't stop touching her daughter. After being checked by the paramedics as well as the child psychologist called in by the FBI, Hannah had been given back to her mother. Though dirty, terrified, and confused, she'd been declared in excellent health.

The man and woman, Bobby and Ava Oates, were now in the custody of the FBI and were being questioned vigorously. With Hannah snugly in her arms, Keeley had stood a distance away and watched them being arrested. Ava had cried; Bobby had cursed.

Cole had taken her to the local sheriff's office and let her hear some of the questioning. It had done little good to listen. Questioned separately, neither acted as if they had any idea who they'd purchased Hannah from, or where Hailey might be. Finally, Keeley had asked Cole to bring her home. She trusted the FBI to get the information, but she was the only one who could take care of her little girl.

She had sat in the backseat of the SUV and held Hannah all the way home. The poor baby had snuggled into her mother's arms and fallen asleep immediately. Other than asking if they were comfortable or needed to make a rest stop, Cole had said almost nothing. He seemed to understand her need to just hold her daughter and absorb the joy of having her in her arms.

An hour ago, they'd arrived home, and despite her intense desire to put Hannah in a bathtub and wash all the filth and vileness from her child's skin, she'd restricted herself to using a damp cloth and wiping off only the worst. Hannah had slept through that, too.

Now, propped up on a pillow, she lay beside her daughter and hummed a tuneless song. Thankfulness and happiness intermingled with an anguish she knew would never be diminished until she had Hailey back, too.

The child psychologist would be by tomorrow to see if anything could be gleaned from Hannah. She didn't want to put her child through any more pain, but she had to find out if Hannah knew anything about her sister. And she needed to know if there was any psychological damage to Hannah. She seemed happy and content, and the psychologist had deemed her well enough to go home. That didn't mean there weren't some issues they needed to work through. Only God knew what she had been through since she'd been taken.

"How is she?"

Keeley looked up at the tall, dark man in the doorway. This man was still a stranger in so many ways, but in other ways, she felt she'd known him all her life. Her chest tightened with emotion. What would she have done without him, Eden, and Jordan?

Swallowing past what felt like a permanent lump in her throat, she kept her voice low. "Still sleeping. She's exhausted."

"She probably feels safe for the first time."

Lifting a strand of her daughter's silky black hair, Keeley rubbed it between her fingers. "I can't believe she's actually here. I have nightmares like this every night . . . that I have them back and then I lose them, then I wake up and realize the nightmares are my reality. I'm almost afraid to go to sleep."

Though his face was expressionless, something flickered in his eyes.

"You know all about nightmares, don't you, Cole?"

"It gets easier . . . eventually."

"Does it?" She looked down at her sleeping daughter. "Only half of my nightmare is over."

"We'll get Hailey back, too, Keeley. I promise."

He said it with such conviction, she got the feeling that finding Hailey was almost as important to him as it was to her.

"Why do you care so much? Is it because of what happened to your daughter?"

Another small flicker, then he lifted a broad shoulder. "Children should never know this kind of fear." He stared at her for several more seconds, as if there was something more he wanted to say. Finally he said, "Why don't you try to get some sleep? I'm going to check in with Honor and see if they were able to extract any information."

"Will you wake me if there is anything?"

"Absolutely."

Laying her head on the pillow, Keeley gathered Hannah closer to her and closed her eyes.

Cole shut the door to the Keeley's bedroom and leaned against the wall. Seeing Keeley with Hannah brought back memories of his own daughter, ones he'd thought were lost for good.

Cassidy had been the joy of his and Jill's life. He remembered the delight they'd shared when she'd first started crawling. Remembered the first time she laughed. And the time Jill called him at work . . . got him out of class to tell him Cassidy had said her first word. For the life of him, he couldn't remember what that word was.

He rubbed at the dampness of his eyes as he headed downstairs for their meeting. Despite Jordan's insistence that Eden lie down once they returned home, she'd insisted on attending.

Cole entered the living room and was glad to see that Jordan had at least gotten her to lie on the sofa. A small bruise was already forming on her jaw, and he knew from experience that she must have a headache. If the harsh, hard look in Jordan's eyes was any indication, Eden was probably feeling better than her husband. He'd been furious when she'd been knocked unconscious.

Eden lifted her head when Cole entered. "How's Keeley?"

An image of her haunted, beautiful face appeared in his mind. "Better, but still hurting."

"And Hannah?" Jordan asked.

"Sleeping. Poor kid's exhausted." Cole checked his watch. "We ready?"

Both Eden and Jordan nodded. Cole pressed the speed dial on the phone beside the couch.

Honor answered immediately, her tone filled with frustrated fury. "They don't know shit."

He'd been afraid of that. Transactions like these were often done anonymously, with as little information given as possible between the seller and the buyer. Cole rubbed his temple where a drum serenade had set up for an all-nighter. "Where'd they get Hannah?"

"Friend of a friend hooked them up." Honor snorted and added, "Husband thought a kid would keep his wife happy. He cashed in his 401(k). Bought her a kid and him a plasma television."

"You're tracking down this friend of a friend?" Jordan asked.

"Yeah. Hopefully we'll have something in a few days. How's the kid doing?"

"Better than anybody else. She's asleep in her mother's arms," Cole said.

Honor's voice softened. "Poor baby. How's Keeley?"

"Ecstatic and terrified," Cole answered.

"Yeah, don't blame her. The child psychologist will be by around noon tomorrow."

"We'll be ready," Eden said.

"Okay. By the way, good work. Though I should have your ass for waiting so long to call me. Don't do it again." Her voice softened once more. "Sorry you got bruised up a bit, Eden."

Jordan growled and Eden laughed softly. "No worries, Honor, I'm fine. We'll see you tomorrow."

The second Cole pressed the keypad to end the call, Jordan stood. "Okay, my love, you stayed and you listened. Now you're going to bed."

"In a minute, Jordan. We need to talk about our next move. Hannah's home, but how do we know that Keeley and she are safe? This person might be ready at a moment's notice to grab them again."

"I'll keep them safe," Cole said.

"For how long?" Eden asked.

Cole shrugged; his priorities were set. "As long as it takes."

"We've got to find the bastard," Jordan said. "If someone hates Keeley enough to have arranged three kidnappings, they won't stop until they get what they want."

Cole nodded. "Yeah, whatever the hell that is. If I didn't think it'd hurt Hannah more than she's already been hurt, I'd recommend we take her away until we find him. Problem is, with the trauma she's had over the last couple of months, doing that might cause irreparable damage."

"No, we're staying here. I'll make sure Hannah stays safe. I won't be careless again."

They all jerked around. Keeley stood at the door. Looking both fragile and brave, she held a sleeping Hannah in her arms.

"Don't blame yourself for what happened, Keeley," Eden said. "No one could have predicted this."

Cole clenched his jaw. Predicted? Maybe not. But if he'd been where he was supposed to be, doing what he'd vowed to do, he could have prevented it.

She pressed a kiss to her daughter's head lying on her shoulder. "Perhaps. But now that I know there's someone out there who hates me that much, I'll be ready for them."

Both Jordan and Eden shot him a look, as if he was supposed to argue with her. Cole wouldn't. Keeley being on guard was a good thing. He planned to teach her some self-defense moves so she could gain more confidence. However, she didn't have to know that he'd die before she'd ever be put in that position again.

"And you still have no suspicions about who it could be?" Keeley asked.

"Not really. We can talk about it tomorrow." Cole glanced at his watch. "It's late. We all need to get some sleep."

Jordan stood and held out his hand for Eden. "Cole's right. Let's catch a few hours and meet again around nine, before the psychologist gets here for Hannah."

Holding hands, Eden and Jordan said good night and headed upstairs.

"So no news? Those people still aren't talking?"

As Cole stood he drew in a deep, controlled breath. The beginnings of a migraine were coming on strong. "Not yet. If they have any knowledge of where Hailey is, we'll get it from them."

"Do you need something for your headache?"

"How'd you know I have one?"

"My mother suffered with migraines. I recognized the signs."

"Thanks. Sleep will work better than anything."

They began walking up the stairs together.

"Would you like . . ." She swallowed, adjusted Hannah on her shoulder, and started again. "I used to massage my mother's neck and shoulders. That seemed to help her. I could do that for you."

A surge of lust hit him hard. *Great—a blinding headache and a throbbing hard-on.* She'd only asked if she could massage his neck, and suddenly the hot, sweet memories of their night together flooded through him, along with images of all the things he hadn't done that he'd dreamed about doing. Dammit. He did not need this.

"Thanks. I just need to get some sleep."

Cole ignored her wide-eyed astonishment as he stomped off. Yeah, he'd been rude, but if she'd seen his arousal at such an innocent offer, she'd be a hell of a lot more than just astonished. She would know that he wanted a repeat performance, only longer, more drawn out, and a hell of a lot more times. That couldn't happen . . . and his body damn well needed to get the message.

Keeley felt as though she'd just gotten into bed when the doorbell clanged. Pulling herself from one of the deepest sleeps she'd had in months, she opened her eyes and gazed down at her still-slumbering child. Hannah always slept so deeply. Hailey was the light sleeper. A pang of grief hit her hard and tears sprang to her eyes. She had to get her baby back.

The doorbell clanged again and then again. Whoever it was appeared to be very anxious. Could it be someone with information about Hailey?

Keeley slid her arms out from under her daughter and slipped her shoes on. She was still wearing her jeans and shirt from yesterday. Combing her hands through her hair, she took one last look at Hannah and ran from the room.

At the top of the stairs, she stopped when saw Elizabeth Fairchild standing just inside the foyer. Damned if she wanted to see the woman this morning . . . or any other morning for that matter.

"Where is she?" Elizabeth snapped.

"If you mean Keeley, she's still asleep. When she wakes, I'll tell her you stopped by." Cole's deep voice was quiet but Keeley recognized the anger beneath the surface.

"I just heard that my granddaughter is home. I demand to see her right now. How could you bring her home and not even call me?"

"How the hell did you even know about it?"

Though Cole's voice remained quiet, his tone was becoming more disgruntled, verging on furious. Keeley didn't know why, but for some reason she liked this Cole much better than the one who'd been so charming and flirtatious with Elizabeth. Maybe because she recognized that this was the real Cole?

"I heard about it on the news." Elizabeth huffed, "The news of all places!"

"Why do you want to see her?" Cole asked.

"Because it's my right. Keeley should have called me and told me what happened. I shouldn't have to watch television to find out these kinds of things."

"Well, she was slightly busy."

Cole's sarcasm brought a lift to Keeley's mouth.

"The reporter didn't even say which one it was."

"Hannah," Cole said.

There was a short pause, and even from a distance, she could see Elizabeth's confusion. "Is that the blond one or the dark one?"

Cole jerked the front door open. His voice, even softer and quieter than before, was filled with a seething fury. "Get out. Now."

Elizabeth gasped but apparently recognized she'd gone too far. She took a step outside. Cole barely gave her enough time to get clear of the door before he slammed it shut behind her.

Elizabeth's insensitivity and arrogance no longer surprised Keeley, but it was obvious that her not knowing which granddaughter was which had hit a hot button for Cole.

She eased down the stairway, wondering if his headache was worse. "Good morning?" She made it a question.

Cole jerked his head up to look at her. "I just threw your mother-in-law out of the house. You got a problem with that?"

Her heart flipped and then melted at her feet for this fierce, protective man. "Absolutely none."

The small twitch to his mouth told her he approved of her answer. "Good." He headed back toward the kitchen. "Breakfast is almost ready."

Something slowly unfurled inside Keeley. That budding crush she already had for this grumpy, gorgeous man became an enormous, full-sized bloom.

Her heart kicking up an excited beat, Keeley said, "I'll go get Hannah." She turned and raced up the stairs.

Elizabeth barely waited for Patrick to open the door before she stormed through it. Of all the overbearing, obnoxious, and rude people, Cole Mathison had to be the worst. How dare he talk to her in such a way? She was a Fairchild, the only one left that mattered. Did he not realize the power she wielded? Two days ago, the man had been absolutely charming, and now he'd become an obnoxious bastard. No doubt that slut's influence.

"What's wrong, Mama?"

She whirled around. Miranda stood in the middle of the foyer, her daughter, Maggie, at her side. These two would probably be thrilled with the news.

"Don't call me Mama. Haven't I told you again and again I don't care for that term?"

Mealy-mouthed child that she was, Miranda said, "I apologize, Mother. What has you so upset?"

"That man staying with that slut insulted me."

Miranda frowned, causing a line to appear on her forehead.

"Miranda, haven't I told you hundreds of times—don't frown. You'll look older than you already do."

"Sorry, Ma—Mother. But what man are you talking about?"

"That Cole Mathison that was here the other day. When he visited, we had a perfectly pleasant conversation. Now he acts as if I'm some sort of vagrant."

"Keeley believes that—"

She waved an irritated hand at her daughter. "I don't care what *Keeley* believes. Why you choose to hang out with such trash is beyond me. When your brother first married her, you were as livid as I was."

Elizabeth waited to see if her daughter would dare defend the slut. She was slightly disappointed when all Miranda said was "We all make mistakes."

She rolled her eyes . . . whatever the hell that meant. "The mistake that man made today won't be forgotten. He's a rude, obnoxious bastard and he'll rue the day he treated me that way."

Miranda's face held a mixture of emotions as she looked down at Maggie. "Why don't you go ask Cook what we're having for lunch today?"

Maggie's green eyes were wide as she stared at Elizabeth, then she nodded and took off running.

"I don't like her running in this house, Miranda."

"Mother, I realize that we're here by your good graces, but please refrain from cursing in front of my daughter."

Elizabeth jerked. "Don't you dare lecture me in my own home. If it weren't for me, you'd be—"

Miranda held up a hand. "I would be out on the streets. Yes, you've reminded me numerous times. And I will be respectful as I can be; however, when it comes to my daughter, I will not have you exposing your hatefulness to her."

Before Elizabeth could speak, Miranda turned and walked away.

Trembling with rage that her daughter was developing a backbone, Elizabeth snarled, "Don't you want to know why I went to see your friend Keeley?"

"Other than to torture her, I can't imagine why."

Triumph filled her that she knew something Miranda obviously didn't yet know. "I went over there to see Keeley's child."

Gasping, Miranda whirled around and grabbed a nearby table. "What do you mean? The kids are back?"

"*Children,* Miranda, not kids. Kids are goats. Besides, just one of them was found. Unfortunately, not the blond one. The dark one that looks like her mother."

"Hannah?"

Elizabeth shrugged her shoulders, found herself frowning at her daughter and smoothed out her face. "Her name starts with an 'H.' That's all I know."

"They both do."

"Whatever. They got her back last night. I heard about it this morning . . . on the television news of all places."

The shock on her daughter's pale face caught her attention. "Oh good grief, you're not going to faint, are you?"

Miranda shook her head. "I'm just so surprised . . . I didn't think—"

Elizabeth headed upstairs. Listening to Miranda's mumblings accomplished nothing. There were things to be done. The slut probably thought her troubles were over. Damned if she would let that happen.

Keeley tugged on the hem of Hannah's favorite princess-print pants. Her daughter had grown and now they were almost too short for her. Thank God the people who'd had her had fed her well. Was Hailey being treated as kindly?

The ringing of the doorbell pulled her from that tortured thought. This would be the second visitor she'd had this morning. For someone who rarely received visitors, she seemed to be getting very popular. Remembering the identity of the last visitor, she amended that word to *unpopular*.

Hannah wrapped her arms around her mother as Keeley lifted her. At some point, she knew she needed to let her daughter walk, but not yet. She just didn't want to let her go. "Come on, sweetie. Let's go get breakfast."

She was just coming out of her room when Jenna and Miranda shouted in unison from the foyer, "Keeley!"

Keeley ran to greet them as they came up the stairs, meeting them halfway down the staircase. "What's wrong?"

"We just heard that Hannah's back." Jenna reached out her arms. "Hannah, come to Aunt Jenna."

It took all of Keeley's willpower to hand her daughter over. Even as much as she loved Jenna, she just hated to let Hannah out of her arms.

Jenna hugged Hannah close to her and kissed her forehead. Tears sparkled in her eyes as she looked up at Keeley. "How did you get her back? Where's Hailey? When did this happen? Why didn't you call me?"

Miranda pulled Hannah from Jenna's arms and hugged her tight. "Hey there, baby doll. Maggie's going to be thrilled that you're home." She pressed Hannah against her shoulder and whispered, "We want details!"

"Come on down to the kitchen and I'll tell you both all about it."

The women turned to head back downstairs, but Keeley put a hand out to stop Miranda. She just couldn't help herself. "Let me take Hannah."

Looking a bit startled, Miranda handed her daughter back to Keeley.

When the warm sturdy body of her child was finally in her arms, Keeley breathed out a sigh and headed downstairs. Her friends followed her to the kitchen where a delightful and familiar aroma emanated.

Keeley skidded to a stop at the kitchen door, almost causing Miranda and Jenna to bump into her. Cole stood at her stove, flipping pancakes. One of her short, frilly aprons was wrapped around his waist.

"Good morning." Eden's words pulled her out of her trance. The knowing amusement in her tone told Keeley she knew exactly what she'd been thinking.

Jordan was pouring juice and coffee at the table and stopped to pull out a chair for Keeley. She flashed him a grateful smile as she tried to ignore the hard thump of her heart at the sexiness of the cook.

"Mama cakes!" Hannah cried out her delight.

She shook herself and smiled at her daughter. "We'll call them Mr. Cole cakes today."

Keeley poured syrup over the fluffy pancakes Cole set before her and cut several pieces for her daughter to eat. Then, aware that Jenna and Miranda were patiently waiting for an explanation, she took a couple of sips of coffee and described what happened.

Jenna gazed around the table, her expression filled with awe. "I can't believe you actually have her back. But what about Hailey?"

Breath shuddered through Keeley. "We're meeting with the FBI later today and hoping they'll have some news for us."

Miranda reached over and pressed a kiss to Hannah's head, but the little girl was enjoying her pancakes so much she didn't acknowledge the kiss.

Jenna laughed. "She acts as if nothing has happened."

Keeley tightened her arms around her daughter. "I'm just hoping she stays that way."

Miranda took a sip of the coffee Jordan had poured for her. "What do the people who had her have to say? Are they the ones who took both girls? Or do they know who did?"

Keeley shook her head. "We think—"

Cole put a hand on Keeley's shoulder as he refilled her half-empty coffee cup. To anyone else, it probably looked casual and meant nothing. But Keeley could feel the tension in his hand. It was a warning. For some reason, he didn't want her to answer Miranda's question. Why?

"We what, Keeley?" Jenna asked.

She jerked her attention back to her friends. "Huh?"

Cole answered for her. "We're almost sure they know something. The FBI are questioning them. We should hear good news soon."

"But that's wonderful," Jenna said.

Too distracted by Cole's lie, Keeley could only nod and say, "We're very hopeful."

Jenna stood and smoothed her hand over Hannah's head. "I've got to get to work. I have three family meetings today. I'll call you later. Okay?"

Miranda grimaced and stood, too. "Yeah, I've got to get back home, too."

Holding Hannah in one arm, Keeley got to her feet and hugged Jenna and then did the same to Miranda. For some reason, Cole wanted to exclude her friends from what was going on. Though she wouldn't argue with him in front of them, she wanted both women to know how much she loved and appreciated them. She would never have gotten through so much, especially the last few weeks, without her best friends.

Keeley waited until she heard the front door close, then she looked at Cole. "What was that about?"

"Until we identify who's responsible, we keep everything we know between the four of us and Honor."

Apparently seeing her dismay, Eden said, "It's nothing personal against Jenna or Miranda."

"Miranda is Hailey and Hannah's aunt. And I've known Jenna since we were in grammar school together. I tell her everything."

"And you can again someday soon," Jordan said. "But until we identify the assholes who took them, we—"

"Jordan!" Eden admonished.

Despite her concern over shutting out her friends, Keeley couldn't help but chuckle as the normally gruff and stoic Jordan Montgomery blushed profusely.

"I'm sorry, Keeley." He shot a concerned look at Hannah and then an almost helpless glance at his wife. "Guess I'd better clean up my language since Paulo will be with us soon."

Laughing softly, Eden kissed Jordan on his still-red cheek. "We both will." She glanced back over at Keeley. "Once this is over, you can explain why we needed to keep things from them. It's just the less people who know what's going on, the better chance we have of targeting the right person."

"But why did Cole lie and say we should know something soon?"

Cole shrugged. "I knew you were going to say we didn't know anything. If Jenna or Miranda talk about it, I'd rather they reveal we're onto someone. That might force him to do something stupid." He shrugged again. "Long shot, I know."

Though she understood, Keeley couldn't help but wish they'd allow her friends in their "need to know" circle. If there were two people she could trust, it was Jenna and Miranda.

fourteen

She pressed Wesley's number into her cellphone, her hands shaking with fury so badly, she pushed the wrong numbers three times.

Wesley answered on the sixth ring, his voice sounding groggy. Lazy bastard was still in bed.

"They found one of the kids."

"What? Stop your squealing and say that again."

Teeth grinding together, she spoke between clenched lips. "I was just there. . . . One of Keeley Fairchild's daughters is back home. How the hell did that happen?"

"Which one?"

"The dark-haired one."

He snorted. "So?"

"So? Are you crazy? If they find out you took them, your ass is fried. And then they'll be coming after me."

"First of all, they ain't going to find out. Nobody can trace either of them kids back to me. Secondly, do you really think I give a fuck what they do to you, if you get caught?"

"If you'd taken them where I told you to go, none of this would have happened. If they catch me, you're going down, too."

"Baby, you threaten me again and that little screwing I gave you the other day will be a pleasant memory compared to what I'll do to you. You got that?"

Dammit. She had no control over the bastard any-more. But there was still something he wanted.

"You still need me to help you get to her."

"I don't need you that bad. I'd advise you to keep a civil tongue in your mouth until our business transaction is complete. Then we'll never have to see each other again and you can swear at me all you want. Till then, I suggest a bit of respect." When she didn't answer immediately, he said, "I didn't hear you."

"Fine," she snapped.

"Good. Now, when you gonna be setting up this little rendezvous?"

An image came to her mind; she made a quick decision. "Do another job for me and I'll arrange it."

"How much?"

"Five thousand."

"Ten and deliver the woman to me soon. Understand?"

She didn't blink an eye. "Fine. Here's what I want you to do."

Wesley hung up the phone, his gut twisting with mixed feelings. Another ten thousand was a good thing. He still had a nice chunk left from the other job. With the extra, he'd be in high cotton.

Despite what he'd said, the fact that one of the kids had been found had him kind of rattled. Not that they could trace him. That transaction had taken place through email. He'd been told where to leave the kid and where to find the money. Nobody had seen nothing.

The other kid would never be found. Hell, he didn't even know where she was, and he was the one who'd sold her. He hadn't asked questions, mostly because he didn't care what happened. Once he'd turned her over to that couple in California and had collected his cash, he'd been gone.

Wes gazed around his sparse bedroom. It wasn't much. Just a tiny, rat-infested hole-in-the-wall apartment, but it'd been his home for a year. This was the longest he'd ever stayed anywhere. Whenever he went out of town on a job, he always kind of looked forward to coming back here.

Uncle John—not his real uncle, but a man who'd raised him—always told him not to get too comfortable, because that's when the shit starts to pour in. He'd been here too long. It was time to skedaddle. Besides, once he got Keeley, he couldn't stay here. FBI and those LCR people would be on him like white on rice.

He wanted to keep her for a few months, if not longer. He already had a nice little cabin ready and waiting in the North Carolina mountains. He'd break her in at a little hideaway he sometimes went to just outside of Fairview. Then, once he had satisfied a few of his most urgent cravings, they'd head to the cabin in the mountains. Nobody would ever find them there. Hell, he might just keep her a real long time.

But first, he had another job to plan.

Cole's feet pounded against the soft, moist earth. Sunlight filtering through the trees created dappled shadows on the ground. The only sounds were his steps and a soaring hawk looking for a late-afternoon meal. He picked up his pace, wanting to get in at least a couple more miles before he headed back to the house.

This trail was perfect for running, and Stephen Fairchild had apparently created it just for his wife. An oddly incongruent gift with what he had learned about Keeley's husband. Why would a man who by all accounts hadn't loved his wife enough to stay faithful to her, do something like this?

Cole had mentioned to Keeley how much he enjoyed running on the trail. She admitted that she hadn't used it since her children had been taken, but he'd seen the glint in her eyes. She missed running. He could identify with that. Running had been his mainstay when he'd been in high school and college. After his family was killed, it had saved his sanity. Keeley needed that outlet, too.

Days of scanning the town's archived newspapers for news of Keeley's running awards had brought more questions than answers. Myron Gurganus had been correct. There had been only one small article when she won the state championship. He had some theories of why the scant coverage. But if she'd won so many awards, where were her trophies? She had to have several. If something meant that much to her, why hide them away? And why had she stopped running? When something was in your blood like that, giving it up was giving up a part of yourself.

The more he knew Keeley, the more he wanted to know her. It was a useless, pointless need that could lead him nowhere; nevertheless, the need was there.

Unless there was some physical reason she couldn't run, he wanted to get her back on the track. Running would relieve some of the stress she was under and would exhaust her physically to help her sleep.

The child psychologist the FBI had sent today had relieved their minds. Hannah had indeed been traumatized by her kidnapping and separation from her mother, but from the gentle, subtle questioning by the psychologist, they now believed she'd suffered no physical abuse. The doctors felt that with a careful watch over the next few weeks to catch any underlying problem they hadn't noticed, Hannah was capable of a full recovery, and could possibly forget most of what happened to her.

The questions the psychologist asked Hannah about her sister had been delicately and carefully worded. No one wanted to cause the child any further harm, and pressuring her could well keep her from being able to remember anything. She'd offered very little, other than she remembered being hungry, cold, and sleepy.

When Hailey's name had been mentioned, Hannah had started crying, prompting everyone to step back from questioning her. Keeley had been advised not to mention Hailey's name for a few days. Cole knew that had to be killing her.

A vibration in his pocket had him reaching for his phone. "Mathison."

"Help."

Keeley.

Cole broke into a sprint. His lungs working at maximum capacity, he raced toward the house and burst through the back door. He heard Keeley shouting at someone near the front of the house. Barreling through the kitchen, he ran down the long hallway to the foyer. He skidded to a stop right behind Keeley, who stood toe-to-toe with Chatam County sheriff Hiram Mobley.

"Get the hell out of my house, you bastard. You are not getting my baby."

"Now, Keeley, I got a court order that says I can."

Hands on her hips, Keeley leaned forward. Since she was several inches taller than Hiram, she towered over him. "I don't care if you have the entire judicial system standing outside my house, you will not be taking my child anywhere."

"What's going on?" Cole demanded behind her.

Keeley turned, relieved to hear his voice. Jordan and Eden had gone out for a while and had made her promise not to open the door to anyone. When the sheriff rang at the gate, demanding to see her, she opened the gate. When he appeared on her doorstep, demanding to be let in, she'd panicked and called Cole. But while she waited for Cole, she'd been stupid enough to let the sheriff inside the house.

"The sheriff says he has a court order to remove Hannah from my care because I'm an unfit mother."

Cole grabbed the legal-looking document from Sheriff Mobley's bony hand. "On what grounds?"

"She's under suspicion for arranging the kidnapping."

Keeley stared in amazement at the stupidity of that statement. "Of my own children?"

"No. Your husband."

Dammit, not again. "The FBI cleared me, Hiram, and you know it."

"Yeah, well, the police force of Chatam County didn't. We still think you done it."

Cole looked down at the paper, a frown deepening the lines on his face. "Who signed this order?"

After an audible swallow, Mobley said, "Judge Albright."

Keeley snorted. "He's been in the back pocket of the Fairchilds for years. Just like you, Mobley."

"Now, see here, Keeley, I'm just doing my job."

"Your job is to protect people, not kowtow to them because they pay you money on the side."

Mean beady eyes narrowed. "You accusing me of taking bribes?"

"That's exactly—"

"Enough," Cole growled. He shoved the paper back at the sheriff. "This isn't signed by Judge Albright or anyone else. Get out."

The sheriff swallowed hard again, his bloodshot eyes skittering from Keeley to Cole. "Well, the judge was busy this morning. I told 'im what I was going to do and he said he'd take care of it when he could."

"Until he does, you have no authority to take the child. Now. Get. Out."

The quiet menace in Cole's voice finally penetrated

Hiram Mobley's thick brain. He began to back away. "I was just doing my job."

Keeley opened the door and barely let Hiram step outside before she slammed it shut. She looked up at Cole. "Can they take her away from me?"

Cole pulled his cellphone from his pocket. "No. I suspect this is just a little payment for me throwing Elizabeth out of the house this morning." He pressed the phone to his ear and turned away from her.

Everything inside Keeley felt as if it would just melt; she wanted to literally sink into the floor and cry. After all Hannah had been through, Elizabeth wanted to take her away. Not because she cared. Not because she truly suspected Keeley of anything. No, the only reason was to hurt Keeley as much as she could. To hell with what it might do to her grandchild.

That brought another thought to the forefront. If Elizabeth hated her that much, could she have arranged the abductions? Did the hatred she harbored have a more sinister and evil agenda than just making Keeley's life miserable?

She had said no before. Now she wasn't so sure.

"I'm as sorry as I can be, Mizz Fairchild, but there aren't any grounds to take that child away from Keeley. She's right. FBI cleared her of anything to do with your son's abduction."

Sitting at her desk, Elizabeth absently sorted through her mail as she listened to Judge Albright whine. At his pause, she huffed out a long, loud sigh to give him the idea that she was disappointed not only in the news, but also in him. The more he felt he had let her down, the more control she had over him.

The sheriff's visit to Keeley had accomplished her goal. Keeping Keeley on edge and in fear was one of the many perks of being the most powerful person in town. She had known there was no basis for removing the child, and she most certainly did not want that child in her house. She already housed Miranda's obnoxious little brat, why would she want another one? Especially one that looked identical to her mother. Elizabeth shuddered at the thought. If one had to be found, why couldn't it at least be the one who looked like Stephen?

"Uh . . . Mizz Fairchild . . . uh, ma'am?"

"That's disappointing, Judge Albright. She's an unfit mother . . . we all know that."

"Yes'm . . . but—"

"Perhaps in the future, you'll be able to make up for your incompetence. For now, goodbye." She ended the call before he could sputter out another apology.

Quite pleased with how the day had developed, despite the unnerving information that one of the children had been found, Elizabeth placed another call.

"Fairview Bank and Trust," said the feminine voice.

"Milton Angle, please. This is Elizabeth Fairchild."

"Oh yes, Mrs. Fairchild. One moment please."

The urgency and deference in the woman's voice pleased Elizabeth. At least someone knew her importance.

"Mrs. Fairchild, how are you?"

"Milton, did we not agree a few weeks ago that you would find a way to remove Keeley from that house?"

"We did, Mrs. Fairchild, but since she's about to put it on the market, I figured you'd want to wait awhile. That way, if you really want it—"

"Are you suggesting that I would offer her money for it?" Elizabeth didn't even have to pretend her disapproval and astonishment. The very idea of paying the slut for that house revolted her.

"Well, um . . ." Apparently realizing he'd said the wrong thing, he backtracked and said, "These things take time. Your son's estate made excellent provisions for Keeley. Even if we figure out a way to say she's not legally entitled to the house, it'll still belong to his young'uns. He—"

"Those *young'uns* are missing. They may be dead for all we know."

So what if one of them had been found. Milton probably didn't know that. The truth was inconsequential to her goal.

"Yes, ma'am, that's true, but your son left Keeley in charge of their estate. He willed everything to her."

"I don't care if he left her the entire balance of the world treasury department, that house should not belong to her. My son would never have left the bulk of his estate to her if she hadn't threatened him in some way." Elizabeth added a small sob. Men could be so weak when it came to a woman's tears. "Just knowing she's living off of his death money is almost more than I can bear."

"Now, now, dear lady. Don't you fret. We'll figure out something. It's just going to take some time."

"Thank you so much, Milton. You've always been a friend to the Fairchilds. When the time comes for your review, I'll make certain the board of directors and shareholders are aware of your professionalism and commitment."

"Why, thank you, ma'am. I do my best."

"You'll let me know as soon as you have some good news for me?"

"Yes, ma'am. The instant I know something."

"Good." Elizabeth hung up the phone, more than a little pleased. For a day that hadn't started well, it hadn't turned out too badly after all.

A small smile twisted at her mouth. Keeley would never be able to sell the house. The Fairchilds were the only family within a hundred miles who could afford to buy it. And Elizabeth sure as hell wasn't going to pay money for it.

Neither the house nor Stephen's money meant anything. What she wanted more than anything was to see Keeley suffer. The slut would rue the day she tried to dig herself out of the garbage she came from.

fifteen

The hum of the desktop computer behind her was a distant buzzing sound, lulling Keeley into a zombielike daze. She was so damned tired.

Hannah had been home for a week, and except for those few hours of peace that first night, sleep had become more elusive than ever. Slumber came in fits and spurts. She was constantly waking up to make sure Hannah was all right . . . that she was really home. And the nightmares had become even more horrendous than before. Now that she knew for sure the girls weren't together, all sorts of hideous images were coming to her about Hailey's whereabouts.

For the first time since this awful waking nightmare had begun, she was beginning to have serious doubts that Hailey was alive.

Rubbing her gritty sleep-deprived eyes with one hand, Keeley clicked through online sites hoping to find some kind of chatter. She'd never known sites like these existed until her girls were taken. Now she perused them every few days. Most of the comments were garbage, but she couldn't not look at them. Someone, somewhere, might mention something that would be helpful. Another long shot, but she had to do something.

Honor had sent over a binder filled with mug shots of known child predators and criminals of all sorts. She hadn't yet been able to show the photos to Hannah. What her little girl had gone through with this monster wasn't known, but she damn well didn't want to add more trauma.

She'd forced herself to look through them in hopes that she could trigger some memory. Maybe she would see someone that looked familiar. Someone she might have offended who had decided to destroy her life in revenge. If only she knew what she had done to have this kind of hatred directed toward her. She would apologize, beg, plead . . . do anything they wanted, if only they would tell her where her Hailey was.

"Mommy, I gotta potty. . . ."

Keeley looked up in time to see Hannah pull down her pants as if she were going to go in the middle of the office floor. Her daughter's independence had taken a hard hit. Before the abduction, both Hannah and Hailey were to the point of requiring very little help in the bathroom other than a gentle reminder to wash their hands.

The psychologist assured Keeley her daughter's insecurities were normal after such a traumatic event. It was just going to take some time.

Holding her hand out to Hannah, she said, "Thank you for telling me, sweetheart. Let's go take care of business."

Hand in hand, they walked to the bathroom together. After taking care of those matters, Keeley saw Hannah's eyes flutter, telling her a nap was necessary. How she would love to lie down with her daughter and let slumber carry her away. But if she slept, she dreamed, and she did not want to dream.

She followed Hannah upstairs to her bedroom and settled her on the bed. Kneeling on the floor beside the bed, Keeley repeated the prayer she'd been saying since Hannah's rescue, giving thanks for her daughter's safe return and asking protection for Hailey and her safe return home.

In the midst of her prayers, she heard a thump. She opened her eyes to see Cole standing beside her, dressed in running shorts and a T-shirt. Her heartbeat went into overdrive. *Oh my.* The man was 110 percent pure masculinity—all gorgeous hard muscle and sinew.

Keeley tore her eyes away from his mouthwatering body with difficulty and looked down at the objects he'd thrown in front of her. Her running shoes.

"Let's go for a run," Cole said.

"What?"

"You're a runner, yet according to Eden, you haven't done any running since this started. It'll relieve some of your stress and help you sleep."

Keeley bit her lip and glanced at her sleeping daughter. "No. I can't leave—"

"Eden and Jordan will watch over Hannah. I've got my cellphone if something comes up. You need this, Keeley."

Could she do this? Take an hour from her worry and give herself this break? She missed running. It had once been her passion, had often been her salvation. On the day her mother died, she'd given up competing in races, but had continued to run to stay in shape and because she loved it so much.

Since her girls had been taken from her, she'd rejected doing anything that made her feel better. Guilt again. Not being able to stop the man from taking her children tore her insides to shreds. She'd trained much of her life to be the fastest runner she could be, yet when it counted the most, she had failed. She'd told herself that the man who had tried to abduct her had slowed her down. While that might be true, it didn't make her feel any better.

She looked up at Cole and shook her head. "I can't."

"It's not up for debate. I need to talk with you and I'm going for a run. Go get dressed."

Adrenaline-drenched anger brought Keeley to her feet. "Now, wait just a minute. I—"

Cole grabbed her shoulders and shook her lightly before letting her go and stepping back. Keeley stopped breathing. This was the first time he'd physically touched her since *that night*. An ache she'd tried to quell built up inside her. How she wanted to have that experience again . . . but only with this man.

"You need this, Keeley. Go."

She found herself headed toward the door before she realized it. His touch had left her so unsettled, she needed some time to herself. When had a man's touch ever made her want to lean into him instead of pull away? *Only this man.*

Even at the beginning of her relationship with Stephen, when she'd thought she loved him, he had never made her heart pound as Cole did with that one small touch. She could still feel the warmth of his hands, the strength of his fingers pressed into her shoulders. Odd tingling sparks of electricity seemed to be attacking her entire bloodstream.

Attributing it to exhaustion and lack of sleep did no good. Her body knew what it wanted . . . she just had no idea how to go about getting it. As she dressed, her heart continued its hard thumping beat. She had asked him once . . . could she build up the courage to ask him again?

Half an hour later, Keeley couldn't believe her exhaustion. She'd barely been able to run two miles before she'd had to ask Cole to stop and walk. He, on the other hand, hadn't broken a sweat. She hadn't realized how quickly her endurance had been depleted. As much as she didn't want to give him credit for practically dragging her from her house, she was glad he did. Staying at home, worrying herself sick, was accomplishing nothing.

"Feel better?"

"Yes. Thanks. Hard to believe I used to run that distance in half the time and barely break a sweat."

"We'll make sure we run every day; your endurance will come back quicker."

She took a deep cleansing breath, already feeling more at peace.

"Was your husband a runner?"

Keeley swallowed a chuckle. The mental image of Stephen in shorts and running shoes brought her an amusement about him she hadn't felt in a long while. "No, Stephen wasn't into physical activity other than the occasional game of golf."

"So this trail was just for you?"

She glanced over at him, saw the questions. She had an easy answer for him. "Guilt."

"What?"

"He bought gifts for me. Cars, jewelry . . . the mansion was a complete surprise. We were living in a very nice house a few miles down the road. About a year after we were married, he said we were going to breakfast and instead brought me to my new home." She shrugged. "I didn't know then that the building of it coincided with a new affair. Apparently every time he started a new one, he appeased his conscience by giving me a new gift. This trail was part of another new affair."

The expression on Cole's face was priceless. She already knew this man well enough to know he would never consider cheating on his wife. He might not necessarily stay in a bad marriage, but she could never see him being unfaithful. He had too much integrity for that.

"How did you find out about the affairs?" he asked.

The disgusting memory caused her to grimace. "I found a pair of thong underwear in his suit coat. He must have forgotten they were in there, because when I confronted him, he looked stunned. He also looked guilty as hell."

"He didn't try to deny it?"

"At first he tried to backpedal, but he couldn't come up with any kind of reasonable answer. When I kept at him, he finally admitted it. Then it was like a dam burst inside him . . . everything flooded out of him . . . like he couldn't stop until he revealed every sordid detail. That's when he explained about the gifts . . . as if that somehow made it better or more forgivable. He told me he started having affairs only a few months after our marriage." She swallowed hard. "I asked him how many. He couldn't remember."

"Bastard."

A small smile tugged at her mouth at Cole's obvious anger on her behalf. "It doesn't really hurt anymore. Not like it did. Though it still makes me angry that I was so incredibly stupid." She sighed. "And then, somehow, after I found out, it seemed everyone knew. I didn't go into town much even then, but the couple of times I went, it was like everyone stopped and stared and then started whispering all at once."

"And that was just days before he was abducted?"

Keeley scrunched her nose. "Yeah, which, looking back on it, had to make me look guilty."

"And you never found out who was spreading it?"

"No. Of course no one would have told me who started it. Neither Jenna nor Miranda knew either."

"Could it have been Stephen?"

"I don't think so. He seemed genuinely ashamed. Though I think he was sorrier that I found him out than he was for actually cheating." Keeley shrugged. "Stephen wasn't the man I thought he was, but he wasn't a bad man. Just very weak and shallow . . . incredibly spoiled. He felt guilty but not guilty enough to stop."

"I'm sorry."

Keeley tilted her head to look up at him. "We all make our choices. Stephen made his." Her mouth moved up into a trembling smile. "Besides, he gave me the most beautiful gifts in the world."

"Hailey and Hannah," Cole said.

"Yes. Even as angry as I was when I realized what he'd done—had been doing for years behind my back—I could never regret the marriage." Weary of thinking about her failed marriage, she said, "You needed to talk with me. About what?"

He was silent for several seconds as if he wanted to say more. Then he said, "Tell me why Elizabeth hates you so much."

Keeley waved a hand at him; they'd gone through this already. "I wasn't good enough for her son."

"That may be part of it, but I'm not sure it's the biggest part. I think that's what she wants you to believe."

"But what other reason could she have?"

"Your mother."

"Mama? What would my mama have to do with it?"

"I've finally found some townspeople who don't mind talking to a stranger. A few of the older citizens of Fairview have opened up in the last couple of days. Judging by some of their comments, I think there might have been something between your mother and Baker Fairchild, Stephen's father."

Keeley jerked to a stop and snarled, "That's a bald-faced lie."

Cole held up a hand. "I'm not saying they had an affair. I'm just saying they had a friendship . . . possibly a light romance?"

"No. My mother never dated. My father died before I was born, but there were never any men in her life."

"What about men who wanted to be in her life?"

Keeley sighed. "Maybe you'd better tell me what you've heard."

"Do you know Robert Mendel?"

"Never heard of him."

"He's retired now, but he used to be in charge of the janitorial services at several of the businesses in town. I stopped for coffee at Amelia's and he came in for lunch. We were sitting side by side at the counter and struck up a conversation. Seems years ago . . . you would've been just a baby . . . Baker Fairchild had a thing for Kathleen Daniels—your mother."

"What kind of thing?"

"I think he called on her from time to time."

Anger surged. The people of Fairview had shunned and whispered about her mother for years. Damned if she'd let that start up again. "Baker was already married to Elizabeth . . . my mother would never—"

"I'm not saying she had an affair with him, but according to Robert, Stephen's father and mother separated a few years after they were married. They eventually reunited, but during the time they were apart, he showed a particular interest in your mother."

Keeley was stunned. Could this be true? Her mother had never mentioned anyone but her father. Could that be the real reason behind Elizabeth's hatred?

"What does Robert Mendel think happened?"

"His memory was spotty, but there were rumors of Baker visiting your mother. Apparently the town gossips put two and two together and decided they were having an affair. Then something happened and Baker went back to Elizabeth."

Keeley shook her head slowly. "This is so hard to believe."

"Robert seemed credible; I detected no malice or spite. Said Elizabeth was publicly humiliated. That the whole town kept waiting for them to divorce, but it never happened."

"Stephen was older than me. Surely he would have known about it."

The palpable silence after her statement jerked her to a full stop. Blood rushed to her face and just as quickly receded. She looked up at Cole and saw he knew exactly what she was thinking . . . and that he agreed.

She didn't want to say it, but it had to be said. "You think that's why Stephen married me, don't you? To spite his mother."

Though she saw the answer in his eyes, he asked, "Do you think it's a possibility?"

Keeley looked away from his compassion and stared sightlessly into space. Stephen's protection of her against Elizabeth had been hit-or-miss. She'd always assumed it was because he was so self-centered. She still believed he was, but with eyes wide open, she saw some of the most damning evidence in a new light.

His charming assurance that eloping and then telling his family about their relationship was the best way. His insistence that she name both of her girls after her mother. The fact that his mother had trash-talked her daughter-in-law for years . . . Stephen had known and had done nothing to stop it. Had never even told her.

She shook her head slowly. "I must be the stupidest person on this planet."

"Naïve, not stupid. You believed the best—"

Furious tears rushed to her eyes; she jerked around to face him. "Stupid. Ignorant. The entire freaking town was talking about me behind my back. Everyone knew about Stephen's affairs. And now I find out our marriage was all about getting back at his mother." She turned away again. "Everyone manipulated me and I had no clue. No. Freaking. Clue."

Cole pulled her around to face him. "Keeley . . .

don't. First of all, you don't know if that's the reason he married you." He raised a hand to stop her when she opened her mouth to argue. "Okay, I agree the evidence looks bad. It may have been a factor . . . I don't know. Thing is, don't take the blame for other people's evil actions."

Breath shuddered through her. Cole was right, but that didn't make her feel any less stupid.

"As small as this town is, I'm surprised you never heard the rumors about your mother . . . no matter how long ago it was."

She snorted. "No one would have told me. When you're the town outcast, hearing gossip firsthand is rare, especially since much of the gossip was about me or my mom." Keeley ticked off her supposed sins. "She was an unwed mother. My father was from Venezuela, so my skin, hair, and eyes are darker than most people's around here and we were dirt poor. Not the best way to gain popularity in a small town."

"Kids can be cruel."

"Kids, yeah. But it was their parents who reinforced it. You know that old saying 'The apple doesn't fall far from the tree.'"

"Where there's smoke, there's fire."

She was surprised to see a rare glint of humor in Cole's eyes. Despite her anger at her stupidity, Keeley felt a lift to her spirits. This amazing man in front of her was trying to make her feel better. Taking a long breath, she set her chin determinedly and eased into the simple game. "Don't put all your eggs in one basket."

A small nod as if he approved. "In for a penny, in for a pound."

"A penny saved is a penny earned."

As they traded adages, they started running again, their pace increasing into a steady jog. While her feet pounded the dark earth, her mind was free to come up with nothing but sayings, and for a few precious minutes, her churning, gut-wrenching emotions were at rest.

Later, when she was alone, she would think about all she'd learned. All that had happened. She had been manipulated in every area of her life . . . did any of this involve the abduction of her children? If so, was the person behind it Elizabeth after all? Could the woman despise and resent her mother so much that she was willing to destroy not only Kathleen's daughter, but also her grandchildren . . . even if those grandchildren were hers, too?

Cole kept a close eye on Keeley's pace and energy level. She hadn't run in over a month and would most likely be sore tomorrow. A slight soreness would be good for her, but too much and she wouldn't get the sleep he knew she needed.

Part of him felt like shit for telling her about the possible relationship between Stephen's father and her mother. Especially when she'd come so quickly to the conclusion he had. But she had a right to know. No one should have their life manipulated and controlled as she had. He had lived a year under the control of a maniac. Every person had a right to control their own destiny.

In the short amount of time he'd been in Fairview, Cole had received several questions and more than a few warnings about his involvement with Keeley. She'd done nothing to deserve their hatred and prejudice other than to have the audacity to marry the town's wealthiest bachelor. He could understand the jealousy, but the hatred had stunned him.

And then he'd talked to Robert Mendel and it all began to make sense. Elizabeth had perpetuated the hate. Did Keeley realize how very dangerous her mother-in-law was?

What kind of man was Stephen Fairchild to marry a

woman to spite his mother and then sleep with everyone he could? Especially when his wife was a woman like Keeley, who was beautiful on the inside as well as the outside.

Hearing Keeley's breathing increase to pants, Cole slowed his pace. She immediately slowed hers as well. A slight sheen of perspiration covered her skin. The black spandex shorts and white T-shirt she wore only emphasized her sleek muscles and luscious curves. A surge of lust swept through him. Unwanted and damn inconvenient.

Every night he passed by her door, he had to make himself not stop and check on her. He was concerned for her, yes. But that wasn't the only reason. Their night together played over and over in his mind. He thought about all the places he hadn't touched her, hadn't kissed her.

His eyes closed briefly to refocus, then he said, "Let's head back."

Trying to keep his mind off what he shouldn't be thinking of, Cole shot her a searching glance. "Why haven't you run since it happened?"

The stricken look in her eyes slashed through him. He'd figured there was a reason other than she just didn't feel like it."

"I trained for years to be the fastest runner I could be, but when it counted the most, I failed. I couldn't catch the bastard. He had my babies and I couldn't catch him." Her eyes swam with tears. "You'll never know how many times I wish I had let that man take me, too. At least I would have—"

Astounded and infuriated, he grabbed her shoulders and jerked her around to face him. "Don't ever say that. Do you have any idea what they would have done to you?"

"Yes," she whispered. "But at least I would have been with my girls."

"And they still would have been sold, Keeley. You would have been raped, maybe even sold yourself or murdered."

"But I—"

"But nothing. Don't fall into the trap of thinking that if you hadn't fought, you could have saved your children. Always fight, Keeley. No matter what. Okay?"

Her eyes closed briefly and then she looked up at him with such pain and longing, Cole gave up fighting the inevitable. Lowering his head, he kissed her gently, softly, renewing their bond in seconds. When she gasped, he swallowed the sound and pressed deeper. Her long arms wrapped around his neck as she opened her mouth under his. With a growl of need, Cole pulled her hard against him and took what he'd been dreaming about for days. She tasted better, even more delicious than before: exotic spice, sweet musk, hot, sexy woman.

His hands had a will of their own as they roamed over the short T-shirt and then slid under to feel the soft, creamy, slightly damp flesh beneath.

The moan she released vibrated through him, urging him on. Desire throbbing hard, Cole's hands had only one destination. What he'd been dreaming and fantasizing about since he'd first seen her. What he had desperately regretted not tasting before, he was now determined to make a reality. His hands covered her breasts and he groaned as the plump, sweet mounds almost overflowed. Her nipples, hard and distended, pressed against his palms. His mouth watered, dying for a taste; imagining the tight, sweet berries on his tongue, in his mouth, he slowly raised her shirt.

Keeley's eyes glittered with desire as she rubbed her body against his. She was panting, wanting him as much as he wanted her. Cole lowered his head to her sweetness.

An obnoxious buzz penetrated the roar of lust in his head. Silent, violent curses thundered through him as he pulled away. The damn phone attached to a strap at his waist was vibrating.

Unable to let Keeley go completely, he grabbed the phone and kept one arm wrapped tightly around her. "Yeah?"

"Cole? It's Elizabeth Fairchild."

Dropping his hands completely away from Keeley, he tried to sound halfway coherent. "Elizabeth . . . what can I do for you?"

As Elizabeth yammered on about inviting him for lunch and making amends over their argument, he watched Keeley's face as she transformed from glowing, gloriously aroused woman back to the pale, tortured woman she'd been minutes before.

"I'll be happy to join you for a late lunch. Say two o'clock?"

"Sounds marvelous. See you then," Elizabeth gushed.

Cole closed the phone. "Looks like I have a lunch date."

Wrapping her arms around herself, Keeley grimaced her sympathy. "Lucky you."

"I want you to come with me."

She gave a small, startled laugh. "I don't think so. On a good day, I don't feel particularly kindly toward Elizabeth. Today I would probably scratch her eyes out."

His mouth tilted as that image came to his mind. "How about we do a little manipulation of our own? She thinks she's in such control all the time. Let's throw her off a bit. Will you play along with me?"

Her eyes darkened and Cole caught a glimpse of the sexy, passionate woman she'd been in his arms. Though his body throbbed with need, Cole couldn't act on those feelings. Hell, he'd told himself time and again he couldn't repeat what had happened before. And what had he done? He'd almost made love to her in the woods. If the phone call hadn't come, they'd be lying in the grass and he'd be inside her right now.

"I would love to play with you." Then, as if she realized how her words sounded, her eyes widened and her face flushed a pretty pink. She swallowed and added, "Manipulating Elizabeth sounds like fun to me. What's our plan?"

The image of her words caused another surge of arousal so hard, Cole had to grit his teeth to concentrate. "We'll double-team her. Whatever I say, no matter what I say, you go along with . . . but remember, it's all an illusion."

The trust in her eyes was almost more than he could handle. Calling himself all kinds of a fool, he held out his hand to Keeley. As they walked hand in hand back to her home, Cole saw a new hell emerging . . . this one of his own making. And there wasn't a damn thing he could do about it. No matter what decision he made, he was doomed.

sixteen

An hour later, Keeley found herself standing with Cole on the Fairchilds' front veranda, waiting for Patrick to open the door. She still didn't know what he planned, but she knew one thing: she trusted him.

She trusted Cole. What an odd thing for her to admit. Trust had never been an easy thing for her. And now, realizing how incredibly stupid she'd been, she fully anticipated it would continue to be difficult. However, she knew in her heart that Cole was a man she could believe in. It felt strange to admit that about someone she'd known for only a few weeks. It was also very freeing.

She'd known Stephen for seven years, had given him her heart and her body . . . and he'd betrayed both. She knew to her soul that would never happen with Cole.

Their kiss still strummed through her senses. Every cell in her body vibrated with sensual heat and awareness. She was suddenly aware of her clothes on her skin; everything felt sensitive, alive. Just the memory of how his hard body had felt pressed against hers as his calloused hands cupped her breasts caused deep flutters in her womb. If Elizabeth hadn't called, would they still be in the woods? Would Cole be making love to her right now? This time she hadn't had to ask. Cole had been the initiator.

Hearing the door swinging open, Keeley took a bracing breath, her focus once more on the reason they were here.

Patrick opened the door wide, a semi-welcoming smile on his face. Since Keeley had never seen him look so pleasant, she was faintly startled. Her surprise quickly changed to anger at his reaction when he saw her standing beside Cole.

Nose tilted upward, Patrick said, "I believe Mrs. Fairchild was only expecting one for lunch, sir."

Watching Cole's fist clench and his jaw jerk fascinated her, so much so that her own resentment at Patrick's rudeness completely vanished. Here was a man who would defend until death what he cared about.

"Keeley and I both want to apologize for our rude behavior the other day. I'm sure Elizabeth could find it in her heart to allow us that." Cole's charming words belied the anger Keeley felt radiating from him.

Before the butler could answer, Elizabeth's voice rang out from the stairway. "Let them in, Patrick."

Cole stepped inside; Keeley came in behind him. "Elizabeth." Cole held out his hand. "Thank you for inviting me to lunch. I insisted that Keeley come, too. We both want to apologize for our rudeness the other day."

Elizabeth moved toward him, her haughty expression melting slightly at the handsome, charming man in front of her.

Keeley couldn't see Cole's face, but the deference in his voice and his apologetic words sounded sincere. She was glad he'd warned her to go along with whatever he said, no matter how it sounded. Otherwise, she would have been appalled at his change of attitude.

Cole moved aside then, allowing Elizabeth to get a glimpse of Keeley.

With a stiff, arrogant nod, she acknowledged Keeley, then she looked up at Cole. "And that's why I invited *you* here. I, too, thought perhaps we could let . . . shall we say . . . bygones be bygones?"

Trying to get into the spirit of things, Keeley said, "Cole was terribly rude to you and I wanted to extend my apologies, too. After all, you are Hannah's grandmother."

Distaste flickered in Elizabeth's eyes before they were masked with an icy politeness.

Uh-oh, wrong thing to say. Diplomacy with this woman had never been her strong suit. Apparently acting wasn't either.

Cole defused Elizabeth's anger by drawing attention back to him. "I was exhausted. Said things I didn't mean. Can you forgive me?"

Elizabeth tucked a lock of hair behind her ear and tilted her head. "Well, we all make mistakes."

Keeley worked hard not to laugh. Hell, the woman was actually flirting with him.

"You're very gracious," Cole said, and then he smiled.

Keeley caught her breath in a gasp. Thankfully, he'd never smiled at her like that . . . she wasn't sure her heart could handle it.

"You know, I've been asking around town and came up with some interesting information. I wondered if you could shed some light on it."

Looking as though butter wouldn't melt in her mouth, Elizabeth leaned toward Cole and practically purred, "I'll do my best."

Okay, this was getting ridiculous. If either of them moved half an inch closer, they'd be touching noses. Being jealous of her former mother-in-law, of all people, might be ludicrous, but that didn't stop Keeley from wanting to step in between them and tell her to stop ogling her man.

"Why don't we make ourselves comfortable in the sitting room. Cook will call us within the next few minutes for lunch." She shot a cold glance at Keeley.

"Patrick, I suppose you might as well tell the kitchen staff that we have one additional . . . guest."

Being treated like a trespasser barely dented Keeley's consciousness. Content to allow Cole to work his magic, she followed behind them, feeling a bit like a wayward puppy.

Cole waited until both Elizabeth and Keeley had sat down before he dropped into a chair across from Elizabeth. And doing what he'd told her he was going to do—keep Elizabeth off guard—he asked, "How well did you know Kathleen Daniels, Keeley's mother?"

Elizabeth jerked slightly and arched a pencil-thin arrogant brow. "We didn't socialize in the same circles, as you can well imagine."

Keeley opened her mouth to growl that her mother was far too superior to socialize with the likes of Elizabeth Fairchild. A quick warning glance from Cole stopped her.

She pressed her lips together. Her mother didn't need to be defended. She'd had more grace and integrity in her little finger than Elizabeth had in the entirety of her too-skinny body.

"But the Fairchilds know everyone, do they not?"

"Well, of course I knew *of* her. She was—" Elizabeth's eyes skittered to Keeley and for once she saw hesitation in them. Something had kept the woman from her normal nasty comment. What?

"She was . . . ?" Cole asked.

"She was known for her sewing."

"Ah yes, Keeley told me. But what I'm hearing from the townspeople involved your late husband. Did he know Kathleen very well?"

Elizabeth's mouth formed an ugly, mutinous sneer. For the first time, the woman actually looked close to her age. Though Keeley could already see the denial and prepared herself for the anger she would probably feel, she also saw the raging jealousy. Stephen's father had definitely had some kind of relationship with her mother. Elizabeth's reaction had been too telling.

A regal wave of her bony hand. "There was nothing to those rumors. She no doubt started them herself."

At those ridiculous words, a growl started inside Keeley; before it could grow into a full-sized bark, she heard a familiar buzzing noise.

Cole pulled his cellphone out of his pocket, looked at the screen and then at Keeley. "Looks like Hannah's up from her nap and wants her mommy. Jordan's outside waiting on you. I'll stay here and have lunch with Elizabeth."

Since Hannah had woken from her nap before they had left the house, Keeley knew it was a ruse. She shot a glance over at Elizabeth, who looked a bit disconcerted that a conversation was taking place in her own home that she had no part of. If this was part of keeping Elizabeth off-kilter, Keeley liked it.

Before she could reply, Elizabeth stood. "I'll call Patrick to see you out."

No doubt to make sure Keeley didn't steal the silver. Before she could assure Elizabeth that there wasn't a damn thing in this mausoleum she wanted, Cole said, "No worries, I'll see Keeley out and be right back."

Looking even more rattled, Elizabeth nodded and watched as Keeley left the room, with Cole right behind her.

Keeley walked out onto the large veranda and waved at Jordan, who stood beside his car, waiting for her. She looked up at Cole. "Is this part of the plan?"

"Yep," he answered in an overexaggerated Texas drawl.

"Was that your version of good cop, bad cop?"

"Give or take a cop or two. She sees you as an

adversary." He grinned. "I'm the good-looking stranger who's paying her some attention."

Keeley definitely couldn't argue with the "good-looking" part.

"I'm sorry you had to hear her comments about your mother again. I would tell you not to let her bother you, but I have a feeling you've been telling yourself that for years."

"Stupid, I know. I can handle her antipathy toward me, but when it comes to my mom or my girls, it's almost more than I can bear."

"Elizabeth is a woman to be pitied. She'll never have a tenth of the happiness you'll have."

"Happiness?"

"Not right now, but you will have happiness again, Keeley. I swear."

The conviction in his expression stunned her. Something told her he would do everything he could to make sure she felt that happiness again.

They broke eye contact and the moment passed. "I'll see you back at your house in a few hours. Now it's time to dig deep and find that charm I was once told I had."

He stalked back toward the house before Keeley could respond.

Returning from Elizabeth Fairchild's house, Cole opened the door to Keeley's home. From one mansion to the other. As the only child of two schoolteachers in the small town of Duncanville, Oklahoma, mansions were something he saw on television but had never experienced.

Wealth had never been of interest to Cole. If it had, he certainly wouldn't have become a teacher himself. History and sports had been his thing, but when it came time to choose between a possible football career and an opportunity to marry his childhood sweetheart and live modestly as a schoolteacher, the choice had been easy.

Though he had to admit, Keeley's house, massive though it was, had little in common with the Fairchilds' pretentious monstrosity. The woman's décor matched her personality. Cold and overbearing. And her sexual overtures during their long afternoon together made him want to take a long, hot shower with a strong disinfectant.

"Any luck?"

Cole turned to see Eden standing at the entryway of the living room.

"Not a lot. She acts like she's the queen and every person should pay her court. In between her pompous bragging about everything the Fairchilds have done for this state—hell, the entire world—we were interrupted about ten times. Every one of them was some big shot in town who acted as though he couldn't wipe his ass without her permission."

Eden laughed but Cole winced. Dammit, years ago that kind of talk would have gotten his mouth soaped down. "Sorry, that was crude."

Eden's twinkling eyes told him she wasn't the least bit offended. "The imagery was a bit gross, but it was funny all the same."

"Where's Keeley?"

"In the children's room." She smiled. "Bath time."

Cole nodded and, taking the steps three at a time, headed to the children's room. What he'd told Eden was true. The visit with Elizabeth had been full of interruptions. But he'd been able to glean enough from her to come up with a couple of interesting theories. He hadn't mentioned it to Eden because he wanted to dig a little deeper first. Maybe his suspicions were all wrong.

Cole pushed the bathroom door open to splashing and giggles. A pain wrenched deep inside him as an unexpected memory sliced through his heart. Jill and

Cassidy and bath time. They used to sing silly songs as
Cassidy splashed and played and Jill giggled. Cole
remembered standing in the doorway, as he was now,
and smiling as he listened to them.

Keeley and Hannah were apparently enjoying their
time together, too, though it appeared that Hannah
liked the splashing part much more than the actual
bath. Keeley was laughing as she tried to dodge the
soak-fest and bathe her daughter.

Not wanting to intrude, Cole backed out of the door.
He must have made a sound, because Keeley looked up
before he had a chance to leave.

"Cole? Everything okay?"

"Yes, sorry to interrupt. Just wanted to tell you I was
back."

Holding on to her daughter's hand, Keeley stood.
"Did you get anything else from Elizabeth?"

Every thought in his head disappeared. The thin white
T-shirt Keeley wore was soaked, as was her bra.
Everything beneath the damp clothing showed in volup-
tuous and explicit detail. Cole clamped his mouth shut
to keep from groaning as he admired what could only
be considered art in its purest form.

Earlier today his hands had been on those luscious
mounds, and now, more than ever, he bitterly resented
the interruption that had kept him from seeing them in
their full beauty. Keeley's breasts were beautiful and
bountiful; brown nipples, hard and peaked, jutted
beneath the shirt.

Lust slammed hard and fast. Turning away before she
could see the evidence of what she was doing to him, he
muttered "No" to her question and shut the door
quickly before she could say anything else.

Keeley pressed a kiss to her sleeping daughter's forehead. After three "Once upon a time" stories, two

"extra special" prayers to bring Hailey home, and a drink of water, she was finally asleep.

Tears pooled in her eyes as she gazed down at her dark-haired angel. Tonight was the first time Hannah had willingly mentioned her sister. The psychologist had recommended that Keeley not mention Hailey's name. And as hard as it had been, she hadn't. Tonight, Hannah had said her sister's name.

Keeley had been listing people for the Lord to bless. She'd said Hannah's name, and without any prompting, Hannah had said, "And Hailey, too." It hadn't been more than that but it was a start.

Unable to resist one more kiss, Keeley leaned down. Cold dampness pressed into her skin and for the first time she realized how wet her shirt was. That thought led her to another: Cole's abrupt answer and his expression when he'd closed the door so quickly. She looked down at her damp shirt and realized that Cole had probably seen an out-and-out peep show. A wet T-shirt contest without the benefit of a bar. No wonder he'd looked so . . . How had he looked? Sexual. Predatory. Hot. His expression had held awareness, desire . . . lust. Those amazing eyes had darkened as they'd zeroed in on her breasts.

Keeley headed to her room for a clean, dry shirt. Despite the warning in her head that being attracted to the dark and dangerous Cole Mathison wasn't like the sensible person she'd always considered herself to be, she couldn't help the increased rhythm of her heart or the tantalizing thought that flashed through her. Would Cole be interested in more than what they'd shared weeks ago?

Even in the first blush of their marriage, Stephen had never looked at her like that. His first priority had always been to pleasure himself. If Keeley happened to find pleasure, well, that was a plus but not something he strived for. Stephen always came first, in more ways than one.

Of course, after what she'd learned today, it made sense that he hadn't cared about her needs. If her suspicions were true, she'd been his pawn to defy and infuriate his mother. Never having had a boyfriend and rarely dating, she'd been the perfect patsy. Her lack of experience and innocence must have seemed like a gift to him.

Cole's heated expression had been completely different from Stephen's lackadaisical interest. The desire in his eyes had been a promise of fulfillment for both of them. She had experienced that fulfillment. Knew how satisfying it was . . . and despite the knowledge that it wasn't wise and sensible, she wanted to experience it again.

Keeley changed to a dry bra, then took a shirt from her closet and pulled it over her head. Her thoughts went back to their conversation this afternoon before Cole had kissed her. Was that really the only reason Stephen had married her? To spite his mother? That seemed extreme, even for someone as shallow as Stephen.

Naïve and gullible she might be, but Keeley resisted believing that was the only purpose for their marriage. Taking a pen and paper from her desk, she sat down in her favorite chair. An image of Stephen popped into her head. Though she knew the greatest blessings from their marriage were her daughters, other thoughts suddenly came to mind—events she hadn't allowed herself to think about since before his death. When she discovered he had been unfaithful, she'd buried any good thoughts of him. Now it was time to determine if her judgment had been totally skewed when it came to her husband.

Her hand flew across the page. Twenty minutes later, she looked down at what she had written—five pages filled with memories of her life with Stephen. While many of them were painful to relive, there were several sweet ones. Movies they had enjoyed together, jokes they had shared. During long walks, they would sometimes hold hands and he would talk about his childhood, how much he'd loved his father and how he was always trying to protect Miranda from his mother's meanness.

One particularly poignant moment was when the twins were born. He'd held them in his arms and tears had rolled down his face.

So she had a choice. She could assume every good thing about their marriage was a lie, or she could accept that while his motives may not have been the purest and he hadn't been the husband she'd hoped for, he'd had some redeeming qualities and their marriage hadn't been a total sham. Keeley chose the latter.

More at peace with Stephen than she had been in years, she stood, the sudden need to see Cole taking over. He'd told her he had learned nothing, but there had to be a reason he came upstairs to see her. The little peep show she'd unintentionally given him might have distracted him from what he had to tell her.

She tried to convince herself that brushing her hair and applying a pale pink lip gloss just to speak with Cole meant nothing—that she would do that for anyone. But she knew that wasn't true, so why lie? She wanted to look nice for Cole.

She made herself walk slowly downstairs. At the entrance to her office, Keeley stopped. Cole sat at the desk, flipping through pages of his notes. Since he didn't seem aware that she was there, Keeley took a few seconds to look at him. Whenever he turned those amazing eyes on her, she had difficulty concentrating. Being able to look at him without his knowing it was a treat. He was a beautiful man; there was no denying that. Well over six feet tall, and built like . . . she mentally shook her head trying to come up with an apt description. Jenna's description of "Greek god" seemed too trite, yet she couldn't deny the appropriateness.

Tall; even to her five feet ten inches, Cole towered over her. Whenever he moved, the muscles rippled under his shirt, and her fingers literally ached to touch his broad shoulders, wrap her hands around a biceps. She regretted not taking advantage of that opportunity when they'd made love before. If she was ever given another chance, she wouldn't make the same mistake.

When she saw him close his eyes and press his fingers to his temple, she came out of her lustful trance. Poor man was suffering from a headache and all she could think about was how gorgeous he was.

"Another headache?"

He opened his eyes and shrugged. "Not bad."

She came into the room and settled on the small sofa a few feet from him. "Have you ever seen a doctor for your headaches?"

A dry, humorless laugh burst from him. "Yeah."

Apparently he wasn't going to share any information about his headaches. That made her sad. He didn't look like he was one to share things with anyone. She was fortunate that she had Jenna and Miranda she could talk to. Who did Cole go to when he needed to get something off his chest?

"Keeley, did you hear me?"

She shook herself out of this odd mood. "Sorry . . . no. What?"

The look he gave her made her think he knew exactly what she'd been thinking earlier. Her insides shuddered and then everything went warm and liquid. Heat rushed to every erogenous zone she had.

"Keeley?"

She watched as he walked around the desk and then stood before her. Unable to stop herself, she got to her feet and found herself within inches of him. When he didn't back away, she raised her hands and pressed her fingers to his temples, using firm but gentle pressure to massage him.

Surprising her, his hands pulled her shoulders toward him as he backed up. She followed him until he leaned against the edge of the desk. Before she knew it, she was between his legs.

Continuing to rub his temples, she watched his eyes close. All sorts of emotions hit her. Gratitude to be able to do something to ease him, along with tenderness, admiration, and a deep yearning to do more than just ease his headache.

Cole opened his eyes and stared into hers. That one look said so much—heat, desire, and caring.

Keeley leaned forward to place a soft kiss to his mouth. Before her lips could touch his, Cole straightened and jerked her hands away from his head. "Thanks. That feels better."

Hurt slammed into her like a freight train. She'd been rejected so many times, this shouldn't hurt that badly. But it did.

Cole went around the desk and dropped back into the chair.

Resisting the urge to just run out of the room and go bury her red face into a cool pillow, Keeley forced herself to stand still. "So you got nothing from Elizabeth."

"More questions than answers."

"What kind of questions?"

"How well do you know Miranda?"

Startled, she sat down on the couch again. "She's been a good friend to me. Why?"

"But what do you know about her life? What she does?"

"She's a full-time mom. Gets involved in a lot of school projects. Does some volunteer work."

"What about the father of her baby? Where is he?"

Keeley grimaced. "Some guy she met in college . . . he took off when she told him she was pregnant."

She hated gossip, but if Cole had questions about Miranda, she'd rather be the one to tell him.

"How does she get along with her mother?"

"She doesn't. She mostly stays out of her way."

"With her money, why can't she live on her own?"

She bit her lip. This was a sensitive subject and one she was surprised he didn't already know. "Miranda doesn't have access to all that money."

"I thought the Fairchilds had millions."

"They do; however, when Miranda's father died, he left Stephen in charge of the finances for both him and Miranda. Miranda has an allowance until she's either married or she turns thirty."

"What happened when Stephen died?"

"The control went back to Elizabeth."

"But why live at home? Expose her daughter to someone like Elizabeth?"

"I think she tries to keep Maggie away from Elizabeth as much as possible, but Miranda left school once she got pregnant and came back home to live."

"Couldn't she get a job . . . live somewhere else?"

Keeley shrugged. "A Fairchild working like a regular person in this town wouldn't go over well with Elizabeth."

"There's a whole world out there, outside of Fairview. Plenty of places for Miranda and Maggie to go where Elizabeth Fairchild has no influence."

"I think Miranda has her reasons for staying. She's private about a lot of things. Maybe she's waiting until she's old enough to inherit all of her money."

"Did Stephen not leave her anything?"

"Some . . . I don't know how much."

"So she could probably use some extra money."

Her head was already shaking before he finished his sentence. "No. There's no way Miranda would be involved with Hailey and Hannah's abduction. She adores them."

His expression unreadable, he shrugged. "Elizabeth rambled on about a lot of things today. One of those was the amount of time Miranda spends away from home, away from her daughter. Elizabeth claims she has no idea what she does. And apparently doesn't care enough to find out."

"Well, whatever it is has nothing to do with Hailey and Hannah, I can assure you."

"I've interviewed her a couple of times . . . she's got secrets."

"Everyone has secrets. You included. Right?"

His eyes went harder than she'd ever seen them as he stood and muttered, "You're right. Good night." Walking around her, he went out the door before she could say anything else.

Keeley bit her lip to keep from calling him back. He had shut her out again. Maybe she'd misread his desire earlier. Maybe their kiss this afternoon had been all about comforting her and she'd projected her lust onto him. Heaven knew she didn't have much experience in the area of attracting men.

She didn't bother to tell herself his rejection didn't hurt; she wasn't that good of a liar.

Wes pulled a beer from his fridge, unscrewed the cap, and guzzled half of it in one swallow. Damn hot summer. He'd be glad to get somewhere cooler. The place he'd picked out to take Keeley was way up in the mountains.

It'd be cooler up there . . . private, too. Not a soul around to hear her scream.

The cellphone on his table buzzed. He didn't want to answer it. She'd be calling for an update. Damned if he wanted to talk to her when he was dripping with sweat. On the other hand, she might have some news on his little rendezvous with Keeley. Taking a chance, he grabbed the phone and snarled, "What?"

"When are you going to do the job I hired you for?"

"Listen, bitch. If you want this done right, you'll give me some time. Setting something like this up ain't as easy as you seem to think. That job I done for you before was a no-brainer compared to this one."

"It's been almost two weeks. What exactly is taking so long?"

He wasn't about to tell her the truth. Cole Mathison was damn hard to follow. Every time he thought he had him, the bastard would somehow disappear. It was like he knew something.

"I can get into Fort Knox a lot easier than I can that damn mansion. He ain't exactly making it easy for me."

"The sooner you do the job, the sooner you'll get your reward."

"I'm going to do it and soon. You just be ready to cough up not only the money you promised, but the woman, too. You double-cross me this time, and it'll take years for them to find all your parts. You got that?"

She was silent for a long time. Finally she said, "You do your job. I'll do mine." The line went dead.

Wes cursed. Damn woman hung up on him. Not that he had anything else to say to her, but he didn't appreciate the disrespect. Maybe once he had Keeley, he'd figure out a way to make the bitch pay for all the aggravation she'd caused. It'd been a long time since he'd done any killing, but it wasn't something he really minded doing.

As long as he didn't get caught, there wasn't a lot Wes wouldn't do.

First he'd take care of Cole Mathison, then he'd get Keeley. Then, before he left town, he'd kill the bitch.

Wes took another slug of his beer. Sounded like a damn fine plan to him.

seventeen

Standing at the window in the girls' bedroom, Keeley leaned her forehead against the cool glass and closed her eyes. She was determined to hold herself together today. She could do this; she had to do this. It was a special day for Hannah. June 20: the twins' birthday.

She would do everything she could to make it as memorable as possible. Hannah was so excited, and Keeley wanted her to stay that way. The little imp had woken before dawn this morning, thrilled that it was her birthday. Now she was asleep in the playroom, but by the time the cake arrived at two o'clock, she would be awake and full of energy for her party.

The presents had been ordered weeks ago. Though Keeley had purchased two of everything, only Hannah would receive her presents. When Hailey returned, she would get hers. And she *would* return. She would!

"What's wrong?" Cole asked behind her.

She straightened and gripped the windowsill, not wanting to turn around and let him see the tears that were streaming down her face. When he touched her shoulder, it was all she could do not to throw herself into his arms.

"Tell me."

She swallowed the sob rising up within her. "My girls are five years old today. I want to make the day as special for Hannah as possible, but I can't stop thinking about Hailey. No one will know it's her birthday. No one will make it special for her." A sob escaped. "Oh God, I don't even know if she's alive."

His hands warm on her skin, Cole pulled her around to face him. The compassion in his expression was her undoing. With a small sob, she leaned forward and Cole's arms locked around her, warm and comforting.

"She's alive. You have to believe that. I do."

Breath shuddering through her, she looked up through tear-filled eyes. "Why do you believe it?"

"Other than I feel it in my bones?"

"Yes."

"Because it makes no sense that she's not alive. The man who took them sold Hannah. There's no reason to believe he wouldn't do the same thing with Hailey."

"If he wanted money, why didn't he ask for ransom?"

"Because money's not his primary motivation, Keeley. We've known that almost from the start."

"But why? What could I have done that was so awful? How could someone hate me that much? Why couldn't they just hurt me . . . why hurt my children, too?"

"I don't know. But we'll find out and we will find your daughter. Don't give up hope."

Taking long, controlled breaths, she finally felt a small measure of control . . . thanks to this man who had come to mean so much to her. "I don't know what I would have done without you."

"You're a strong woman. You would have survived, no matter what."

Risking rejection once again, Keeley rose up to kiss him. It was brief and meant as an act of appreciation. The moment her lips touched his, that changed.

He grasped her shoulders. To pull her to him or push her away? She didn't know, didn't care. Making the decision for him, she wrapped her arms around him and pressed her entire body against his.

With a deep growl that went through his body and vibrated against hers, he pulled her closer and returned the kiss. As his mouth moved over her, his hands moved from her shoulders to her bottom and pressed her lower body against him. Feeling the hard desire, Keeley gasped. Cole took advantage and swept his tongue inside.

Standing on her toes, Keeley fitted herself against him. As if he knew what she needed, he fit his erection at the top of her sex, exactly where she was aching for him the most. Rubbing and pressing, she felt hot, scorching need erupt within her. Without conscious thought, she began a slow, sensuous ride against the rigid length of his penis; little gasps, muffled by his mouth, echoed in the room. A pulse-pounding intensity swept through her as her entire body tensed; she wound tighter and tighter.

Cole lifted his mouth to whisper, "That's it, sweetheart. Let go."

That whispering growl pushed her to the very edge. She was so into the moment, she barely comprehended that Cole had picked her up. Her legs naturally wrapped around his waist as if they belonged there. He held her back against the wall as she rode harder . . . harder. The gasps rasping from her lungs grew louder. A wild, uncontrollable urgency tightened everything inside her. On the precipice of sheer ecstasy, it slammed through her. With a keening cry, Keeley exploded.

Slowly, as if reluctant to let her go, Cole lowered her feet to the floor. She peeked up at him. He'd just given her yet another amazing orgasm, but he was still aroused, unfulfilled. Self-denial once again etched his face. And as before, she refused to be the only one to receive pleasure. Cupping him gently through his clothes, she glided her hand down his length with a slow, firm stroke.

He grabbed her wrist. "No. We can't."

The erection throbbing against her hand was something he couldn't deny; he wanted her. "Why not?"

"Because I—"

"Sorry to interrupt," a deep voice said.

Keeley peeked around Cole's broad shoulder and saw Jordan standing in the doorway. Though he looked somewhat uncomfortable, his face held grim determination.

Without turning, Cole said, "What's up?"

"Need to talk to you . . . can you come downstairs for a few minutes?"

"Yeah, be right down."

Cole waited till Jordan left the room and then breath shuddered through him as he took several steps away from her. "I'm sorry, Keeley. I shouldn't have done that."

"Why not?"

"Because, I just can't . . . it won't happen again." He stalked out of the room.

Keeley stared at the doorway Cole had disappeared through. What had that been about? Why couldn't it happen again? Was it because of the case, or something more? All those insecurities she did her best to ignore came back full force. Was there something about her that Cole didn't find appealing after all? Had he just been trying to comfort her and she was the one who'd turned it into something else once again? His arousal had been obvious, but when a woman threw herself at a man, was that just a normal response? Was she falling in love with a man who really didn't want her at all?

Needing some recovery time before he went downstairs, Cole stomped to his room, leaned against the closed door, and cursed silently for a full minute. What the hell had he done? And how the hell was he going to get out of it? He couldn't deny he wanted her . . . she'd held that desire in her hand. Cole shuddered at the memory of how she had stroked him.

He'd been on the verge of giving in, allowing those desires free rein. And if Jordan hadn't interrupted them, he would have. He would have let her continue stroking and it would have led to another amazing sexual experience. Something he'd told himself he couldn't allow again.

Knowing Eden and Jordan were waiting for him, he gritted his teeth and headed downstairs. He'd face what he'd done later.

Stopping at the door of the living room, he wasn't surprised to see Jordan and Eden in an embrace. They were an affectionate, demonstrative couple. When he heard a soft sob, he froze. "What's wrong?"

Eden pulled her head from Jordan's shoulder. The tears in her eyes were like a gut punch he felt all the way to his soul. They'd found Hailey. She was dead.

"Is it Hailey?"

"No."

The relief he felt at that one word was almost more than he could handle. Having to tell Keeley her daughter was dead would have been his worst nightmare come true.

"What's wrong?" he asked.

"It's Paulo." Eden swallowed. "He's sick . . . in the hospital. We need to go to him."

Keeley appeared beside him and said, "Of course you do."

Still disturbed by what had just happened with her, Cole forced himself to focus. "Anything I can do?"

Jordan jerked his head in a nod, indicating he wanted to talk privately. While Keeley went to Eden and hugged her, Cole and Jordan retreated to a corner of the room.

"You okay?" Jordan asked.

"Hell no."

"You going to be able to do this?"

"You mean, am I going to be able to keep my hands off our client? Yeah, I'll make damn sure I am."

"That wasn't exactly what I was asking. But I trust you to know what's best."

Cole swallowed a snort. Good thing Jordan trusted him, because he sure as hell didn't trust himself. He glanced over at Keeley, who was talking in a low voice with Eden. Keep his hands off her? Yes, he would do that. But how to tell Keeley without hurting her? He didn't have an answer for that one.

Keeley's determination that Hannah's birthday be one of joy was a success. Miranda arrived with Maggie, who carried in a giant stuffed giraffe. Jenna brought a doll and a half-dozen books. Eden and Jordan had given her a dozen or more DVDs of children's movies. And Cole surprised everyone, including Keeley, when he disappeared in the midst of the party and returned a few minutes later, pushing a small pink bicycle into the room. Hannah had squealed with glee, causing everyone to laugh.

Hannah had only mentioned Hailey once. Before she blew out her candles on her cake, she expressed her wish out loud: "I wish Hailey would come home."

Tears sprang to her eyes before Keeley could stop them. She swallowed a sob, tried to speak and found she couldn't. Cole had been the one to press a kiss to the top of Hannah's head and say, "That's a good wish, Hannah, and one we'll make come true."

Still unable to speak, Keeley smiled her appreciation at Cole.

Eden and Jordan left early the next day. Despite Eden's worry for her son, Keeley could tell that she felt guilty for leaving. She'd assured her that she would be fine. And she would be. With Cole here, somehow she still felt that optimism that Hailey was alive and they would find her.

Out of necessity, Cole, Eden, and Jordan had met with Honor to update her.

It no longer hurt as much that Honor had been relocated to Greenville. She didn't resent it because she knew there were other cases just as important to them.

She did wonder if LCR would begin to feel the same way, though. Yes, she was their client and paying them well, but they were used to action. Used to getting things done and going on to another job. Nothing had happened with this case. Finding Hannah had been a miracle, but the longer Hailey was gone and there were no real clues, the less their chances of finding her.

She knew Cole didn't feel that way, but how long would that last? He wouldn't stay here forever. And she would never stop looking. He'd said he wouldn't leave until they found her, but she was realistic enough to know that he couldn't stay here indefinitely, no matter how much she wanted him to.

"Want to go to the park?"

Keeley jerked at the suddenness of Cole's voice. She pulled her gaze away from the website she'd been staring sightlessly at for several minutes. She'd zoned out again and hadn't even known he was in the house.

"What?"

"It's a beautiful day outside. Let's take Hannah and go for a picnic in the park."

Her stomach twisted. How could he ask her to go to the place where this nightmare had begun?

"Don't look like that, Keeley. I know what I'm asking, but you've never gone back since it happened. I want you to see if you might remember something. Even as young as Hannah is, she might remember something, too."

"No, it would upset her too much."

"She'll be fine. If she looks the least bit upset, we'll bring her home."

"But the psychologist said she didn't appear to remember anything."

"And she could be right, but let's try it and see what happens."

Keeley stood. He was right. Nothing would get accomplished if they didn't have the courage to do everything they could.

"I'll go get her dressed." She stopped at the door, took a deep breath for courage, and said, "You know, we need to talk about what happened."

"No we don't."

"Why?"

"Because it can't happen again, Keeley. I'm responsible, I know. I got carried away again. But I can't have a relationship with you. And you're not the type of person to have sex with someone and just forget about it."

"You mean the way you did with Honor."

There was both guilt and embarrassment in his expression. "You know about that?"

She shrugged. "I didn't mean to. I overheard you apologizing to her. You didn't even remember being with her."

His mouth flattened into a grim line. "It was a long time ago."

"Do you sleep with so many women that you can't remember them?"

His face shut down . . . he didn't intend to say anything else. He would neither deny her accusation nor defend himself. It was none of her business; she knew that. If Cole wanted to sleep with an entire fleet of women, it shouldn't be her concern. But if he did sleep with so many women he couldn't remember sleeping with a beautiful woman like Honor, then why wouldn't he sleep with her?

In a year or two, would he have forgotten that one night with her? No, she refused to believe that . . . it had been too incredible . . . too special. But had it been that special to him?

Keeley had worked hard at overcoming the insecurities Stephen's betrayal had caused her. It hadn't been easy. She knew she wasn't unattractive, but there were certain things she didn't like about herself. Things Stephen had sometimes made a point of mentioning.

"Keeley, I don't want to hurt you."

She suddenly realized she'd been standing in the middle of the room staring at him. Cole had probably read every expression on her face as an indictment against him. She held no rancor toward him. How could she? He'd done nothing but try to find her children, defend her against Elizabeth's spitefulness, offer his body to her as solace, and give her hope. Just because he didn't want a repeat performance wasn't something she could hold against him. If she couldn't even keep her husband's interest, how on earth could she expect to attract someone like Cole?

"Thank you for being honest with me."

As she turned away, she couldn't help but wonder why he flinched.

eighteen

"Mommy, higher . . . push me higher!"

Despite his bleak feelings from their earlier talk, Cole couldn't help but smile as mother and daughter figuratively butted heads. Hannah wanted to swing higher; her overprotective mother was giving her only the lightest of pushes.

He'd hoped coming here would trigger some kind of memory for Keeley or Hannah. Though Keeley had a haunted look in her eyes the first half hour, Hannah had acted as if nothing bad had happened here. The resilience of children always amazed him.

He wanted to give both of them a little time to get more comfortable before he started his questions. If they were relaxed, perhaps they might remember something.

Admittedly it was a long shot, but he was running out of options. Hailey had been gone almost three months. The press had gone, with only a weekly call from a few of the major television stations to ask for updates.

The FBI was still on the case, but Honor was their only local agent. And even she was working on other cases and was basically waiting for something to break on this one.

Cole was convinced nothing would break unless they forced it. Hailey wasn't coming home on her own. Her picture had been flashed on every television station from here to Australia. People all around the world knew about her case, and not a damn one of them had given them a clue they could use.

Even their sadistic emailer seemed to have lost interest. It had been almost a week since Keeley had received a cruel reminder of her loss. Was this a final indication that everyone assumed Hailey would never be found? He refused to allow that to happen. He would never give up and neither would Keeley.

"How about we stop for a few minutes and talk?"

Hannah looked disappointed, but Keeley looked scared. Cole hardened his heart.

Keeley pulled Hannah from the swing and headed toward Cole. He spread a blanket on the ground under a giant oak. Opening the picnic basket Keeley had packed, he pulled two bottles of water out and handed one to Hannah and one to Keeley.

They both took a sip and then he asked, "Tell me about that day, Keeley."

Keeley swallowed the water, took a breath, and said, "It was sunny . . . not as sunny as today. And warm. One of those early spring days that makes you realize winter is completely over."

"What time did you get to the park?"

Her brow wrinkled in concentration. "Not as early as we'd planned. Jenna was supposed to meet us here. She was bringing lemonade and cookies. When she called and told me she couldn't come, I took some extra time and baked cookies from some frozen dough I had in the freezer."

"Where was Jenna?"

"Mr. and Mrs. Pointer had died in an accident the day before. Jenna had to meet with the family to make arrangements for a double funeral."

"And Miranda and Maggie. Weren't they supposed to come, too?"

"Yes . . . but I knew the night before that they

wouldn't be coming with us. Maggie was running a fever."

"Okay, so what time did you get here?"

"About ten-thirty, I think."

"Was anyone here when you arrived?"

"There were a few people. Not as many as I expected, considering the weather. Hailey and Hannah had the playground to themselves."

"And you saw no strange men lurking about? Men you'd never seen before?"

"No. The few people I did see were people I'm acquainted with."

"How long were you here before it happened?"

"Not long. Maybe about forty minutes or so."

"Show me where you were and where Hannah and Hailey were."

She stood and walked over to the monkey bars. "I was standing between the girls. Hailey was playing on the bars. I heard her giggle and turned to see her trying to climb higher. She's such an adventurous rascal. I pulled her down and told her not to do that anymore. She just grinned at me." She closed her eyes as if the memory was painful.

"Then what?"

Opening her eyes, she concentrated on what Cole knew was the most horrific moment of her life. "Hannah asked for some juice." She walked a few steps to a bench. "I pulled a juice box out of the bag. She took it and went toward her sister. I knew Hailey would want some, too, so I was getting out another one when I heard the screams."

Cole stiffened his resolve and looked at Keeley's daughter. "Hannah, do you remember that day when the bad man took you?"

He ignored Keeley's gasp and concentrated on the

little girl, who seemed to be totally absorbed with her water. He said again, "Hannah, do you remember?"

"He gave us cookies and juice."

Keeley jerked. Hannah had never mentioned that before.

"Was it good?" Cole asked.

She scrunched her nose up and shook her head emphatically.

"What else do you remember?"

"We got sleepy."

They'd pretty much determined that both girls had been drugged, most likely to keep them quiet until they could be gotten rid of.

"Do you remember what the man who took you looked like?"

Another emphatic shake of her head and then, "Mommy, can I swing again?"

Cole held back his impatience. As much as he wanted to push her, he couldn't. Hannah was five years old. It was a miracle that she had suffered no apparent emotional trauma from her abduction. The last thing he wanted to do was hurt her.

As Hannah stood, she looked at Cole and said, "He had a boo-boo like that."

Cole looked down at the inside of his forearm where he had a long, slender scar. A scar caused by a whip. His heartbeat kicked up. It wasn't much but it was something. The man who'd taken the girls had a scar.

His heart still thundering, he kept his voice only slightly curious and said, "Really. Where was it?"

As if she didn't know that the two adults were hanging on her every word, she said, "On his hand."

"Did he have dark hair like you and your mommy's?"

She shook her head.

"Was it like Eden's?"

"Like Hailey's and Daddy's."

"You mean blond . . . kind of like Aunt Miranda's?"

She nodded her head and said, "Can I go swing again?"

Cole looked up at Keeley. There were tears in her eyes and gratitude on her face. Wanting nothing more than to pull her into his arms and hold her, he stood and said, "I'll call Honor," and walked away.

Keeley followed Hannah to the swings, her emotions close to eruption. Her baby had remembered something. No, it wasn't a lot—hair color and a scar—but it was more than they'd had before. Anything at all to help narrow down the suspects was progress. And she owed it all to Cole. She hadn't wanted to come here. Hadn't wanted to put Hannah through more questioning. Hadn't wanted to relive the horror of that day, even though it was ingrained into her mind. But Cole had done the hard thing, and thanks to him, they had something they didn't have before.

"Mommy, who's that with Unca Cole?"

Last week Hannah had started calling Cole "Unca Cole." She should discourage it. He wouldn't be here forever, and having Hannah attach any kind of nickname to him meant she could easily form an attachment.

So far she hadn't told her not to call him that. . . . She should, she knew . . . but not yet.

Keeley twisted her head to see Cole standing beside a truck and being hugged by a beautiful auburn-haired woman. A man with shoulder-length golden-blond hair, about Cole's height, stood beside the woman. He gave Cole a brief manly hug. They talked for several seconds and Cole did the most extraordinary thing. He pulled the woman back into his arms and swung her around, the golden-haired man grinning the entire time. Then Cole set her down and placed his hand on her belly.

A lump formed in Keeley's throat. The universal

signal of a woman expecting a baby. Everyone wanted to touch the tummy.

As if they knew they were being watched, all three of them looked over at her. She should be embarrassed to be caught staring, but couldn't force herself to look away. This was the most emotion she'd ever seen from Cole. Even when they'd had those passionate encounters, he'd been aroused but so very controlled. It was obvious this couple meant a lot to him.

As the small group headed toward her, she took her daughter's hand and led her to the blanket Cole had spread. Hannah pulled out her new doll and Keeley waited for Cole and his friends. The woman was even more beautiful than Keeley had first thought. Vibrant auburn hair, creamy magnolia skin, and twinkling emerald eyes.

Keeley glanced over at the golden-haired man and could only stare. To say he was unusual-looking would be an understatement. His long hair was a mass of different colors—blond, brown, and golden—and he had a scar on the left side of his face. The scar did nothing to detract from his striking looks.

"Keeley, I'd like you to meet Shea and Ethan Bishop. They're with LCR, too."

As Keeley shook their hands, she was surprised at the way Shea kept looking at Cole, as if assessing him for something. A slight furrow of her brow told Keeley she was concerned for him for some reason. Why?

"And this must be Hannah," Ethan said.

Hannah raised her head to give an adorable grin and then resumed playing with her doll.

"Are you here to work with Cole?" Keeley asked.

Shea smiled. "If he'll let us. We just got off an op and were at loose ends."

"You mean we couldn't wait to come here and tell Cole the news," Ethan said.

"Well, that, too."

"Congratulations," Keeley said.

"How'd you know?" Shea asked.

"Cole put his hand on your stomach. When I was pregnant, that seemed to be the first thing people wanted to do, too."

Shea laughed. "That'll take some getting used to."

"So you guys going to stay awhile?" Cole asked.

Ethan glanced at his wife and then back at Cole. "If you think we can help."

"We just learned something new. Maybe you could help with that. Research. Not any action."

"Ethan needs a rest." Shea shot her husband a teasing grin. "He pulled a muscle chasing down our ride in Chile."

Ethan snorted. "If I hadn't, we'd still be walking. Damn stubborn mule."

Keeley watched their exchange in awe. Their kind of life was so foreign to her. Before her world was torn apart, her daily routine consisted of meals for the girls, play and nap time, reading bedtimes stories, and the occasional grocery store run.

She watched Cole's face as he talked with his friends. Their world was his. Adventure and danger. No wonder he didn't want to become involved with her. How boring she must seem to him. Even though he'd been a history teacher in the past, he'd left that life behind. Had even told her he was a different person and could never go back to it.

"You okay, Keeley?"

Cole's concerned frown pulled her from her wistful thoughts. Getting both her girls back was all she needed. Hoping for any kind of permanent relationship with a man like Cole would be futile.

"I'm fine." She smiled at Ethan and Shea. "It's great to have more LCR people on my case."

"We'll do all that we can," Shea said.

"How'd you know we were at the park?" Cole asked.

"We stopped at Keeley's house and Mrs. Thompkins told us where to find you," Ethan said.

Keeley felt a tug on her shirt and looked down at her daughter's angelic face. "Mommy, I'm hungry."

"I am, too." She glanced up at Cole's friends. "We were just about to have a picnic. We have plenty of food to share."

As if sitting down with a five-year-old was the highlight of their day, they grinned at each other and then Ethan said, "I'm starving."

And with that, three LCR operatives sat down on the blanket and ate the peanut butter and jelly sandwiches and drank their milk as if they did it every day.

Pacing across his bedroom suite, Cole waited for Ethan and Shea to join him. Keeley had put an exhausted Hannah to bed and had already bid good night to everyone. She looked worn out. Reliving the girls' abduction today at the park hadn't been easy.

He was beginning to feel as helpless and useless as an old shoe. There had been no leads in weeks. The most hopeful thing that had happened was Hannah remembering the hair color and scar on the hand of the bastard who'd grabbed her. It wasn't much, but it was more than they'd had before.

That's why Ethan and Shea were meeting with him. He intended to put as much description as he could together and give it to Shea. She was a gifted artist. Yeah, they'd done this already with the FBI, but he wanted to try it again. With Keeley's descriptions of height and weight, along with the little Hannah had given them, he hoped something else could be discovered from Shea's talented hand.

He looked up at the knock on his door. Shea and then

Ethan entered. They were practically glowing they looked so damned happy. Once again he was reminded that even if he wouldn't wish what happened to him and Shea on his worst enemy, he was glad something good and right had come out of all of it. Shea and Ethan had loved each other for years. The pain they'd gone through to get to that happy ending made them appreciate it all the more.

Ethan eased down onto the sofa with a grimace.

"You did hurt yourself in Chile, didn't you?" Cole asked.

"You try running with sixty pounds of equipment on your back after a skittish mule, with Shea laughing hysterically behind you."

Cole chuckled. They'd had good times together once, before they'd all screwed it up. Shea with her insecurities, Ethan with his guilt, and Cole with his damned interference.

"Don't let him fool you, Cole. He's faking most of it."

Ethan's expression was a mixture of indignation and guilt. "Hey, it does hurt."

Shea rolled her eyes. "He's worried about me. He's hoping that if we get involved in this case, it'll keep me from suggesting something with more action."

Ethan shrugged, but didn't deny her claim. Cole understood completely and concurred. The miscarriage she'd suffered the first time she was pregnant wasn't something any of them would ever forget.

Cole sat in the chair at his desk; leaning forward, he took in both of their gazes. "I could use your help. Especially you, Shea. Hannah remembered something about her kidnapper. I'm hoping we can ease her into remembering even more. I have a vague description from Keeley. The bastards were wearing ski masks, so Hannah is probably our best bet to find out what their faces look like. If we can put more time on it, we might be able to come up with something we can work with."

Shea nodded. "I'll do whatever I can. This has got to be killing that poor woman, not knowing where her daughter is."

"Finding Hannah helped, but you're right, it's killing her not to find Hailey. She's a strong woman. Just one of the things she's gone through in the last few years would have broken most people. Everyone has a breaking point, though."

"You sound . . . fond of her," Shea said.

Cole shrugged. "I admire her strength."

He ignored the exchange of concerned glances between Shea and Ethan. He wasn't about to explain that his admiration for Keeley went far beyond just her strength. Nothing could come of it, and having to answer questions about his feelings wouldn't change anything. Especially when he had no answers.

"How can I help?" Ethan asked.

"I need you to be Keeley's shadow. I still think she's in danger. She doesn't go out much, but Eden was with her whenever she did, and you're a hell of a lot more intimidating-looking than Eden."

"Shea and I read the file and talked with Eden and Jordan before they left for Thailand. You still believe this could be some sort of vendetta against Keeley?"

"Yeah. Unfortunately, the only person who publicly despises her would probably be the last person to invite all the publicity this case has garnered," Cole said.

"Elizabeth Fairchild," Shea said.

Cole nodded. "She's a bitch and loves to make Keeley's life miserable, but it's brought the Fairchild name up for public scrutiny and that's the last thing a woman like her would want."

"Maybe her hatred is stronger than her need to protect the family name."

"No. Nothing is stronger than that. I know—I've spent way too much time in her company."

"Oh really?" Shea didn't bother to hide her amusement. "Have you become cougar bait?"

Cole's stomach twisted. Having Elizabeth attracted to him gave him an advantage, that didn't mean he had to like it.

"I think I'm a little too old to be considered cougar bait. However, staying on her good side has been helpful. She's revealed some things I don't think she meant to. I'm going to stick—"

The bedroom door flew open. Cole looked up to see Keeley standing in the doorway, tears streaming down her face. He was at her side in an instant.

"What?"

She held a piece of paper in her shaking hand, but seemed unable to speak. Taking the paper from her, he wrapped his arm around her shoulder and read the vile email.

I got your little girl, Keeley. You'll never see her again. Never get to dress her in that pink and green jumpsuit with the baby elephants on the front. How sad . . . boo hoo. Maybe I'll send her body back to you so you can bury her in it.

Rage bubbled inside Cole but he forced it back. Keeley needed his support, not his anger. He looked down at her ravaged expression. "I'm assuming Hailey has a pink and green jumpsuit with elephants on the front?"

He watched her throat work as she tried to speak and couldn't. Finally she nodded.

"You've received sick emails like this in the past, but this confirms what we already suspected. It's someone you know . . . apparently very well for them to have information about what's in Hailey's wardrobe."

A shudder ran through her as she visibly tried to compose herself. When she spoke, her voice was thick with emotion. "You don't understand. I bought that outfit the day before the girls were taken. She never even wore it."

"Where did you buy it?"

"At the children's store in town."

Shea took the paper from Cole's hand and said, "So anyone who saw you buy it there could have—"

"No." She winced as if embarrassed. "The owner, Cindy Brackett, knows I don't like to be seen in town that much. She sometimes let's me come in after hours to shop."

Cole tamped down additional fury. First they'd focus on finding Hailey, then he'd work on the antipathy Keeley had been putting up with for far too long.

"So Cindy Brackett could be a suspect," Ethan said.

Keeley shook her head. "Cindy's seventy-nine years old. There's no way she would be involved in anything like this."

Cole didn't respond. He'd question Ms. Brackett before he cleared her. If she was innocent, there was only one other explanation. One he had never considered. He hoped to hell he was wrong and cursed himself for not thinking of it before.

Breath shuddered from Keeley as she worked to control her emotions. Just how much more could this woman take before she completely lost it? He didn't want to find out.

"I'm sorry I interrupted you . . . didn't I?" Keeley asked.

"Not at all," Shea said. "We were just discussing how we can best help."

"Thank you both for being here." She brought her gaze back to Cole. "I think I'm going to sleep with Hannah in her bed tonight."

"No." Cole inwardly winced at his abruptness, especially when Keeley flinched. "I want you to sleep in one of the guest rooms with Hannah. Just for tonight. Okay?"

Her eyes glittered with tears and questions, but Cole was humbled by her faith in him when she just nodded and said, "Okay."

Keeley said "Good night" to Shea and Ethan, then left the room.

Following her out into the hallway, Cole couldn't have stopped what happened next if an earthquake hit. He pulled Keeley into his arms and held her close. Breathing in the beauty of the fragrance that was Keeley, he whispered, "I promise you, Keeley. It will all work out and we will get Hailey back safely."

She held him tightly for several seconds and then pulled away. Her heart in her eyes, she whispered, "I believe in you, Cole."

Holding her face in his hands, Cole leaned down and pressed a soft kiss to her lips. "Get some sleep."

Cole waited until she disappeared into her daughter's room and then, seconds later, reappeared with Hannah in her arms. Whispering another soft "Good night," she went into the bedroom suite across from the girls' and closed the door.

His eyes closed for a long second as he acknowledged what he'd been denying for weeks. It wasn't just desire he felt for Keeley. It was more, so much more.

He'd thought he knew every level of hell that existed. He had been wrong. Falling in love with the widow of the man he had killed was like free-falling into the fiery pit and looking up to see heaven and knowing he didn't have a chance in hell of attaining it.

nineteen

Cole parked in front of the Bows and Britches children's clothing store. After he and Ethan had made a preliminary surface search of Keeley's house that morning with no results, he decided to come into town and talk with Cindy Brackett. Once he eliminated her as a suspect, he'd go back and break the news to Keeley.

She would be upset that her house might be bugged, but not surprised. He'd seen the knowledge in her eyes last night when he'd requested that she and Hannah sleep in another room. But until they did a thorough search of the house, any serious discussions needed to be done outside.

He'd left Shea in charge of showing Keeley some self-defense moves. He was determined she'd never be left defenseless again.

LCR operatives would soon arrive to do a more thorough search of the house. After his interview with Cindy Brackett, Keeley and Hannah would be moved to a safe house. Ethan was making those arrangements now.

He opened the door of his Jeep and got out slowly, his eyes searching the perimeter. Ever since he had arrived in Fairview, he'd felt as if he were being watched. Small towns were notorious for wanting to know people's business. This felt like more. Almost as if there was a malevolent presence eyeing him. Other than the normal goings-on of a small, prosperous town, Cole saw nothing out of place.

Shrugging off his unease for now, he opened the door of the store and walked in. An elderly white-haired lady with a sweet smile, twinkling eyes, and a cane hobbled toward him. If this was Cindy Brackett, he immediately eliminated her as any kind of threat. Nevertheless, perhaps she'd mentioned Keeley buying the clothes to someone. He was here. Might as well ask some questions.

Dressed in a mechanic's overalls and wearing a stringy black wig with an attached cap, Wes sauntered over to the black SUV that Cole Mathison had just exited. Why the bitch wanted the man dead wasn't something he concerned himself with. She'd called him last night and insisted it had to be done today. Fine with him. Wasn't like he didn't want to do the job, he'd just been looking for the right opportunity.

He'd already picked out a spot where he could watch the entire show. Last time he performed this particular deed for her, he hadn't been around to watch the results and wished he had. He'd heard that the car had exploded on impact; the couple inside never knew what happened. Damn, he would've liked to have seen that explosion. He'd seen the results afterward, though—car had been burned to a crisp. And no one had suspected a thing.

He had more incentive for this job than the other. The sooner he took care of this deed, the quicker he'd get his reward. With that kind of incentive, why the hell would he ask questions or procrastinate?

Acting as if he had every right to be there, Wes walked around the SUV. His eye out for any real curious people, he went to the front of the vehicle. If anyone asked, he was just a mechanic from Gary's Garage on the other side of town, giving what Gary prided himself on: good customer service.

He didn't know why Mathison had gone into the kids' store, but Wes figured he wouldn't be in there long. Not that he needed a lot of time for a job like this. He took one last wide glance around, squatted down, and then eased under the front of the vehicle.

Attach, click to activate, and slide out. Quick. Easy. Deadly.

Getting to his feet, Wes whistled tunelessly, his gait slow and unhurried as he disappeared behind the building. If anyone was questioned later, they'd just claim to have seen a man with long, greasy black hair in a mechanic's suit seemingly admiring the sleek lines of the SUV and nothing more.

A grin slid up on his mouth. Now to get on his dirt bike and head to his spot to watch the fireworks. Cole Mathison was about to meet his maker for his heavenly reward. And very soon, Wes would be getting his earthly reward.

Despite the seriousness of his reasons for questioning Cindy Brackett, Cole chuckled as he left the store. Not only was the elderly woman as sharp as anyone half her age, she was also a huge supporter of Keeley's. That, in Cole's book, made her even more special.

Unfortunately, Mrs. Brackett could shed little light on who might have known about the clothes Keeley had purchased for Hailey. Which meant only one thing— Keeley's house was bugged.

Cole backed out of the parking space and rolled out onto the almost empty street. It was just past six o'clock and the small town's businesses were closed for the evening.

As he headed back to Keeley's house, his mind wrestled with how the bugs had been placed in her house in the first place. If no outsiders had been in her house in a while, then the house could have been bugged for years. Possibly from the time it was built. Which brought all sorts of questions to mind about the husband who'd had it built for her.

Cole tapped his brakes as he rounded a curve. He heard a small pop, felt a minute thump and then nothing else. Wondering if he'd hit something, he looked in his rearview mirror. Nothing. About to round another curve, he applied the brake again and nothing happened. The vehicle didn't slow. Frowning, he pressed again. Nothing. His foot went all the way to the floorboard. Dammit. No brakes.

Steering toward the edge of the road, hoping the gravel would slow his descent, Cole checked the rearview mirror again. Empty of traffic. If he was going to wreck, he didn't want to involve anyone else.

His speed picked up as he continued down the hill. As long as he didn't lose control, he'd wait till he got to the bottom of the hill, then he'd find a safe place to apply the emergency brake. He turned the steering column. "Shit," he whispered. No brakes and now a locked-up steering wheel. Out of options, Cole pulled the emergency brake. Nothing happened.

A sharp curve loomed ahead of him. With no way to steer and no way to stop, the vehicle was headed straight toward a sharp drop-off. He had two choices, both shitty: stay in the vehicle and probably die or jump out.

Unbuckling his seat belt, Cole opened the door. The ground was a blur of green and brown. The vehicle zoomed down hill, picking up speed. Seconds before it took flight, Cole threw himself from the SUV. He landed on his side and rolled. Adrenaline helped to detract from the impact of the hard earth and the rocks jabbing into skin.

Winded, he lay silently for a couple of seconds. Then, pulling in a deep breath, he sat up. A thunderous crash echoed through the hills as the SUV hit the bottom of the ravine.

The booming noise almost overwhelmed the sound of the gunshot blast above him.

What the hell! In one fluid movement, Cole rolled, pulled his gun from his ankle holster, and sprang to his feet. Adrenaline surging, he stayed low and ran toward the direction the shots came from.

twenty

Hannah's hand in hers, Keeley walked along the drive back to the house and breathed in the fresh air of summer. How she loved the change of each season. A fragrant hint of the magnolia trees about to bloom blended with the scent of the early roses lining the trellis of the small gazebo at the side yard. In about a month or so, the magnolias would be in full regalia, covered with large white flowers that carried the sweetest lemony scent.

A movement at the front of the house caught her eye. Ethan was running toward his truck. Her heart thudding with dread, she watched as he started the truck and zoomed toward them. She caught a glimpse of his expression and fear slammed deeper. Something was very wrong.

The truck stopped beside them and Ethan slid the window down. Keeley braced herself for bad news.

"Cole's had a little car trouble. I'm going to go pick him up."

His grim expression told her it was something more than car trouble. The glance he shot Hannah was one of concern. He didn't want to scare her.

Keeley turned to her daughter. "Hannah, go on to the house and ask Shea if she'll give you a bowl of ice cream. Okay?"

The delighted expression on her face an indication she

hadn't picked up that anything was wrong, Hannah took off running. As soon as she was out of hearing range, Keeley turned back to Ethan. "What's happened?"

"Cole's brakes failed. He had to jump out of the Jeep."

Keeley grasped the side mirror for something to hold on to. "Is he hurt?"

"He's fine. Some bruises and scrapes, nothing more." He grinned and added, "I'll bring him home and let you fuss over him."

Though she knew Ethan's teasing words were supposed to ease her fears, she couldn't help but feel the need to go see for herself that Cole was truly all right. She cast an anxious glance toward the house, torn between wanting to go with Ethan and the need to stay with Hannah to make sure she was safe.

Ethan recognized the look. "Stay with Hannah and Shea. As soon as you get inside, turn on the security alarm."

"Something else happened, didn't it?"

"Just get inside, Keeley. Everything will be all right."

She backed away and watched Ethan speed out of the drive. The instant the gate closed, Keeley sprinted toward the house. Her heart in her throat, she burst through the door, slammed it shut, and punched in the security code.

Needing to see Hannah, she ran into the kitchen and jerked to a stop at the incredibly normal and calm scene. Hannah sat at the table devouring a bowl of chocolate ice cream. Shea sat across from her, eating a small bowl of vanilla ice cream.

Her smile serene, Shea said, "It's delicious. Want some?"

Breaths almost coming in spurts she was feeling so panicked, she shook her head. "Cole, he—"

"Is fine," Shea finished for her. "Just a bit bruised. Nothing's happend that he can't handle. Okay?"

Without knowing how she got there, she found herself sitting at the table. Her knees were shaking so badly, she knew she would have fallen if she hadn't found a seat soon.

A ragged sigh scraped against her lungs as Keeley admitted something she hadn't allowed herself to think about. Cole had become important to her. Very important. If something happened to him . . . No, nothing could happen to Cole. She couldn't bear it. She'd lost too much already. She couldn't lose Cole, too.

Cole stood at the side of the road and waited for Ethan to pick him up. The shooter was long gone. Cole had only been able to get off a couple of shots before he was out of range. The dust kicked up from the guy's dirt bike obscured him, but in the split-second glimpse Cole got of him, he'd been able to see a man about six feet tall, with long, black stringy hair. Not a hell of a lot to go on.

The shooter had been waiting for him. The small pop he'd heard underneath the vehicle must've been a device that disabled the brakes and the steering column. Apparently he hadn't been sure his first attempt would work, so he'd had a plan B.

The sound of a vehicle approaching brought his gaze away from the totaled SUV at the bottom of the ravine. Cole dropped behind a small boulder and waited. Damned if he'd give the bastard another chance at him.

At the sight of Ethan's grim face, Cole expelled a sigh and headed toward the vehicle. The truck rolled to a stop; Ethan opened the door and jumped out. He gave Cole a sweeping glance, then went to the edge of the drop-off and looked down at the wrecked Jeep. He turned around and asked, "You piss somebody off?"

Cole shrugged and then winced slightly. "Apparently."

"You okay?"

"Yeah." He looked down at his ripped clothes. "Couple of bruises and a lot of dirt."

"What happened?"

"Brakes failed. Steering locked up."

"Sabotage?"

"That'd be my guess, since the second I jumped out, somebody took a shot at me."

Ethan gazed around with more interest. "Damn, you did piss somebody off. Got any ideas?"

"Not yet." He opened the passenger door and eased inside, ignoring his bruised hip and shoulder.

Ethan got in beside him. "You need to go anywhere else?"

Meaning did he have injuries that needed tending.

"No. I want to get Keeley and Hannah out of the house as soon as possible. The search team will be there in a couple of hours. I'd just as soon Hannah not see strange people going through her house. She's been through enough already."

"What about your Jeep?"

"I've already called a mechanic I know here. He'll tow it to his shop. If he can't confirm what happened to the brakes, I'll ask Honor to have her people take a look."

"Safe house is set; just waiting for us to arrive."

Cole nodded, grateful that Ethan and Shea were here to assist. Since Keeley and Hannah's safety was his primary concern now, the more help he had from LCR, the better.

Targeting him had upped the stakes. Someone wanted him out of the way; he didn't have to question why. If the house had bugs, any kisses or conversation would have been picked up. Whoever was behind this knew

Keeley had become more than a client to him. And apparently they didn't approve.

Anxiety streamed through Keeley as she stood at the front door and waited for Cole. She'd talked to him on the phone only moments ago, and he'd assured her he was fine. Until she saw him in person, though, she wouldn't be able to relax. He hadn't said, but the grimness in his tone gave her a hint of what might have happened. Someone had tried to hurt or kill Cole. And it was because of her.

The horror that someone hated her that much was almost more than she could bear. Was she destined to lose everyone she had? Should she tell Jenna and Miranda to stay away from her?

The instant she spotted Ethan's black truck, she pressed a button on the wall to open the gate. Normally the numbers were keyed in at the gate entrance, but Keeley couldn't wait for that. She had to see Cole as soon as possible.

Before the truck could roll to a stop in front of the house, Keeley was out the door and running toward the passenger side. Cole opened the door and she let out a little cry. The left side of his face was scraped and his khaki pants and light blue shirt were torn and filthy.

She raised a trembling hand to his bleeding cheek and whispered, "I'm so sorry."

Instead of answering her, he gave Ethan a hard look. "Find Shea and Hannah. I'll be there in a minute."

Giving a sharp nod, Ethan ran up the steps to the house.

Before she could say anything, Cole grasped her shoulders and said, "Do not ever think this is your fault, Keeley. You understand me?"

Tears blurring her vision, she nodded. "I can't bear the thought of anyone else getting hurt."

He pulled her forward and pressed a kiss to her forehead. "He's making mistakes and he's getting desperate. That means we're getting closer than he'd like."

"Close how? We still know nothing."

He shrugged and then winced as if in pain. A fresh wave of guilt washed over her. Here she was letting him reassure and comfort her and he'd almost been killed.

"Are you sure you don't need to go to the hospital?"

"I'm fine."

"Let me at least get some antiseptic and Band-Aids for your face."

"Where's Hannah?"

"She and Shea are in the playroom." She smiled faintly. "I think they're both taking a nap."

As if his mind were a thousand miles away, his eyes were distant as he nodded slowly. "Go get the bandages and stuff . . . meet me in the girls' bedroom. Okay?"

Even though she thought it was a bit odd to take care of his injuries in the girls' bedroom, Keeley didn't question him. Something told her that no matter what it was, Cole always had a purpose and a reason. One of the many things she admired about him.

Cole pushed open the door to the children's bedroom. He went to the middle of the room and stood. It was large and open; most of the toys were kept in the playroom except for a few favorites. Two twin beds, about five feet apart, were against a large wall, with a giant double window between them. Two large dressers, one on either side of the room, were bare with the exception of a few dolls. There was a desk, a tall bookcase filled with books and various stuffed animals, a small sofa and chair, and a long, narrow shelf that held an antique doll collection. And there was enormous potential for a hidden camera.

Cole went to work.

Barely five minutes later, he found it. A giant stuffed monkey tucked up on the top shelf of the bookcase. Out of reach from little hands, it had probably been considered a safe place to hide a camera. He'd taken down each animal individually and examined them closely. So far, this one was the only one he'd found. If there were more, the team coming in would find them.

In the meantime, Cole couldn't resist relaying a message to the bastard. He placed the monkey back on the shelf and looked into its eyes. "I'm coming for you. You're going to pay for what you've done. If you're smart, you'll give Hailey back before it's too late."

"Cole, who are you talking to?"

Cole moved away from the toy. He had considered taunting the creep with Keeley tending his cuts, but he couldn't make himself do it. His warning had been enough. He held out his hand to lead her from the room.

Whoever had done this wanted to see Keeley suffer. What better way to do that than to spy on her most private grieving moments? Remembering how she often came in and collapsed on the floor after one of her nightmares made him so livid he could barely function. The bastard had watched it all . . . and enjoyed every single fucking moment.

In the hallway outside the room, he put his fingers on her mouth and whispered softly, "Let's go. Not one word till we're outside."

Her eyes widened briefly, then dulled with acceptance. She dropped the antiseptic and bandages on the hall table and followed him down the stairs and out the door.

They were halfway down the long driveway before he spoke. "Okay, this should be safe."

She wrapped her arms around herself and said, "My house is bugged."

"I found a camera in a stuffed monkey in the girls' room."

He eyes were wide with horror. "The monkey?"

"Where did it come from?"

Her throat worked as she swallowed. "Stephen," she whispered. "He gave it to Hailey on her second birthday. He gave Hannah a stuffed panda . . . she keeps it in the playroom."

That wasn't an answer he expected. Stephen was one of the few people Cole knew for damned sure hadn't taken the girls. Somehow at least one of the toys had ended up with a camera device. Hell, maybe Stephen had set it up to watch the girls. Maybe the camera wasn't even active anymore.

"Do you remember where he got them?"

"No. He would often bring gifts home. I never asked where they came from." She shrugged. "Never had a reason to ask."

Revulsion churned in Keeley's stomach. She had suspected something like this last night, when Cole had asked her to sleep in a guest room with Hannah, but hadn't allowed herself to dwell on it. Now she had to face the horrifying facts. She'd been on display for this person. Her privacy invaded . . . her daughters' privacy invaded. Possibly everything from showering and getting dressed to conversations she'd had were all being watched. Who could be doing this?

"I just don't understand. Why?"

"It goes pretty well with our theory that someone wants to see you suffer. What better way than to see your private pain?"

He was right. If someone hated her enough to take away the most precious people in her life, then they'd definitely want to see her suffer. She'd tried to be brave in front of cameras and her friends, but in private, when no one could see, she'd broken down and sobbed her heart out numerous times.

A horrendous thought hit her. "That's why you're being targeted now. We kissed in the girls' room . . . within view of that camera."

Fascinated, she watched a myriad of powerful emotions flash across his face. She recognized anger and determination. There was more, though. There was heat and desire, too. He was remembering those kisses.

Despite her revulsion at being spied on, she couldn't regret what had taken place. Even if the creep had watched, that moment had been special and she'd be damned if she felt anything but joy.

"He's made several mistakes in the last few days. I'm betting he'll make more."

"Like what?" She swallowed a sob. "Not killing you?"

"That and the fact that he's revealed the camera. Something set him off . . . made him out himself."

The fierce satisfaction she saw in Cole's expression grounded her. He was right. This person had made mistakes; now they needed to figure out how to capitalize on them. Keeley drew in a breath. "What do we do now?"

"We've got experts arriving in about an hour. They'll comb the house and the grounds. Ethan's already got a safe house ready for us. We'll pack a few things and get out."

As much as she didn't like being forced from her own home, Keeley knew she wouldn't be comfortable until every nook and cranny was searched.

"Can the cameras be traced?"

"If we can find the place of purchase, we can find who bought them."

Though he sounded confident, it didn't sound that

easy to her. "Isn't that kind of like a needle in a haystack?"

"Not necessarily. I don't know that much about cameras, but this one looked expensive. And if we find more throughout the house, so much the better. I'd be willing to bet there are only a few places in the state that sell it in quantity."

A slight optimism surged through her. Even though it sickened her to know she'd been spied on for God knows how long, if substantial information was gained from it, she'd be glad about it.

"I'll get Hannah's things together."

"Try to say as little as possible inside. If Hannah asks where you're going, just tell her it's a surprise." He smiled and she knew he was trying to make her feel better. "We'll just pretend this is an adventure. Hannah will love it."

"You're right, she will." She reached up to touched his face that was still bloodied. "We need to get some antiseptic and bandages on you."

"It's just a few scrapes. I'll take care of them while you pack."

She headed back to the house. Cole's voice stopped her.

"The more mistakes he makes, the better our chances. We're getting closer. I promise you."

Gratitude and affection blended with desire and a thousand other emotions she could barely recognize. Unable to stop herself, Keeley came back to him and pressed a soft kiss to his mouth. Numerous words came to mind. Some would embarrass him; others would probably scare the hell out of him. He wouldn't want to hear that she was falling in love with him. So she settled for "I'm glad you're here with me." Lukewarm words, compared to her real feelings, but true nonetheless.

Before he could respond, she whirled around and ran to the house.

Gnawing at her lip as she stared at the screen, she ignored the fact that her red lipstick was probably staining her teeth. Cole Mathison's warning had unnerved her. Not only because he'd found the camera. Dammit, he was supposed to be dead.

Making the decision to get rid of him hadn't been that easy. It'd been a long time since a man had stirred anything in her other than antipathy and disgust. Cole had the looks and the charm to make any woman, no matter how jaded, want a taste of him. But he'd become entirely too important to Keeley . . . which meant he had to go.

Once again the freak of a pervert Wesley had failed. The bastard had become undependable. He'd screwed up the last two jobs she'd given him. Their association had been a long one and he'd done some damn fine work for her. However, every business relationship had to end sometime. Theirs would end with Wesley's death.

Finding the camera wasn't that unexpected. She'd known when she sent the email to Keeley about the elephant jumpsuit that Cole would suspect something. Of course, if he'd been killed, that would've taken the focus off the camera.

She shouldn't have sent the message, but that passionate little love scene she'd witnessed between them had pissed her off. How dare Keeley be getting off when one of her kids was still missing? Especially when she'd been wanting a taste for herself.

Keeley had needed a painful reminder and the email had accomplished that. Too bad it had outed the camera, but what was done was done.

Despite her unease, a little chuckle escaped. Keeley would be racking her brain, trying to figure out how the camera got there. And since Stephen had given the stuffed animals to the girls, there was no way in hell she'd ever figure out where it had really come from.

Just another hard but painful lesson to be learned. Life was like that—full of pain-filled, sometimes devastating surprises. Keeley should know that by now.

twenty-one

The move to the safe house was handled with relative ease. Cole was right. Hannah was excited to be going on an adventure, and had been promised an extra bedtime story when they arrived at their hideaway.

Finding a safe house in a small town should have been impossible. Trust an LCR operative to make it seem easy. Ethan had found a lovely lake house about twenty miles from Fairview. It apparently belonged to an older couple who used it for vacations and family get-togethers. With five bedrooms, including a child's room with cartoon character décor, it was the perfect size.

Tucking her daughter in, Keeley pressed a kiss to her forehead. After two "happily ever after" stories and an hour of mindless television, Hannah's eyelids were drooping with exhaustion.

Double-checking the baby monitor by the bed one last time, Keeley tiptoed out of the room.

Her heart racing, she went to her own room and took a long look in the full-length mirror. She felt like a geeky teen about to ask the captain of the football team for a date. On the ride over here, she'd made a decision. Actually, that wasn't the truth. Days ago, when she'd been picking up a prescription at the drugstore, she'd made an additional purchase that cemented what she'd been thinking about for weeks, since the night Cole had selflessly offered his body to her in comfort.

Hopeless it might be, but she was hoping he might reconsider a relationship.

While packing, she'd thrown that additional purchase into her suitcase. Unfortunately, she hadn't packed anything remotely sexy. Not that she had a lot of sexy clothes or even considered herself the type who could wear sexy clothes. True, the jeans hugged her curves nicely, and leaving the two buttons open at the top of her lavender shirt allowed a hint of cleavage to show.

Thanks to Jenna's gentle urging to eat more and Cole's insistence on running every day, she'd gained a little weight and had a healthier color than she'd had in months. She scrunched her nose at her image. Still she was no sexy siren.

Determined to make the best of what she had to offer, Keeley brushed her teeth and her hair and then applied a small amount of mascara and colorless lip gloss. She stepped back to view the results. As long as Cole was attracted to the somewhat pale plain-Jane type, she had it made.

Tucking the small packet of condoms into her jeans pocket, she grabbed the child monitor she never went without. If Hannah stirred at all, she'd be able to hear. Her chin set with determination, Keeley took a deep breath, steeled her backbone, and marched out the door. Now or never.

As she knocked on his door, she fought the urge to dash back to her room. Before meeting Cole, she'd never come on to a man. This would be the second time she'd asked him to make love to her. No, she was being silly. She wasn't *absolutely* going to ask. If he acted the least bit uninterested, they'd just talk awhile and then she'd leave. And he never had to know that—

The door swung open and all thoughts of any kind of seduction vanished. Cole's expression told her it wasn't a good time to talk, much less anything else.

He held a cellphone to his ear and the icy coldness in his eyes had her backing away. "Sorry to bother you, I can come back later."

Without a word, he grabbed her arm, pulled her into the room, and closed the door.

Keeley stumbled in, astonished. Before she could ask what was going on, he spoke into the phone.

"I'm not that person anymore, DeAnn. I haven't been for a long time."

It was impossible to act as though she couldn't hear the conversation, since the voice on the other end of the line spoke rather loudly. Keeley couldn't understand every word, but from the sound of it, a woman was trying to convince Cole to come home where he belonged.

The tic in his jaw was a good indication that he wasn't happy about the call.

"Look, I'll try to come back for a visit in the next few months. Give Larry my regards. Goodbye."

He closed the phone and kept his back to her for several tense seconds. She watched him rub the back of his neck and suspected that he had a headache.

"Are you okay?"

"Yeah. Sorry about that."

"Was that someone in your family?"

"My mother-in-law. Rather my former mother-in-law. She thinks I should come back to Texas and teach again. Try to get back to my old life."

"You don't agree?"

"No way in hell."

Sensing that he needed to talk, Keeley took a seat in a chair and watched him pace. When it didn't appear he was going to say anything, she asked, "Why did you become a teacher?"

"My parents were teachers. It seemed the most natural thing in the world to follow in their footsteps."

"Do they live in Texas, too?"

"I lost both of them right after Jill and I got married. My dad died of a heart attack, my mom got sick a few weeks later. We thought it was a bad cold. Turned into pneumonia. She was gone before we knew it."

This man had suffered so much loss. First his parents, then his wife and daughter. Keeley hadn't yet been able to ask him about the scars on his back, but something horrific had to have happened—the pain would have been tremendous. Cole's amazing strength astounded her.

"I'm sorry about your parents."

"Thank you."

"How long were you a teacher?"

He dropped into a chair across from her. "Counting my internship in college, about seven years."

"Was your wife a teacher, too?"

"Sort of . . . she was a stay-at-home mom." His mouth twisted in a bitter smile. "Jill's degree was in criminal justice. After college she wanted to go into law enforcement. I convinced her it was too dangerous, too risky. We moved to Dallas so I could teach in a larger school system. That way I could make more money and she could stay at home with Cassidy." His face darkened. "Hell of a note that she ended up getting killed because of my non-dangerous job."

Keeley hurt for him. Life was so damn unfair sometimes.

"Tell me about Cassidy."

She instantly regretted asking. The stark pain she saw in his eyes was a reflection of what she saw in hers each time she looked in the mirror. Only she still had hope. Cole didn't even have that.

Unable to see his pain without doing something to comfort him, Keeley slid from her chair and went to her knees in front of him. "If it's too painful, you don't—"

"Sorry. I should be able to talk about her . . . I need

to be able to talk about her." He took a breath. "What can I say but that she was the light of my life. The light of our lives. She had the kind of young, innocent curiosity that made me want to talk with her for hours. Her favorite thing was story time. She used to make up stories for us and keep us in stitches."

"She sounds like a beautiful child. Do you have pictures of her?"

Cole shook his head. "Not on me. I have some back home in Tampa."

"Tell me about Jill."

"She was funny and smart." He smiled. "Much smarter than me."

"Where did you meet?"

"Grammar school. First grade . . . first day of school. She spilled her milk at lunchtime and I gave her mine. We were best friends from then on. We didn't date until our senior year."

"Why not?"

"I think we were too busy being best friends to see each other as anything else."

"What made the change?"

"She got her heart bruised by a friend of mine. I comforted her, but realized how glad I was that they weren't together anymore. Somehow she saw me differently, too."

"What was she like?"

Cole closed his eyes as he tried to remember the woman he'd forgotten for months while in captivity. He'd seen photographs of her, recalled some events, but the majority of his memories were still sketchy and probably always would be. "She had vibrant auburn hair, green eyes, and a beautiful smile."

"You just described Shea."

Time for a small confession. "Shea's my ex-wife."

"What?"

He chuckled at her astonishment. It felt good to be able to laugh about his stupidity. "Long story short . . . Ethan, Shea, and I were friends. Ethan acted like an ass back then and I was looking for someone to take care of. Ethan broke it off with her and Shea was going through a bad time."

"So Mr. Knight in Shining Armor came in and rescued the damsel in distress?"

"Something like that. We both realized it was a mistake and ended up having it annulled."

"I'll bet that made things slightly awkward between you and Ethan."

Cole winced. That was one memory he'd just as soon not have. Seeing Ethan's hurt had been hard to take, but his acceptance of the marriage had been even harder. The idiot had believed Shea was better off with Cole. " 'Slightly awkward' would be an understatement. Though we did our best to hide it, since we still worked ops together."

"How did Ethan and Shea finally get it right?"

They were headed in a direction best kept for another day. After his conversation with his former mother-in-law, Keeley's warmhearted compassion had already made him share things he hadn't thought of or talked about in years. Telling her anything more would lead to an area he couldn't yet discuss.

He shrugged and gave a vague answer, hoping she'd let it go. "They both came to their senses."

There were questions in her eyes, but she seemed to sense he didn't want to talk about it any longer. There would be a time he'd have to tell her everything. Now wasn't that time.

"How's Hannah?"

She stood and began walking around the room as if

she was suddenly nervous. "Enjoying herself." She laughed. "That kid is amazing. Give her a snack and a few fairy tales and she's content."

"And how are you doing?"

"Feeling violated, on top of everything else. The one place I thought I had some privacy was in my own home. Now to know that whoever this person is planned this so well that they could actually install a camera or cameras to record my pain . . ." She stopped pacing for a second and looked at him. "And it's apparently someone who knew Stephen, too."

And that made him even more suspicious that the two abductions were related in some way. Had the same person who'd commissioned Stephen's abduction also arranged for the children's kidnapping?

"Since the house is so large, we won't know for a couple of days the extent of the bugging. Who has access to your house?"

"Very few people. Everyone who does is someone I'd trust with my life."

"How old is the house?"

"About six years old." Her eyes widened. "Wait. I had a plumbing problem last year. It took almost two weeks for them to get everything fixed. The girls and I stayed with Jenna while they were making repairs. I'm sure there were all sorts of people coming in and out of the house. Any of them could have put in cameras."

Hell, she was right. The list had just grown larger.

"Give me the names of the contractors. If more cameras are found, I'll contact them and see what we can come up with."

She nodded and then dropped down onto the bed. Everything inside Cole went still except for the one body part that went on high alert anytime Keeley was near. Did she realize where she was sitting? He'd been dying to get her back in bed for weeks. Now that's where she was and it was taking all of his considerable willpower not to join her.

"Cole, do you find me attractive?"

He almost glared at her. What the hell did she think the rigid bulge in his pants meant? And what did she think the incredible sexual encounter they'd had in her bedroom was all about? Not to mention all those kisses they'd shared, orgasm included. Did she think he reacted that way to just anybody? Hell yeah, he found her attractive . . . more than just attractive. But there wasn't a damn thing he could do about it.

He could have told her that and a whole lot more. Instead he said simply, "Yes."

She wrapped her arms around herself in a defensive, self-conscious movement. "I didn't date in school. . . . Stephen is the only man I've ever been with, until you." A blush, bright red and almost painful to look at, covered her face. She was obviously embarrassed by what she was saying, but for some reason she forged on. "But he didn't . . . I rarely . . ." She swallowed convulsively. "I guess what I'm trying to say—and very badly at that—is—until you—until we—that night we—I've never really enjoyed—" She broke off, unable to finish.

Holy hell, what was he supposed to do now? He wanted this woman with every fiber of his being, and from what he could tell, she was, in an awkward but incredibly sweet way, telling him she wanted to have sex with him again.

"I know I'm not really the type to attract men in that way, but—"

He jerked at the most ridiculous statement he'd ever heard. "What the hell are you talking about?"

She jumped to her feet. "I'm sorry I brought it up. I'll go now."

Cole moved in front of her to block her exit. No way

could he let her out of this room now. She looked hurt and humiliated.

Unable to keep from touching her, he lightly caressed her arm. "Keeley, you are one of the most beautiful women I've ever known, inside and out. How in hell could you believe that you're not attractive?"

Her eyes glittered with uncertainty. "I'm too big."

"Too big where?"

"I'm too tall, my hips are too wide, and my breasts are too large."

Cole snorted his disgust. "Says who?"

"All sorts of people."

Fury built inside him. "You mean Stephen?"

She shrugged defensively. "Not just Stephen, though he liked to encourage me to run as much as possible since I have a tendency to gain weight if I don't stay active. But guys used to make comments all the time. And the girls were even worse."

"Let me tell you a little something about people, Keeley. Guys for one . . . when they make crude and cruel comments, it usually means one thing: they're attracted but know they don't have a chance in hell. Women . . . it's pure jealousy, nothing more."

"But Stephen—"

"You said yourself that Stephen was a spoiled child in a man's body. He got what he wanted, but didn't know how to appreciate the gift."

"Stephen was constantly encouraging me to lose weight. If I exercise and eat right, I can keep my weight off, but when I got pregnant, I was sick a lot and couldn't work out. I gained weight. Stephen liked my body even less when I was pregnant."

Cole couldn't be glad the bastard was dead, but he could wish him alive so he could beat the shit out of him. How could a man with any kind of intellect at all

think about treating his wife that way? Especially someone as beautiful and special as Keeley?

"He was an idiot. And you deserved someone a whole
lot better."

"Make love to me, Cole."

Aw hell.

She was biting her lower lip in nervousness and he
wanted to join her. More than anything right now, he
wanted to hold this beautiful woman in his arms and
show her how wonderful she was and how she deserved
the very best. But he was the very worst person to even
be around her, much less make love to her.

"I can't."

"Why not?"

"You're vulnerable right now and I won't take advantage of that."

She tried for a teasing grin but he saw the fear in her
face—fear of his rejection. But what choice did he have?

"I'd be taking advantage of you, too. I'm not asking
for promises. But we're attracted to each other. We're
adults. We're both single. And we both have known
loss."

His mouth tilted in amusement. "So basically it'd be
mutual pity sex."

A surprisingly sultry smile replaced the fear as her
expression became one of knowing. Not that it'd take a
genius for her to know he was turned on. The obvious
bulge in his pants sure as hell wasn't his gun.

"Not pity sex. More like spectacular sex between two
people who are very attracted to each other. I haven't
stopped thinking about that night. How wonderful it
was."

Her eyes were filled with desire and vulnerability. It
had taken a lot of courage for her to make this offer.
And in that moment, all the reasons he shouldn't be

with this beautiful woman vanished. With a low growl of need, Cole pulled her into his arms.

Inches from her mouth, he stopped. If he was going to do this, then he'd damn well do it right this time. His eyes holding hers, he lowered his mouth to her luscious lips and feathered a soft, slow kiss. Relearning her textures, her flavors. She tasted better than he remembered, better than he had dreamed.

With a soft, sweet moan, she opened her mouth and Cole lost his sanity. He plunged in. He went harder, was ready for her in an instant . . . wanted to push her back on the bed, strip her clothes off, and taste every sweet, curvy inch of her.

Their hands seemed to want to be everywhere at once. She pulled at the buttons on his shirt as his hands glided down her body and went under her shirt. The second his fingers touched soft, silky flesh, he pulled away. This he needed to see to experience. He opened each button slowly, then slid her shirt off and dropped it on the floor. The catch in his breath wasn't something he could control. Her white lace bra covered her breasts with an old-fashioned modesty. His hands literally shaking, he unhooked the front clasp and uncovered beauty.

He swallowed hard. "Keeley, you're perfect." The words sounded as if they were torn from his lungs.

"Really?"

Aroused to the point of explosion, he still recognized the insecurity and wonder in her question. And despite the desire hammering at him to get her naked and himself inside her as soon as possible, Cole took the heat down a notch. Their experience before, though hot and wild, had been about comfort. Tonight was different. Tonight he would savor.

This beautiful woman had never known the touch of a real lover. A man who could and would appreciate and cherish every sigh she gave and every peak she reached. If he did nothing else for Keeley tonight, she would leave this room assured that she was a beautiful, desirable woman.

Pulling away, he turned her gently around to face the full-length mirror attached to the door.

Her eyes wide with fear, she stiffened and tried to pull away from him. "Cole. No."

His arms locked around her, he held her still and pressed a kiss to her soft, silky bare shoulder. "Yes, sweetheart. I'm going to show you what I see when I look at you."

Ignoring the trepidation in her expressive face wasn't easy, but he had to give this woman the knowledge of what she did to him. Probably did to just about every man who came in contact with her.

Pulling her bra off her shoulders, he let it fall to the floor. His hands cupped her breasts, the generous mounds almost overflowing his big hands. His eyes on the beauty in front of him, he leaned down and whispered in her ear. "Do you know what I see when I look at your beautiful breasts?"

She shook her head.

"Art in its purest form." He rubbed his thumbs against her nipples and delighted in her gasping sigh. "Sweetheart, your breasts are beautiful." He pinched the nipples lightly and enjoyed another gasping sigh. "My mouth waters from wanting to taste them, lick them, suck them."

Her eyes fluttered closed.

"Open your eyes, Keeley. See the beauty I see."

She opened her eyes again and he watched her expressive face as his hands left her breasts and drifted lower. Her warm skin felt soft, firm, resilient under his gliding hands. Encircling her waist, he gently bit the lobe of her ear and growled, "Unzip your jeans."

Her eyes locked on his in the mirror, she obeyed him.

"Now slide them down those gorgeous legs."

Again she obeyed, allowing the pants to drop to the floor. He almost lost it when he saw the white cotton briefs she wore. Just like most of her clothing, there was nothing remotely sexy about the garment, but on Keeley, it suddenly became wet-dream lingerie.

His hands slid over her hips, caressed the silky soft skin at her thighs. "Your legs are perfect, too. Long and beautifully shaped. I love how your sleek muscles ripple when you move." He bit her ear again. "Do you know how often I've fantasized about having those legs wrapped around me again?"

"Really?"

"Oh, sweetheart, you have no idea how badly I want you. You're a fantasy woman . . . the kind that men dream about but know they can never have."

"You can have me."

The shaky, breathy confession almost undid him then and there. "Thank you, Keeley."

More than anything, he wanted to strip off her briefs, lay her on the floor, and plunge into her. But this moment was too important. The fact that she'd gone for so long not knowing how incredibly sexy she was seemed almost impossible. But he'd seen the evidence in her expression. She was totally unaware of her innate sensuality. The way she walked, moved . . . even her slow smiles made him think of sex with her.

Desire strumming hard, Cole took a ragged breath and allowed his hands to glide up and down her luscious curves several times, loving the way her eyes followed his movements. He stopped at her briefs and hooked his fingers into the cloth, taking them down as he continued down her legs. They dropped to the floor, on top of her jeans.

"Step out of them."

As if her legs were weak, Keeley took a small

stumbling step. Cole's arms held her as she moved away from the clothes, her last barrier against him. Knowing what he would see when he looked back in the mirror didn't prepare him for the reality. She was a goddess. An olive-skinned, exotic beauty from the top of her silky head to the bottom of her long, narrow feet.

She needed to hear the words as much as he needed to say them. "Look at yourself, Keeley, and never, ever, doubt your beauty again."

"I feel beautiful in your arms."

His eyes on her face, he gauged her reaction as his hands moved over her, stroking. Dark brown nipples, peaked in arousal, hardened even more, and Cole knew he wouldn't be able to hold out much longer from tasting her. His control in serious peril, he continued to caress as he expressed his thoughts.

"Watch my hands glide over you . . . you're softer than satin. Soon, very soon, I want to taste every inch of that sweet, silky skin."

Watching her eyes follow his hands as they glided up and down her lush curves was one of the sexiest turn-ons he'd ever had. A pretty flush of pink covered her entire body, tiny breaths panted from her, and the glaze in her eyes told him she was finding pleasure in watching.

"Have you ever watched yourself come?"

"What?"

The startled surprise in her expression told him no. He wanted to give that to her, too. Not only to see herself as the beautiful, sexy woman she was, but also to help her see she could explore her sexuality with him. He wanted her to feel safe and secure in his arms and with herself.

"Will you do that for me? Come for me . . . here, in front of the mirror? Watch yourself fall apart in my arms?"

A bright red flush covered her face. "Cole, I don't know . . ."

"Trust me, sweetheart." His conscience reared its ugly head at that comment. Hell, when she found out what he was keeping from her, would she ever trust anyone again? He'd been stupid for starting this, but damned if he would stop it. When she found out, he'd make sure she realized that in this he was telling the truth.

One of his hands glided to her breasts and caressed firmly, the other slid to the short ebony curls at the apex of her thighs. Her body trembled as her eyes followed his hand to her sex.

"Open for me."

His breath hitched as she parted her legs. Cole's hand shook as he placed it on her sex and felt the heat. He inhaled deeply, searching for control; the scent of her arousal almost pushed him over the top. As his fingers parted the soft folds, he groaned as heated moisture coated his fingertips. She was already throbbing, close, on edge.

"Let go for me, sweetheart. Watch me pleasure you."

Delving his fingers deeper, Cole had to close his eyes for a second as he slid inside and felt her inner muscles clenching, drawing him in.

"So hot and ready for me." He pressed a firm finger against the hard kernel of nerves at the top of her sex and groaned when she gasped and moved with sensuous grace against his finger. "That's it, Keeley. Feel me inside you. Think about how I'm going to fill you."

"Cole . . . I don't . . . Oh . . ." She gave a low, sexy moan and began a dance of sheer beauty. His finger delving deeper, Cole watched her face, saw the flush of deep arousal as her dark eyes went black with heat.

Sliding two fingers inside her, his other hand cupping her right breast, he took her nipple between his finger and thumb and pinched gently. The answering throb inside her sex had him plunging deeper. Tension filled her body as she began a wilder dance.

Locking his eyes with hers, he plunged and retreated over and over. Her eyes went wide with shock, her mouth opened on a long, low moan as she shuddered and came against his fingers.

He let her ride for several more seconds, loving how she clenched and spasmed; imagined how she'd feel against his cock. When she gave one last shuddering sigh, he asked, "Do you want me, Keeley?"

Her eyes half closed, she moved her head in a languid nod. "More than ever."

Clenching his jaw for control, he pulled his fingers from her hot moist core, turned her around, and covered her mouth with his, plunging and thrusting, devouring.

Keeley wrapped her arms around Cole's neck and pressed against him. Though she was nude and he was fully clothed, it didn't bother her in the least. This was Cole, and anything and everything they did together was perfect. What she'd just experienced with him was unlike anything she had ever dreamed, or fantasized about. . . . She wanted, needed to experience everything. But only with this man.

Cole pulled away slightly, fire glinting in his eyes as they roamed over her body. "I want to be inside you so badly, I can't wait any longer."

"Don't wait. I feel like it's been a lifetime already."

Letting her go, Cole began to strip. Keeley helped him as much as she could, but had to stop several times to caress the hard silk of his skin. When his shirt landed on the floor, her fingers roamed over him, loving the furred mat of hair that covered his chest and tapered down to his hard, flat stomach and then to his groin. Before he could unzip his pants, her hand slid beneath his waistband, searching for the hard masculine length that could give such pleasure. Throbbing began anew between her legs as she remembered how it felt to have that hard length coming inside her.

Cole pushed her gently away and growled, "Let me get out of these clothes."

A hot flush of heat swept through her as she anticipated seeing him nude for the first time. Her legs shaky, Keeley backed up until she felt the bed at the back of her legs. She dropped onto it and watched Cole strip down to his briefs. If she'd thought him beautiful before, she now amended that to magnificent. Only in her deepest, wildest fantasies had she ever imagined a man who looked like Cole Mathison.

"Lay back, sweetheart."

Keeley lay down and watched as Cole walked slowly toward her. She was surprised when he stopped suddenly, his face a blend of hot desire and a touching uncertainty. "I don't have any protection. We took a big chance before, but I—"

"Check the pocket of my jeans."

The smile on his face almost distracted her from watching his incredible body move as he stooped down to pick up her jeans. Muscles rippled and flexed and it was all Keeley could do to sit still and not go to him. She literally could not stop staring. If ever there was a physically perfect man, it had to be Cole Mathison.

Her heartbeat went into overdrive when he pulled down his last piece of clothing, his underwear, and Keeley saw him for the first time. She hadn't thought he could turn her on any more than she already was. But seeing him fully nude, fully erect, and to know that desire was for her . . . she swallowed a groan as he slid a condom over his long, hard length.

Her entire body throbbing with arousal as Cole approached her, Keeley scooted up farther on the bed to give him room. Instead of joining her, he dropped to his

knees beside the bed and growled, "Come here."
Grabbing her legs, he pulled her toward him. Before she
could fathom his intent, his mouth was on her, his
tongue in her. She clapped her hand over her mouth to
muffle her screams as she zoomed toward full climax
again in seconds.

Before she had recovered her breath, Cole loomed
over her. His face tender and aroused at the same time,
he asked again, "Are you sure?"

Pulling him down to her, she whispered against his
mouth, "Yes."

And then he was inside her, moving, thrusting. Her
legs wrapped around his waist, Keeley rose up to meet
every thrust, glorying in the overwhelming and unbelievable pleasure he was giving her. Eyes closed, she let
her mind accept what her heart had known for days.
She was in love with Cole Mathison. For the first time
in her life, she was truly and completely in love.

twenty-two

The night was quiet and peaceful . . . the aftermath of not only incredible physical pleasure, but an intimate exploration of her sexuality. Her body, though limp with exhaustion, felt reborn, renewed.

The baby monitor she'd placed on the bedside table transmitted the sweet sounds of Hannah's deep, even breaths of sleep. And for just those few precious moments, despite the pain she continued to feel for Hailey, Keeley felt a small measure of tranquillity.

Cole had switched off the ceiling light, and the small glow from the bedside lamp revealed his expression of relaxed contentment. She had never seen him look so at ease. He held her tight in his arms as her hands glided over his shoulder, then his back. Tears pooled in her eyes as she felt the scars beneath her fingers.

"How did it happen?"

He didn't pretend not to know what she was talking about. Releasing her, he rolled over onto his back. "On an op with Shea and Ethan. I had my mind on something else and screwed up . . . ended up getting captured."

The words were so calm, sounded simple. The experience had to have been horrifying and the pain immense. She swallowed back the emotion and asked, "What did they do to you?"

He gave a hollow laugh. "Whatever the hell they wanted. Drugs, beatings, torture."

"But why?"

"Because they could."

"How long?"

"Almost a year."

Dear God, a year! Her heart bled for him. "How did you get away?"

"Shea and Ethan rescued me."

Wrapping her arms around him, she pressed the side of her face against his chest; his heartbeat, a strong, steady thud in her ear, was a gift. "Thank God they did. Did the person who did this . . . were they caught?"

"I killed him."

She wanted to say "Good," because for the first time in her life, she was glad that someone was dead. Whoever had done this deserved death. However, the pain in Cole's voice made her think he somehow regretted killing him.

"You sound sad."

He breathed out a long, low sigh. "Not sad that he's dead . . . and not even sad that I was the one to do it." He stopped for a second and then added softly, "But killing should never be easy, no matter how much the bastard deserved it."

"I'm sorry you went through something like that."

"Keeley, there's something you—"

She climbed on top of him. "Shh." Her mouth feathered down his face, pressing soft little kisses.

With a groan, he grabbed her ass and kneaded it, pressing her against him. Keeley straddled his hips and took him inside; Cole grabbed her hips and pushed deeper.

She sat up and gasped at the incredible fullness. Her eyes closed as she began a slow, steady ride.

"Look at me, sweetheart."

She looked down and watched Cole's eyes deepen to a dark ocean blue. His hands moved her hips, up and down, giving her a quicker rhythm. A gasp of need had her leaning forward to lie over him.

He caught her shoulders before she reached him. "I can't believe I haven't even tasted you yet."

She jerked, the growling words startling her, and then gasped as he pulsed within her. Her eyes fluttering closed for a second, she opened them to see his gaze focused on her breasts.

"Can I?" he asked softly.

Desire strumming so wildly she could barely function, she answered him in the only way she could. Holding her left breast in her hand, she brought it to his mouth and watched as his lips closed over her nipple. His tongue lashed across the sensitive bud and she shivered at the sensation. And then he opened his mouth wider, took her deeper, and began a strong suckle. Keeley cried out at the incredible sensation of his hot mouth drawing on her. An answering throb deep within her had her moving up and down on his hard length.

Cole pulled his mouth from her breast and whispered, "Now give me the other one."

Her hands shaking with need, she took her right breast and held it to his mouth. Cole opened and the sheer eroticism of placing her nipple on his tongue almost sent her over the edge. And when his mouth closed over her and sucked hard, she arched her back and groaned his name, pleading with him.

Climax slammed through her so fast and hard, she caught her breath on a gasping scream. As her womb throbbed, Cole sucked at her nipple harder; lightning flashed . . . exploded behind her eyes, in her body, and once again Keeley came apart in his arms.

Returning to earth, she opened her eyes to see Cole's expression fierce, almost feral with need. He seemed to be asking her a question. Though not sure what the question was, she trusted this man above all others.

Whatever he wanted, whatever he needed, if it was hers to give, he could have it all. She nodded her head and then, in case he didn't understand, she said softly, "Anything."

With a low, deep growl, Cole rolled her to her back, spread her legs wide, and plunged deep, pistoning into her over and over.

Keeley held on tight, glorying in giving not only her body but also her heart to this remarkable, wonderful man.

Cole woke on a strangling nightmare. Jerking awake, his heart pounding with panic, he searched the room for a threat. Dawn was breaking, lighting the room to give him just enough vision to see there was nothing wrong. The room was calm and serene; the woman beside him deeply asleep.

Pulling away slightly, Cole gazed down at the beauty of Keeley. She had given him her body in the sweetest, sexiest way he could imagine—an irresistible combination of innocent wonder and earthy sensuality. Watching Keeley explore her own sexuality had been an exercise in self-control and patience. Explosion had been imminent at the first touch, but as she'd watched him in the mirror, those dark, beautiful eyes heated with desire, he'd come as close as he'd ever been to losing control.

He sighed as he settled his head back onto the pillow and tightened his arms around her. A multitude of emotions writhed through him, but not one of them was regret. No matter what happened in the future with him and Keeley, their lovemaking last night was not something he could ever be sorry about.

He'd come to Fairview to help find two little girls, not fall in love with their mother. There were a dozen reasons why their relationship was wrong. He was six years older—not a lot of years, but in many ways, Cole felt ancient . . . way too old and damaged to have fallen in love with such an innocent. He'd seen and experienced things few people had—evil, hideous things. Keeley was a small-town girl, with small-town values and a tender, generous heart. And Cole often wondered if the beatings, torture, and drugs he'd endured had demolished everything good in him. What did he have to offer her but a scarred body and a severely hardened heart?

What did he and Keeley have in common other than the fierce determination to find her children and a burning desire for each other?

Keeley made a soft moaning little sound in her sleep. A sound that should turn him on . . . and it did, but it also clutched at his heart. Whether it was right or wrong, whether they had anything in common or not, and whether she would understand when he told her the truth, he didn't know. All he knew was that for this moment in time, with this beautiful, sensuous woman, he'd found a contentment he never thought to feel again.

Gathering her in his arms, he held her close and allowed himself this happiness. How long it would last, he didn't know, but for right now, Cole had found peace.

Wesley picked up his ringing cellphone. "Yeah?" He made his tone belligerent and challenging. Damned if he'd cower to the bitch.

"Cole Mathison is not dead."

Hell, he'd done his best; no way would he apologize. And he sure wasn't going to admit it to her, but the guy had scared the shit out of him. What kind of man reacted to almost being killed the way Cole Mathison had?

When he'd seen Mathison jump out of his Jeep, Wes had known he'd failed. So he'd panicked and shot at him. Any other man would have taken cover or run. But what'd the giant do? He'd rolled to his feet, pulled his gun, and shot back. Hell, Wes had no experience with that kind of man. Anybody he'd ever tried to kill, he'd always succeeded. And they sure as hell had never fought back. Was it Wesley's fault that the guy was hard to kill?

Not that she needed to know that; her opinion didn't matter, but he still had his pride. "So what?"

" 'So what?' That's all you can say?" she screeched. "I hired you to do a job. You failed."

"I ain't asking for the money. Big damn deal that he ain't dead."

"You know he's screwing her, don't you?"

That got his attention. "Why didn't you tell me that?" Damn, he might've tried even harder if he'd known the bastard was getting for free what Wes had been working so hard for.

The exasperated huff that came through the phone line pissed him off and sealed her fate. He was tired of her bitchy, arrogant attitude . . . always acting as if she was better than him.

"Would that have made a difference?" she asked.

"It don't matter. Once I have her, she'll forget all about him."

"You didn't do the job. There's no need for me—"

"Don't you even think about backing out. If Mathison ain't dead, that's your problem, not mine. Killing him has no bearing on me getting the woman. Now, either deliver her to me or I'll be telling the entire town exactly who hates Keeley Fairchild so bad she had her children kidnapped and sold."

He could almost hear her teeth grinding together. Finally she snapped, "All right, fine."

"Good."

"She almost never leaves the house anymore. And she's got one of those LCR guys with her when she does."

"Ain't my problem. Don't tell me about the labor pains . . . just give me the baby. No, wait, I already got her babies." He couldn't hold back the laughter from his little quip. When she didn't join in, he snarled, "You better make sure those men aren't with her or I'll blow them to hell, along with the woman, and then I'll come looking for you."

"I'll call you as soon as I know something. Do you have what you need?"

Rubbing his crotch, he laughed. "Baby, you know better than anybody that I got everything I need and more."

"Not that, moron. Are you going to do her there or take her somewhere else?"

"Why?" Then comprehension hit. "You want to watch, don't you?"

"Of course not. I just want to make sure you keep your end of the bargain. Once you're through with her, you have to let her go."

She was lying. He heard the excitement in her voice. Damn, he wished again that the bitch wasn't such a bitch. They had so much in common.

"I'll do her at my cabin. I can arrange a little hiding place for you. You'll be able to watch the show and she'll never know you're there."

"And no killing. Right?"

"Baby, I ain't ever killed anyone I screwed. At least not yet." He let the threat hang in the air. She knew if she betrayed him again, he'd do more than kill her. Before he finished with her, she'd be begging to die.

Her tone a little more wary, she said, "How long are you going to keep her?"

"Till I get my fill."

"Unless you want the FBI back on your ass, you'd better be happy with no more than a few hours."

She didn't need to know he had a place all ready for Keeley, hundreds of miles away from Fairview. His secluded cabin would be impossible for anyone to find, including the FBI and those LCR people. "I'll just make sure I enjoy myself for the short amount of time I have."

"I'll call you as soon as I make the arrangements."

"I'll be ready for her."

Keeley stood in the giant foyer of her house. Though she'd never loved this house the way Stephen had, it had been home.

Five more cameras had been found, placed strategically throughout the house. The person who had planted them had known exactly which rooms Keeley used the most: the kitchen, her bedroom, her office, the twins' playroom, and the small sitting room at the back of the house. Every one of those rooms had been her haven, a place of total security for her and her children. She felt violated; she was furious. And that fury was directed not only at the unknown sadistic voyeur but also at herself.

How incredibly clueless could one person be? It wasn't so much that this freak had spied on her, though that was bad enough. But her babies . . . they had been exposed, endangered. If she'd been more aware, less trusting, could she have prevented her children from being taken?

She had purchased the most up-to-date security system to protect her home and hadn't even considered that it had already been invaded.

"Don't do this to yourself, Keeley. Don't blame yourself for someone else's perversion."

She whirled around to Cole, who stood at the entrance. "How can I not blame myself? Here I was, living in this house, thinking my family was protected, and apparently we've been the object of someone's sickness for as long as we've lived in this house."

Cole's expression was a mixture of fury, sadness, and compassion. "We're contacting the builder, along with every contractor that was involved in any of the construction. Someone had to have seen something."

She whirled back around and gazed at what might not have been her dream home, but had been home all the same. Now it would be the place she and Hannah would live until Hailey returned. She had planned to move anyway . . . she wouldn't wait till she sold it. As soon as Hailey was back home, they would be gone.

A warm, hard body pressed against her back, and long, muscular arms wrapped around her. "I know I keep saying this, but it's the truth. We will find this person, Keeley. And we will find Hailey."

Turning in his arms, she gazed up at the man who'd become so important to her. For almost a week, they'd stayed holed up in the safe house. Ethan and Shea had left to go home for a few days, leaving Keeley, Cole, and Hannah together. While Keeley had worked on her laptop, Cole had played games with Hannah. They'd cooked meals together and Cole had taught Keeley how to make the best hamburgers she'd ever eaten. And every single night he had loved her into oblivion.

Standing on her toes, Keeley leaned into him and pressed a soft kiss to the beautiful mouth that had given her such pleasure. "I'm so glad you're here with me. I don't know what I would have done without you."

Cole returned the kiss and then pulled slightly away. "You would have managed. You're a hell of a lot stronger than you give yourself credit for."

Since most of the time she felt like a basket case, she silently disagreed with his assessment. "What are you going to do today?"

His frown one of distaste, he said, "Have lunch with Elizabeth."

"Again?"

"She claims that our last lunch together was interrupted too many times to really talk." He shrugged. "She's the one who allowed all the interruptions. However, she said that Miranda will be joining us. I'm looking forward to getting to know her better."

Keeley shook her head. She knew her friend had nothing to do with any of this, but Cole needed to be convinced.

"I told Mrs. Brackett that I'd come in today and look at some new dresses for Hailey and Hannah. And then Jenna's coming over for a late lunch." She grimaced. "I think finding out where I've been the last few days is number one on her priority list. I hate having to lie to her."

"I know, Keeley, but until this is over, we keep everything within our small circle. Just tell her what we discussed—that I took you and Hannah away for a few days of rest."

She sighed. Even though she understood, it was still difficult holding anything from her best friend. "Okay, I will."

"And make sure you stay with Ethan the entire time you're out, okay?"

She leaned in again and placed a kiss on his stern, stubborn chin. "Will do. And please, you be careful, too. You're as much of a target as I am."

A slow smile, sweet and incredibly sexy at the same time, lifted his perfect lips. She traced the beautiful curve with her finger. "Why are you smiling?"

"I was just thinking how good it feels to have you worry about me." Desire heated his eyes. "I like it."

Wrapping her arms around his neck, she whispered, "Good."

Cole covered her mouth with his, and for just a little while, Keeley blanked out everything but the beauty of what this man could make her feel.

"Thanks for bringing me to town, Ethan. I know you'd rather be back home with Shea."

Ethan grinned. "Are you kidding? I left her in our bedroom reading baby name books. Believe me, I'd rather be just about anywhere else. That woman has changed the baby's name at least twenty times in the last twenty-four hours, and we still don't know if it's a boy or a girl."

Keeley laughed, remembering how she'd agonized over the very same thing. Choosing your child's name was an important decision.

She pushed open the door to Mrs. Brackett's children's store.

"Miss Keeley, how are you?"

Keeley hugged the fragile, elderly woman. She was one of the few older townspeople who wasn't afraid of Elizabeth Fairchild's wrath and had been kind to Keeley from the moment they met.

"I'm doing fine, Mrs. Brackett." She pulled away and nodded toward Ethan. "This is a friend of mine, Ethan Bishop. Ethan, this is Cindy Brackett, one of the sweetest ladies ever born."

The white-haired, pale-cheeked Mrs. Brackett blushed like a schoolgirl as she shook Ethan's hand.

"I'm going to look around a few minutes." Keeley winked at Ethan. "If you really want to see Shea's eyes light up, why don't you take a look at those newborn clothes over on the far wall."

The delighted look on his face tugged at her heart. This giant of a man was thrilled that he would soon be a father. She watched as he walked away, making sure he was headed in the right direction. Then, turning to Mrs. Brackett, she said, "You found some things for me?"

"Yes, I just got a new shipment of dresses in last week. They're the sweetest things." She headed to the back room. "I put a few away for you to take a look at. I'll go get them for you."

Keeley spotted a giant stuffed pink poodle she couldn't resist. And then, unable to stop herself, she pulled down a stuffed monkey the same size. Her eyes blurred as she looked down at the goofy face on the stuffed animal. Hailey adored monkeys. They'd had to destroy the one with the camera; this one would be a good replacement.

Mrs. Brackett's voice came from the back room. "Keeley, can you come back here, please?"

Putting the animals aside to pick up before she left, she walked through the door into the stockroom. Boxes were neatly stacked on shelves, and clothing hung from every available hanging space. Keeley glanced around, not seeing Mrs. Brackett. "I'm here, where are—"

A hard arm wrapped around her from behind and a cloth covered her face. She tried to open her mouth to scream and inhaled a sweet, sickly scent and everything went dark.

twenty-three

"I'm afraid Mrs. Fairchild is indisposed and has to cancel the luncheon," Patrick said.

Cole stood at the door of the Fairchild mansion, surprised that Elizabeth had broken protocol. Not notifying him that the lunch was canceled until he arrived seemed like the complete opposite of the proper decorum she required from everyone else.

"Why wasn't I notified?"

"Mrs. Fairchild took ill suddenly . . . a migraine. She asked me to call you at Mrs. Stephen Fairchild's residence. Which I did, but you had already left."

"Perhaps I could visit with Miranda then."

"Miss Miranda informed me she has another appointment."

"I see. Then please tell Elizabeth I hope she feels better."

Patrick's sour face never changed its expression as he nodded and closed the door, leaving Cole on the porch.

As he headed back to his vehicle, his mind whirled. Was Elizabeth faking an illness? If so, why? And Miranda . . . if she was supposed to join them for lunch, why had she made other plans?

A movement out of the corner of his eye caught Cole's attention. He turned to see Miranda coming out of a side door. Purse and keys in hand, she was apparently headed to the "other appointment" she'd made.

Cole called out to her, "Miranda."

Her entire body jerked as she whirled around. "Cole."

"Sorry to hear about our lunch plans being canceled."

Her expression indicated she wasn't thrilled to see him, making him all the more determined to talk to her.

"Even though your mother can't join us, why don't we go grab a bite somewhere?"

"I can't . . . I . . ." She cast a longing look at her little silver BMW parked at the side driveway. "When Mother told me she was canceling, I made plans with someone else."

Her excuse would have been more believable if she didn't look as though she was dressed for a hike in the woods. She wore a pair of faded jeans, a ragged T-shirt, and sneakers. Whoever it was that she was meeting, she apparently wasn't trying to impress him or her.

"Where you headed?"

"I . . . uh . . . lunch with a friend."

"Mind if I join you?"

She shot an uneasy glance at the house and then back at him. "It's kind of a date."

"Must be pretty casual." He gave her body an up-and-down look. Yeah, kind of insulting, but he was hoping to piss her off. It worked.

Her spine straightened. "I'm not sure what you're insinuating but I don't like your tone."

"Your mother says you go out quite a bit at night. Seems kind of rotten of you to leave your little girl home alone."

Tears filled her eyes and Cole felt like he'd just kicked a sick kitten.

"Maggie is my number one priority."

"How can she be your number one priority when you leave her alone with your mother?"

"Not that it's any of your business, but my mother has very little contact with Maggie."

In his experience, making people angry was one of the best ways to get them to say something they never planned. Ignoring the tears sparkling in her eyes, Cole went for the kill. "Seems like getting rid of Keeley's daughters would be a great way to get you some money and perhaps torture a woman who got your family's money."

Her eyes widened with shock. "My God, are you crazy?"

"Did you?"

Cole finally got the fury he'd been angling for. Her pale cheeks bloomed with color. "For the record, no, I did not have anything to do with their disappearance. No, I do not resent Keeley for having more money than me. And it's none of your fucking business where I go or what I do. Is that clear?"

A smile twitched at his mouth. At last he'd gotten some truth from her. He backed away and said, "Have a nice lunch."

As he slid behind the steering wheel, he could feel her eyes on him. He made his way down the long drive and knew she stood and watched him. Turning onto the main road toward town, Cole drove for a few yards, then pulled over onto a dirt road. He could see the Fairchild entrance from here. Almost convinced that Miranda had nothing to do with the abductions, Cole had to make sure. Following Miranda should give him an idea of what secrets she was keeping.

He saw her little BMW peek out from the drive, then turn left, shooting away from town. Cole waited a few seconds, allowing three other vehicles to pass by, then he pulled out to follow her. With three cars between them, he should be safe from her spotting him.

Miranda was definitely hiding something. If it had nothing to do with Keeley and her children, it was none of his business. But until he was sure it didn't, in his eyes, she was still suspect.

Elizabeth, on the other hand, continued to be at the top of his list. Nothing he could prove yet, but based on her mindless, pompous meanderings, several thoughts and theories were coming together. Very soon he intended to have a private and explicitly frank talk with the woman. She wasn't going to like anything he said.

When his phone vibrated beside him, Cole kept his eyes on the car ahead of him and answered with an absentminded "Yeah?"

"Keeley's gone," Ethan said.

Cole's entire body went into overdrive. "What do you mean, she's gone?"

"I brought her to that children's store. She went back into the stockroom with Mrs. Brackett. When she didn't come out, I went looking for her. I found Mrs. Brackett on the floor. Someone had knocked her out. And Keeley was gone."

Barely glancing in the rearview mirror, Cole made a sharp twist on the steering wheel and made a U-turn to head back to town. "How's Mrs. Brackett?"

"She's got a bump on her head, but said she was fine. Wouldn't let me call an ambulance."

"Did Mrs. Brackett see anything?"

"Said a man held a knife to her neck and told her to call Keeley's name. Next thing she knew, I was helping her up."

"You call the sheriff?"

"Based on what you told me about him, didn't think it'd do any good."

"You're right. Idiots would only get in the way. I'm five minutes away from you."

"I'm sorry, Cole, I should have been more aware."

"Hell, Ethan, she was just a few feet away from you. The bastard's damn cocky. Was Keeley's purse there?"

"No. It was one of those shoulder bags that hangs from your neck and shoulder. She probably still has it on her."

"Good. Hopefully he won't throw it out and we can track her cellphone."

"I'll wait for you here."

Cole closed the phone and shut down every emotion he had. If he allowed himself to think about what the bastard had done with Keeley, he wouldn't be able to do what needed to be done. Once it was over and she was back in his arms, then he would explode.

He had to stay sane. If this was the same creep who'd taken the kids, this might be their best chance to also find Hailey. Just please God let Keeley's cellphone be on so he could track it.

Consciousness returned slowly. She became aware of whispered mutterings, as if there was an argument, which blended with sounds of birds twittering and the buzz of a low-flying plane. Keeley moved her head and groaned at the stab of pain.

"Wakee, wakee, my beauty."

Her eyes flickered as she tried to focus. Something or someone stood over her. She moved slightly; agony exploded in her head. Her blurred vision made out what looked like the back of a car seat. Squinting, she tried to look around without moving. She was lying in the back of a car. Her hands braced against the cushion, she pushed to sit up; nausea surged and a whimper left her mouth.

"Yeah," an unfamiliar male voice said. "That damn stuff always gives you a headache and makes you want to puke. It'll get better."

Dry, rough hands grabbed hold of her arms and pulled. Keeley found herself standing outside. Swaying back and forth, she leaned against the car as she struggled to get her balance. Wavy images appeared in her blurred vision. She rubbed at her eyes, finally able to see a man standing in front of her. Grogginess vanished as fear seeped into her bones. Her eyes roamed the area. Woods surrounded them; a small cabin stood a few yards away.

"Welcome to our little love shack, Keeley."

Her heart almost exploding out of her chest, Keeley forced her fuzzy mind to focus and did her best to not show her fear. Both Shea and Cole had recently taken turns giving her advice on how to protect herself.

Shea had told her that to keep people off guard, act the opposite of the way they would expect you to act. No doubt about it, she should look terrified . . . and she was. She would do her best not to let the creep know it. "Who are you and what am I doing here?" she demanded.

"Aw, Keeley, I'm hurt. Don't you recognize me? We went to school together. And remember, I used to come into the diner where you worked?"

She squinted hard; recognition came in a flash. Yes, she did know him. Wesley something . . . Tuttle? That was it—Wesley Tuttle. He'd even asked her out a few times. She'd always said no . . . thankfully. This creep looked as though he'd done some hard living.

"What do you want?" she asked.

"Just what you refused to give me years ago."

Her eyes shifted left and right, looking for any kind of escape. "You're crazy."

"Crazy like a fox." He gave a sly grin. "Don't you want to know where that little girl of yours is?"

She jerked around and then gasped as his face wavered in front of her. Gritting her teeth, she said, "You know where Hailey is?"

"Maybe." He shrugged. "If you're nice to me, I might just tell you where you can find her."

"How do you know?"

" 'Cause I'm the one who took 'em . . . and sold 'em."

Fear and nausea forgotten, Keeley focused on the man in front of her. He was about the right height. Her gaze went to his arms. A thin, silvery scar lay on the inside of his right hand, just as Hannah had described. He was the one! She pasted a doubtful expression on face. If he thought she didn't believe him, maybe he'd tell her more. "How do I know you're telling the truth?"

The grin grew into an evil smirk, making Keeley want to plant her fist into his face.

"Come on into the house. We'll get comfy and talk." He grabbed her arm and pulled her toward the cabin door. "Let's go get acquainted."

If he got her inside, chances were slim she would get out before she was raped or worse. She had to figure out a way to overpower him, and then she'd make the creep talk.

Using the few skills she'd picked up from Shea, Keeley swung her right fist up, connecting with Wesley's nose, and followed it with a kick to his shin.

Yelping, Wesley swung his arm and slapped her across her face. Keeley felt herself falling and grabbed at Wesley, hoping to do some damage to him on her way down. Her fingernails dug into his skin and she felt a brief triumph when she heard him howl. Then his fist slammed into her jaw and there was darkness.

She woke to a pounding headache and nausea clawing at her stomach like little gremlins. Heavy eyes barely opened; daylight pierced her skull and she closed them quickly.

"Now, now, no going back to sleep again. We got some reacquainting to get done."

Keeley forced her eyes open as memory reemerged. *Wesley. He knew where Hailey was.*

She pulled in a breath to focus. The terror building inside her would do her daughter no good. She had to find out as much as she could. "Where are we?"

"All in good time. Want to sit up now?"

The soothing tone had an oily quality about it, causing the nausea to increase. Keeley tried to sit up as bile rose to her throat. Pain exploded in her arms, stopping her forward progress. Dammit, she was tied to a bed.

"Easy now. I got you harnessed in tight, but I'll loosen the restraints once we get a few things straight."

The bile almost clogging her throat, Keeley swallowed hard and then said, "Who are you?"

"Come on now, Keeley. I didn't hit you that hard, did I? It's Wesley, baby." The overexaggerated petulant tone held amusement. "I've been hot for you for so long and you forgot me all over again? That don't bode well for our future, now does it?"

She glared up at the tall blond man. "Did you really take my daughters?"

As if she hadn't spoken, he said, "Do you remember me asking you for a date, over and over again?" Before she could speak, he continued, "Once that body of yours bloomed, guys were asking you out left and right and you didn't say yes to any of them. I always admired you for being so discriminating. That's the only reason I didn't take you in school. As much as I would have liked to have been the one to pop that cherry of yours, I figured you weren't quite ready for the fun I had in mind."

A cold shudder of revulsion and horror permeated Keeley's being. This man had kidnapped her and planned to rape her? What did that have to do with his taking her babies?

"Dammit, did you take my daughters or not?"

"All in good time, Keeley."

"Why are you doing this?"

That petulant tone came back. "You got a hearing problem or something? I just told you. I've had the hots for you since high school."

"And you thought abducting and selling my children would make me like you more?"

His face loomed over her. "It don't matter whether you like me or not. I just figured it'd be easier for you if we did a little talking first. But if you'd rather get to the good stuff, that's more than fine with me. I've been waiting too long already."

She restrained her fury. If she made him angry, chances were he'd rape her immediately and she'd learn nothing about Hailey.

"No . . . uh . . . let's talk. Uh . . ." She swallowed hard and tried to come up with something. Hard to do when you were terrified. How did you talk to a lunatic?

Apparently he didn't see her lack of conversational skills as a problem. "Let's sit you up and get you more comfortable. We'll catch up." He grinned, revealing perfect white teeth, which seemed oddly incongruent with the face of evil. "Be kind of like foreplay."

She heard him move behind her and then her arms loosened. Determined to make the most out of any opportunity to escape, she shot up straight and then screamed as he yanked her back by her hair.

"Not so fast, baby." He laughed. "But it's good to see you're as eager to get started as I am."

Her head dropped down to where she was lying on the pillow again. He came around to stand in front of her. She took a breath and asked quietly, calmly, "Do you really know where Hailey is?"

"Sure I do . . . I sold both of them." He grinned. "Got fifteen thousand for the dark-haired one and twenty-five for the blond one."

Keeley gritted her teeth; the bastard was bragging

about selling her children. Forcing herself to remain calm, she asked, "Where is she?"

He turned and pulled a chair closer to the bed. Sitting down, he crossed one leg over the other in a casual, friendly way as if he planned to have a normal conversation with her. When he reached out and touched her hair, she jerked away.

"Now, Keeley, you're hurting my feelings, acting as if you aren't pleased to see me."

"Where is my daughter?"

"You got one of them back already, didn't you? That should make you happy."

Torn between sobbing her heart out and screaming obscenities at the freak, Keeley swallowed hard, determined not to lose control.

"My daughter Hailey . . . the blond one, is still missing. Do you know where she is?"

"You sure do have purty eyes."

Bile rushed toward her mouth. Oh, sweet heaven. Was he trying to flirt with her? She closed her eyes briefly. *Concentrate, Keeley!* "Why did you take my children?"

"Do you remember how I used to ask you out when you worked at the diner?"

"Yes."

"You always said no. That stung, but I was okay with it 'cause you didn't go out with nobody else either. Leastways that's what everybody thought. Then what'd you up and do but marry that no-account Stephen Fairchild. That really gnarled my balls, Keeley. I wasn't good enough for you, was I? Or was it I wasn't rich enough?"

Had he had something to do with Stephen's abduction, too? "What do you know about Stephen?"

"I didn't have him nabbed, if that's what you're asking."

"Then why take my daughters?"

"I tried to get you to come with me, too. Ever think what would've happened if you'd just come along peaceful like? You would've been with your kids."

She blinked against the tears. How many times had she asked herself that question? Out loud . . . in her own home. Her eyes flew open. Yes, it made sense that he was the one.

"How did you get the cameras into my house?"

His expression froze for a second and then he let out a loud guffaw. "Damn, now that's funny." He tilted his head and an evil, sickly grin spread slowly across his face. "You give a good show when you're home alone, don't you?"

She clenched her teeth. "How did you do it?"

"Now, that's one secret I ain't going to give up. Let's get back to getting reacquainted."

"Why didn't you ask for ransom money? I would have given you every cent I had."

"I told you, Keeley, it wasn't just money I wanted. Your girls brought in a nice chunk of change and I'd planned for you and me to have some fun. But you got away from me." He rubbed his crotch. "I might've just let them go if you'd given me what I wanted."

"If you've wanted revenge for this long, why did it take you years to come after me and take my girls?"

"You hardly ever left the house and I can't get inside that fort you built. Me and my friend were driving by the park that day and saw you. It was like a dream come true."

"Where did you take them?"

"I sold the dark-haired one to somebody over in Grantham . . . never knew their names." He grinned. "Guess you know 'em better than I do, since you got the kid back from them."

"What about Hailey?"

"Let's just say you'll probably never see her again."

Tears flooded her eyes. Her voice barely audible, she whispered, "You killed her?"

Wesley leaned over her. The hurt in his eyes would have looked almost genuine if it weren't for the smirk. "I think you must be getting the wrong impression of me, Keeley. I don't kill kids." He shrugged. "Dead kid ain't worth nothing,"

She believed the bastard. And that meant Hailey was alive. Despite the horror of what lay ahead, a profound relief gave her an almost euphoric feeling. If Hailey was alive, then she would find her. With Cole's help, she would find her baby.

Cole. He would be looking for her. Ethan probably knew by now that she'd been taken. A horrific thought hit her. "What did you do to Mrs. Brackett?"

"Just gave her a little tap on the head." He leaned forward, his expression one of feigned sincerity. "I ain't really a killer. I mean, yeah, I've done some, but it ain't like I do it on a regular basis."

"Did you try to kill Cole the other day?"

"I made an exception for him. Seems like every time I turn around, you're flaunting men in my face." Hard meanness glinted his eyes. "Bastard escaped."

He talked so casually about kidnapping children and murder. And she had no doubts that this animal intended to rape her. She would fight to the death to prevent that, but if he knew where Hailey was, she needed to keep him talking until Cole could find her. She refused to ask herself how he would even know where to look. It didn't matter. Cole was smart and resourceful. And he would be relentless.

"If you didn't kill Hailey, where is she?"

"She's in another country."

Keeley pulled in several shallow breaths to center herself. Grateful for the first time to know someone like her mother-in-law, she opened her eyes and, in her best Elizabeth Fairchild imitation, demanded, "Let me go right now or you'll spend the rest of your days in jail."

Delight brightened his face, scaring Keeley more than his dark looks. "Damn, girl. I like that bitchy attitude. Shit like that can make for some good rough loving." He rubbed her arm almost gently. "It don't have to hurt bad, Keeley, if you just cooperate a little. Let's just have a little fun, and when I'm through, I'll let you go. Scout's honor. That cheating husband of yours has been dead a long time, and I'll bet that Mathison guy can't give it to you as good as I can."

Keeley shrank as far away from him as she could get. Since she was still tied to the bed, she knew it would do no good. Pulling in the last of her reserves, she swallowed the bile of revulsion and said, "And you promise to tell me where Hailey is?"

The way his eyes lit up told Keeley he honestly believed she was going to let him rape her without a fight. She added *delusional* to his list of evil traits.

Nodding eagerly, he said, "Course I will. Give me a few good screws and I'll tell you everything. I know you're worried sick about her. You give me what I want . . . I'll give you what you want."

The slimy bastard was lying. Well, so could she.

Since she was close to throwing up, there was no way in hell she could act like she wanted him. But if she could hold herself together long enough to get him to believe she'd let him do whatever he wanted, then she could take him off guard. "If you keep your promise to tell me where my daughter is, I'll do whatever you want."

He eased down beside her on the bed. "Oh yeah . . . now, that's the kind of talk I like."

She tugged at the bindings on her wrists. "Do you want me to touch you?"

A hand covered her left breast. Keeley closed her eyes and swallowed a sob. She could do this . . . she had to do this. If Wesley knew where her child was, she would do whatever it took to get him to talk. Though she was able to control the scream building up inside her, she couldn't control the tears that seeped from her eyes.

"Aw, baby, don't cry. I can make it good for you." His voice had turned crooning and raspy.

She tugged at her hands again. "Do you want me to touch you?"

He untied one wrist and placed her hand on his crotch. Keeley swallowed thickly and forced her hand to cup him firmly. Once both hands were free, the bastard would know what real pain meant.

"Oh yeah . . . feels good," he muttered.

Teeth clenched with fury and revulsion, she caressed the hard bulge at his crotch. Her heart almost jumped from her throat as Wesley moved forward and touched her other hand. He was going to untie her!

A cellphone rang. Not hers. Someone was calling him.

With a curse, he rolled away from her and got to his feet. Stomping over to a table, his back to her, he grabbed the phone and snapped, "What do you want?"

Keeley quickly untied her other hand and eased off the bed.

Listening to his remarks, she surmised he was having an argument about some kind of agreement that had gone wrong. She couldn't pay too much attention to it, since her focus was to find a weapon and disable him. Her eyes roamed the filthy, dank room, and her heart jumped when she spotted a flashlight three feet from her on a small table. She reached for it.

A hand pulled at her hair. "Dammit, come back here!"

She screamed and, stretching with all her might, managed to grab hold of the hook hanging from the end of the flashlight with one finger. It wasn't enough to get a good hold on the handle, but she had no choice. Agony ripped through her head as he pulled her backward by her hair. Keeley whirled around and flung the flashlight toward Wesley. Triumph flooded her when she watched it smash into the side of his face.

Blood spurted from his mouth. A feral inhuman growl emerged from his throat and he let go of her hair.

Keeley took a running step toward the door. Wesley leaped onto her back and they both fell. She slammed onto the hard planks of the floor; breath whooshed from her.

"Fucking bitch! You're all alike. I knew I shouldn't've trusted you."

Stunned, unable to move, Keeley heard a rip . . . felt cool air wash over her back. His knee ground between her shoulder blades.

"You want it rough? Then, baby, that's what you're going to get."

Hands closed around her neck. Keeley raised her head and searched for something else. The flashlight . . . it was only inches from her. She could reach it . . . she had to! She stretched out her arm; her finger snagged the hook at the end of the handle. She inched it toward her. The hands around her neck tightened; the knee pressed deeper into her spine. One chance only . . . that's all she would have. Vision dimming, Keeley closed her hand around the long narrow cylinder.

On the edge of unconsciousness, his naked skin touched her bottom. Superhuman desperation giving her impetus, she tightened her hand around the flashlight and swung it hard behind her. A vibrating thud— a direct hit to something hard. She dimly heard a yowling sound and then his body collapsed on top of her.

Keeley jerked his hands from her neck; gasping, she

tried to get air back into her tortured lungs. His body, a dead weight, pinned her down. She lifted up to dislodge him. Wesley moved slightly. She lifted again; he slid off.

Sobbing, she crawled toward the door. *Hang on. Get out of here. Don't lose consciousness.* She had to find help. Her mind muddled, she inched closer and closer to the door. Daylight wavered in front of her . . . *just hang on* . . .

A sharp, agonizing pain speared her head and she knew nothing more.

Disgust filled her as she looked down at Wesley's unconscious body. His pants were unzipped and the head of his penis stuck out. It took every bit of self-control she had not to take a butcher knife and cut off that pathetic appendage he was so damned proud of. Stupid bastard couldn't even rape a woman.

She kicked Wesley in the ribs. He groaned but didn't wake. She kicked harder. "Get up, idiot. They'll be here for her soon."

He blinked. "Uh? Wha . . . ?"

"Those bodyguards of hers will be here any minute. Why didn't you throw her cellphone away? If you don't want to get caught, you'd better damn well get out of here."

He got to his feet and weaved like a sloppy drunk. "The bitch hit me."

"Yeah, she did. And you're going to get your ass kicked for good if you don't get out of here. I'm betting those guys have a GPS on her cellphone. They'll be able to pinpoint her exact location."

"Shit," he mumbled. "Let me get her and let's go."

She almost laughed in his face. That would come later. Right now she had to act as if she had his best interest at heart. "We don't have time for that. They'll be here any minute. If you want to save your ass, you'd better get up and get out of here now."

Blood dripped from Wesley's mouth as he stumbled toward the door. He looked like something from a slasher horror movie, and it was all she could do not to pop the idiot right here, right now.

A soft moan brought her attention to Keeley. Cursing under her breath at the screwup Wesley had once again made, she pulled Keeley's cellphone from the purse she'd taken from Wesley's car and pressed the key to turn it back on. No doubt Mathison had some sort of tracking device. By the time he pinpointed this location, she and Wes would be long gone.

When Keeley realized there was someone close by who knew where her baby girl was, she'd be crazy frantic with the need to find him. How would she react when they found Wesley dead?

A burst of happiness swept through her.

twenty-four

Cole slammed on the brakes in front of a dilapidated, ancient cabin. SIG Sauer in hand, he opened the car door. Ethan exited from the passenger side, his gun at the ready.

Both men went in low, running. Ethan headed toward the back of the cabin; Cole approached the front. There were no sounds coming from inside. As hard as it was, Cole resisted the urge to slam through the door. Him getting his head blown off wouldn't help Keeley. He peered in a front window; his heart dropped. Keeley lay facedown on the floor.

Jumping up on the small porch, Cole shoved the front door open. His eyes searched for a threat as he ran to Keeley. Seeing no one, he dropped to his knees and felt for a pulse. Slow and steady.

Turning her over gently, he brushed the hair from her face and lightly tapped her check. "Keeley?"

Her eyes fluttered open and Cole felt as if the entire world had just gotten brighter.

"Cole?" she mumbled.

"Stay still, sweetheart. Let me check and see where you're hurt."

"That man . . . where's that man?"

"There's no one else here," Ethan said from the doorway.

His hands running down her body in search of anything broken, he asked, "Where do you hurt?"

She grabbed his arm. "Stop . . . listen to me." Tears glazed her eyes. "We have to find him . . . Wesley Tuttle . . . he's the one who took the girls. He knows where Hailey is . . . we have to find him."

"We will, sweetheart. I promise. Tell me where you're hurt."

"Just my head, I think."

Cole examined the lump on her head, then noted the dark bruises already forming around her neck.

"Let's get you to the car."

Her eyes glazed with pain, she shook her head. "But we have to—"

"And we will, Keeley, but you're in no shape to do anything right now. Let me get you to the hospital and then we'll—"

"No hospital." She swallowed and grabbed his arm. "Take me home. I need to think . . . we need to find him."

Lifting her in his arms, he turned to Ethan. "Call Honor and let her know we found her. See if she'll give you an address on a Wesley Tuttle." He glanced around at the dump of a cabin. "See if you can get any intel from this place; call when you're through. We're going after the bastard."

Ethan nodded.

Holding her as close as he dared, afraid he'd hurt her if he touched the wrong spot, Cole stalked out of the cabin and put Keeley in the backseat.

"I can sit up front."

Close to explosion from the churning emotions inside him, Cole cupped her face in his hands. "Let me take care of you for now. You can argue about how well you feel later."

Apparently seeing the need and fear in his eyes, she pressed her palm against his face. "I'm okay, Cole." Her hand caressed his jaw. "Thank you for finding me."

Cole gave her a soft kiss and pulled away. Jumping into the driver's side, he started up the engine. First order of business was taking care of Keeley. Then he would hunt down Wesley Tuttle and beat him within an inch of death.

Shea met them at the door, her eyes swimming with tears. If there was anyone who knew how Keeley felt, it would be Shea.

"How is she?"

Cole carried Keeley through the doorway. She'd started shivering in shock halfway home. He had pulled over and covered her with a blanket he found in the trunk.

"Bruised, exhausted, terrified." He swallowed hard and added, "Alive."

Shea stroked Keeley's hair. "Ethan called and told me you were coming. I went ahead and ran a bath for her, but . . ." She swallowed hard and said, "Keeley, I know this is hard to face, but you need to go to the hospital. They need to examine you . . . to be able to press charges. Then, you can get clean."

Keeley raised her head, her eyes searching. "Where's Hannah? I don't want her to see me like this."

"She's in her playroom watching a movie. But you really need to go to a hospital for an exam, Keeley."

"No . . . I'm fine . . . he didn't rape me." Keeley raised her head and took in both Shea's and Cole's gazes. "I just want to clean up and then we need to talk."

If her teeth weren't chattering so hard it was difficult to understand her, Cole would have been more convinced. He headed up the stairway.

Shea called out, "Do you need help?"

Keeley shook her head and tightened her arm around Cole's neck. "Thanks, but Cole can help."

Cole took the stairs two at a time. Keeley's shivering was tearing him apart. He needed to get her into some warm water and then warm clothes. He pushed open the door to her bedroom and went straight to her bathroom. The tub was steaming and a floral scent filled the air.

After sitting her down on the chair beside the tub, he dropped to his knees and started to untie her shoes. He looked up to see that she was just staring into space, in a daze. Should he have taken her to the hospital after all?

"Keeley?"

Her eyes refocused as she turned to him. "I'm fine, really. Just so exhausted." She shuddered. "And cold."

"I know, sweetheart. We're going to get you warm soon." He lifted her slightly and pulled her pants off. Scooping her into his arms, he lowered her into the hot water.

She leaned her head against the back of the tub. "He knows where Hailey is. He's the one who took the girls."

Smoothing the hair away from her face, Cole checked the lump on her forehead, examined her eyes. No signs of a concussion but they'd need to keep an eye on her. Wake her every hour or so . . . check vital signs. He'd get Shea to watch her. Make her some tea, maybe some toast.

"Cole, did you hear me? He knows where Hailey is."

He took the sponge from the side of the tub and proceeded to bathe her.

"Cole? Talk to me."

"Keeley, I'm doing everything I can do to not lose control. Ethan's getting an address, gathering evidence. As soon as you get out of the tub, we'll talk. But for right now, just for five minutes, take care of yourself. Then we'll talk."

"Okay," she whispered. Tears seeped from her closed eyes as Cole tenderly bathed her; he muttered soothing little sounds when he reached a particular painful spot and she whimpered.

A few minutes later, he was through and Keeley looked more peaceful. And Cole had to admit, the bubbling rage inside him had lowered to a slow simmer. Once they talked and he put Keeley to bed, then he'd go back into explosion mode.

"Okay, sweetheart. You ready to get out?"

She nodded and stood. Cole wrapped a towel around her and lifted her from the tub. He dried her gently, trying to ignore not only the bruises now forming all over her body, but also how her body always made his react.

Turning away, Cole grabbed her robe hanging from the door. "Let's get you settled in bed, then Shea's going to come in and you're going to give us a full description. Okay?"

Relief flickered on her face. She allowed him to help her put the robe on, and then he picked her up, carried her into the bedroom, and settled her on the bed.

"Where's Hannah?" Keeley asked.

Cole turned to find an anxious Shea holding her sketchpad and pencil, along with a steaming cup of liquid. "She's having a snack in the kitchen with Mrs. Thompkins. She's fine, doesn't suspect a thing." Handing the cup to Keeley, she said, "Hot tea with loads of sugar; it'll help with the shock."

Flashing her a grateful look, Keeley took the tea and sipped.

Shea sat on the chair beside the bed, flipped open the pad, and said, "Describe him."

As Keeley gave a full and vivid description of Wesley Tuttle, Cole took his phone out and called Ethan. "You finished?"

"Yeah. Honor's got a team headed this way. She gave

me his address but I had to promise her he'd be alive when they got there."

Cole didn't argue. He wouldn't kill the bastard, but he'd damn well do enough damage to make him pray for death.

"You get any evidence from the cabin?"

"Nothing helpful. Don't think the guy lives here. There're only a few clothes, a couple of cans of food . . . nothing else. Found plenty of blood leading out the door to the front of the cabin. Keeley managed to do some damage."

"Yeah, but why'd he leave?"

"Guess we can ask him when we find him. You ready to go get him?"

"I'm headed to pick you up right now." Cole hung up the phone and listened as Keeley finished giving a description. He stood over Shea as she finished the sketch. The man didn't look familiar. The guy who'd tried to kill him had long, black stringy hair . . . but that could've been a wig.

As Shea added final strokes, he sat on the edge of the bed beside Keeley. "What else do you know about him other than his name?"

"I went to school with him. Didn't know him very well. He only attended occasionally. He used to come into the diner I worked at during college. He asked me out a couple of times. I said no and that was that. I haven't seen him in years. Not since Stephen and I were married."

"And he said he took the girls?"

"Yes."

"You believe him?"

"He knew where we found Hannah . . . said he sold her for fifteen thousand dollars. Remember, that's the amount Robert Oates said they paid? The FBI didn't release the amount to the press. He laughed when I asked him about the cameras in the house . . . told me I put on a good show when I'm alone. He also admitted that he tried to kill you. And he has a scar on his hand, like Hannah said . . . and he has blond hair . . . the way she described him." She paused and added, "He said that Hailey was alive . . . and was in another country. He wouldn't tell me which one. I'm not even sure he knows."

"Did he say why he did it?"

"For money . . . I told him I would have paid him, but he said that money was only one of the reasons." Tears filled her eyes. "He said if I had cooperated and gone with him that day, he would have let the girls go."

Shea stopped sketching for a moment. "Don't buy into that, Keeley. You did the right thing by fighting him."

"You're right, I know," Keeley said.

"We've got his address. I'm going to pick Ethan up and then we'll find Tuttle."

"I know this is a stupid question," Keeley said. "But should we call the sheriff?"

Cole shrugged. "Not stupid if you lived anywhere other than Fairview. The sheriff has made it too damn clear he's not going to help you with anything. Honor is headed here with her team. Ethan and I will hold him till she gets to us."

Leaning down, he kissed her softly. "I'll call you as soon as we find him. In the meantime, if you remember anything else, tell Shea. She'll call me if there's something she thinks I need to know."

Keeley grabbed his hand and pressed a kiss to his palm. "Please be careful."

Cole caressed her cheek gently and pulled away. "Get some rest. I'll call you soon."

Taking the finished sketch from Shea, he turned and

stalked away. The fury reemerged full force, lighting a fire that wouldn't diminish until Wesley Tuttle paid.

Four hours later, weariness dragged at him, but anger continued to boil within him. Wesley Tuttle had disappeared. The little apartment he'd occupied had been cleared out except for the empty beer cans and candy wrappers left on the floor. They'd searched everything, but could find no evidence to lead them to Hailey or to Tuttle's current whereabouts.

A bulletin had been issued with the sketch Shea had made, and Honor had brought several other agents with her to aid in the search. Soon Tuttle wouldn't be able to go anywhere without being recognized.

Cole pushed open Keeley's bedroom door; she was sleeping. Her face was still too pale, making the hideous bruises on her forehead, cheek, and neck stand out all the more. Rage bubbled; Cole reined it in. She didn't need his anger; she needed his support.

Her eyes flickered open. "Did you find him?"

"Not yet." He sat beside her on the bed and took her hand. "We went to his apartment. Looks like he hadn't planned on returning. He left nothing behind."

Tears seeped from her eyes, rolled down her pale face.

"We'll find him, Keeley. There's a bulletin out for his arrest and Honor has some extra people working with her. He won't get away."

"What if he's already left town?"

"With that bulletin and our contacts, the man won't get far."

"I was so close. I should have figured out a way to make him talk."

"No. You did exactly what you should have done. You knocked him out and survived. That's the most important thing."

"Do you think he was telling the truth? About Hailey being in another country?"

"Yes. That's not something we haven't already discussed. We've got people in every major city in the world. That's one of the many advantages of LCR. No one can hide from us long. Photographs of Hailey are in every corner of the globe. We'll find her. You just have to believe that."

"I believe in you, Cole."

More than aware that when she learned the truth, she would most likely change her mind, he reached into his pocket and pulled out a slender oblong box.

"This is something I want you to wear and promise to never take off."

"What is it?"

He opened the box and showed her.

She frowned her confusion. "It's a watch."

"Yes, it's a watch, but also a cellphone. I ordered it a few weeks ago from an electronics developer in Germany that LCR works closely with. Timing sucks, since it was delivered today." He took the watch from the box. It was an innocuous-looking white-gold watch with a stretch band. It was also state-of-the-art. LCR was one of the premier testers for new electronics for the German manufacturer. This little watch had proven to be one of their best new inventions. Cole showed her the little hidden button on the side. "Stays on all the time, doesn't need recharging. If you ever need me, all you have to do is touch this button once." He pressed the button and a jingling sound came from his pocket. He took his cellphone out and showed her the screen display that said *Keeley*.

Her mouth curved up. "Cool."

"It's waterproof and tough as nails. One push . . . no matter where I am, you can get me. You don't have to hold it to your ear or mouth like a regular phone. And it has the most up-to-date GPS device available. I can track you anywhere."

Throwing her arms around his neck, she whispered in his ear, "You're the best man I've ever known."

Dread growing inside him, Cole held her tight.

Wesley pressed a cold compress to his sore jaw. Bitch had broken two teeth, split his mouth open, and maybe even cracked his jawbone. How he wished he could have stayed and given her what she deserved. But he couldn't. Those LCR people would have found him. Dammit, why hadn't he thought to take her cellphone and throw it in the river?

Now he was holed up in this shitty motel until he could think straight. Even though he was out of Fairview, he wouldn't be able to stay here long. He'd seen the news reports already. That sketch they'd done of him was too damn close for comfort. Just a few hours' rest, and then he'd have to hightail up to his hideout.

"You all right?"

Wesley turned, startled to realize he wasn't alone. "How the hell did you get in?"

She grinned. "I'm good with a lock pick." She flung the hair of her blond wig over her shoulders and batted her eyes dramatically. "One of my many talents."

"Get out of here. I got nothing to say to you."

"Now, don't be mad; I know your head hurts." She held up a grocery sack. "Look, I even brought you some things to tide you over."

Wesley grabbed the bag and pawed through it. Beer, aspirin, potato chips, sardines, hot sauce, and condoms. "This'll help a little. I need to get as far away from Fairview as I can, but my brain feels like it's about to explode out of my skull."

"Sit down and I'll get you some aspirin and a beer." She took the bag from him. "And a snack."

Wesley dropped onto the bed and watched her, his suspicions sky high. "What're you being so nice for?"

Her back to him, she shrugged. "I feel kind of guilty. I should've tried to help you, but I couldn't afford to have her see me."

"I hope you make the bitch pay for that someday."

She turned around and smiled. "Oh, she's already paying." She held several aspirin in one hand, a cold beer in the other. "Here, this'll help with the worst of it."

He threw the pills into his mouth and swallowed them down with the beer, guzzling it till it was empty. Damn, he hadn't realized how thirsty he was. A belch erupted as he leaned back against his pillows and watched her prepare the sardines and chips on a paper plate. His dick suddenly decided if it couldn't have what it wanted, it would settle for a substitute. "If you really want to make it up to me, why don't you come over here and make me feel better?"

"Food first, then we'll see." She handed him a plate and another beer. Then, after pulling one more beer from the bag, she popped the top and took a long swallow.

Wesley attacked the sardines and chips. He hadn't eaten since that morning, and though the salty food stung his sore mouth, he didn't let that slow him down. Chugging down his second beer, he began to feel much better. Relaxed and sleepy, he blinked at the woman in front of him. Why was she smiling like that?

"What's got you so happy?"

"Just like to see a man enjoy his food. Want another beer?"

"Not right now." He belched again and patted the

bed. "Bring some of them rubbers over here and give me some dessert."

"Okay." She grabbed her purse. "Let me go to the bathroom first."

As she shut the bathroom door, Wes was surprised to realize he was glad she was here. It'd been a long time since anybody had taken care of him. Leaning back against the headboard, he was relieved that the worst of the throbbing had stopped, but now he was suddenly very sleepy. His eyes closed . . . he'd just grab a nap till she came back.

Inside the bathroom, she pulled on plastic gloves and then removed the gun from a plastic baggie she'd put in her purse. After attaching the silencer, she waited. The sleeping pills she'd disguised as aspirin should be working by now. The two beers would have helped them along.

Catching a glimpse of herself in the mirror, she fluffed the blond strands of her wig. Maybe she should let her hair grow out a little more. This style made her look younger, less serious. She could ask Wesley what he thought, but since the idiot would be dead in a few minutes, his opinion didn't really matter.

Checking her watch, she determined seven minutes had to be enough time. She needed to get this done and get back home before anyone missed her.

Carefully, not wanting him to see her, she eased the door open slightly and looked out. Wesley's eyes were closed and he was snoring softly. Good.

The gun behind her back, just in case he was playing possum, she advanced toward the bed. Wes didn't move a muscle.

She walked around the bed and stacked up the pillows. Now came the tricky part. "Wesley."

"Huh?"

"Sit up a little."

"Later." He grunted and then snored louder.

As out of it as he was, it took waking him twice before she finally got him to scoot up the necessary inches to where he was propped up against the pillows. If this was going to look like a suicide, it'd be more convincing if he was sitting up.

Taking both his hands, she wrapped them around the gun, and placed his finger on the trigger. Then, holding his face, she opened his mouth slightly and placed the muzzle in his mouth. He opened his eyes wide at the feel of the steel against his tongue, but was too groggy to react quickly enough, She pressed his finger against the trigger and pushed hard.

He jerked and slumped back against the wall with a satisfying thud of finality.

She grimaced at the blood on her new blouse. Dammit, she'd never get the stains out and she certainly couldn't take it to the cleaners. She'd have to throw it away.

With the efficiency she was known for, she quickly cleaned up any evidence that Wesley hadn't been alone. A suicide note would be a nice touch, but seemed too organized and convenient, not in keeping with a man of Wesley's sordid, soulless reputation.

Sure, there'd be speculation that he wasn't alone, but no one could link them together. In a day or two, when the stink got to the outside world or a maid came in, Wesley would be discovered. Of course, it might take a few days to identify him, since a good part of his forehead and the top of his head were mangled and lying on the floor under the bed.

Feeling quite satisfied with the day's outcome, she took one last look around the room and stepped outside. At this time of the night, not a soul was around.

She opened her car door, and got in thinking about what she'd gotten accomplished today. Keeley was at home, bruised and traumatized. Wesley, who'd become a major pain, was dead. And best of all, when Wesley was found, there would go Keeley's last hope of ever finding her daughter. She would be devastated.

Yes, all in all, a most successful day.

twenty-five

Turning from the computer screen, Keeley grabbed the flyers she'd just printed. She'd been out of it for a couple of days and had neglected her regular office routine. Just because there was finally some hope of finding Hailey didn't mean she could drop her normal activities. These flyers should have gone out yesterday. She would have to double up on hours until she was caught up. Until Hailey was home, the work could not stop.

"Keeley!"

She jerked her head up to see Jenna and Miranda rush toward her. She jumped to her feet and met them in the middle of the room. "What's wrong?"

Miranda practically screamed at her. "What's wrong? You were attacked two days ago and we just heard about it? That's what's wrong."

Flashing Miranda a stern look, Jenna touched Keeley's shoulder. "Are you okay, sweetie? Why didn't you call me? When you canceled our lunch the other day, I thought you had a stomach virus . . . I can't believe you didn't tell me what really happened."

Guilt filled her once more for keeping her friends in the dark. She had known Jenna and Miranda would have been here in minutes and would have enjoyed mothering her. She'd asked Cole to cancel her lunch date with Jenna using the excuse of a stomach virus. She hadn't liked lying to her friend, but had needed the time to herself. As much as she loved Jenna, she had a tendency to hover . . . as did Miranda.

She hugged both women and said, "I'm sorry. I just needed some rest. All I have are a few bumps and bruises. Nothing more. And I didn't want either of you to worry. I'm fine . . . really."

Miranda shook her head. "Cole said that you'd been attacked, abducted. What happened? Who was it? Why did—"

She took both of her friends' hands and pulled them down to sit beside her on the couch. "It was Wesley Tuttle. Do you remember him?"

Her forehead furrowed in concentration, Miranda said, "I don't think I've ever heard of him. Who is he?"

Keeley figured Miranda wouldn't remember him, since she was a few years younger, but the expression on Jenna's face told her she remembered him.

"I thought he left town a year or so after high school," Jenna said.

"Unfortunately, he came back."

Jenna shuddered. "I remember how he always gave me the creeps, like he was looking through my clothes or something." Her eyes filled with tears as she spotted the bruises on Keeley's neck. "Oh, sweetie, he really hurt you, didn't he?"

"Not as bad as it could have been."

"But why did he attack you?" Miranda asked.

"He's the one who took Hailey and Hannah."

"He took them . . . and then he attacked you? But why?" Jenna asked.

"I know it sounds weird—it *is* weird—but I know he's the one."

Miranda jumped up, hands on her hips. "Why would he do that?"

"I really don't know other than he held some kind of grudge against me for not going out with him."

"From all those years ago?" Jenna snorted. "Now, that's about the dumbest reason I've ever heard."

Miranda nodded. "I agree with Jenna. Carrying a grudge like that for years seems really crazy. And why take your kids? That's even crazier."

"I agree . . . but that's what he told me. And he knew things only the kidnapper would know. The FBI is looking for him. Once we find him, he can tell us where he took Hailey."

Jenna touched her shoulder again. "That's wonderful, sweetie. I knew it would all work out for you."

Miranda's eyes narrowed as she searched Keeley's face. "There's something else going on, isn't there?"

"What do you mean?"

"You've got a spark in your eyes you haven't had for a very long time."

"That's because we're about to find out where Hailey is," Keeley said.

"Maybe." Miranda's tone held doubt.

Jenna nodded. "I think Miranda's right. There is something there. What's going on?"

For some reason, she hadn't mentioned anything to her friends about her new relationship with Cole. She wasn't sure why, other than she didn't want to share it with the world yet. It was her secret to savor and relish. But that was silly. Her two best friends deserved to know that she had fallen in love with a wonderful man. They would be thrilled for her.

"I'm in love with Cole."

"What?" they squealed in unison.

"I know it sounds strange. The last few months have been the most horrific of my life, but . . . " She shrugged, unable to explain how in the midst of this nightmare, she'd actually found love. "He's the most amazing man. And as determined as I am to find Hailey."

Jenna's worry was reflected in her words. "This isn't some kind of hero worship, is it?"

Keeley shook her head. "I admit that I admire him tremendously, but I'm also in love with him."

"Well . . . I guess he's handsome and all . . . but isn't he a little old for you?" Miranda asked.

Keeley laughed softly. "He's thirty-five . . . that's not exactly elderly."

"But does he feel the same way?" Jenna asked.

"I think so. We haven't talked about the future, because there is no future until I have Hailey back. But once we do, I think there will be."

Jenna grasped Keeley's hand and squeezed it. "Well, I think it's fabulous. It's about time something good happened in your life."

Keeley was surprised that her normally unromantic friend Jenna was the one who seemed the happiest for her, while the usually idealistic Miranda looked so doubtful.

Cole leaned against the wall, across from the closed door of Keeley's office, and waited for Miranda and Jenna to come out. As Keeley's best friends, they'd be able to tell him how they thought she was doing. She still looked too damned pale to him, but she'd assured him she was well enough to work. He wanted to get their input.

He couldn't deny a secondary reason for calling them over. The conversation he'd had with Miranda a few days ago continued to hammer at him.

Now that they knew Wesley Tuttle was behind everything, Cole no longer suspected Keeley's sister-in-law of being involved in her nieces' abduction. However, she was hiding something, and by the continued worried expression on her face, it was something big.

They hadn't exactly parted on good terms the other

day; Cole was probably the last person she wanted to talk with. But Miranda was a young single mother, and she was important to Keeley. Maybe there was something he could do to help her. First, she had to tell him what her problem was.

He straightened when the door opened and both Miranda and Jenna emerged. Jenna gave him a quick smile and then turned to look back inside the office. "Get some rest and I'll call you tomorrow." She whirled around to Cole. "She looks exhausted."

"I heard that." Keeley's amused voice came from inside the office.

Jenna grinned. "Good, you were supposed to." She closed the door and shook her head. Tears glinting her eyes, she said, more quietly, "I can't believe what that bastard did to her. Do they have any leads yet?"

"Not yet, but the FBI's got his sketch out everywhere. He won't get far."

"Good." Jenna glanced over at Miranda. "I've got to get back to work. You coming?"

"I—" Miranda started.

"I'd like to talk to you, Miranda, if you have a few minutes."

Her mouth tightened but she nonetheless nodded and said, "Of course."

Jenna gave both of them a curious, searching look. "Well, I'm outta here. Cole, make sure Keeley gets some sleep. I'll call her later."

He nodded and waited until he heard Jenna go out the front door before he said, "Let's go into the sitting room."

Her expression a mixture of defiance and worry, Miranda followed him into the room and then perched on the edge of the sofa as if she might take flight at any minute.

Leaning forward, he tried to make his expression as

unintimidating as possible. "Miranda, is there something going on that I can help you with?"

Surprise replaced the anxiousness in her eyes. "What?"

"Keeley cares a lot about you . . . and I care for Keeley. If you're in trouble, or need help, I'd like to offer assistance."

"That's very kind of you." She straightened her spine. "But I don't know what you're talking about."

"Where do you go at all hours of the day and night?"

"I told you the other day, it's none of your business."

"You're right, it's not. But LCR has a lot of contacts. If you need help . . . assistance, we'd like to offer it."

When she smiled, he saw the beautiful woman she might be someday if she didn't have worries weighing her down. "Now I see why Keeley is so fond of you." She rose to leave. "Thank you for your concern. But sometimes, offering help isn't in the best interest of the person you're offering it to." Walking past him, she added, "Tell Keeley I'll call her later."

Cole stayed seated. Whatever her problems were, he admired her for wanting to handle them without assistance from others. And as long as they brought no harm to Keeley, they were her secrets to keep.

The call came three days later. Holding the phone to his ear, Cole stood at the window overlooking the backyard where Keeley played on the swings with Hannah. As he listened to Honor's report of how Wesley Tuttle's body had been discovered by the weekly maid at a motel miles from Fairview, he watched the two people who'd become so important to him look up at the same time, wave and smile.

Cole couldn't manage a smile, but he waved and turned around, unable to look at the sweet scene as he heard the news that would crush Keeley once more.

With Wesley's death, there were no apparent leads to find Hailey.

"You're sure it was a suicide?"

"Cases like this rarely give an absolute certainty." Honor sounded as tired and dispirited as Cole felt. "There's no suicide note, but no evidence that he had company either. The place wasn't wiped clean of prints. So far, other than Tuttle, there're at least two dozen other prints. It isn't exactly a higher-end motel; these rooms are rented by the hour. We'll keep running the prints." The frustration in her tone was an indication that she didn't expect anything good to come from the prints.

"The gun was stolen a couple of years ago from a pawnshop in Raleigh. We'll wait for the official word from the coroner after he does the autopsy. But for right now, it's looking like a suicide."

Knowing it was useless, he asked anyway. "And there's nothing he left behind that gives any clues?"

"No. The suitcase was filled with nothing but clothes, toiletries, and about two thousand in cash. No receipts or credit cards. Nothing that tells us anything about this guy. You saw his apartment . . . it was nothing but a garbage dump of beer cans and food wrappers. Neighbors say they rarely saw him, and when they did, he was always alone. Landlord only knew he was paid up in his rent . . . that's all he cared about.

"The cabin where he took Keeley belonged to him, but that's the only thing we know about it. It wasn't really habitable, even for a pig like Tuttle, so he apparently didn't spend a lot of time there." She took a long breath and added, "I'm sorry. I know this is going to upset Keeley."

Major understatement, but Cole said, "Yeah. Listen, call me if anything—even the most inconsequential-looking evidence—shows up. I've got to figure out a way to break this to her. It'd be nice if I had something even remotely hopeful to tell her."

"I'll try, but don't count on it."

"Thanks." Cole closed the phone. Before he headed outside, he went looking for Shea. Keeley wouldn't want Hannah to be anywhere close by to hear a discussion about Tuttle.

The instant smile Keeley gave when she spotted him and Shea coming toward her made Cole's chest tighten. He hated having to tell her this news. No, it wasn't the death knell to their investigation, but the small amount of optimism they'd felt at finding Tuttle and getting him to talk had disappeared. It was now back to square one.

Keeley saw something in his expression, because her smile slipped and her eyes went somber. She stood and Cole could see her visibly preparing for bad news. Looking down at her daughter, she said, "Hannah, why don't you go with Shea and let her read you a story?"

Since story time was still two hours away, Hannah looked thrilled with the idea. She jumped up and ran toward Shea, who held out her hand and led the little girl to the house.

"What is it?"

"They found Wesley Tuttle."

She wrapped her arms around herself. "And?"

"He's dead. Self-inflicted gunshot wound."

Her head shook slowly in denial. "That makes no sense. Why would he kill himself? Why not just get out of town?"

"I don't know. The coroner's doing an autopsy."

Keeley shuddered and closed her eyes. "We were so close."

He wrapped her in his arms. Her words muffled against his chest, she said, "Getting Wesley was our last chance, wasn't it? We'll never find Hailey."

"That's not true, Keeley. A week ago, we didn't even

know about Tuttle and we still had hope. Yeah, it would've been great if we could have asked him, but that doesn't mean we won't find her."

She pulled away and worked at a brave smile. "You're right. At least he told me she was in another country. That's something."

His heart hurt for her because it might be something, but it was a piss-poor substitution for being able to question the bastard himself. Finding out Hailey had been transported out of the country wasn't even a big surprise. Human trafficking to various parts of the world had become big business. She could be anywhere.

"So what's next?"

"There's something else. I hate to bring this up right now, but with Tuttle dead, the threat against you and Hannah is over. Shea and Ethan will probably get a new assignment."

She nodded. "That makes sense." Her throat worked convulsively as she asked, "Are you leaving, too?"

He pulled her against him again. "Hell no. We're getting Hailey back, sweetheart. I promise. I won't leave until we do."

"But what about your job?"

"This is my job until she comes home. Period."

A soft, sighing sob shuddering through her body, Keeley burrowed against him.

With the threats against her gone, Cole was more than aware that there was one more thing Keeley needed to know. The reason for withholding the truth from her no longer existed. She had to know who had killed Stephen.

Tightening his arms around the woman who'd come to mean the world to him, Cole closed his eyes against the reality of what he must do and the burning question of how Keeley would react.

Would she still want him in her life, knowing he had killed her husband?

Cole sat alone in Keeley's darkened office. Hannah was being tucked in; Shea and Ethan were packing.

The dismal news of Wesley's death had cast a dark cloud over everyone. In an effort to give Keeley and Hannah a bit of relief, he had insisted the three of them go to a movie of Hannah's choice that afternoon. Sitting in a darkened theater on a Tuesday afternoon with Keeley and Hannah had been the most fun he'd had in years. It hadn't been the talking animals on the screen, but hearing Hannah's laughter and seeing Keeley's corresponding smiles at that laughter, that had given him a sense of enjoyment he'd thought he'd never feel again.

After the movie, they'd picked up a pizza, carried it home, and watched cartoons. Now an exhausted Hannah was being tucked in and Cole was about to do one of the most difficult things he could remember ever having to do. How did you tell the woman you loved that you were her husband's murderer?

The fact that it had been unintentional and he hadn't known what he was doing at the time didn't lessen the sin of his not being truthful with her at the beginning. He had his reasons, but would her anger and hurt keep her from understanding them?

With Tuttle dead and the threat against Keeley and Hannah gone, the only real reason for him to stay here was to give Keeley support. Hailey was still out there somewhere and Cole would never give up looking for her. The contacts LCR had all over the world gave him up-to-the-minute accounts in the search for Keeley's daughter. He would bring Hailey home to her mother if it was the last thing he did. But whether he stayed here while that search continued was entirely up to Keeley.

"What are you doing down here in the dark?"

Shea stood in the doorway. The light from the hall-way highlighted the concern in her eyes.

"I'm going to tell Keeley the truth," Cole said.

Silently she stepped inside the room, turned on the light, and then closed the door. As she dropped into a chair across from him, he read her expression perfectly. She was almost as torn as he was. Shea and Ethan had come close to losing each other because Ethan had kept secrets.

"How do you think she'll handle it?" Shea asked.

"I have no idea, but there's no reason to keep it from her any longer."

"Would you like me to talk to her? I could help her to understand what happened."

"Can you make her understand why I lied to her in the first place?"

"You didn't lie . . . you just didn't tell her everything. And you had your reasons."

"Kind of the way Ethan did?"

Tears glazed her eyes. "I forgave him . . . she'll forgive you."

"Maybe. I don't know. How do you tell a woman you killed her husband and oh, by the way, sorry that you didn't happen to mention it sooner?"

"It wasn't your fault, Cole."

He wished he could believe that. "It was my decision to go into that warehouse without backup. If I hadn't done that, Stephen wouldn't have died and you wouldn't have gone through hell."

"You were tricked, Cole. You thought you were sav-ing a life. And you can't live your life filled with what-ifs and if-onlys. Ethan and I suffered through that already. Living in the past, letting regrets color everything, is no way to live."

Cole got to his feet. "I may be leaving tonight . . .

depending upon Keeley's response. Can you stay a day or two extra if she needs you?"

"Absolutely. But don't borrow trouble. Tell her everything; make her understand. I'm sure it will be all right."

Wishing he was as confident, Cole twisted the doorknob. It was now or never. Might as well get it over with.

He opened the door, then jerked to a stop. Keeley stood in front of him, her face death pale; tears and accusation filled her eyes. His gaze dropped down to her hand. She was holding Hannah's baby monitor.

"I left the other monitor in my office . . . was about to come get it." She swallowed a small sob. "Guess I should have left it down here sooner, huh?"

Shit.

"I'm sorry." Since she'd apparently heard everything, what else could he say?

She took a breath and said, "I guess you'd better explain."

"Do you want me to stay?" Shea asked behind him.

Unable to look away from Keeley's accusing stare, Cole answered without turning. "No. I'll handle this."

Nodding, she passed Keeley, who flinched as if she thought Shea would say something. Shea just shook her head and walked past her. There was more than one bridge to mend here.

"Let's go inside." He turned back to go into the office.

"So I guess you were coming up to tell me?"

"Yes, I'm sorry, I—"

"No excuses, Cole. Just the truth."

He went back into the office and waited for her to come in. He'd be damned if he'd stand in the middle of her hallway while he spilled his guts.

He watched as Keeley came inside, closed the door, and then leaned against it with her arms crossed defensively in front of her. Several emotions crossed her expressive face; the one that tore at him the most was the look of betrayal. She'd been betrayed so many times already. How was he going to convince her this wasn't just one more?

She took a deep breath as if preparing herself and said, "Tell me."

Cole sat on the edge of the sofa. While he hated relaying his hellacious experience, if anyone deserved to hear about it, it was Keeley. "Remember I told you I was kidnapped and drugged?"

She nodded.

"It was Donald Rosemount."

"The same man who kidnapped Stephen?"

"Yes."

"Noah McCall told me that another victim of Rosemount killed Stephen. You were that victim."

"Yes."

"How . . . why?"

"I was on an op with Shea and Ethan. Did something stupid and got captured. After Rosemount had his fun with me, he drugged me with one of his new concoctions. It was a cocktail of drugs designed to erase all memory and free will. I had no cognitive thought . . . only did what the bastard ordered me to do. I was supposed to abduct Stephen, not harm him. Only they gave me too much of the drug . . . I went berserk . . . and killed him."

Her gasping sob tore at his heart. Cole swallowed past the mountain of regret building in his throat and continued, "I didn't realize what had happened for a long time, because they drugged me every day. Then . . . something happened and they stopped dosing me for a while. That's when I realized I'd killed someone . . . an innocent man. I had killed others, but this one I remembered because somehow I knew it had been wrong."

Keeley could feel panic and hysteria building inside her, and she couldn't seem to tamp it down. "Why didn't you tell me?"

"I wanted to . . . so many times. My number one priority was finding your daughters and making sure you stayed safe. I figured if you knew, you wouldn't want me here." He stood and faced her. "I had to be here."

Cole's beautiful eyes were filled with sadness. Lying eyes. She felt like such a fool. Once again, she was the last to know. Once again, the only one left in the dark.

When was she going to learn her lesson? She freely admitted that she was naïve, but only recently had she realized how much that naïveté crossed over into stupidity.

And in front of her was the best man she'd ever known. The only man she thought she could love after what Stephen had done. The one man she thought she could trust. And now, she didn't know what was the truth and what was shaded by his guilt. She had thought they had a future together, but how far had his guilt taken him?

"That's why you came here? Out of guilt?"

"Guilt. Responsibility."

"Is that why we . . . why you . . . " It hurt too much. She couldn't finish the thought.

"Dammit to hell, no! I don't fuck out of guilt."

She jerked at his crudeness but refused to back down. "Then why?"

His head shaking slowly, he let out a laugh so bitter, Keeley flinched at the grating sound.

"You know, I've been through this scenario in my mind a hundred times. Not once did I think you'd accuse me of a pity hard-on. For your information, Keeley, men don't get erections because they feel sorry for someone."

"Then why, Cole?"

"If you have to ask that question . . . if you really can't figure it out for yourself, then there's no reason for me to stay."

She couldn't think straight . . . couldn't deal with the hurt and the betrayal. "After the things Stephen did, I never thought I'd be able to trust another man . . . but I trusted you."

"If I had told you the truth, what would you have done?"

"I don't know, but I would have liked to have been given a choice."

"What do you want me to do?"

Moving away from the door, she walked shakily to the middle of the room. She kept her back to him, unwilling for him to see the agony in her face. An ache was building up inside her, hurting so badly she could barely whisper, "I think you need to leave."

She heard him walk toward the door and then stop. "No matter what you feel about me, I'll never stop looking for Hailey. I will find her for you and I'll bring her home." He turned and walked out the door, closing it softly behind him.

Sobs exploded from her lungs; deep ugly sounds of anguish. Keeley clamped her hand over her mouth to stifle the awful noise. Her legs giving out, she dropped to the floor.

twenty-six

Operating on automatic, Cole rang Elizabeth Fairchild's doorbell. Yeah, it was after ten o'clock . . . way past time to visit decent folk. Elizabeth didn't fall into the "decent folk" category. Keeley might never forgive him for keeping the truth from her, but he could damn well do one final thing for her before he left town.

Patrick answered with his usual look of snobbery. "Yes?"

"I need to see Mrs. Fairchild."

"She's retired for the night." He pushed the door to close it.

Cole's hand shot out and stopped the door from being shut in his face. "Then tell her to damn well un-retire. I'm coming in . . . get out of the way." When the butler seemed to hesitate, Cole barked, "Now!"

Patrick's throat worked as he obviously debated whether he should suffer what was sure to be his employer's wrath or a sound beating from Cole. Choosing his physical well-being over his employment, Patrick backed up and allowed Cole to step inside. "I'll let her know you're here."

Cole stood in the giant foyer and watched Patrick run up the winding stairway. The man was halfway up when Elizabeth's voice snapped, "Who is it, Patrick?"

"Cole Mathison, ma'am."

"Oh, tell him I'll be right down."

Cole wasn't surprised to hear delight, almost genuine

warmth, in her voice. The woman had made it clear more than once she'd like to get to know him a hell of a lot better.

Patrick returned and stopped at the bottom step. With his usual imperious nod, he announced, "Mrs. Fairchild will be glad to receive you in the sitting room."

Any other time, he might have laughed at the ridiculously formal statement. His laughing days were behind him.

Cole followed Patrick to the sitting room. Standing beside the sofa, he waited for Elizabeth to come through the door. Ten minutes later, he was still waiting. Was she doing this on purpose? If so, he had no real issues with dragging her downstairs. Just when he thought he might have to do exactly that, the door opened.

She glided toward him, her hand out in welcome. "Cole, how wonderful to see you again."

Cole ignored her hand. "I'm leaving town. I won't be back. There're some things you need to hear and it's about damn time someone said them to you."

Shock replaced the smile she'd greeted him with. "I beg your pardon?"

"You will stop your harassment of Keeley. Do you hear me?"

"How dare you! Get out of my—"

"I'll get out when I've had my say. You've had fun these last few years torturing a woman whose only sin was to be the daughter of the woman your husband was obviously in love with."

"That's a lie."

Cole glowered at the woman who'd caused Keeley so much misery. For days he'd been mulling in his mind some theories, and had come to some interesting, albeit outrageous, conclusions. He'd only recently started listening to his gut again, and despite the lack of evidence to back up his suspicions, he was certain he was on the right path. "I know you're the one who arranged for your son's kidnapping."

Before the expected self-righteous indignation took over, he saw a flicker of fear. "You're insane. Why on earth would I have my own son kidnapped?"

"You tell me." He cocked his head and went with his instincts. "You've hated Keeley and her mother for years. Stephen had to know this. I'm thinking part of his marriage to Keeley was to spite you."

She wrapped her thin arms around herself. "Stephen was a rebellious young man with a skewed sense of humor. He knew I wouldn't approve."

"So you did your best to make Keeley's life miserable by turning the town against her. And then, when she was publicly humiliated about his affairs, you decided this was a perfect opportunity to teach him a lesson. Having him abducted would scare the hell out of him, and Keeley would be considered the prime suspect. Only it didn't work out the way you planned, did it?"

She glared at him. "You can't prove any of this."

"A new diary has been found in Rosemount's belongings . . . evidence points straight to you."

Shock replaced the haughtiness. "That can't be true . . . I went through a—"

Triumph filled him. Lying had never felt so good. "You went through what? A broker? Yeah, the broker told Rosemount. He recorded it in his journal."

Recovering quickly, she straightened her shoulders. "My word—the word of a Fairchild—will be believed over any hoodlum who claims I had anything to do with Stephen's abduction. And I'll have you up on defamation charges if you even—"

She stopped on a gasp as he loomed over her. There were certain things he *could* prove. "The ransom was one million dollars. Rosemount took forty percent; the person who hired him took sixty. A week after Stephen's body was found, you made sizable donations to ten different charities."

Her thin lips tightened. "And that proves I had my own son kidnapped?"

"You're not a generous woman, Elizabeth. That's the first charitable contribution you've ever made. Did donating the money clear your conscience for getting your son killed?"

Her face went white. "I had nothing to do with my son's death."

"You had him kidnapped."

"They said they wouldn't hurt him. He wasn't supposed to—" She broke off, apparently realizing she'd said too much. Her face stiffened into a cold mask. At last she looked like the embittered middle-aged woman she was. "You can't prove anything."

"I don't have to. What I can do is put a bug in the ear of the FBI. They'll crawl up your ass six ways to Sunday until you won't know which end is up."

She shook her head. "They weren't able to uncover who was responsible when it happened. Nothing's changed."

"Keeley didn't have me then . . . she does now." He leaned over her and growled, "You've got a choice. Not only will you stop vilifying her to the entire town, you'll stop trying to contest her husband's will, the sheriff's office will stop their harassment, and oh yeah, you will stop those emails that begin with 'Bad Mama Bitch.'"

Shock widened her eyes. "How did you . . . ?"

He hadn't . . . until now. Now that he knew everything, this woman would rue the day if she ever said anything against Keeley again.

"Leave Keeley alone or suffer the consequences. Your choice."

"Are you threatening me? I'll have you arrested."

"Threats have no backbone . . . this is a warning. The

only one you'll get. If you don't comply, this town will turn against you so fast, you'll have to move out of the state. I'll contact every newspaper in the South and feed them information about Elizabeth Fairchild that'll make your hair stand on end. The famous Fairchild name will be made a laughingstock. All because of you."

"I'll sue you for slander."

"Go ahead, I've got nothing to lose. You don't stop, it'll be like shit on a skunk. No one will be able to determine what stinks more, you or the Fairchild name."

"You disgusting, vile man."

"You've not seen disgusting yet." He leaned even closer; within inches of her pale face, he snarled, "Stop. The. Harassment. Now."

Elizabeth's mouth twisted and pursed as she tried to come up with another threat. He didn't give her time. Satisfied he'd made his position clear, Cole turned and stalked out the door.

Keeley stared blindly out her bedroom window, every particle of her body hurting, especially her heart. She had told him to leave . . . and he had left. And now she felt so incredibly empty. Hollowed out and alone.

She heard the door open and turned to see Shea stride into the middle of the room, her expression an odd mixture of compassion, anger, and determination.

"He left," Keeley whispered. Why she said it, she didn't know. And didn't know what she expected Shea to say, to do. It just hurt so damn much.

"I know," Shea said.

Leaning back against the window, she faced Shea with her hurt. "I trusted him."

"He made a mistake by not telling you. You deserved to know."

"Yes, I did."

"I'll let you wallow in your anger and self-righteous

pride in a few minutes, if that's what you really want. But before you do, I think you need all the facts. Then you can decide who should be apologizing to whom."

Keeley straightened her spine. She had known there was more. Cole had given her the briefest, barest facts. He hadn't tried to sugarcoat anything but she knew he'd been through hell. She'd come this far in learning, she'd damn well hear it all.

"Tell me."

"Not to be too melodramatic and quote movie lines, but are you sure you can handle the truth?"

"I've survived a hell of a lot over the last few years. I'll survive this."

Her eyes narrowing slightly, Shea tilted her head. "You've had it bad, Keeley. There's no denying that. A lot of the things that have happened to you aren't fair or right, but that's the way life is sometimes and you deal with it."

A dry, humorless laugh burst from Keeley's mouth. "Deal with it? That's your best advice?"

"You think you're the only one life has screwed over in some way?"

"Of course not."

"Here's what I see: a girl who lost her mother too soon, the most important person in the world to her. Then the girl, still grieving, fell for a charming smile and a slick line. A man you might not have paid attention to if you weren't so vulnerable. He cheated on you, humiliated you. Damaged your trust and your heart . . . then he died.

"What happened next is probably the most horrific thing a person can know . . . your children are taken and it seems like all is lost. But then, like out of a Hollywood movie, a mysterious stranger comes to help. Bigger than life, movie-star handsome, heroic, brave, and kind. Everything a woman might fantasize for her dream man. He matches your determination and drive to save your children. It appears he can do no wrong. He treats you with respect and tenderness. He's your hero and you fall in love with him."

Keeley swallowed. She wanted to deny Shea's words, but she couldn't. Every one of them was true. Cole had seemed so incredibly perfect.

"And today, you find out your perfect man is not so perfect after all. He's human. Those fantasies you cooked up about him aren't all true. You find out he's flawed."

"I wasn't looking for a perfect man. But we were as close as two people could be, and he still didn't tell me. I was married to a liar . . . I can't be with another one."

Shea's brows arched and a cold light entered her eyes. She spoke softly, but Keeley heard the fury. "You're comparing Cole to your sleaze of a husband?"

Tears she'd been fighting for hours overflowed. No, God, no. Cole Mathison and Stephen had nothing in common. *Nothing!*

Pushing away from the window, Keeley straightened her shaky legs and walked to the middle of the room. Holding her hand out to Shea, she said softly, "I need to know everything. . . . Help me understand him."

Her smile incredibly lovely, Shea took her hand and they sat together on the couch.

Ethan appeared at the door. "Everything okay?"

"We're just having a little heart-to-heart," Shea said. "I'll be fine."

Ethan nodded but didn't move away from the door. His expression was one of concern and protection; he knew his wife was upset and was determined to be close if she needed him.

Keeley was beginning to realize the men of LCR were very protective of their loved ones. As Cole had been with her.

"Tell me," Keeley said.

"We were on an op together . . . Ethan, Cole, and me . . . and some other operatives. Ethan was running the op. We'd set up what we thought was a good sting to bring Rosemount in. Only he somehow found out about it." She took a breath and asked, "Did you know that Cole and I were married at one time?"

"Yes, he told me that."

"We had just signed the annulment papers right before we went on the op. I think we were all emotionally ravaged at the time . . . Cole and I shouldn't have gone." Shea shuddered another breath and Ethan was by her side in an instant, his hand on her shoulder.

Shea smiled up at her husband, but when she turned back to Keeley, her eyes swam with tears. "It was my idea to go. . . . Cole didn't want to, but I talked him into it."

"What happened?"

"Cole and Ethan had an argument. . . . Cole walked out, saw something he thought he could handle by himself, and went inside a warehouse . . . the building blew up. We thought he died."

"But instead he was captured?"

"Yes . . . for a year he was tortured and drugged."

Keeley swallowed and closed her eyes. She'd seen the scars. That wasn't something Shea needed to tell her. "I've seen his back."

"Do you know why he has the scars on his back?"

"He told me he was beaten."

"They missed giving him the drug for one day, and he was able have some kind of cognitive thought. He was ordered to break a woman's neck . . . he refused. He was beaten and then whipped."

"Oh dear God," Keeley whispered.

"He was Rosemount's puppet . . . his killing machine. He murdered on command because he didn't know anything other than what Rosemount put in his head. But that one time, when he had a moment of clarity, he knew it was wrong. He refused and was tortured."

As if Shea no longer saw Keeley, her eyes glazed over and she spoke in a dull monotone, "He almost died. They started drugging him again. He had no conscious thought, no will . . . " She took a long, sobbing breath. "He lost all memory of who he was, what he was. I went after Rosemount . . . wanted to make him pay. I ended up getting captured, too. I was given the same drug as Cole. He watched while Rosemount abused me, tortured me, and he did nothing to stop it."

Tears rolled down Shea's face as she refocused her gaze on Keeley. "Knowing the kind of man Cole is, how protective he is . . . can you imagine what that did to him when he realized he'd watched my torture and hadn't tried to save me?"

As if unable to watch his wife share her story without holding her, Ethan sat beside Shea and wrapped his arms around her.

Shea nestled into her husband's arms as she continued, "After he was rescued, came off the drugs, he woke up to a living nightmare. Had to relive losing his wife and daughter all over again. He remembered the bad things first . . . that's how the drug works. The good things either never come back or are sketchy. All of this might have destroyed a lesser man. Cole took it on all over again, because there was one thing he couldn't let go of, couldn't stop thinking about. Do you know what tortured him the most?"

Frozen, unable to speak for the mounting sorrow building inside her, Keeley could only shake her head.

"The knowledge that he'd killed an innocent man. It happened after the very first drugging. The dosage was wrong . . . the pain almost killed him. He was crazy with it . . . didn't know what he was doing."

Barely able to whisper, Keeley said, "He told me."

What Cole had been forced to do, what had been done to him, was tragic and horrendous. Keeley couldn't blame him for Stephen's death. It hadn't been his fault.

"When he was well enough, he came to check on you," Shea said.

Keeley shook her head. "I never met him before—"

"He did it from a distance . . . he was worried for you, for your children. He couldn't let go of the fact that he'd killed your husband and felt as if he needed to take on the responsibility of seeing to your safety."

"How did he do that?"

"He kept an eye on you for days, trying to determine if there was a threat. You seemed to be getting your life back together. He could detect no danger."

"Why didn't he tell me any of this?"

"He didn't want to hurt you . . . bring you more pain. Getting your children back for you was his only priority."

"He should have been the one to tell me everything."

Shea nodded. "You're right, he should have. But Cole is human, just like the rest of us. He screwed up. Couldn't figure out how to tell the woman he was falling in love with that he'd been her husband's killer." Her green-eyed gaze direct and challenging, she said, "The question is, are you going to let that one mistake destroy everything? Because, if you are, then you don't deserve him."

Keeley hurriedly stuffed clothes into a small duffel bag. Of all the mistakes she'd made in her life, and she had made plenty, telling Cole to leave had been the worst.

Everything Shea said was true. She had imparted Cole with perfection, and when he'd ended up having flaws, she'd turned on him. If there was anyone who should be apologizing, it was herself.

Years ago, she'd dreamed about a man of integrity and courage coming into her life. Her mother had told her about her father, about what a wonderful, strong man he'd been. Keeley had dreamed about finding a man like that. Instead she'd settled for a shallow, handsome man with a charming smile.

The reasons Stephen had married her no longer mattered. Whether he'd done it to spite his mother; whether he'd actually loved Keeley at all. It was all in the past. Stephen was gone and her only goals were to have both her children back with her . . . and to go after the man she loved.

Cole was the man of integrity and character she'd longed for, and what had she done? She'd accused him of making love to her out of pity. Told him to leave.

Her mind went back to all those beautiful moments they'd shared. How he'd made love to her with such tender ferocity. Her fantasies hadn't come close to the reality of how Cole made her feel, what his lovemaking had done for her . . . not just the pleasure, which was immense, but also the confidence she'd gained.

She had wanted perfection and now with her eyes wide open, Keeley realized how very imperfect she herself was. She had wanted a hero . . . a white knight . . . a savior. What had she gotten? A flawed, imperfect man who was good and decent and had done everything within his power to help her. Had sacrificed himself time and again to make up for something that hadn't been his fault in the first place. Every time she'd turned around, Cole had been doing things for her. What had she done for him? Nothing.

Would he forgive her?

She loved him. He hadn't told how he felt with words, but his action had been full of love.

It wouldn't be easy . . . nothing worthwhile ever was, but if she could convince him of her love and sincerity, would he give her a second chance to make it right? To be worthy of his love?

She'd already called Jenna and asked her to come stay with Hannah. Now all she had to do was convince Shea to give her Cole's address. Hopefully, she wasn't so angry with her she wouldn't tell her where he was.

Grabbing the duffel, she took one last look at her hastily dressed self. The black jeans and white shirt were comfortable and would hold out for however many hours she would need till she got to the man she loved.

A soft knock on her door had her turning around. "Come in."

Shea opened the door. The expression on her face was one Keeley had never seen before. Her entire face glowed with excitement. "We have news."

Her heartbeat quickening, Keeley ran toward her. "What?"

"You know that Eden and Jordan are in Thailand?"

Unable to speak, Keeley could only nod.

"Since they can't bring their son home yet, they decided to do a little snooping in some of the lesser-known houses that are suspected of selling children."

Keeley's heart was ready to leap out of her chest.

"They think they've found Hailey at one of them."

Her finger gripped the dresser behind her as her legs threatened to give out. "Are they sure?"

Shea grinned. "Almost one hundred percent sure. You know they've seen numerous pictures of Hailey. They would know."

"Oh my God."

"How do you feel about going to Thailand?"

"Thrilled. When do we leave?"

"Can you be ready in an hour?"

"I'm ready right now." Heart racing and insides shaking, Keeley tightened her grip on her duffel bag and followed Shea out the door. She was really going to get her baby back!

twenty-seven

Bangkok, Thailand

"What the hell is she doing here?"

Keeley almost didn't recognize the man standing in front of her with a glare that could melt steel. Gone was the man who'd thrown her daughter up in the air, laughing at her antics. The man who'd held her so gently in his arms, tended her bruises and cuts when she was attacked, and made love to her with a fierce tenderness she'd felt to her soul. In front of her stood a man primed for battle—ready to fight, defend, and protect. A warrior.

The Cole Mathison she'd fallen in love with had disappeared. Or had he? Was this the real Cole, or the man he had to be to do what needed to be done? The man she'd told to leave?

Keeley felt a wailing begin inside her, similar to the one she'd felt since her girls were taken. Now the wailing was for a different reason. Had she destroyed her only chance for happiness by not being brave enough and wise enough to grasp what was in front of her?

Swallowing past the pain, Keeley glanced around the large room. They'd set up shop in a small warehouse. A dozen or so people, men and women, milled around, each doing various jobs. A few worked at computers. Two were deep in conversation in a corner. Several had weapons in front of them that they were cleaning and checking. Cole was with this last group. Except for the one time when he snarled out the question of why she was here, he hadn't spared her a glance.

She had to find a way to get him alone, to tell him how sorry she was and that she loved him. Straightening her shoulders, Keeley took a breath and started toward him.

A young woman stalked into the room, catching Keeley's attention and halting her. Dressed in jeans and a T-shirt, she was below average height and slender. Her bleached blond hair was shorter than some of the men's, but the short cut only emphasized her incredible bone structure and natural beauty. She was young, maybe early twenties, but she looked at home here. Confident and capable.

Cole looked up when the woman approached him, and he gave her a smile. Cole's smiles had always been so discriminating and rare that Keeley somehow believed they all belonged to her.

The woman held herself back from the others, but with Cole she seemed to loosen up. The other men surrounding Cole backed off, as if they knew she didn't want them around. They seemed to respect her need for distance, and when they spoke to her it was from several feet away. She looked serious and competent, as if she'd been in the midst of battles many times and had come out a winner.

Even though this operation was to rescue her daughter, Keeley felt awkward and out of place. As if she were the only one who shouldn't be here. She fought that sensation. She had every right to be here. But the feeling lingered, as it had many times when she felt out of place back home.

The woman said something to Cole and he let out a dry laugh.

Keeley's heart lurched at the sexy, familiar sound. Was

Cole attracted to this kind of woman? A woman who understood his world . . . could live and work in it?

"So the mysterious Ghost is on the case."

Keeley turned to see Shea smiling.

"Ghost?"

Shea nodded, her eyes still on the slender woman talking to Cole. "That's her nickname. Her real name is McKenna. She's an LCR operative but no one but Noah knows anything about her. She shows up, sometimes unexpectedly, does her job and leaves."

"Cole seems to know her."

Shea snorted softly. "Not really. He saved her ass once during a raid. She'd been shot. Cole picked her up and carried her out of the building. She was kicking and biting at him the entire time."

"But why?"

A compassionate flicker of understanding gleamed in Shea's green eyes. "She doesn't like to be touched. Cole ignored her and saved her life."

"So they developed a friendship?"

"Not hardly. In a few minutes, she'll be just as distant with him as she is with everyone else. I suspect this is the first time she's seen him since he was rescued. Being halfway friendly to him is her way of saying 'I'm glad you're not dead.'"

Compassion suddenly replaced Keeley's jealousy. "She's been hurt, hasn't she?"

"Most LCR operatives have." She paused for a second and said, "Maybe you should consider joining our ranks."

With those intriguing words hanging in the air, Shea winked and walked away.

"You okay?"

Stunned at Shea's suggestion, she hadn't realized anyone was behind her. She turned to see Eden standing there with a warm smile of welcome on her face and tears in her eyes. With a soft sob, she threw herself into Eden's arms. "Thank you. Thank you."

Eden laughed softly and held her tight. "It was a long shot, but it paid off."

She pulled out of Eden's arms and reached up to press a grateful kiss to Jordan's cheek as he stood beside his wife. "And you're sure it's her? How does she look? Does she look healthy?"

"Her hair's been colored a dark brown, so we didn't recognize her at first," Eden said. "And yes, though she looks like she could use a bath and hairbrush, she looks healthy."

"What kind of place is this?"

"Black market adoption," Jordan said. "We think they've only had her a few weeks."

"Why do you think that? Where has she been?"

"Jordan and I went inside, pretending to inquire about an adoption. Most of these places actually do a few legal ones. We told them some specific features we were looking for, hoping if they hadn't seen Hailey themselves, someone had. The second agency we went to, they'd just gotten in a child about the age and physical description we said we were looking for." She grinned. "They warned us she was a handful and that the people who'd had her before returned her. She apparently was a little more rambunctious than they anticipated."

Hailey!

"I remember your description of Hailey included her tendency to be a bit of a daredevil. We told them this was exactly the kind of child we'd love to have. They let us meet her."

"And she was healthy?"

"Yes. She looks like she's been well fed, not abused, but she had quite the attitude. Refused to come when they called. Glared at me and Jordan the entire time we were there."

"Oh God, I can't believe I'm finally going to see her again."

"I'm glad you could be here. Who's with Hannah?"

"Jenna's staying with her."

"I'm sure she'll be thrilled to have her sister back home."

Keeley shivered as she glanced around at all the busy people. "Will everyone here go in?"

Eden shook her head. "No more than three or four. The less we send in, the better our chances of getting out without anyone getting hurt."

One again, people would be putting their lives on the line to save her child. Cole included. Another shiver swept through her. "How dangerous will this be?"

"Nothing we haven't done before. They've got a good plan. Everything will be all right." She grabbed Keeley's hand. "Okay?"

"Yes . . . thanks." Shaking her head, she said, "I haven't even asked about Paulo. How is he?"

Pure happiness lit up Eden's face. Keeley had never seen her look more beautiful.

"He's perfect. He's still in the hospital but we've been spending time with him each day. Yesterday Jordan asked him if he'd like to come home and live with us."

"What did he say?"

"He asked if Fred could come, too."

"Who's Fred?"

Jordan grinned. "The stuffed bear we gave him. When we assured him that he could come, he said that would be fine then."

"That's wonderful. When can you take him home?"

"In another couple of weeks. He's still too weak to travel and the last thing we want is for him to get sick again."

"I—" Her words caught in her throat as she saw Cole striding toward them. Would he say anything to her?

Cole had worked hard to keep his eyes off Keeley. He understood why she had to be here, but seeing her was a simultaneous gut punch and heart stab. He'd blurted those unwelcoming words without thinking. Keeley's corresponding flinch had made him feel like shit.

He'd wanted nothing more than to go over and reassure her that everything would be okay and she would soon have her daughter back, but he'd forced himself to stay on the other side of the room. She might not have looked as if she hated him when she saw him, but her mind was on Hailey, as it should be. If she felt anything other than hatred for him, it was only gratitude. Nothing more.

Once she had her daughter back with her, she could go home and hopefully never have to worry about their safety ever again.

Still, the need to reassure her that things would soon be over propelled him toward her.

"Everything set?" Eden asked.

"Yes. We'll do a quick review in a few minutes." He glanced toward Keeley and then back at Eden. "Mind if I talk to Keeley?"

"Not at all." She gave Keeley a reassuring squeeze to her arm, then she and Jordan moved away.

Before he could speak, Keeley said, "Cole, please forgive me. I'm sorry, for so many things. Thank you for all you've done. I don't know how to thank you enough."

The tension inside him eased. She might not feel the way he'd like for her to, but knowing she didn't hate him helped a hell of a lot. "None of that matters now, Keeley. We're going to get Hailey back. Then everything will be as it should be."

"What does that mean?"

"Just that you can finally get your life back on track."
He glanced at the small group of LCR operatives gathered in a corner. "Those people over there are here for
only one purpose. To rescue Hailey."

"Thank you . . . but—"

"I've got to go review with the group. I just wanted to
tell you that it'll soon be over."

Before she could say anything else, Cole turned away
and headed toward the group waiting for him. She
looked so worried and sad. If he stayed any longer, he'd
try to take her in his arms. He wouldn't make that mistake again.

His eyes took in the three operatives who would be
going in with him. Five others stood behind them. They
would provide technical support and backup if needed.
He stood in the middle of the room and reviewed their
plan.

"We know this adoption agency is a front for the ille-
gal one going on in the back." He shot a glance at Eden.
"Eden, you'll go in the front and express an interest in
seeing the child you looked at before. From what you
said, there're only two or three people who work out
front. One will probably go in the back with you. Once
you neutralize him, give us a click on your mic."

He shot a glance at the man leaning against the wall
as if too lazy to stand up straight. Cole's first impression
of Dylan Savage hadn't been a good one. He'd soon
learned how wrong he was. The man's laid-back, "I
don't give a shit" attitude was a front for one of the
toughest and hardest-working operatives LCR had.
Cole felt damn lucky to have him on this op. "Dylan,
once you hear the click, you come through the back
door. If there's anyone else in the back besides the kids
and Eden, they'll try to go through the back to escape."

His expression never changing, Dylan gave a slow
nod of understanding.

Turning to McKenna, Cole said, "You and I will go in as a couple looking for a legal adoption. Once Dylan and Eden give us the all clear, we take the people up front."

To the rest of the group, he said, "Once we neutralize any threat, you guys come in and let's round up the kids. The authorities will come along with you. Any questions?"

A soft, hesitant voice spoke up from the other side of the room. "Should I be close by?"

Cole turned to Keeley. Forcing himself to see her as only a client of LCR, he said, "Eden will grab your daughter and bring her to you. We're about a block away from the agency."

"But couldn't I—"

"You'll stay here." She flinched at his hard voice, but he didn't care. Having her in harm's way even the slightest amount wasn't something he was willing to risk.

Shea wrapped her arm around Keeley's shoulders and whispered something. Keeley's eyes never moved off Cole. He kept his face deliberately harsh and unreadable. If Keeley wanted to think him a hard-ass, that was her problem.

He turned back to the group. "Any other questions?"

When everyone shook their heads, he said, "Let's get ready. We go in half an hour."

Keeley tried her best not to be hurt as she watched the small group disperse, each getting ready to save her daughter. They were putting their lives on the line, and to resent being treated like a civilian was not only incredibly selfish, it was pointless. She was a civilian. She had no idea how to help apprehend these people, and getting in the way of saving her daughter wasn't something she would risk. But she so wanted to be as close to Hailey as possible. Her little girl would be terrified and God knew she'd been traumatized enough over the last few months as it was.

Shea's quiet reassurance in her ear had helped, but still a small part of her smarted from Cole's attitude. Stupid, really. After the things she'd said to him, he had every right to act that way. She was lucky he hadn't just said to hell with the job and given it over to someone else. Of course, he wouldn't do that for one very simple reason: he was a man who kept his promises. Cole had said he would rescue Hailey and that's exactly what he was doing.

But then what? Despite the joy of knowing she'd soon be holding her daughter, Keeley couldn't stop thinking about Cole. Had she ruined his feelings for her completely?

She'd done a lousy job of telling him what was in her heart. All the things that had been eating at her had come out in one giant, gushing, bubbling wave of words. Only she hadn't said the one thing she probably should have said. She hadn't been able to form the words, because if she'd said "I love you" and he hadn't responded in kind, she would have been devastated.

As she watched the small group of operatives head out the door, going to save her daughter, she saw Cole's stoic expression and cried inside. Did it matter if he didn't love her? What if something happened and she never got another chance?

Sitting in a car just down the road from the adoption agency, Cole heard Eden open the door to the building of the agency. The mic in his ear picked up the sounds perfectly.

"May I help you?" a gruff-sounding female voice asked.

A young and seemingly timid Eden said, "I was here

the other day . . . with my husband. We were looking at a child for a special adoption."

"Oh yes. I remember you."

"I was wondering if I could see her again. My husband is on a business trip and suggested I take one more look before we made up our minds. Would that be okay?"

Eden was playing it just right. The bastards would be caught off guard by her innocent-young-woman act. If Jordan had gone in with her, they might be more wary. No one who looked at Eden would suspect that behind that slender, delicate-as-a-flower façade was a lethal and dangerous operative.

There was a long pause and Cole tensed. Had they suspected something? Had he underestimated their intelligence? He released a relieved breath when a male voice said, "She's asleep. You can go in and look at her, but don't try to wake her up."

Cole's jaw clenched. They'd likely drugged Hailey to keep her quiet.

Footsteps sounded and then there was total silence. He held his breath.

Finally Eden's voice came through loud and clear. "Oh, she looks so peaceful, doesn't she?"

"Yeah. You going to get her or not?" the man asked.

"Oh yes, we want her. In fact, I think I'll take her right now."

Several successive noises followed, as if Eden was delivering a few blows. Then he heard a grunt and a thud. Silence again. Then Cole heard the sweetest sound of all come over the mic—a definite and distinctive click. Their "go" signal.

Cole shot a glance at McKenna. "Let's go."

As he and McKenna headed to the building, Eden spoke low: "Okay, I got him tied up and out of the way. Don't see anyone else. We got five kids here. They're all asleep, probably drugged. I— Shit, someone's coming. Dylan, he's coming your way."

"I see him. Hold on, everybody." Once again there was silence, then sounds of a scuffle, a groan of pain, and then a thud.

"Okay. He's out," Dylan said.

"See anyone else?" Cole asked.

"Clear," Dylan answered.

"Clear here," Eden said.

"How many up front?"

"Two. Man and a woman," Eden said.

"Cameras?"

"Didn't see any."

"Okay, we're heading in."

He shot a glance at McKenna as they walked up the steps. He'd worked with her only a couple of times. After saving her life once, he probably knew her about as well as almost anyone, which meant not at all. She was one of LCR's most secretive operatives.

Despite her odd quirks, she was a damn good operative and had saved a lot of lives. Besides, there weren't any LCR operatives he knew of that didn't have a few oddities. Seeing and experiencing hell seemed to have that effect on people.

Since she usually dressed like a teenaged boy or a punk rocker, he was surprised to find that when she dressed like a woman, McKenna was actually very attractive. There was an elegance and femininity he'd never noticed before. She, like so many LCR operatives, was a chameleon, becoming what she needed to be to get the job done.

They reached the top step, gave each other a slight nod, and then Cole pushed the door open for McKenna to go ahead of him.

The office was one of understated elegance. An attractive middle-aged woman sat behind a desk. A man, probably in his late twenties, stood beside the desk talking to her.

The woman smiled up at Cole and said, "Can I help you?"

"Yes, we'd like to inquire about an adoption," Cole said.

"Do you have paperwork?"

Pulling a legal-looking document from his pocket, Cole unfolded it and handed it to the woman. Something dropped from the document and the man beside the desk went to pick it up. Cole hit him on the head; the man collapsed to the floor. The woman behind the desk sprang to her feet and then yelped as McKenna grabbed her arm.

Cole gave the woman a cold stare. "Anyone else in the building?"

Jerking at the hard grip McKenna had on her, she snarled, "You don't know who you're dealing with."

"Maybe after this is all over, you and I can sit down and you can tell me exactly who I'm dealing with," Cole said.

"You'll pay for this."

A small, wry smile tilted McKenna's mouth. "That line never gets old, does it?"

Cole held a gun on the woman while McKenna tied her hands behind her back.

Cole's gaze swept the small office. No indication of cameras, but he wouldn't rule that out. "Okay, guys. We all clear?"

"I'm clear," Dylan answered.

"Me too," Eden said.

He looked at McKenna. "Stay here. Alert me if you see anything odd."

Barely giving McKenna an opportunity to nod her agreement, Cole pushed open the door to a small hallway. His heart lurched and then went into overdrive.

Eden stood at the end of the hallway holding a small, brown-haired girl. The child appeared to be asleep, but even from a distance Cole recognized the sweet face of Hailey Fairchild.

Peace like he'd never known flowed through him. Keeley was finally getting her daughter back. Cole's pledge had been fulfilled.

twenty-eight

Keeley couldn't sit still any longer. She'd stared at the radio left in the room and had heard every word. Hailey had been found. Without asking permission, Keeley ran through the door. No one tried to stop her and if they had she would have knocked them out of the way.

She stood on the street, unsure which direction Cole would be coming with Hailey. People milled around her, dodging her. Some looked at her strangely. She saw nothing, her mind only on one thing. And then, like the parting of the Red Sea, the crowd divided into halves and Cole strode toward her, a small child in his arms. Keeley's heart stopped. The closer he came, the more her heart dropped. She looked nothing like Hailey. How could they have thought . . . ?

Cole murmured something to the child who had her arms wrapped around his neck. The little girl lifted her head to peek around, and Keeley saw an angel's face. Her angel—Hailey.

Sobbing and laughing all at once, Keeley took off running; Cole stopped and put Hailey on the sidewalk.

"Hailey!" Keeley screamed.

"Mommy!"

Keeley scooped up her daughter in his arms and swung her around. Tears pouring from her eyes, she buried her face against Hailey's soft neck and cried.

She held her for several long seconds, absorbing the

wonder of having her baby back in her arms. Finally able to raise her head, she looked over to where Cole stood. Only he was no longer there. Keeley whirled around. She saw Eden and Jordan standing a few feet away. Shea and Ethan were walking toward her . . . but where was Cole?

A few hours later, Keeley was tucking Hailey into the small bed they'd set up on the plane. After LCR doctors had examined Hailey and declared her healthy, the two of them had been hustled onto a private jet. It had been done quietly, efficiently, and quickly . . . and Cole hadn't been anywhere to be found.

Even Shea and Ethan didn't know where he'd gone. Eden said that he'd stood for several seconds watching the mother and daughter reunion and then had turned around and disappeared into the crowd.

She hadn't said goodbye. Hadn't said thank you. And most important, she hadn't said, "I love you."

Would she ever see him again? Keeley straightened her spine. The last few months she had learned a lot about herself. Some of the things she'd learned, she hadn't liked. She realized that until her children had been taken, she'd never truly fought for anything. But when they had disappeared, she had stood her ground on more than one occasion. Now it was time to fight for herself.

She'd always been stubborn and an optimist, but had never had the confidence to demand respect. Which was one of the reasons she'd allowed Elizabeth to treat her as she had. And one of the reasons she'd stayed in a bad marriage.

That Keeley was gone. Forever. She'd survived one of the most unspeakable horrors a woman could know— losing her children. She had never given up hope they would be found. And now, that fortitude and determination would see her through for Cole. She would not give up on him.

There were things to be done, issues that had to be addressed. The doctors had said Hailey was fine physically, but they had urged her to make sure she received a thorough exam from her pediatrician. And the child psychologist would want to see her as well.

Once she was assured that Hailey was indeed fine, she would turn her attention to finding Cole and making sure he knew that she wanted to be a part of his life if he still wanted her.

She refused to allow herself to believe he didn't. That would be a final break to her heart. One she would never recover from.

Jenna looked out the window as Hannah played in the backyard. Her heart broke for the little girl who would soon lose her mother. It would be a devastating blow to her and to little Hailey . . . especially after what they'd gone through already this year.

She had no choice, though. It was time for it to end. She couldn't put up with the inequality any longer. After years of being in the shadows, always receiving Keeley's leavings, it was time for her to step up and take her rightful place.

She had hoped to avoid this. Had hoped Keeley would see how much she needed her friend. See how important Jenna was to her survival, to her happiness.

Jenna's importance had always been predicated on what Keeley wanted and needed. And had Keeley appreciated that? Had she been grateful for the things Jenna had done for her, allowed her to have? Of course not. She had taken and taken until Jenna didn't have anything left to give.

None of this had turned out the way it was supposed to. Keeley should have turned to Jenna for comfort and strength. Taking her kids hadn't created the emotionally needy Keeley that Jenna had expected. Instead, she had become self-sufficient and stronger. That emotional support Jenna had been primed to offer her friend had never really been needed.

And now, it had come full circle, but was so much worse than before. Keeley not only had both of her children back, she'd also fallen in love. Why was it that everything always worked out for Keeley? It was so damn unfair. And it had to stop.

It hurt Jenna deeply; she couldn't deny that. She loved Keeley and would miss her tremendously. Hailey and Hannah would need her to stay strong for them. They were her daughters now. She would take care of them, mother and nurture them. She'd never allow something to happen to them the way Keeley had. She would be a good mother.

The townspeople would praise her for taking in two orphan girls. They'd tell their friends when she passed by, "Oh, that's Jenna Banks, she took in Keeley Fairchild's children after Keeley suddenly disappeared. She didn't have to, you know . . . but that's just the kind of person Jenna is." People were finally going to realize how special she was. So much more special than Keeley.

The newspaper would run an article on her. Maybe the television stations would come and interview her the way they had Keeley when the girls first disappeared. Everyone would admire Jenna for her self-sacrifice and her loyalty to her missing-and-presumed-dead friend.

And then there was Cole. He had always been nice to her, always seemed interested in what she had to say. With Keeley out of the way, he would be able to see how special Jenna was. How much better she was for him than Keeley.

Which proved the point: life might not turn out the

way one plans, but sometimes, if one works very very hard, it can turn out even better.

Tampa, Florida

Cole stared down at the notes he'd just scribbled. He'd gotten in last night and hadn't been able to sleep. Knowing Keeley now had her children home with her should have given him the peace he'd searched for. For some reason, that feeling had only been temporary. Something was ripping at his insides. Wesley Tuttle was dead. There was no longer a threat to Keeley or her children. So why the hell did worry keep hammering at his brain? Something had been bothering him and he couldn't get a grasp on what it was.

As soon as he walked in the door of his home, he grabbed a soda from the fridge and started writing. In his previous life, before LCR, he used to work out problems this way. He remembered that Jill used to tease him about his method.

He still missed her . . . would always miss her. She'd been a beautiful, special person. Had been a part of his life since he was a little boy, and he'd planned to spend the rest of his life with her. But that hadn't been possible, and though a piece of his heart would never heal from her death, he knew she would want him to move on and be happy again. That happiness would only come with Keeley.

Whether she would give him another chance, he didn't know. He would give her and her daughters a chance to bond again, and then he would go back and see if there could be a future for them.

He let his pen move across the paper without any plan on what he would write. And suddenly he wrote Jenna's name. Snatches of conversation he'd had with Keeley

over the past few months passed through his mind; Cole
jotted them down.

*"Jenna and I used to run together. After her knee
injury, she couldn't run anymore. Her mother broke her
kneecap. She wore a brace for years. By the time she
could afford surgery, it was too late, the damage had
been done."*

"Jenna knew about Stephen's affairs and didn't tell me."

*"Running has always been my panacea. Whenever I
was at my lowest point, I could run and everything
seemed just a little bit better. It made me happy."*

*"I stopped competing in track because my mom died
when I was running a race. Jenna was with her. I came
home with a first-place medal and no mother."*

*"Jenna's always been there for me. At the most dev-
astating times of my life, she's been right at my side. I
don't know what I would have done without her."*

Cole shot out of his chair.

Jenna!

Keeley pulled her car up in front of Jenna's house. For
some reason, her friend had decided to bring Hannah
here. Which actually worked out better for everyone.

She had called Miranda and asked her to take care of
Hailey while she picked up Hannah from Jenna's. She
wanted to tell Hannah that her sister was safe before
she brought them together again. One psychologist had
suggested that the shock of seeing each other so suddenly might have a negative effect and bring back memories they weren't ready to deal with yet.

Twisting the doorknob, she was surprised when the
door opened as if it hadn't been closed all the way.
Sticking her head in, she called out, "Jenna? Hannah?"

No answer.

Keeley went from room to room, puzzled at first and
then becoming increasingly concerned. Every room was

pristine, organized and beautifully decorated. But still no Hannah or Jenna. That was odd. Jenna knew she was coming. She'd called her less than an hour ago and told her she was coming by to pick Hannah up. Where could they be?

On the second-floor landing, Keeley heard a soft sound from below. Running down the stairs, she called again, "Jenna?"

"In here."

Keeley ran down the hallway. As she pushed the door open to the kitchen, shock jerked her to a stop. Jenna stood at the center of the kitchen behind the butcher-block counter. Hannah lay on the counter, her eyes closed. What chilled Keeley to the bone was the knife Jenna held against Hannah's throat.

"My God, Jenna. What are you doing?"

Jenna's brown eyes glittered with hatred as a sick smile spread across her face. "What I should have done years ago. You never deserved the good things that happened to you, Keeley. You never appreciated them. You gave me up . . . lived without me . . . did things without me.

"Every time I let you have something, you took it and never thanked me." Tears filled her eyes and she wiped them away with the back of her hand, all the while keeping the knife at Hannah's throat. "You even ran away and got married. You called me before you left, but it wasn't the same. I didn't get to be your maid of honor like we'd always planned."

Keeley could barely register Jenna's crazy words. All she could concentrate on was the butcher knife pressed against her daughter's tender neck.

"Jenna, whatever I've done to you, however I've hurt you, I'm sorry. But don't hurt Hannah because you hate me."

"I don't hate you, Keeley. I love you. You're my best friend."

"Then if we're best friends, we should be able to talk things over." She took a step forward. "Let's sit down and talk it out."

"Oh, we'll do plenty of talking, and if you move any closer, your darling Hannah is going to bleed all over my nice clean kitchen. She's asleep right now . . . she'll just never wake up. Is that what you want?"

"No! Please . . . tell me what you want me to do."

"I want you to drink from that cup on the counter in front of you."

Keeley's eyes darted to the cup at the edge of the counter and then back to the horrifying scene before her. "Why?"

"Because I said so, Keeley. From now on, I tell you what to do. You've had your way for too long. Now it's my turn."

"What's in the cup?"

"Not poison, if that's what you're afraid of."

Keeley took a breath to steady herself. This was a woman she'd known most of her life. Had shared every secret and every sorrow with. That couldn't have been a lie. Somewhere inside the crazed woman staring at her was still the young girl she'd giggled with and told all her secrets to.

Keeley placed her hands in front of her. They were shaking so badly, she didn't know if she could hide what she was doing, but she had no choice. The watch Cole had given her and made her promise never to take off might be her only hope. Crossing one hand in front of the other, Keeley pressed the button Cole had showed her would reach him immediately. The button next to it was the mute button. If Jenna heard Cole answer, there was no telling what she might do.

She couldn't hear him answer; she could only hope he would hear her.

Keeley raised her hands and walked slowly toward

her in a nonthreatening way. "Jenna, please listen to me. Whatever I've done to you, please, I'm begging you, don't hurt Hannah."

"I won't as long as you do what I tell you to do. Now, drink what's in the cup."

"I—" Keeley choked back a cry when Jenna seemed to press the knife harder against Hannah's neck.

"Don't make me have to do it, Keeley. If I kill her, it's your fault."

Keeley picked up the cup in front of her. It was filled with a dark liquid. "If I do this, what happens to Hannah?"

"I'll make sure she's okay, her and Hailey. I love them, Keeley . . . just like they were my very own. That's why I had two good families all picked out for them. They would have been happy . . . well cared for. Instead the bastard sold them to buyers who could pay more money. He didn't die soon enough for me."

Fury replaced the shock. "You hired Wesley to take them, didn't you? And you killed him?"

She laughed. "Finally, after all this time, you figured it out. You know, you're not nearly as smart as people think you are."

"But why?"

"Drink!"

Her hands shaking, knowing she had no choice but to do what Jenna said if she wanted to keep Hannah safe, Keeley put the glass to her mouth.

"All of it, Keeley. If I see even a little remaining, I'll cut one of Hannah's ears off."

Keeley took a sip, surprised it was her favorite herbal tea. It was tepid and she finished it quickly. Whatever had been in the drink would most likely disorient her soon. Could she get to Hannah before she passed out?

She set the glass down and took a step toward Jenna. The room wavered in front of her. Whatever had been in the drink was faster acting than she anticipated. She blinked again and forced her eyes to focus enough to see that Jenna had moved away from Hannah and was no longer holding the knife to her neck.

Her vision tunneling toward darkness, Keeley flew across the room in the direction she thought Jenna was. Before she reached her, pain slammed into her head and she dropped to the floor.

twenty-nine

Keeley woke to ink-black darkness. Her mind tried to comprehend where she was . . . what had happened. In a flash, she saw Jenna's face, saw the knife pressed against Hannah's throat. Dear God, it had been Jenna all along.

Where was Hannah? Had Jenna hurt her?

She tried to lift her head. Couldn't move. And not only was her entire body frozen, she was enclosed in something. Her shoulders touched the sides of something. Where was she?

Was anyone here? She willed her mouth to open. Oh God, it was as frozen as the rest of her body. She screamed through her barely opened lips. The sound, eerie and inhuman, bounced off the walls of whatever held her.

An awful thought came to her, followed immediately by a flood of mind-numbing panic. *No . . . it couldn't be.* Despite the silent scream of denial roaring through her head, Keeley knew she had to face the truth. She was inside a coffin.

Sheer terror gave her the impetus to lift her pounding head. When she did, she butted up against the satin lining, confirming the fear. Her heart felt as though it would explode from her chest. Breath panted from her; a roar in her ears told her she was going to pass out.

Stop it, Keeley. You can't panic. You have two little girls depending upon you to be strong. Depending upon you to survive.

The panic within her subsided. She had just gotten her children back; damned if she'd allow herself to be defeated like this.

Cole.

Before she drank the liquid, she'd pressed the tiny button on the watch. Had she been able to reach him? She refused to believe she hadn't gotten through. He'd said the phone could reach him anywhere. Was he still in Thailand? If so, he wouldn't be able to reach her in time. But someone could. He was her only hope.

Concentrating as hard as she could, she willed her hand to move. Almost crying from the strain, she managed to raise her wrist. Jenna didn't know about the watch. Cole had made her promise to tell no one. Her hand was stiff and uncooperative as her fingers crawled slowly across her stomach until she reached her other arm. She searched, feeling for her wrist. Yes, there was her watch. Her fingers stretched and felt around until they reached the tiny button. Now she could only hope. She held her breath. Praying he was there, Keeley forced her mouth open to speak.

Cole shoved his fingers through his hair. He'd heard every word. Every. Damn. Word. And he hadn't been able to do anything. Keeley had pressed the mute button . . . he was sure of it. But he'd heard and he had listened to the most terrifying conversation imaginable.

How the hell had he missed it? Damn it all to hell, how had he missed it? Jenna, her best friend. The woman who'd been more like a sister to her than just a friend. The woman she'd trusted her children with.

He was still half an hour out of Fairview. He was hoarse from calling Keeley's name. He'd heard every word that was said, he knew where she was, what had happened . . . everything. He had listened to Jenna's grunting and muttering as she moved Keeley's body. And hadn't been able to do a damn thing but listen.

Honor had been his only hope, but he'd only gotten her voice mail. He left a detailed message, but had no idea if she would get it in time.

He had called Miranda from the plane, claiming to be looking for Keeley, and had been relieved to hear Miranda say that Jenna had dropped Hannah by the house. She'd told Miranda that Keeley had never shown up. At least he knew Keeley's daughters were safe.

Miranda sounded surprised to hear from Cole, but he hadn't told her what was happening. If Jenna knew they were onto her, there was no telling what she might feel forced to do.

His cellphone rang: Keeley's ringtone. A faint sound sounded in his ear. "Keeley? Can you hear me?"

There was only silence.

"Keeley, is that you? Talk to me."

The faint sound he heard . . . was it Keeley or just his imagination?

"Keeley, dammit. Say something."

"Help."

She sounded far away, but he heard her.

"Keeley, I can barely hear you. Scream if you have to."

He heard only a few words. "Jenna." "Inside." "Coffin."

"Listen, Keeley, I'm on the way . . . almost there. I heard you when you called before. I know Jenna's the one. And I know where you are. You're at the funeral home. Listen carefully. I'm just a few minutes from touching down at the airstrip. I will find you and I will save you. Just hold on."

Her faint voice said, "Hannah. Hailey."

"Miranda has both of them. They're fine."

"Hurry."

He heard another sound.

Jenna, her voice eerily calm, said, "Keeley, are you ready to see your mama again?"

Keeley squinted against the harsh fluorescent light that blared in her eyes. Jenna's voice. How could she sound so normal, so sane? So much like the friend she'd known forever? Why didn't she sound like the crazed lunatic Keeley now knew her to be?

Thank God Miranda had both girls. However, if she didn't mention Hannah, Jenna would wonder.

"Where's Hannah?"

"So you *are* awake. I thought I heard some sounds. Should have known a cow like you would have to have more drugs to keep her out."

"What did you do with my daughter?"

"Relax, Keeley. I wouldn't truly hurt Hannah. I dropped her off to stay with Miranda. Stupid bitch didn't even bat an eye when I told her you'd never come for Hannah. Guess all of your friends have deserted you, haven't they? Even Cole's not around. Did he finally see behind that innocent façade? See that you're nothing but a user?"

Tears seeped from Keeley's eyes. Hannah and Hailey were safe. That was the most important thing. And Cole was on his way. But she wouldn't wait for him. If she had a chance to get away, she would. She was stronger than Jenna, always had been. She should be able to take her without any problem. Keeley ignored the inner voice that whispered, *Yeah, if only you could move.*

She'd been able to move to call Cole. Already she could feel her limbs loosening up. Another few minutes and she would be able to act. Until then, she would stay still and allow Jenna to believe she had her whipped.

"What did you give me? I can't move."

"Just a little something to ensure your cooperation.

It's nice having contacts in the pharmaceutical world. Finding one who'll put those pesky ethics aside was a bit difficult, but once I did, he hooked me up with major cool drugs." She shrugged. "I couldn't have you loose and moving around while we have our final girl talk."

"Why, Jenna? What did I ever do to you?"

"The question should be, what haven't *I* done for *you*?" She shook her head. "You couldn't be happy with what you had . . . you had to have more. Whenever I let you have something, you took it and acted as if it was due you."

"What are you talking about?"

"We were the same, you and me, Keeley. From the same background. We were like that old song—it was you and me against the world. But that wasn't enough for you, was it? You had to do more, have more. And what happened to me? I got left behind. Who wanted a pale, washed-out cripple around?"

"Jenna, I never—"

"Don't try to deny it. You started winning all those awards for running. Got all that attention." Keeley saw genuine pain in her eyes. "I couldn't run like you. I wanted to, but you were tall, so much faster. I couldn't compete with you, but I hated losing. So I went home after practice one day, took a hammer and cracked my knee."

"My God," Keeley gasped. "You said your mother—"

Jenna snorted. "That bitch was so drunk most of the time, she could barely lift a bottle to her mouth, much less a hammer."

"And all because I could run faster than you?"

"You still don't get it, do you, Keeley? We were supposed to be the same. We shared everything. And then you became something special and left me out."

Despite her horror at what Jenna had done with her children and what she intended to do with her, Keeley couldn't stop herself. "I'm sorry, Jenna. I didn't know."

"Of course you didn't. You were too busy being special. And then you started getting attention for a whole new reason. You got boobs and a butt. Boys noticed you. We could be standing together and not a damn one of them even knew I existed."

"Why didn't you say anything?"

"What did you want me to say? 'Keeley, stop being prettier than me? Stop being taller than me? Stop growing tits'?"

Jenna lifted her hand and Keeley swallowed a gasp. The knife she'd held against Hannah's throat was in her hand. She waved it as she spoke, as if she didn't even realize she had it. "And the thing was, you never even appreciated it, Keeley. Boys would ask you out and you'd say no. You got all this extra stuff and didn't do a damn thing with it."

Tears glazed her eyes again. "And Mama. She was so proud of you. Acted like you were some kind of princess. Always bragging about you . . . she used to love both of us equally until you started doing all those special things."

"Jenna, I was hardly ever around your mother."

"I'm not talking about her . . . I'm talking about Kathleen. She was my mother, too. Maybe not by blood, but she took care of me the way a mother is supposed to. Then she got sick and I took care of her . . . the way a good daughter should. And what did you do? You went and competed in that race."

Keeley closed her eyes. Her biggest shame. At her mother's and Jenna's urging, she had competed in the race and had come back home to find her mother had passed away.

"I knew you would come home with a medal. Knew you would be bursting with pride . . . I allowed you to have that but I had to take something away from you, Keeley. You do understand that, don't you?"

"What do you mean? What did you take away?"

"Mama, of course."

Oh. Sweet. Lord. Sick nauseating horror flooded through her body; her throat clogged with emotion, she could barely get the words out, "What did you do, Jenna?"

For the first time, Jenna looked defensive. "She was dying anyway. I just held a pillow over her face for a couple of minutes. She didn't really try to fight me or anything. I think she was ready to go."

Her mother. Her sweet, precious mother had been killed by this lunatic and she never saw it. Never suspected. Jenna was right in one thing, Keeley realized. She was stupid . . . supremely stupid to have had this woman as her best friend for years and not once suspected her of anything remotely bad.

Her voice husky with tears and pain, she whispered, "Did you have Stephen kidnapped, too?"

"Now, that's something I can't take credit for. Wish I could. He was such a bastard." She scrunched her nose up in such a cute Jenna way that Keeley let out a whimper. "He was terrible in bed, too. Even Wes was better than him. Stephen and I only did it for a few months. And every time, I had to do most of the work. You should've let Wes do you so you could have some kind of comparison."

"You set it up so Wesley could rape me?"

"You needed to learn a lesson. He wasn't going to kill you or even hurt you that bad . . . but you needed a reminder, Keeley. Seems like every time I turned around, you were forgetting about me. When you were happy, you didn't need me." She shrugged and gave a small, self-deprecating grin. "I like to be needed."

There was nothing more she could say that could hurt her. Jenna had taken her beautiful mother from her. The doctors had said she only had a few weeks left. Dammit, if only she hadn't run in that race.

Keeley forced away the pain and took a controlled breath to refocus. "So you had an affair with Stephen. When?"

A smug smile brightened Jenna's face. "A month or so after you were married, I showed up at his office. I was there barely five minutes before I went down on him, then we did it on his desk." She grimaced. "Not the most romantic encounter, but it accomplished what I wanted. After that, we'd meet in a hotel outside of town."

She leaned down inches from Keeley's face. "You really should thank me, because I'm the reason you got that nice fancy mansion. He felt so damn guilty for doing your best friend. And he made it so easy for me to hide those cameras, too." Pride and glee glinted in her eyes. "I saw it all, Keeley. Every argument, every time you cried. And the day you found that pair of panties in his jacket. Oh, Keeley, I cackled like a wet hen for hours. That was so much fun."

She lowered her voice. "You want to know what the best part of sex with your husband was? Knowing that finally I had something you didn't have. When Stephen was in bed with me, you didn't have him."

Since the coffin covered her legs, Keeley squirmed, working her stiff muscles. She had to be ready when the right moment came. "If you didn't have Stephen kidnapped, who did?"

Jenna shrugged and backed away. "My money has always been on Elizabeth. I don't know that for sure . . . don't really care. Seeing you hurting like that . . . " Her eyes went vacant as an expression of absolute joy transformed her face, making her look like the young, pretty Jenna. "You needed me so much then." Her gaze focused on Keeley again. "Remember, we talked about me moving in with you, but I knew if I did, you'd somehow figure out about me. Then what do you do? A year or so after Stephen's death, you start getting your life back together again. You said you were going to sell your house, move away."

"That's why you had Hailey and Hannah taken?"

"I knew once you lost them, you'd never recover. You would always need me. Never leave me." Her eyes glittered with tears again. "And I would have been there for you. Always. 'Cause that's what best friends do."

Her head shook slowly. "But Keeley, you didn't need me as much as you should have. Your babies had been snatched. You should have been inconsolable . . . should have needed me even more. But you didn't. You started doing all sorts of things on your own to get your kids back." She swallowed a sob and added, "You really disappointed me."

Then, as if she hadn't had an emotional moment, she sneered and said, "That bastard Wesley wanted you, too, but I double-crossed him. Remember I was supposed to be on that picnic with you? Only I had to work because Mr. and Mrs. Pointer had been involved in that terrible accident? Remember?"

"Yes."

"Wes arranged that."

Keeley gasped. "He killed the Pointers?"

Jenna shrugged defensively. "Well, I had to have a good excuse not to be there, didn't I? Besides, they were real old and it wasn't like they suffered or anything. Car exploded on impact." She shrugged again. "Wes just thought I wanted them dead . . . he didn't know I was going to use it as an excuse not to come to the park. I was supposed to bring the lemonade. Remember?"

"Yes."

"It was supposed to be drugged. Wes and his friend were just going to be able to come and pick all of you up without any problems. Of course, if I had been there, I would have been slightly hurt, trying to battle the two big, bad men." She chuckled. "Wes was so pissed when he only got the girls and not you, too."

Keeley raised her one knee until it touched the top of the casket, then she raised the other one. She fought to keep the relief from her face as she asked, "If you hated me that much, why not just get rid of me?"

Jenna's face showed genuine surprise. "I don't hate you, Keeley. Why do you keep acting like that? I love you. I even chastised Stephen for marrying you to spite his mother."

"You mean because his father was in love with my mother?"

Jenna jerked a little, apparently astounded that Keeley actually knew something. And her taunt cemented Keeley's suspicions of why Stephen had married her. She had to be the worst judge of character in the world. A voice inside her whispered, *Cole is for real. He may have kept the truth from you, but he's the real deal.*

"Aw, Keeley, don't cry. It won't hurt much. You'll eventually just run out of air and stop breathing."

"What are you saying?"

"Well, duh. Did you think I put you in the casket just so you could take a nap? This is your final resting place. And it's the nicest, most expensive coffin we offer here. Are you comfy? I've been in the business for a long time and never even tried one out."

"So you're just going to bury me alive?"

Jenna rolled her eyes. "You always were the drama queen. Besides, I'd have to have help to bury you, so I'll have to cremate you instead. I'll make sure you're not breathing, though."

The horror of Jenna's words barely registered as she continued to work her legs up and down. The top of the casket kept her from bending them far, but it was enough for her to realize that much of the drug had worn off. Soon she'd be able to push herself up and out of there. She just needed to keep Jenna talking for as long as she could.

"How do you plan to explain my disappearance?"

"Why should I have to explain anything? I was keeping Hannah, like the good friend that I am. You never came to pick her up. Someone must have nabbed you on the way to my house." An exaggerated sigh. "Such a tragedy. And since I'll be taking in little orphans Hailey and Hannah, I'll be the hero."

"I have a will, Jenna. You won't get my children."

"What are you talking about? I'm supposed to get them."

"I know we talked about it, but it made sense that Miranda get them. She's their aunt and she has Maggie."

Jenna's eyes bulged with fury; her face went purple with rage. "You bitch!"

Before Keeley could move, the top of the coffin slammed down on her again and she was once more in darkness. She screamed but refrained from pounding at the top like she wanted. If Jenna knew she could move, she'd lock her in.

Under the roar of panic and the triple pounding of her heart, she heard Jenna's muffled words: "Scream as much as you want, Keeley. There's no one left to hear you."

The instant the plane landed, Cole was at the door, pounding to get out. He glared at the attendant. "Get out of the way and let me open the damn door."

"Sir, regulations say—"

"Fuck regulations. I want the door open. Now!"

Though this was a private charter, the crew members weren't LCR people. The flight attendant looked at Cole as if he were a dangerous lunatic. If that door didn't open soon, he'd live up to her suspicions.

She scooted out of the way. Cole twisted the lever, shoved open the door, and pushed the metal steps down. He clanked down the stairs, his heart almost bursting. Panic as he'd never known was threatening to take over. He'd heard every word Jenna had said. She had closed the coffin; there was no telling how much oxygen Keeley had left.

In desperation, he'd called the sheriff and had gotten the answer he expected. "I ain't going on no wild-goose chase for you, Mathison. You think that woman's in trouble, then you go after her."

The sheriff had hung up on Cole's threats to have his ass fired. After Keeley was safe, he was going after the sheriff. The man would either resign on his own or Cole would beat the shit out of him until he did. Either way, he would no longer be in the position to take bribes from Elizabeth Fairchild or pick what crimes he chose to respond to.

Cole was halfway across the tarmac, running full steam toward the small building of the Fairview airport, when a black SUV zoomed toward him. *Honor.* Cole changed directions and ran toward the speeding vehicle. It skidded to a stop beside him; Cole jumped in the passenger seat. The SUV took off again.

Honor shot him a grim look and Cole acknowledged it with a grimmer nod. They both knew they were up against the tightest of deadlines. If Keeley ran out of air before they got there . . . No, Cole refused to even finish that thought.

And now that Honor was here, she would see to Keeley's safety. If he didn't survive, Honor would save Keeley. Fate had brought him here to keep this family safe, and he'd failed repeatedly. Not anymore. Keeley had suffered enough because of his failures. And she'd damned well suffered too much from Jenna Banks.

thirty

Jenna stared at the mirror in the funeral home's small restroom. Grieving family members frequented this bathroom, often breaking down and sobbing their hearts out right here. She'd always thought that so odd. Grief should be contained, held within so no one could see it, question it, judge it.

Today she almost understood their lack of control, the inability to keep it locked up. Killing Keeley would be like killing part of herself.

Her lip trembled uncontrollably as she stared at the vacant-eyed, pale-faced stranger. Could she do this? Keeley had been a part of her life since she was six years old. They'd shared everything. She loved her as if she were her own sister. But time after time, Keeley had betrayed her. Tried to break free of their bond. When Keeley was happy and content, she didn't need Jenna. At least not the way she should.

Just how many times was she supposed to forgive Keeley?

Every time something good happened in Keeley's life, Jenna felt shut out, pushed away. Sure, Keeley had shared those happy moments with her, but it hadn't been enough. Jenna wanted that happiness for herself . . . that feeling of euphoria that Keeley had. When she couldn't feel the same thing, she realized Keeley was only sharing a small amount. Jenna wanted to feel it all, the same way Keeley did.

But she now knew that wasn't possible as long as Keeley existed. With Keeley finally gone, she would take over her friend's life, feel what she felt, experience what she experienced. Only Jenna would live it better, enjoy it more.

She took a trembling breath. Hailey and Hannah were young enough that they would soon forget their mother and, in a few months, would be calling Jenna their mommy.

She would sell her business . . . maybe leave town. No, she couldn't do that. If she left, then strangers wouldn't know what she had done . . . what she had sacrificed by raising her best friend's children. No one would know how heroic she was if she went somewhere else. She would stay here and be the martyr who took in two orphaned children.

Keeley had said Miranda would get Hailey and Hannah. . . . She couldn't let that happen. Miranda might have to die, too. Jenna was the only one capable of taking care of Keeley's children. That's what a good sister and a best friend would do.

She straightened and watched the pale-faced stranger change before her eyes. Once more she was strong and certain. Sure of her goal, confident in her plan to get there. As much as she hated it, it was time to say good-bye to her dear friend Keeley. And though she would miss her, everything would be so much better when she was dead.

Keeley eased open the coffin lid. She hadn't heard any sounds from Jenna in at least five minutes. She needed to get out of here before Jenna came back. She would go to the police. If Hiram didn't want to help her, she'd call Honor.

Rising slowly from the casket, Keeley looked around

the large room filled with nothing but closed coffins. She refused to wonder if there were bodies in them.

Pulling her legs from beneath the wooden cover, Keeley swung them around and lifted one leg out, then the other. A door slammed shut. Her head jerked up; Jenna was headed toward her.

Determined to be at least standing for the confrontation, Keeley jumped from the coffin. Her legs collapsed like limp noodles; she fell to the floor.

Jenna huffed an exasperated sigh. "Dammit, Keeley. Do you know how long it took me to get your oversized ass into that coffin?"

Sitting on her bottom, staring up at her former friend, she said, "Gee, Jenna. I'm so sorry I'm making killing me so difficult."

"Sarcasm never was your forte."

Since Jenna knew she could move, she saw no need to pretend. Besides, she needed to figure out how strong she was or wasn't. Willing herself strength, she managed to get to her knees.

Her hands on her hips and an expression of frustration on her face, Jenna said, "I don't suppose you'd be willing to climb back into the coffin for me, would you?"

"You first," Keeley said.

"I was afraid you were going to say that."

Jenna turned and reached for something on a table behind her. Keeley sprang up and forward. Since her legs would still barely hold her, she only managed to fall on top of Jenna.

With an earsplitting shriek, Jenna somehow managed to throw Keeley off and scramble to her feet. Keeley sat up to see that Jenna was not only furious, she now held a gun in her hand.

"You're actually going to shoot me?"

"That's up to you." Jenna raised her other hand, which held the butcher knife. "I also have this knife, if you prefer." Waving both the gun and the knife at the coffin behind Keeley, she said, "Get back in or it's going to get really messy."

Several feet behind Jenna a shadow moved. Keeley couldn't see who it was, but it was definitely a person. Cole?

Determined to keep Jenna's attention until Cole could do what he needed to do, Keeley asked, "Why did you marry Frank?"

"What?" Surprise replaced the crazed glint for a moment.

Keeley shrugged. "I've always wondered. I figure if you're going to kill me, you wouldn't mind me knowing why you would marry a man twice your age."

"You never saw my father, did you?"

"No. You said he left your mother when you were only a baby."

Her eyes took on a faraway glaze. "We were living in Elkhart, Indiana. Daddy just never came home from work one day."

"What does that have to do with Frank? Did he resemble your daddy?"

"Kind of. He *was* my daddy."

Shocked at Jenna's statement, Keeley gave her full attention to the woman in front of her. "What?"

Jenna giggled. "Gotcha."

Keeley almost started crying. That was a game they used to play when they were kids. Two lies, one truth. Each had one guess, and if a lie was guessed as a truth, it was a "gotcha" moment. How could her best friend have turned into this fiend in front of her?

The shadow came closer, approaching Jenna slowly from the back. Keeley focused on keeping Jenna's attention. She still couldn't yet see who it was . . . but it had to be Cole.

"So Frank didn't resemble your daddy?"

"I have no idea. I don't remember what my daddy looked like. Mama tore up all the pictures she had of him." She shrugged. "Frank didn't have any family. He wasn't much to look at and was kind of a limp-noodled perv in bed, but we made a deal. I'd marry him, do whatever he wanted me to do, and then when he died, he'd leave everything to me."

"Did you kill him, too?"

Instead of being insulted, Jenna cackled with laughter. "You'll never know how many times I thought about it . . . most especially when I was having to fulfill my end of the bargain. But no, Frank died from a stroke . . . and I got to be the tragic young widow for a few months."

Amusement abruptly gone, she glared at Keeley. "Then, you know what happened to make people forget about me again?"

Already knowing, Keeley asked anyway. "What?"

"You had the twins. I had to take a backseat again."

"Jenna, dammit. Almost everyone in Fairview hates me. My husband cheated on me, my mother died, how could you be jealous of me?"

"Don't trivialize my feelings by saying I was jealous. When something good happened to you, I was happy for you, I really was. But it was all about you. The spotlight was always on your accomplishments and achievements. No matter what I did, I couldn't compete with them. That's why I had to balance it out."

Finally the shadow moved so she could see . . . it wasn't Cole; it was Honor with a gun pointed at Jenna.

Desperate tears filled Keeley's eyes. No matter what Jenna had done, she didn't want her friend to die. "Jenna, please. I'm begging you from the bottom of my heart. Whatever I've done, however I've hurt you, I'm so very sorry. But please don't do this."

Jenna shook her head. "It's not enough, Keeley. No

matter what, you always come out on top. Maybe it's not your fault . . . it doesn't really matter anymore." She raised the gun. "It's got to stop."

Cole stooped behind a coffin where neither Jenna nor Keeley could see him. Keeley had spotted Honor and was doing a good job of keeping Jenna focused, but if Honor got an opportunity, she would take the shot.

Though his goal was to rescue Keeley, Cole would do everything in his power to keep Jenna alive, too. If it came down to choosing, there was no choice but to save Keeley; Cole hoped not to have to make that choice.

Keeley had lost too much already. Jenna had done some vicious, hideous things and deserved to pay for each one, but Cole would rather her pay for it by going to jail than to hell.

As he crept closer, Cole kept an eye on the gun in Jenna's hand. She was shaking, clearly nervous.

He dared a glance at Honor, who looked prepped to shoot. Unable to get her attention, Cole prepared himself to lunge.

"Drop the gun, Jenna," Honor yelled.

Whirling around, Jenna fired wildly toward Honor. Honor ducked behind a coffin.

Jenna turned around and snarled at Keeley, "See, that's the way it's always been. Everybody wants to protect Keeley. Everybody wants to help Keeley. When is it my turn? When do I get to feel special?"

"Jenna." Keeley was sobbing her words. "You've always been special to me. I love you and I'm so sorry for making you feel like you were unimportant." Her voice so thick Cole could barely understand her, she said again, "I love you."

Cursing, Jenna shot toward Honor again. Taking advantage of the distraction, Cole jumped from his cover and leaped toward Jenna.

As he took her to the ground, he wrenched her wrist,

forcing her to drop the gun. Since she was so much smaller than him, Cole did his best not to land directly on her. They both landed facedown on the floor. Jenna let out a long, loud wail and then was ominously silent.

Cole got to his knees quickly; Jenna lay unmoving.

Aware that Keeley was crawling toward him, tears streaming down her face, Cole protected Jenna's neck as he rolled her over. The handle of a butcher's knife jutted from her side.

Keeley's soft cry of horror was like a dagger to his soul.

His hand unbelievably shaky, Cole checked Jenna's pulse. It was there—but too damned weak.

A distant surreal setting floated around him. He heard Honor on her cellphone, calling 911. Heard Keeley crying over her friend. His heart pounded with denial as a cold, painful ache permeated his body.

Getting to his feet, he watched Keeley bend over and whisper something to Jenna, then she looked up at Cole. Tears flowed down her face and agony sliced his gut as she whispered, "She's dying."

No. He couldn't do it . . . couldn't deal with it. He hadn't meant to kill her but had done it all the same. His entire system on meltdown, Cole slowly backed away.

Honor appeared beside him. "Cole, you okay?"

Shaking his head, he said, "I can't do this." And with every particle of his soul disintegrating, Cole turned and walked out the door.

thirty-one

Two weeks later
Tampa, Florida

Her heart pounding so hard she could barely think straight, Keeley kneeled down in front of her daughters. She rarely dressed them alike, but they'd both fallen in love with the frilly red-and-white polka-dot dresses and so had she.

The only difference in their outfits was their hair ribbons. Hannah had wanted to wear white; Hailey had wanted green. Thankfully, Hailey had compromised with red.

They both looked healthy and absolutely adorable, even if she was a bit biased. Both girls still saw a counselor twice a week; no matter what happened here today, that would continue. Their strength and resiliency amazed and humbled her. No, life wasn't perfect for them. They still had nightmares, Hailey more so than Hannah, but with help from professionals, careful watch, and mountains of love, the outlook was good.

Now her angels looked up at her expectantly and she didn't know quite what to say to them. How did you tell your five-year-old children that you were taking them to see a man you desperately hoped would want the job as their father? A man who in every way, shape, and form was a hero. A man with a heart as big as

Texas whose greatest strength wasn't in physical form but in compassion, integrity, and decency.

Tears pooled in her eyes, but she battled them back. The time for tears was over. Now it was time to move forward and, if she had to, battle for a future with the man who'd saved her life, her children's life, and the life of her best friend. The greatest man she'd ever known. But would he still want her?

Keeley stood. Holding her hands out, she grasped their small hands and marched toward the two-story red-brick home . . . Cole's house. He didn't know she was coming. Probably didn't even know she'd been in touch with every LCR operative she'd ever met in an effort to find him. Shea and Ethan had refused to tell her; Eden and Jordan had, too. All were of the opinion that when an LCR operative wanted to disappear, that was their prerogative. Thankfully, Noah McCall had caved.

Okay, so Noah hadn't exactly caved. She had called him every day for the last two weeks. Yesterday, he asked the same question he'd asked her each day when she called: "Why do you want to talk to Cole?"

Every time he had asked before, Keeley had always said that she wanted to thank Cole for all the things he'd done. Which was true . . . but there were so many other things she wanted to say. Private things that should only be said to him.

Yesterday, tired of getting the same question and no help, she'd had enough and shouted, "Because I'm in love with him and I think he's the most wonderful man in the world. That's why!"

In the next second, she had not only his address, but the promise of a chartered jet picking her up the next day to take her to him.

Taking a breath, Keeley rang the doorbell. She knew she was hedging her bets by having her girls with her.

Cole might slam the door in her face, but he wouldn't do that to her daughters. Dirty trick, yes . . . but she was planning on shooting everything in her arsenal at him today. Might as well start with her strongest weapons.

Cole opened the door and stared at the three most beautiful females on the planet. He was grateful Noah had forewarned him they were coming. He didn't know why they were here. McCall had just said he'd given Keeley his address and that was that. Since the man was infamous for shocking the hell out of people, he was fortunate to be able to prepare. Still, it was hard as hell to prepare to see the woman you loved if you had no idea whether she wanted to slap you in the face or kiss you.

"Hello, Cole." Her voice was shaky and a bit husky, her eyes searching and vulnerable.

Aware that two little faces were looking up at him expectantly, Cole went to his knees and said, "Hi, Hailey. Hi, Hannah."

As usual, they each responded differently. Hannah grinned, then went shy and turned her face against her mother's leg. Hailey giggled and said, "Hi."

Cole stood and moved aside to let them in. Looking even more uncertain than before, Keeley passed by him and it was all he could do not to grab her.

As the three entered his home, he said, "Would you like something to drink?"

Keeley shook her head. "We had something on the flight over . . . we're fine."

Feeling as awkward as a teenager on his first date, he said, "Come on in." He led them into the living room, and Hailey and Hannah immediately spotted the gifts he'd gone out and bought them after Noah had called. Coloring books, crayons, dolls, and stuffed animals of all shapes and sizes filled half the room.

A soft sob from Keeley brought his gaze back to hers. She shook her head slowly. "It will take me a lifetime to tell you all the many reasons I love you."

His heart so full he thought it might burst, Cole asked huskily, "Can we start now?"

With another sob, Keeley ran into his open arms.

Hours later, two exhausted little girls slept in the bedroom down the hallway, while Keeley waited for Cole to lock up for the night and join her in bed. She still couldn't believe she was really here. That Cole really wanted her; wanted to be a family.

He came into the room and her heart rate tripled in speed. She sat up and watched him approach. Had she ever seen his eyes so heated and full of emotion? Months ago, when she'd met him, she had thought him expressionless and cold. And now, she realized that beneath the façade of uncaring was one of the most gallant and loving men ever placed on this earth.

Sitting on the edge of the bed, he said, "I didn't want to ask in front of Hailey and Hannah, but how's Jenna doing?"

Her heart twisted as it always would when she thought about her friend. "She's out of the Fairview hospital and is in a psychiatric hospital in Greenville until her trial."

"Has she said anything yet?"

"Not since the first time I saw her in the hospital when she screamed at me to die." Her lips trembled. "I guess our friendship is officially at an end."

"I'm sorry, Keeley, I—"

Keeley leaned forward and put a finger on his mouth to stop his apology. "You have no reason to be sorry. My incredibly poor judgment brought this on . . . not you."

"And you shouldn't be blaming yourself either. She fooled people for years."

Her voice shaking, she said, "You could have killed her . . . and you didn't."

"If it had come down to killing her to save you, I wouldn't have hesitated . . . the choice would have been easy. But I couldn't bear to see you lose someone else you loved . . . even if she was a maniac. And killing isn't something I'll do if there's any way to avoid it. I've taken too many lives already."

"You saved my life again. Thank you."

"I'm sorry I walked out on you. . . . " His mouth twisted. "I thought she was dying . . . I couldn't bear to see the pain in your face."

Keeley wiped impatiently at the tears pooling in her eyes. Damned if she would cry now. "If Jenna had died, it wouldn't have been your fault. Just like you weren't responsible for Stephen's death. It was tragic and I hate that it happened, but Donald Rosemount is to blame, not you."

"And Stephen's mother," Cole said softly.

Keeley nodded. She'd had a lot of time to think in the last couple of weeks. And as bizarre and crazy as it seemed, it made sense. Elizabeth would have seen that as a teaching lesson for Stephen. Unfortunately, it had gotten him killed.

"Jenna might be insane, but her comment got me to thinking about it all. Elizabeth saw an opportunity to scare the hell out of Stephen and make it look like I was responsible."

"Unfortunately, Rosemount never revealed who hired him, so I don't see it ever being proven that she was involved," Cole said.

"Elizabeth will remain a vicious, embittered woman, but she'll always have the knowledge that she was responsible for her son's death."

Cole's beautiful eyes roamed her face; he looked so solemn. Hoping to break the tension a bit, she added, "A lot of things have changed in Fairview in the last two weeks."

"Like what?"

"Let's see. Hiram Mobley is officially out of office, along with two of his deputies. I think Honor had a lot to do with getting him fired. And, according to Miranda, who heard it from a reliable source, Elizabeth told her lawyers she no longer wants to contest Stephen's will. And, wonder of all wonders, I saw Elizabeth at the courthouse three days ago and she asked how the girls were doing."

Cole snorted. "Did she actually know their names?"

Keeley grinned. "Well, she called them Hilary and Holly, but I'm counting it as progress." About to impart another bit of news, she became nervous again. "And, I, uh . . . I gave my house away."

"You did what?"

Going to her knees, she placed her hands on his thighs, took a breath, and explained, "I gave my house to Miranda. You know you thought she was keeping secrets? Well, she was. Turns out, she's been secretly working to find a place for unwed mothers to live. Working night and day on a small house about ten miles out of town. She and a couple of other people were trying to fix it up without anyone knowing about it. She knew Elizabeth would have a fit, so she told almost no one what she was doing. That's why she was so evasive when you questioned her in front of Elizabeth. So, since my house was a gift from Stephen to appease his conscience and I was going to sell it anyway, I deeded it over to Miranda so she could use it."

"I'll bet Elizabeth will love that."

Keeley giggled. "I have to admit, that was extra incentive."

"So where are you and the girls planning to live?"

More vulnerable than she'd ever felt in her life, she whispered, "Wherever you are . . . if you'll have us."

"Keeley," he said simply, his voice thick with emotion. Then he pulled her into his arms and covered her mouth with his.

Keeley opened her mouth to his thrusting tongue. Never had she felt so blessed, so fortunate, as to have this remarkable man in her life.

He broke their kiss to breathe against her lips, "I don't think I've told you yet . . . but I love you."

Tears of joy swam in her eyes. The words sounded wonderful but hadn't really been necessary. Everything this man had done for her showed his love. "And I love you . . . so much. I'm sorry I sent you away . . . sorry I treated you the way I did."

"I should have told you about Stephen sooner . . . I just couldn't allow anything else to happen to you. I figured if you knew, you'd send me away. I had to protect you . . . and then I fell in love with you."

"Thank you for saving my girls . . . and for saving me."

He placed another soft kiss on her lips and then asked, "How do you think Hailey and Hannah will feel about having a new daddy?"

"I think they'll feel like the luckiest little girls in the world."

"Where do you want to live?"

"Anywhere you are."

Cole lowered his head to devour her mouth. Locking her arms around his neck, Keeley gave herself up to the absolute ecstasy that only this man could create inside her. How she'd gotten so fortunate, she didn't dare question. She'd made so many mistakes. Had trusted the wrong people, made the wrong decisions. From now on she vowed, once and for all, to get it right. She had her angels back and the most amazing man in the world in her arms. No woman had ever been so blessed.

The night, velvet and warm, cocooned them in darkness. Cole held Keeley in his arms, listening to her soft, even breaths of sleep and reveled in the gift of her love. Three doors down, two precious little girls, who would soon be his daughters, slept deeply, knowing they were at last safe from harm.

He never believed he could love again, feel happiness or contentment. But because of this beautiful woman in his arms, Cole realized that he had been given something incredible, had been granted a miracle he'd never expected. He'd been given a second chance.

acknowledgments

Special thanks to my wonderful family for putting up with my crazy hours and nervous mutterings and ramblings the closer I get to deadlines.

Thank you, Kate Collins, my fantastic editor, for your insight and kindness. And thanks, also, to the entire Ballantine team, especially Beth Pearson and Kelli Fillingim.

My sincere and deep appreciation to my agent, Kim Whalen, for your support, encouragement, and wonderful words of wisdom.

And thank you to the readers of the Last Chance Rescue books, especially those who sent emails regarding Cole, insisting that he have a happy ever after. I do hope you enjoy his story.

Read on for a preview of

LAST CHANCE

the sixth novel of sexy suspense and
thrilling adventure in
Christy Reece's *Last Chance Rescue* series!

Present day
London, England

He was tired of chasing a ghost. More than once he'd told himself she was a figment of his overactive imagination or a hallucination caused by too many blows to his head. That some three-hundred-pound bruiser by the name of Rudolph or Hans had rescued him, not a delicate-as-air blond angel named Ghost.

But she wasn't a figment; he'd felt her, touched her, smelled her. And he couldn't get her out of his head.

On his return from Brazil, he'd launched two investigations. One was to determine who else had been involved in his abduction other than Victor Lymes. The other was to find his mysterious rescuer.

The investigation into his abduction had taken less than a week. Lymes, working with two of the hotel employees where Lucas had been staying, had seen an opportunity and took it. The plan had been to ransom him and split the earnings. The two conspirators had confessed quickly when confronted by the authorities.

The second investigation hadn't gone as well. It was as if the young woman who'd aided in his rescue didn't even exist.

"Kane, do you agree?"

Lucas jerked his head around. Staring out the window like a new employee didn't exactly inspire confidence. The twenty board members of Kane Industries stared at him as if he had a third eye.

"Yes, the takeover should go through without a hitch. Just make sure we have jobs for everyone." He sent a pointed stare at Stanley Humphries. "If I hear that even one worker was displaced, heads will not be the only body parts rolling."

The stiff nod of agreement was belied by the mutinous expression on Humphries's face. Lucas noted it and added it to his growing list of concerns. The man had become increasingly belligerent and uncooperative over the past few months. Lucas knew he was going to have to do something about him soon.

Though Humphries wasn't a member of the board, he'd been with Kane Industries for well over thirty years and had earned his spot in making decisions. However, Lucas had become aware of recent shortcuts and mismanagements that the man was directly responsible for.

When Lucas had taken over his family's empire, he'd been determined to do a few things differently. That included making sure no one was adversely impacted as Kane Enterprises thrived. Humphries apparently didn't like that concept.

Lucas needed to make a decision about the man's involvement in future projects. Times like this, he wished for his father's tough-minded decision making. Lucas could kick ass and kill with the best of them, but when it came to dealing with wayward employees, he was at somewhat of a loss.

Harbin Nickels, CFO of Kane Industries, stood. "I think that about wraps up everything we needed to review with you, Lucas. Anything else that comes up, we can go through your assistants. When do you leave for your trip?"

His mind occupied between finding a ghost and disciplining an employee, Lucas answered with a careless "A few hours" and then fell silent.

They stared at him for several seconds before they made their way out of the room. Being distracted wasn't good for morale. A leader distracted led to uncertainty in his employees. He'd worry about that when he returned. Now he needed to get on his flight to Paris and talk with the one man he believed could help him.

Paris, France
Last Chance Rescue Headquarters

"Noah, did you give Micah another piece of chocolate?"

Before turning his gaze from the computer screen in front of him, Noah swallowed the remaining evidence. Turning to her, he gave his most innocent look. "Mara, why would you say that?"

Hands on her hips, amazing eyes flashing, Samara advanced toward him. "Because he's as hyper as a wildcat. Angela's with him in the conference room, chasing him around the table."

Before he could proclaim his innocence of giving their two-year-old son chocolate, Samara added, "And because you have chocolate on your chin."

He sighed. Nothing got past his Mara. "So, come over here and lick it off for me."

Her eyes darkened and she got that look on her face that could heat his blood in an instant. She came toward him and then stopped. "Wait. What time is Lucas Kane supposed to be here?"

Noah groaned and looked at the clock. "Fifteen minutes. Not near enough time."

"Here." She handed him a tissue from a box on his desk. "Get the chocolate off for now and we'll stop at the store on the way home."

He grinned, already anticipating the night ahead. "Deal."

Settling into a chair across from him, she returned to the topic of their upcoming meeting. "So, you really just want my observation on the man. Nothing more?"

"Right."

"Are you planning on telling him you know McKenna?"

"No. Her association with LCR must remain private. But I want to meet with him before I mention his search to her. When she relayed the details of his rescue, it got me interested in him even more."

"How so?"

"Hard to say, other than it sounds to me like he handled himself a little too well for a British billionaire. About as well as any LCR operative. There's got to be more to him than just inherited wealth and a keen eye for the next money-making venture."

"Think he has military training?"

Noah shook his head. "Records show that he spent most of his years collecting degrees and prepping himself to take over his family's empire. Military training hasn't been mentioned."

"Perhaps he had someone train him. As high profile as he is, maybe he felt he needed to know how to defend himself."

"Could be. That's where you come in. I want your impression. I may be biased."

She smiled. "That's because you're protective of McKenna."

"I'm protective of all my operatives."

"True, but whether you want to admit it or not, you have a special fondness for McKenna."

Noah couldn't deny it. He did feel much more like McKenna's big brother than he did her boss. Not that he was technically her boss, since she still wasn't officially employed by LCR. Even though all active LCR operatives were freelance and could work when they wanted, he considered them full-fledged employees. McKenna not so much.

LCR's first encounter with McKenna had been unusual. One day, during the middle of an op involving the rescue of a young teenager, McKenna had just shown up. One of his operatives had been injured, unable to assist. McKenna had gone after one of the kidnappers, jumping on his back and taking him to the ground. Dylan had been on the op, along with Shea and Ethan. All three had regaled him with accounts of her bravery. Problem was, she'd disappeared as soon as the rescue was complete.

She had assisted once more, this time in Paris. Noah had been on the op and had cornered her before she could disappear. She hadn't liked being trapped. Had been almost feral in her fear, as if she thought he was going to hold her. They'd talked . . . at least, as much as McKenna would talk. Noah had learned enough to know that not only was she incredibly brave and surprisingly skilled, she was also the most alone person he'd ever met. And he'd met a lot of alone people since starting LCR.

Though McKenna had never officially become an LCR operative, most of his people thought she was. Noah gave her that support and allowed her the anonymity for one very important reason: McKenna needed to feel that she was part of this organization, whether she realized it or not. Even though she turned him down every time he asked her to become an operative, he had high hopes that someday she would change her mind.

Thanks to McKenna, Skylar Maddox, Gabe's wife, had been rescued several months back. Since the same person who'd held Skylar had also abducted Lucas Kane, McKenna was able to rescue him as well.

No one knew where McKenna had come from or even where she lived. Though Noah was more than aware that he could do his own investigation, he continued to refrain from it. At some point, he might have to. For right now, he wanted to allow McKenna the anonymity she obviously needed.

Samara had gotten to know her better than anyone at LCR, which was one of the many reasons he wanted his wife to meet Lucas Kane. The man had not stopped looking for McKenna from the moment he arrived home after his rescue. Noah wasn't about to give up any secrets about McKenna, but he wanted Mara's opinion on Kane. He trusted his wife's judgment over anyone's.

"So McKenna has no idea he's looking for her?"

"She knows he's looking. As you know, she got good instincts about that." He and Samara both believed McKenna was hiding from someone. But until she was ready to ask for their help, all they could do was wait until she chose to trust them. "I just don't think she knows how determined Kane is to find her."

"Why do you think he is so determined?"

Noah shrugged. "Could be as simple as he wants to thank her, but somehow I think it's more. With his contacting LCR, he either suspects we have an association with McKenna or he's desperate and wants us to do something we don't do as a rule. He knows we only search for people who are endangered in some way. . . . I'm interested in your observations. What you think he's looking for."

The buzzer sounded, alerting them that Kane was on his way. The man had called him three times before

Noah had agreed to see him. That he was being allowed to come to LCR headquarters was almost unprecedented. Only LCR operatives, or those Noah knew he could trust, were aware of this location. But Noah had an instinct for people. He'd met Kane years ago at a social event and had never forgotten that meeting. There was more to Lucas Kane than the man allowed most people to see.

Noah didn't worry that Kane knew where LCR headquarters were. What did concern him was the man's unusual fixation on McKenna. He wasn't known to be obsessive . . . so why this time?

McKenna had given Noah the barest of facts on her rescue of Kane. Just that all three men holding him were killed. She'd reported that Kane was shot but only slightly wounded, and that she'd left as soon as Dylan Savage, another LCR operative, had picked him up. She also indicated that Kane had assisted in his own rescue.

Noah hadn't pressed McKenna for more details. If she were officially with LCR he would have. However, with McKenna he treaded softly. Yes, he wanted to hire her as a full-time operative when she was ready, but that wasn't the biggest reason. If he pressed, he greatly feared she would just up and disappear. The young woman needed LCR even if she wasn't aware of it.

After the rescue, Dylan had dropped Kane at a local hospital before he regained consciousness. The official story was that Kane had been in Brazil on business and was jumped by some thugs. Having no publicity was better for LCR and, for that matter, Lucas Kane.

If one ignored nuances and went only on words, McKenna's rescue of Kane had taken less than an hour. Noah sensed there was more. Something had happened in that time frame that had her even more skittish than usual. Even more reason to want to meet with the man.

At a knock on the door, Noah went around the desk and stood by Samara.

The instant Lucas entered Noah McCall's office, he knew he'd get little or no cooperation from the head of Last Chance Rescue. And the petite, dark-haired woman at his side looked just as reticent.

Didn't mean he wouldn't try to persuade them otherwise. Lucas held out his hand. "Thank you for seeing me, Noah. It's been a few years."

As Noah shook his hand and introduced him to his wife, Lucas felt Samara McCall's eyes assessing him. He was being given some kind of test, and apparently the lovely Mrs. McCall would be giving the final verdict. *Interesting.*

He settled onto the overstuffed chair McCall indicated and waited. As expected, Noah led the interrogation while his wife observed.

Seated across from him, McCall leaned forward. "You said you were looking for a young woman?"

"You may have heard that I had a bit of trouble in Brazil a few months back."

McCall's expression didn't change as he nodded.

"Truth is . . . while I was in Peru on business, I was abducted from my hotel room there and ended up in Brazil. With help from the authorities, I kept it quiet . . . conducted my own investigation. The people who assisted in the abduction were caught. However, there was a young woman there . . . she rescued me, but disappeared before I could thank her."

"This young woman . . . what was her name?"

Frustration and admiration dueled within Lucas. Going on nothing but instinct, he was almost certain his ghost had some sort of association with LCR. McCall was apparently going to pretend otherwise.

"She gave no name . . . other than Ghost."

McCall's mouth quirked slightly. "Ghost?"

"Yes. Unfortunately I lost consciousness before I could inquire further. When I woke in the hospital, she was nowhere to be found. I was told a man brought me there, leaving no information other than my name."

"I'm surprised you came to us. You know we only search for those who have been abducted or are missing."

"I'd like for you to make an exception in my case."

"And why would I do that?"

"I think she may be in trouble."

McCall's expression didn't change, but his wife's shoulders stiffened, confirming Lucas's suspicions. They did indeed know her.

"What sort of trouble?" McCall asked.

Lucas shrugged. Even as much as he wanted to find her, he felt an odd loyalty to his ghost. Describing the expression in her eyes . . . How do you describe a look that on one hand has the innocence of a fawn, but at the same time reveals a stark hell?

His innocence was long gone; he had a familiarity with hell. That look was something he'd seen in his own eyes from time to time. Along with hollowness, emptiness. Extreme sadness. He would mention none of these. Odd really, but he felt as if a secret had been shared between them. He was loath to break their silent bond. Those naked moments with his ghost would remain theirs alone.

Aware that McCall waited for an answer, Lucas shrugged. "She looked as though she needed a friend. I'd like to be able to help her in whatever she needs."

"I'm sure you've hired your own investigators to find her. Why come to us?" McCall asked.

"For one, LCR is the best at finding people. My investigators have come up dry."

"And the other reason?"

"I thought perhaps she was affiliated with your organization."

"Why would you think that?"

Lucas shrugged. "She rescued me."

McCall frowned. "We are hired to rescue. We rarely become involved unless asked."

While he knew that was true, he also knew that LCR would and had rescued when they saw a need, whether they were paid for it or not.

"How did your rescue go down?"

This was the first time Samara McCall had asked anything. Her question surprised Lucas. He had figured Noah would be the more direct interrogator. So far, McCall had been subtle; Samara McCall cut to the chase. Did her question hold a secret agenda?

Nevertheless, he described how he'd been abducted from his hotel room while he was on business. He glossed over the disgusting details of his sickness, along with the infuriating information about the beatings he'd endured while he'd been ill. He explained his first meeting with the young woman who had rescued him, along with her apparent association with Victor.

"Could this woman have not just decided that she'd had enough of Victor and turned on him?" McCall asked.

That's exactly what Lucas had told himself many times since then. She was just one of Victor's people who'd decided to betray him, and Lucas happened to benefit from that. None of that rang true. She'd let him go instead, saved his life. Seemed genuinely concerned for his welfare. And she'd asked for nothing in return.

Lucas lifted his shoulders in a casual shrug. "It's possible. However, I'd like the opportunity to talk with her—ask her myself."

McCall shook his head. "I'm sorry, but I don't think LCR can help you."

With a nod, Lucas stood. Noah McCall wasn't known for changing his mind once a decision had been made. Lucas saw no point in trying to persuade him. However, he'd gotten at least a piece of the answer he'd been searching for. This woman did indeed have some sort of connection with Last Chance Rescue. That was apparently the only thing he was going to get.

Holding out his hand, he shook Noah's hand and then Samara's. As he walked to the door, Samara McCall's soft voice stopped him. "Mr. Kane, if you don't mind my asking . . . If given a chance to see this young woman again, what would you say to her?"

He turned and gave her the truth, hoping that it would get to his ghost. "I would thank her and tell her that if at any time she ever needs my help in any way or for any reason, I would be there for her."

With a slight smile, she said, "Very nice to meet you, Mr. Kane. Have a good trip home."

Lucas nodded again and walked out the door.

Noah waited several seconds until he was sure Kane had gotten on the elevator, then he turned to Samara. "So what do you think?"

"I think he'll keep looking until he finds her."

"Did you also get the impression he knew we weren't be exactly truthful?"

She scrunched her nose. "My fault. He surprised me when he said the words that you and I both feel about McKenna. That she needs help in some way."

"Don't worry about that. His knowing she has some kind of association with LCR won't get him any more information than he had before."

"Something else is bothering you though . . . what?" Samara asked.

"I just think it's interesting that Kane picked up on McKenna's vulnerability. When she's on an op, she's excellent at hiding her true self. Which makes me even more curious about what really happened during the rescue. When she gave me the details, I sensed she was disturbed about something."

Samara nodded. "I talked to her a couple of weeks after it happened. She glossed over the entire event, but I got the feeling she had a distinct admiration for Lucas Kane."

"He's done some admirable things since he took over his family's dynasty. Did you get a feel for why he's so intent on finding her?"

A smile curved his wife's mouth, and Noah couldn't resist the opportunity to feel it under his. After several breathless moments, he pulled from the kiss and said, "Sorry, got distracted . . . you were saying?"

Her smile now even bigger, she said, "I think in the short amount of time that Lucas and McKenna spent together, they both felt a strong attraction for each other."

"You may be right." He picked up the phone. "Now lets see if McKenna wants to do anything about Kane continuing his pursuit."

McKenna hung up the phone. Refusing to acknowledge the racing of her heart at the knowledge that Lucas Kane was in Paris, searching for her, she went to her closet. Pulling her duffel bag from the top shelf, she immediately began to pack.

His hunt for her had gone further than she anticipated. She'd become aware of questions being asked about her in Brazil. Based upon the physical description the people searching for her had given, she had known they were Kane's people. She hadn't expected him to expand beyond Brazil, nor had she expected him to go to LCR. That was a little too close to home.

Why did he continue? Did he believe she was involved in his abduction? Was that the reason, or was there more? Noah had indicated that Kane wanted to thank her. Perhaps that was all. She hoped so. Silly really, but she hated for Lucas Kane to think badly of her by believing she'd actually been in cahoots with Victor.

She'd had plenty of time to relive those moments during his rescue. *His rescue?* How laughable. Other than taking out Victor, she'd done very little. Pretty damn bad when the victim becomes the rescuer. Of all the damn times to pass out. Any other time she'd been forced to kill someone, she usually became nauseous. Not pleasant, but at least she was usually able to function to finish the rescue. Passing out was not only embarrassing; it was damn dangerous. They both could've been killed.

When she awoke, one man was dead. Thankfully she'd managed to distract the other one, but Lucas Kane had still been able to take care of him, even with a bullet hole in his shoulder.

After the excitement had passed and she was far enough away from Kane to think straight, she acknowledged that if she had never shown up, Lucas Kane would have gotten out of the situation all by himself. Which made her fascination for him even larger. Something she definitely hadn't needed.

McKenna rushed around her little apartment, collecting the few things she wouldn't leave without. She'd stayed here longer than she did most places. . . . It was past time to leave anyway. No use looking around and bemoaning the frilly little curtains she'd hand-stitched herself or the painting she'd found at a flea market that reminded her of home. She'd hung it over the television and found herself looking at it more than what was on TV.

She would leave those things, of course. Taking the minimal belongings was the only way she traveled and the only way she'd survived this long.

Being hunted wasn't a new thing for her; she just had a new predator. No, she could never call Lucas Kane a predator. Noah's words continued to whirl around in her head. "He wants to thank you . . . wants you to know that if you ever need anything, you only have to ask."

McKenna snorted as she grabbed a handful of underwear. Maybe she should just go to Kane and tell him that for years she's been hunted by a crazed maniac and would he mind hiring an army to kill him. She could just see his handsome face as she gave him her request. He probably wanted to give her a box of chocolates or a basket full of bath salts as a thank you, not a paid assassin.

No, she would never ask someone to do something she would one day have to do herself. There would be a final confrontation. And she would be the one who would end his sorry life. If she had to lose hers in the process, that was only fair. At some point she would stop being such a chickenshit and do the deed.

Standing on her rickety kitchen chair, she opened the cabinet above the refrigerator. Moving aside the bargain-sized jar of peanut butter, she pulled at the loose board behind it and opened the small area she'd created only hours after moving in. She took the nylon pouch and unzipped it and checked its contents, though she knew nothing had been moved. Six passports, five driver's licenses, twenty-eight thousand dollars, and a small black wallet with three photographs. She no longer looked at the pictures . . . they were carved into her mind, seared into her soul, but she would never go anywhere without them.

She stepped down and returned the chair under the table. Zipping the pouch, she dumped it in with her clothes and toiletries. Placing her notebook computer on top of everything, McKenna closed the bag and straightened. With a long, silent sigh, she took one last glance at the landscape above the television, grabbed the duffel bag, and walked out the door.

Lucas Kane needed to stop looking for her. There was only one way to ensure that he did.

ETERNAL
ROMANCE

FIND YOUR HEART'S DESIRE...